TOUCH OF FIRE

"Fire Dancer," Mackenzie whispered, kissing him gently on the mouth.

"This man will never forget you." He kissed her back, harder, and pulled her closer.

"Never," she answered, lost in the moment.

He drew her onto his lap and she made no protest. All she wanted was him. In the desperation of the moment, she wanted nothing but to touch him, to be touched by him.

They kissed again and again. He laid her back on her bed and she sighed and moaned with pleasure, reveling in the feel of his body pressed against hers.

His hands burned a path on her bare skin. Any sense of modesty she might have felt in the past was gone. All that mattered was Fire Dancer and the pulses of pleasure that surged through her veins.

"This is what you want, heart of my heart?" he whispered in her ear.

"Yes, yes," she whispered. "It's what I want." She opened her eyes, staring into his. "I'll never love another the way I love you . . ."

Books by Colleen Faulkner

FORBIDDEN CARESS
RAGING DESIRE
SNOW FIRE
TRAITOR'S CARESS
PASSION'S SAVAGE MOON
TEMPTATION'S TENDER KISS
LOVE'S SWEET BOUNTY
PATRIOT'S PASSION
SAVAGE SURRENDER
SWEET DECEPTION
FLAMES OF LOVE
FOREVER HIS
CAPTIVE
O'BRIAN'S BRIDE
DESTINED TO BE MINE
TO LOVE A DARK STRANGER
FIRE DANCER

Published by Zebra Books

FIRE
DANCER

Colleen Faulkner

Zebra Books
Kensington Publishing Corp.

http://www.zebrabooks.com

Prologue

Pennsylvania
Winter, 1801

"Close the window, Abigail." Mackenzie glided soundlessly across the polished wood floor of the parlor. "You want your old grandmother to catch her death!"

"Old, indeed." Ten year old Abby's black eyes flashed with sassiness as she obediently closed the glass shutter windows of the log cabin. "Grandpapa says you're as spry as the day he met you."

"Grandpapa is a foolish old man." Mackenzie ran fingers that smelled of linseed oil over the latch of the lock to be certain it was secured. She grasped her granddaughter's hand and helped her jump down off the wing-backed chair. "I thought you were supposed to be in the kitchen helping Cook with the bread."

Abby released her grandmother's hand and walked away, her lower lip stuck out in a sulk. "But I'm bored, Grandmama." She trailed her finger along the chair rail partially embedded in the plastered log walls. "I don't want to help Cook."

"There are books in my bedchamber. You're welcome to any one of them so long as you're careful with the pages."

Abby swung around, her black braids flying out behind her. She was a mirror image of her mother. The thought made Mackenzie smile. As spunky as her mother, too.

"I don't want to read, and I don't want to paint." She leaned against Mackenzie's precious cherry sideboard. "I just don't feel like it." She crossed her arms over her chest. "Do you know what I mean?"

Mackenzie eased herself in the upholstered chair. "Restless, are you?"

"*Ah*. Grandpapa says I'm always restless. He says that when I grow up I should go west."

Mackenzie sat back in the chair and her doeskin moccasins peeked from beneath the hem of her gown. "West is it?"

"*Ah*." Abby's face lit up. "Grandpapa said that if he wasn't a year shy of his eightieth birthday and feeling it in his bones, he'd take me himself."

Mackenzie laughed and clapped her hands together in amusement. "That sounds like your grandfather. I told you he was old and foolish."

Abby wandered across the parlor. "I'm glad I got to see your cabin, Grandmama. I like it much better than the house in Baltimore. I'm glad I got to come."

"This woman is glad you came."

Abby ran her fingers over the cherry sideboard and stared at the oil painting that hung on the plastered wall above it. It was Mackenzie's favorite portrait.

Abby studied the painting with the careful eye of a budding artist. "The colors are excellent. Very realistic earth tones."

"Thank you."

Abby still stared at the painting. "I realize the man is Grandpapa and the woman is you and the little boy is Uncle Fox." She dropped her hands to her hips. "But Grandmama, I have a question."

Mackenize raised an eyebrow. She had known the question was coming. She was surprised it had taken this long. "And what is that, my inquisitive one?"

Abby faced Mackenzie, her mouth drawn up. "Why don't you have any faces? The painting is so beautiful, but there are no faces." She took a moment to study the portraits that lined the log cabin's parlor walls. "None of them have any faces, Grandmama."

"Well, that, my love, is a long story."

Abby drew up a stool and sat at Mackenzie's feet. "That's all right. We have all afternoon. Grandpapa said he wouldn't return from hunting until supper." Abby took Mackenzie's hand. "Please, will you tell me?"

Mackenzie squeezed the little girl's hand in her own wrinkled one. Her eyes grew misty. Already she could feel the sands of time slipping . . . slipping back.

"It all began one afternoon," she said softly to the wide-eyed child. "It was during the French and Indian war . . . before the colonists' war for independence. My father was escorting me to a fort called Belvadere." She gazed at the portrait. "It was my very first commission . . ."

Chapter One

August 1759
Somewhere in Penn's Colony

Mackenzie Daniels stared up into the tree limbs overhead, fascinated by the patterns of light and dark that poured through the dense foliage and swirled on the forest floor in a kaleidoscope of colors and textures. The warm wind blew in her face, and the smell of honeysuckle was strong in her nostrils.

Her horse moved rhythmically beneath her at an easy pace. In front and behind her rode a dozen British soldiers, her escort to Fort Belvadere. Her father, Franklin, brought up the rear in his wagon, which was filled with trading goods and her precious art supplies.

"We can stop and rest if you're tired, Mackenzie." Joshua Watkins met her gaze with those cow-brown eyes of his.

She loosened the reins in her gloved hands, encouraging her mount to pick up the pace.

She sat astride a man's saddle, rather than sidesaddle because Major Albertson, the commander of Fort Belvadere, had ordered it so. He had warned her father that it would be easier for her to escape in case of an Indian attack.

Indian attack. She shuddered at the thought.

"Mackenzie? Did you hear me? I said that if you're fatigued—"

"I'm not tired." Mackenzie met Josh's gaze again. She'd completely forgotten him. "I'm fine."

Rather than being flattered by his attention, as her father suggested she should be, she was annoyed. She didn't care if Joshua was the only man interested in her. She didn't want a man. What did she need a husband for when she could ride, shoot, fish, chop wood and skin out her own deer? "I told you I was fine half an hour ago, Josh," she continued. "And I told you an hour ago."

"I . . . I know. I was just checking. It's been a hard journey."

She frowned. He was just trying to make her feel *womanly* again, as if she were his delicate flower. Glancing at her clothing, she snickered at the thought. She wore a blue tick skirt and her father's shirt with a pair of men's leather riding boots made by the saddler. In clothes like this, she wasn't exactly a picture of femininity.

"Oh, it has not been hard. It's been nothing like you and Father tried to warn me." She tugged off her straw bonnet by its flat ribbon and shook her mane of auburn hair. Then she looped the reins over the pommel and passed the hat to Josh to hold while she swept loose strands from her face and secured them in a ribbon at the nape of her neck. "I've quite enjoyed the journey. I've seen none of the dangers you warned of."

She held the ribbon in her teeth as she tugged on the unruly handfuls of hair. "The birds, the deer, those foxes we saw yesterday. The rivers, the clouds, the moon at night. It's all grand, Josh, just as I imagined. I haven't seen a single redskin since we left the Chesapeake." She caught a stray lock of hair that blew in the breeze. "I swear, I'm beginning to think you men made up this whole story of hostile Indians so that you could traipse off into the forest with your guns and sit around at night and drink and spit and scratch."

"You might not believe it now, but just you wait 'til we reach the fort," he responded anxiously. "The soldiers say the place is swarming with the devils."

"I'm not afraid of Indians." She lied. She was afraid. Her father's whispers behind her back had made her afraid.

"Which is just why I don't think you belong here, Mackenzie. With the fighting all over the colonies, it's too dangerous. You don't know enough to realize when you're in danger."

"My first commissioned portraits," she scoffed, "and you think I should have turned Major Albertson down because a few scalps have been taken?" She drew the ribbon from her teeth and wrapped it around the thick ponytail of hair. "That's just why it will never work between you and me, Josh. This is a perfect example of why I could never marry you."

He looked behind them to see if anyone had heard her. "Shhhh." He lowered his voice. "I thought we weren't going to talk about that. I thought we were just going to see how things went on this journey."

She took her bonnet from his hands and slapped it on top of her head. "You and Father made those plans, not me. I already gave you my answer, Josh." She whipped the ribbons through her fingers to tie the hat down. "I'm not marrying you. I'm not marrying anyone. I just want to—"

Gunfire erupted from the forest and her horse shied and danced in place.

"Indians!" a soldier shouted.

Mackenzie grabbed her reins tightly, keeping control of her horse. The soldiers immediately formed a tight circle around her. She crouched and stared up into the trees waiting for the Indian attack.

Joshua drew his musket from his leather saddlebag, his face pasty with fear. "Oh, God. Oh, Jesus God. I knew we were going to be massacred." He shook. "I knew it."

"Get a hold of yourself, Josh," Mackensize snapped. She jerked her mount around and faced the nearest soldier. "What's happening? Are we under attack?"

"Don't know, ma'am." The soldier checked the prime on his pistol. "It's Lieutenant Burrow's weapon that discharged up ahead. He must have come upon something, but I don't 'ear Indians. They usually hoot and holler when attacking."

Mackenzie glanced over her shoulder, craning her neck to

see her father. He was still pulling up the rear in his wagon, but his musket now lay across his lap.

"Lieutenant?" one of the soldiers called into the forest. "You all right, sir?"

"I've got him," came a shout out of the trees. "I got the bloody, horse-thieving bastard!"

Mackenzie's heart pounded and her hands were sweating inside the calfskin gloves as she and the soldiers rounded a bend in the road. *Were they under attack or not?*

She spotted Lieutenant Burrow holding his musket on a red man. She took a second look. The Indian was just a boy.

"He the only one?" one of the British soldiers called as he looked up into the trees suspiciously.

The other soldiers dismounted and ran toward the prisoner, their muskets pointed at him.

"I believe so," the lieutenant answered, his perfectly pronounced speech seeming out of place here in the Colonial wilderness. "I caught him riding out with Major Albertson's horse. I believe we ought to hang him right here. Cassidy, get me a rope."

"Hang him?" Mackenzie jumped down from her mount.

The Indian was less than five feet tall, dressed in buckskins with sea shells tied into his long ebony braids. He looked to be about ten, the same age as Josh's younger brother. The Indian boy appeared frightened, yet he was brave enough to glare at the lieutenant with defiance in his black eyes.

"Mackenzie, come back here!" Joshua shouted. "He's dangerous."

"Dangerous?" She gave a little laugh, though she was still shaking from the scare. "Dangerous? He's a boy." She left her mount's reins dangling and marched toward the child.

One of the men grabbed the boy by a hank of his hair and shoved him onto his knees.

She walked right through the middle of the soldiers. "You men afraid of this little boy?" she dared, irate at their handling of him. "You ought to be ashamed of yourselves."

"I must ask you to stand back, Miss Daniels. My men and

I are trained to," the lieutenant cleared his throat, "deal with the enemy."

"Leaping apes in hell! He's a boy." She lifted her hand. "Children can't be enemies." Then she spotted blood on the sleeve of the boy's buckskin tunic. She stared at Lieutenant Burrow. "You shot him?"

"He stole the major's horse. He was trying to get away."

Mackenzie glanced at the bay casually nibbling on a bush. It was bridled with rough leather straps and saddled with a deerhide blanket. There were Indian symbols painted across its haunches in red ochre. It didn't look like a soldier's stolen horse to her.

She turned back to the Indian and reached for his arm, but he pulled back, saying something in his foreign tongue.

Mackenzie looked into his eyes, speaking slowly. "It's all right," she murmured. "I won't hurt you. I just want to look at your arm."

He relaxed a little, his gaze locked onto hers.

"That's right," she soothed. "I only want to look." She peeled back the blood-soaked leather of his sleeve. To her relief, the sun-tanned skin had only been grazed. It was an ugly, bloody wound, but clean, with no lead embedded in the flesh.

She called over her shoulder. "How do you know he stole Major Albertson's horse?"

"That's Major Albertson's horse, indeed." Burrow nodded. "I would know it anywhere. It has the white star on its forehead."

She snatched a water can from a soldier's saddle, opened the lid, and poured some of the water on the boy's arm. She hiked up her cotton tick skirt and knelt in the deep leaves to get a better look at the wound. "The major's horse is missing and you're certain this is it?"

"It's missing now, isn't it, Miss Daniels?" The lieutenant's tone was sharp and belittling. "Now please, if you will just step back and—"

"This man did not steal," the Indian boy said so softly that Mackenzie wasn't certain she heard him.

She looked up at his face, startled by the thickly accented English. "What did you say? You spoke English. I heard you."

He stared right into her face. "This man no steal soldier horse. Uncle's."

She blinked. "You didn't steal the horse?"

He stared at her with his black eyes. Her father had taught her to fear the redman. To avoid him. Now up close to one, the Indian boy seemed no different to her than a white boy. His blood ran the same color: red. She saw the same fear as white men's in his eyes.

"This man not steal," the boy repeated softly. "Take horse to fort. Uncle's horse."

"All right," she whispered so that only the boy could hear her. "I won't let them kill you. I swear it." Mackenzie reached under her skirt to tear a strip of muslin from the hem of her shift. She tied the muslin strip tightly around the boy's arm, speaking loudly. "Which way was he headed, Lieutenant?"

"Miss?"

She rose from her knees and whipped around to face the English officer. "The question was simple enough."

"Mackenzie, please. It's not our place to interfere," her father warned as he pushed his way through the crowd of soldiers.

She had done it again. She'd stepped over the line of female propriety. She could hear it in her father's voice. Yet she didn't care—not when she was all that stood between the boy and death. Mackenzie ignored him. "Lieutenant, I want to know which direction the boy was headed when you came upon him. Was he headed north toward the fort, or south toward us?"

The lieutenant avoided eye contact with her. "You do not know these scurvy red rats like I do, Miss Daniels. They can be rather crafty."

"I see." She swept off her bonnet to wipe the sweat from her forehead. "They're so crafty, these Indian boys, that they can be riding one way, but make it look like they're going another?" Her sarcasm was so thick that several of the soldiers snickered.

Lieutenant Burrow flushed. "Miss Daniels—"

A soldier approached them. "I got that rope ye asked for, Lieutenant. You want us to string 'im up right here on the road so the other redskins can see we're serious when it come to horse thievin'?"

Mackenzie took a big step backwards putting herself between the Indian boy still on his knees and the soldier with the rope. Her bonnet fell to the ground, but she left it where it lay. "You hang this child, and I'll have you stand trial for murder," she threatened.

The soldier glanced at the lieutenant. The lieutenant looked at Franklin Daniels, as if to ask why he couldn't control his own daughter.

Franklin cleared his throat. "Mackenzie, honey, step back and let the soldiers do their job."

"Do you hear yourself, Father? You sound just like them." She pointed at him. "We don't know if this horse is Major Albertson's or not."

"Mackenzie, I'm certain that Lieutenant Burrow has more experience with these matters than you or I do. He's lived in these woods. He's dealt with these hostiles."

"You always taught me to stand up for what I believe, Father." She stared him down. "I won't let them kill this boy for theft without a trial. We don't even know if that is the major's horse!"

She grabbed the Indian boy's hand and backed away while still remaining between him and the soldiers. "There's no reason why the lieutenant can't wait until we reach the fort to sort this matter out. Major Albertson can witness for himself if this is his horse. If so, than I agree the *boy* must be punished, but I doubt our friend would agree to hanging a *child*, Father."

Franklin studied her for a moment, then reluctantly turned to the lieutenant. "Ed, she's right. We'll be at the fort in a few hours. If he stole the horse, what's the difference if you hang him now, or at sunset?"

The soldiers waited for the officer to respond.

The lieutenant frowned, silent for a moment. "Cassidy," he shouted. "Tie the redskin up to your saddle. Let him trot a few hours. We'll give our major the satisfaction of hanging the little bastard himself.'' He walked away.

Mackenzie let out a sigh of relief. ''They're not going to hang you,'' she told the boy quietly. ''They're going to take you to the fort. Do you understand me?''

The soldier called Cassidy pulled the boy roughly to his feet and bound his hands together in front of him.

The boy looked at her, his ebony eyes filled with both fear and relief and gratitude. ''My uncle will speak the truth. *His* horse. Gift from English *manake* soldier many moons. This man no take the horse.''

She smiled grimly. ''We'll get to the bottom of this, I swear we will.'' She gave Cassidy a rough push on the shoulder. ''Easy there. That's tight enough. You'll cut the blood off to his hands if you make those knots any tighter.''

''Mackenzie,'' Joshua called as he lead her horse toward her. ''You'd best mount up.'' He kept his gaze lowered as if he were embarrassed by her forward behavior.

Not that she gave two snaps.

''I'm not riding.'' She snatched her hat up off the ground and beat off the leaves clinging to the straw.

''N . . . Not riding?''

She shook her head. ''No. The boy walks. I walk. If I don't, you know they'll move too quickly. They'll be dragging him behind a horse in less than an hour's time.'' She walked away before he had time to think of an answer.

As she approached Fort Belvadere Mackenzie could smell raw sewage and unwashed bodies.

The fort itself seemed rather unimposing here in the middle of such a grand wilderness. The fifteen-foot palisade walls were cut from nearby gum and sassafras trees. As big around as a man's forearm, the tree trunks had been sunk into the ground with the bark still attached and sharpened to points on the top.

A lookout high on the wall cried a warning and the gates swung open to allow the group inside. Mackenzie walked beside the Indian boy, her eyes and mind taking in all she saw and smelled and heard.

Inside the walls, one large, two-story log building ran east to west, its rear wall attached to the palisade. Smaller, even cruder buildings were scattered in the muddy yard.

Men in red uniforms hurried back and forth through the filthy compound. Pigs and geese ran freely, turning the entire yard into a slop pit. She nearly gagged at the smell of refuse that was piled everywhere: rotten cabbage, rancid meat, bean shells—all just tossed into the yard on top of animal droppings. Yet she was fascinated at the same time.

Her father's tavern and trading post saw some activity during the traveling months, but there were never more than a dozen people there at a time. Here, there had to be nearly one hundred soldiers, all milling about, most appearing bored.

Mackenzie felt trapped as the gates of the fort swung shut behind them. She understood the walls were for protection against the warring Indians, but she wasn't sure they made her feel any safer.

"Franklin! You're here at last. Mackenzie, dear." Major Albertson rushed across the compound, his arms outstretched to hug her.

Instead of looking at the major's familiar face, her gaze was immediately drawn to the man who strode beside him.

A redman.

A savage.

The most glorious man she had ever laid eyes on.

Chapter Two

Major Albertson wrapped her in his arms in a bear hug, his full beard scratching her face as he kissed her. "You made it. I knew you would." He was a big man, as tall and wide as a doorway. His laughter was warm and genuine.

He and her father had been friends as boys living together on the Tidewater. As adults, they had gone their separate ways but stayed in touch. Franklin had built the tavern and trading post. Harry had bought himself a commission in the king's army.

Mackenzie lifted her arms automatically to her friend's embrace, but her thoughts were not on the major's welcome. She didn't know what it was about the Indian that mesmerized her so, but she couldn't tear her gaze away from him.

Major Albertson released her and held out his hands to Franklin Daniels.

Mackenzie just stood there in the ankle-deep mud watching the Indian. He stared back with the darkest obsidian eyes she had ever seen. He made her feel self-conscious. Her appearance had never been of importance to her in the past, but suddenly she wished she weren't so dirty and travel-worn. She pushed

back a lock of droopy hair, hoping she improved her appearance
a little.

"Ah, Franklin. You did come with Mackenzie." Major
Albertson shook her father's hands vigorously. "I knew you'd
not be able to resist my invitation." The two friends embraced,
and then the major stepped back. "I want to introduce to you
one of our delegates."

Still, the Indian stared at her. Still, she stared back, taking
in every ripple of the sun-bronzed muscles on his bare arms
and legs. Sweet heavens, the man was nearly naked and not a
bit ashamed. The setting sun sparkled off the ornamental copper
bands that accentuated the girth of his biceps. His face was
fine-lined, as if molded by a master potter, his skin the color
of rich, red clay. His eyelids, fringed by black lashes never
blinked. He had the most fascinating lips she had ever noticed
on a man, thin and firm. Lips she imagined pressing against
her own. What would they feel like? How would they taste?
Mackenzie knew she blushed. She lowered her gaze, and
focused on the men's conversation. *Fire Dancer?* Was that
what the major had called the redman? She thought the major
said he was an Indian prince or something.

The Indian dipped his noble chin in something akin to a nod
to her father.

"And this is Mackenzie Daniels, his daughter," the major
continued jovially.

Mackenzie didn't lift her torn skirts to curtsy as would have
been proper. Instead, she nodded regally, imitating him.

She could have sworn she saw the barest smile cross his
lips. Was he mocking her, or was he just amused?

"Major! I've a matter here that demands your attention."
Lieutenant Burrow sloshed through the mud toward them, picking his way around a sow with a fetid cabbage in her mouth.
Piglets squealed and scattered but for one that hung tightly to
its mama's long teat.

"Lieutenant, can it not wait?" The major addressed his
officer with good-natured impatience. "I'd like to offer my
good friends a drink and a decent hot meal after their arduous
journey."

"It cannot wait, sir, I assure you." The lieutenant planted himself before the major.

"Very well. Make it quick."

The lieutenant indicated the native boy with a nod of his chiseled chin. "We caught that redskin stealing your horse, sir. I intended to hang him there on the trail as a sign of our intolerance for thieves." He eyed Fire Dancer who stood silently beside the major. "But . . . but I thought better of it, sir, and decided to allow you the honors."

Mackenzie's eyes widened at the man's lie, but she kept her mouth shut, waiting for the major's response.

"Stole my horse?"

"Aye, sir." The lieutenant flicked an imaginary speck of dirt from his uniform coat. "But as I said, I've the culprit under custody."

"That boy stole my Johnny?" The major glanced over his shoulder at a private who stood behind him. He barely looked old enough to be off his mother's lead lines. "Somebody stole my horse and you didn't tell me, Private O'Donaho?"

The private immediately came to attention. "I . . . I didn't, I didn't know your Johnny was missing, Major."

"There's your stolen horse, sir." The lieutenant thrust out his chest. "Laden with Indian accouterments, but in good shape, nonetheless. We've returned him to the paddock."

"How the hell are we losing horses again with gates locked day and night?" The major pushed passed the lieutenant. "This thief one of yours, Fire Dancer?" He took long strides toward the paddock intent on getting a better look at the horse and the boy who'd stolen it.

The Indian brushed past Mackenzie as he walked at the major's side. He passed so closely to her that she felt the warmth of his skin.

"This man knows the boy," said Fire Dancer. "He is not a thief."

Mackenzie followed Fire Dancer with her gaze, fascinated by the sound of his voice. It was smooth like honey and lilting, each syllable pronounced in slow, perfect English. Then he let out a string of gibberish, and the boy called back in the same tongue. It must have been their Indian language they spoke.

Mackenzie ran a couple steps to catch up with Major Albertson and Fire Dancer.

Her father called her name, warning her to stay out of it, but she pretended she didn't hear him. "I knew you would want to take care of this matter yourself, Harry," she said as she reached his side. "I didn't think you'd want a child hanged."

The major lifted a thick brow. "What made me guess you were somehow involved in this?"

She looked away quickly, feeling self-conscious as the Indian watched her. The lieutenant and the escort soldiers all followed her and the major and the Indian to the paddock near the entrance to the fort.

"There, there he is, sir. Sound and safe."

Major Albertson leaned on the split rail fence. "Where?"

"There, sir. Still wearing the trappings. I wanted you to see how the savage tried to disguise your mount. The little heathen has even painted pagan symbols on the hindquarters."

"Hell, that isn't my Johnny!" The major spun around. "Have you lost what little sense you possessed, Burrow?"

The lieutenant paled under his superior's gaze. "I . . . I was certain that was your horse. It . . . it's a roan gelding with a star on its forehead."

"And boots, for heaven's sake! Does my Johnny have white boots?"

"No, sir," said Private O'Donaho standing beside him.

"No sir, I guess not, sir," echoed the lieutenant.

Fire Dancer stood at the rail of the paddock. "My horse," he said quietly. "The boy is son to my sister. He is called Tall Moccasin. Tall Moccasin brings the horse to his uncle."

The major nodded toward the Indian boy bound at the hands and pinned between two redcoats. "That's your nephew?"

"*Ahⸯ.*" Fire Dancer nodded.

"*Ahⸯ,*" Mackenzie mimicked under her breath. She didn't know why, but she liked the sound of the word.

"Well, why the hell didn't you say so?"

"This man knows that all English *manake* suspect we *sav-*

ages.'' He emphasized the word with sarcasm. "I wanted you to see the truth for your own eyes."

The major gave a snort. "Don't just stand there," he shouted to the soldiers. "Let him the hell go!" He waved his hand impatiently. "Didn't you just hear our guest? It's Fire Dancer's horse!"

One of the soldiers hurriedly began to untie the boy.

"I apologize for the mistake," the lieutenant said. "I saw the redskin, and I knew he couldn't actually own a horse. I—"

Fire Dancer glared at the Lieutenant.

The major held up his hand to silence his officer. "If I were in your boots right now, Burrow, I think I'd shut my mouth. You're in deep enough horse crap as it is." He lowered his voice so that only the lieutenant and Mackenzie heard him. "You're lucky old Fire Dancer didn't scalp you right here. Now get out of my sight. I'll see you at *Report* tonight."

Fire Dancer turned and walked toward his nephew.

"I apologize, Fire Dancer," the major called after him. "You get these men barely weaned from their mama's tit and they want to make an impression on their superiors. Bring the boy to the evening meal, if you like. I want you both to be guests in my quarters for supper."

Fire Dancer nodded. His black hair, as long as Mackenzie's and tied in a queue, blew in the late afternoon breeze. "This man thanks you." The sarcasm was gone from his tone. "There are no bad feelings. I also have men who do not think with their heads."

"See you for supper, then," the major called. Then, turning his attention to Mackenzie, he took her hand. "Come on, girl. Let's see about that drink, you and I. Your father looks parched."

"You mean he looks mad." She dragged her gaze from the Indian as she and the major walked side by side through the mud and refuse of the fort yard. "He doesn't like me interfering in *men's* business. He's says I'm going to get myself injured or worse."

The major looked at her. "And your father's a wise man."

"Harry, I couldn't just let that lieutenant hang that boy." She raised her voice in anger at the thought of what could have happened. "It wasn't even a stolen horse."

"I know, I know." Harry patted her hand. "It was wrong for that young man to jump to conclusions, but you don't know the whole story here. You don't why they're all so scared, why we're all scared," he said cryptically. "Now smooth your dander. I was going to say your father is right, that you risk getting hurt, but I admire your grit." He smiled. "You're one ballsy woman. And I know you won't be offended by me saying so. That's why I knew this would be the perfect job for you."

She smiled. "The portraits. You want me to get started right away?" she said, so excited that she could barely contain herself. "Who will I be painting? You, of course. But who else?"

He laughed. "Let's get you settled in first. There'll be plenty of time tonight after supper or tomorrow to talk of business. There's your father now. Gads, who is that pale boy with him?"

Mackenzie couldn't resist a giggle. "That was to be my betrothed, Joshua Watkins."

"Was to be?" He raised eyebrows so bushy that they met as one in the middle of his forehead. "You turned him down?"

"It would never work. I don't want to marry Joshua, or any other man, for that matter."

Major Albertson chuckled. "Just wait, sweetheart. You've just not met the right man yet."

Her father approached them, interrupting their conversation. "I'm sorry, Harry. I had to see to my wagon. Josh got it stuck trying to move it." He shot an impatient glare in Mackenzie's direction. "I do apologize for my daughter's interference in your business."

The major waved his free hand. "No apologies necessary. I know her as well as you do. Now let Private O'Donaho take you to your quarters to get cleaned up. It isn't fancy, but it's a sight cleaner than this yard." He kicked a blackened potato with the toe of his boot. "You and the boy, Franklin, will be bunking with the officers because space is tight, but I had a nice corner storage room cleaned out for Mackenzie on the second floor. She'll be safe and well-guarded there. After you get settled in, we'll talk in my quarters. I got a hind of bear sizzling on the spit as we speak. The meat with a nice Madeira will make us all forget our troubles.'' He winked.

''Thank you,'' Mackenzie mouthed silently. And then she allowed her father and the private to lead her away.

The quarters Major Albertson provided for Mackenzie were more than adequate. The rustic room was small, perhaps eight feet by eight feet, the walls horizontal logs with the bark still on them. There was a narrow rope bed with a feather tick that would be perfectly comfortable once she added her mother's blue and white quilt. The room had no fireplace, but it was already warm enough that she wouldn't need one. A stump serving as a table and a canvas camp stool occupied one corner. Iron nails had been pounded into one wall for her to hang her clothing. But the best thing about the room was its small window.

Mackenzie kneeled on her bed, pulled the iron pin on the shutter, and pushed it open. A warm breeze from the trees blew in, chasing away the stench of the fort. She pressed her face to the wooden bars, breathing deeply. The window faced west, giving her a view of the sun beginning to set over the treetops in a glorious ball of blazing red and yellow.

Mackenzie smiled to herself, bouncing up off the bed. This room would be ideal for her painting. She already knew where she would place her subjects—there, in the corner of the room, and here . . . here she would place her easel. She glanced at the window. The only problem would be whether or not she would have enough natural light. It was almost dusk now and already necessary to illuminate the room with several smelly, fat-back candles. She would have to wait until daylight to see how much sun filtered through the chinks in the log walls.

Someone tapped at the door and Mackenzie answered it. It was Private O'Donaho with her trunk.

''Just put it right there,'' she said as she held open the door. The boy dropped the trunk beside the bed and made a hasty retreat to the doorway, obviously shy. "Will . . . will there be anything else, Miss?"

She followed him to the door. "It's Mackenzie. And, no. I don't need anything else. Thank you for bringing up my trunk."

"Your . . . your father says he'll have your painting supplies sent up whilst you're at supper." He stole a quick glance at her before returning his gaze to his boots. "I . . . I'll see to it myself, Miss . . . um . . . Mackenzie."

She smiled. "Thank you. It's Charlie, right?"

He scuffed his boot. "Private Charlie O'Donaho."

She rested her hand on the door, anxious to change out of her dirty travel clothes and get downstairs to the meal Major Albertson promised. She was looking forward to seeing the Indian again. "Well, thank you again."

"My . . . my pleasure." The private backed out of the room and closed her door behind him.

Mackenzie immediately went to the trunk. She hadn't brought many pieces of clothing with her, and what she had brought was rather utilitarian. As silly as it was, she wanted to look presentable tonight. She told herself it was because she had displeased her father today, and she knew how he appreciated it when she at least made an attempt to appear feminine. But she knew that wasn't the whole truth. What she really wanted was to look nice for *him*.

Mackenzie changed into her leather skirt and a white linen shirt she'd confiscated from her father's clothes press years ago. She added a wide leather belt she'd bought at the Chestertown fair. The clothing was plain, but from what she could see in the small looking-glass she brought with her, the white was becoming against her suntanned skin and the skirt form-fitting enough to flatter her figure.

She brushed out her hair and on impulse, left it down but for a braid she twisted on the crown of her head. After she rubbed off most of the mud that had dried on her boots, she was ready.

Giddy with excitement, Mackenzie made her way down the narrow, cloistering hallway and down the steps, carrying a candle for light. At the bottom of the steps, she found a redcoat soldier, obviously on duty.

"This way, Miss." He led her through a labyrinth of narrow passageways. Squeaking rodents raced ahead of them. She ducked as a bat flew overhead. The soldier paid no mind to the pests, so neither did she. She'd have no one saying Mackenzie Daniels was a cowering female.

Mackenzie heard the men laughing before she reached the major's quarters. She recognized Harry's boisterous voice and her father's own quieter one.

The soldier swung open a crude planked door and stepped back to let her enter. He reached for her candle. "I'll take it, Miss."

"Thank you." She lifted her leather skirt to step over the sill, and entered the noisy dining room.

"There you are." Joshua hurried toward her.

He was still wearing the same dusty clothes, his hair uncombed, his face unwashed. She could smell his body odor an arm's length away.

"Are you all right?" he asked anxiously.

"Fine. Why?"

He lowered his voice so that no one else could hear him. "The quarters your father and I are sharing with the officers are dreadful."

"My room is fine." She lifted her shoulder. "Small, but quite nice. I can paint right there, if I wish."

"I think your father should sell his goods, and we should turn around and go home to the Chesapeake. This is no place for a woman."

"Mackenzie!" Major Albertson waved for her to approach. He stood on the far side of the room near a stone fireplace, a mug in his hand.

"I rather like it here," Mackenzie answered Joshua as she waved back at Harry. "Now, if you'll excuse me." She nodded politely and left him to join the major.

"A drink, Mackenzie?"

She smiled up at Major Albertson as he crossed the plank floor to greet her. "You promised me a good Madeira."

"Charlie! Get Miss Daniels a Madeira." He turned back to her. "Your room satisfactory?"

"Perfect. I appreciate the window." She wrinkled her nose. "I prefer the scent of the forest to that of the fort, I fear."

He laughed heartily. "You get used to it after awhile, dear." He accepted a glass of amber wine from O'Donaho and pushed it into her hands. "Let's eat. I'm starving."

Mackenzie took the seat Major Albertson indicated next to her father, who sat next to the major at the head of the table. Joshua sat further down with the other officers. The table quickly filled, save for two empty chairs directly across from Mackenzie.

After a quick blessing, they began their meal. A young woman appeared through a doorway with the first course. She was a pretty native woman dressed in a stained English bodice and petticoats. Her black hair was pulled back and tucked haphazardly under a mob cap. As the only other woman Mackenzie had seen at the fort so far, she immediately intrigued Mackenzie. If it hadn't been for her bronze skin, she'd have looked like a serving wench in Franklin Daniel's tavern.

"Mary makes the best damned roast bear south of the Adirondacks."

She had a Christian name? How odd. Mackenzie smiled as the woman gave her a portion of soup. "Thank you, Mary."

Mary kept her eyes averted.

Mackenzie took a corn biscuit and passed the plate to the young lieutenant beside her. She glanced at the empty chairs. "Missing guests?"

The major slathered butter on his three biscuits. "Indian time."

"Sir?"

Albertson chuckled. "Our Shawnee delegate moves on what I call Indian time. It's not that he can't tell time. He's even got himself a silver pocket watch. He just doesn't pay attention to it. Comes and goes as he pleases. It drives our French delegate Major DuBois mad." He reached for the stewed squash her father passed. "The Indian and his nephew'll be around after awhile."

Mackenzie lifted her fork to taste the bear meat. "And where is the French delegate?"

"Called away." Albertson took an enormous bite of his biscuit. "Had to go north to settle some uprising. Seems a pack of his own redskins turned on one of his forts. He's expected back within a fortnight, though."

Mackenzie nodded. The bear meat was strong but moist and savory. She cut off another slice as her gaze wandered to the empty chairs. She listened as her father and the major struck up a conversation.

The meal was half over when the outside door swung open, and Fire Dancer and his nephew entered. Obviously, they had bathed. Fire Dancer's hair, pulled back in a sleek queue, was still wet. He had changed into a knee length skirt, tall moccasins and a soft buckskin tunic that was beaded with the most beautiful work she had ever seen. The boy was dressed similarly.

Mackenzie smiled to herself, lowering her gaze to her plate. From the smell of the room, there were a few others who should have followed the Indians' example.

"Major Albertson." Fire Dancer nodded.

"Sit. Sit. You know the drill." The Major rocked back in his chair. "Mary!" he shouted. " 'Nother guest."

Fire Dancer took his seat directly across from Mackenzie, allowing the boy to sit beside Major Albertson.

"This is my sister's son, Tall Moccasin," Fire Dancer introduced.

Major Albertson stuffed another piece of biscuit into his mouth. "So sorry about the mix-up, boy. You weren't injured, were you?"

The Indian boy looked to his uncle, as if asking permission to speak.

Fire Dancer nodded slightly.

"This man was not injured," the boy said simply. Then he pulled his knife from his belt and dug into the slab of bear meat Mary served him.

Fire Dancer's gaze moved across the table and settled on Mackenzie. He said nothing.

She had no clue as to what he was thinking. She said nothing.

She couldn't tear her gaze from his deep, soul-searching black eyes.

"Mackenzie?"

She blinked. "I'm sorry, Major. What did you say? It's been a long day, and I fear I wasn't paying attention."

"I said you'll be painting Fire Dancer. Me, Fire Dancer, and Major DuBois, when he gets here. We will settle this fighting here, and our portraits'll be hanging in Whitehall in London."

Mackenzie grinned at the thought. "I'll do my best, Harry, I swear it."

"I know you will."

Dinner progressed quickly. The officers were so pleased to have female companionship that they all vied for her attention. Here, it didn't seem to matter that she wasn't very feminine. She was flattered by the attention, but a shameless part of her wished it was coming from the Indian.

One by one, the men began to rise and excuse themselves. They had duties to attend to, or pipes to smoke. Fire Dancer and his nephew left, and Mackenzie was disappointed that she didn't get to speak to him—not that she knew what she would say to an Indian. She was disappointed, nonetheless.

For half an hour, Mackenzie listened to her father, Joshua, the major, and a few others discuss the war. Bored with the conversation, she finally excused herself.

"Let me escort you." Joshua jumped up.

"Thank you, but that won't be necessary. I can find my own way." Mackenzie stretched and yawned. She was anxious to get a good night's sleep. Tomorrow, she would set up her easel and begin searching for the perfect spot to paint the portraits.

Joshua glanced at Franklin. He pleaded with one hand. "Sir, you're not going to let her—."

"Hell, let her go, Josh. Women need time to themselves. She's safe, isn't she?" her father questioned the major.

Albertson nodded. "Safe as long as she's inside these walls."

Mackenzie said goodnight and taking a candle from Mary, she stepped out into the dark hallway.

"Need an escort, ma'am?"

Startled by the soldier's voice, she pressed her hand to her pounding heart. "Goodness, no. But thank you." Lifting the candle, she started down the narrow passageway, but instead of heading straight for the staircase, she made a slight detour. She needed a breath of fresh air before she went to sleep.

Mackenzie pushed open a heavy door and stepped out onto a wooden walkway. She leaned on a rail and breathed deeply. The yard was quiet now except for the sound of horses naying and the occasional squeal of a piglet. The tiny windows of the fort were illuminated with light. The watch soldiers' pipes glowed in the darkness on the palisade walls across the open yard. High in the sky above the fort walls, the stars glimmered.

Mackenzie sighed at the beauty. She had enjoyed sleeping outside so much during her journey that she hated the thought of sleeping in a dark, storage-closet-turned-bedchamber.

"It is beautiful, *Tapalamawatah's* sky, no?"

Mackenzie didn't know where he came from. She'd never heard a sound, and yet, suddenly the Indian was standing beside her, gazing up into the heavens. Her heart gave a little trip.

"It is beautiful," she whispered. He was so close that his bare arm brushed her sleeve. He smelled clean, like the forest, and the streams she'd crossed to reach the fort. The smell of him and his nearness made her feel strange inside, but not bad.

"I was just thinking that, in coming here, we slept outside under these stars," she said hesitantly. "It was the first time I ever slept outside. I'm going to miss it."

Fire Dancer took his time in responding. It was as if he actually considered her words before formulating his own reply. "In the winter, when it is cold and I sleep in my wigwam, this man misses the sky."

"So we have something in common." She smiled at him in the darkness. "I really didn't get to talk to you at the supper table."

He tapped his thumb and forefinger together in a rapid motion. "The officers, they chatter like magpies. This man wanted to speak to you. To thank you."

She didn't look at him because she didn't want him to know how nervous she was in his presence. "For what?"

"The soldiers could have hanged Tall Moccasin for what he

did not do. You had courage to speak for him when your men did not.''

She lifted her hand lamely. ''It was nothing. I only wanted to see justice done. The boy didn't look like a thief to me and the lieutenant seemed too quick to accuse.''

''To some, it was nothing. To me, much. This man loves the boy as he would love a son of his own loins. This man will not forget what you did for the boy . . . for me.''

Mackenzie could feel the Indian staring intently at her. She didn't dare meet his gaze. How odd a man he was, speaking of love so freely. She wondered if it was the Indian way. It certainly wasn't the colonists way. Even her father, who she knew loved her a great deal, never actually used the word.

Fire Dancer was silent for so long that she thought he might leave. But she wasn't quite ready for him to go. She had to think of something to say to keep him a little longer. ''I . . . I was wondering why you were here.'' She balanced the candlestick on the rail. ''I mean, I know you're a delegate, but how were you chosen to come to the peace talks?''

When he didn't answer right away, she was afraid she had said something to offend him. ''I'm sorry. Now I sound like the magpie. It's really none of my business. I shouldn't have asked.''

''No. You have said nothing to anger this man. I am just surprised that you would have this question. Other white women I know do not speak of such matters.''

She could feel her face growing warm. ''Another fault of mine. I like politics.'' She smoothed her rough hands nervously. ''Not very womanly.'' Then she raised her hands. ''Like these.''

To Mackenzie's surprise, Fire Dancer took one of her hands in his. She knew the proper thing would have been to pull away, but she couldn't help herself. His hands were the same size as hers—warm, gentle, but firm.

''This man does not think these hands are unwomanly.'' He smoothed them in something akin to a caress.

Now Mackenzie knew she was blushing. Surely he hadn't meant his comment to be a compliment, but she took it as one.

He let go of her hand. "You ask why I come? I come because the chief sent me. But the chief is also the parent to this man."

"Your father is the chief of your tribe? He must be very important." For some reason, she wasn't surprised. Fire Dancer had a quiet, commanding way about him.

He smiled. "Chief of my village, but an important chief. One who represents our—" he paused, obviously looking for the right word—"clan, as well."

"I see. And your clan wants peace. You don't want to fight with the French against the British anymore."

He lifted a finger to correct her. "This man and his clan did not choose sides. Not yet."

She nodded. "But you will?"

"This man wishes for peace. No sides. No enemies."

She smiled grimly. "I understand." They were both silent for a moment, but it wasn't an uncomfortable silence. "Well, I'd better go inside before someone starts looking for me, thinking I've been kidnapped by wild Indians." She swallowed a laugh as she realized what she'd said. Now she felt like a complete fool.

"I'm sorry," she said softly. "I didn't mean that. It's only that—"

"It is what you know. What you have been told by your men."

Ashamed, she hung her head. "Yes. I fear I've not really been left to make my own judgments." She lifted her chin. "But I am now, and I'm thinking that maybe my father has been wrong." She reached for the candle, lifting it to illuminate his face. "You don't seem so dangerous to me."

"No?" He raised a feathery black eyebrow, his face without emotion. "Do not be so sure."

Then he walked away as silently as he'd come.

Chapter Three

Mackenzie stood on the palisade walkway, her hand on one hip, her sketching pencil poised. Major Albertson sat perfectly still on a camp stool, his face turned so that the light struck his red-bearded face at just the right angle.

Mackenzie paused, drew a line, and glanced at her subject again. It was important to her that these portraits be good. She needed to prove to her father that she could make money as an artist. She had to prove it to herself.

"Another sitting and I should be done with my sketching," she told the major. "Then I can begin painting." Her grandfather had taught her to paint and had advised that making polite discourse helped the subject to relax. It was easy enough to talk to Harry. She'd known him since she was a little girl and he was a green lieutenant like Burrow.

"I hope you're sketching me to be the good-looking hound that I am." He reached up to pinch his own ruddy cheek. "Not too fleshy."

"I sketch and paint what I see." She eyed him carefully, trying to judge the angle of his jawbone. "And what I see is a handsome, caring bear of a man."

He chuckled. "You could make a man very happy, Mackenzie. If I were a few years younger, I'd marry you myself."

She laughed at the ridiculous thought. "I don't make most men happy. My father's cross with me again. He doesn't think I should be standing up here, even though he knows that I need the direct sunlight. He's positive a sniper is going to murder me." She rolled her eyes. "Joshua is barely speaking to me because, two days ago, I refused to let him carry my slop bucket. Now, apparently, your Shawnee delegate is angry with me because he failed to show up for his sitting this morning. That's two in a row he's missed."

Major Albertson frowned, ruining the line of his mouth. "That Fire Dancer, he's a hard one to figure out. I'll speak to him, but I can't make any guarantees."

She nodded and reached out to lift his chin slightly. "Good. Right there." She sketched another line on her canvas. "You said he's a hard one to figure out. What do you mean?"

"He's an Indian. They don't make sense. I mean, I think he's honest enough. I believe he's really looking for peace, but how can you trust a man when you don't know what he's thinking? He just stares at you with those heathen black eyes of his. You can't read them like you can a white man's. DuBois doesn't trust him, and hell, they're supposed to be on the same side."

"I thought Fire Dancer wasn't on either side."

Albertson turned his head, ruining his pose. "Who told you that?"

Mackenzie thought before she spoke. She kept her gaze fixed on her canvas. "Fire Dancer and I were making conversation after supper that night in your quarters. I asked him why he was here. Could you please turn back? I need you to sit still."

He turned his head. "You shouldn't be having private conversations with savages. Especially not him, prince or not. And you shouldn't be alone with him, either. He's dangerous."

Fire Dancer's words echoed in her head. He himself had suggested that he was dangerous. Mackenzie wrinkled her nose. "Dangerous, how? He's a peace negotiator, the same as you. Besides, just what do you think he's going to do to me? Kidnap me?'' She laughed. ''He's surrounded by the King's armed soldiers, for sweet heaven's sake. You said yourself—no one can get in or out of this fort without your men knowing it.''

''He's an Indian.''

''Oh.'' She plucked a bit of lint from his red wool uniform coat. ''And that automatically makes him a dangerous man, no matter how honest he may be, or how honorable?''

His reply was firm. ''Yes.''

She turned back to the portrait sketch. ''Now you sound like my father.'' She licked her finger and rubbed the canvas where she'd made an error. ''I swear, you men, you're all alike. You draw these lines in the sand and they're thick black lines. Don't you ever see the gray area? Don't you ever think that our side might be just a little wrong?''

The major rose. ''You're saying we should let the Frenchmen take our land?''

''*Our* land?''

''Our people began colonizing in the name of England first. It's our land.''

''And who was here before these colonists arrived, before the French arrived?''

He rolled his eyes. ''This is why women shouldn't discuss politics. You don't understand the complexities.'' He threw up his hand impatiently. ''I have to go. Duties to attend to.''

Mackenzie smiled as he retreated. She seemed to have a knack for annoying people. She wasn't worried, though. She and Harry had shared many disputes over the years, and they always forgave each other later. ''See,'' she called after him. ''I told you I'd make a lousy wife!''

Late in the afternoon, Mackenzie sat on her camp cot, toying with a piece of writing charcoal and a bit of paper. She intended to sketch the fort walls, as she saw them, from the inside, but instead, she found herself sketching Fire Dancer's horse in the paddock below. The horse had returned sometime this afternoon, with its owner, she presumed. Perhaps Fire Dancer could meet with her tomorrow to let her begin her sketching. She thought she'd give Harry a day to cool off before she called for him again.

Bored, Mackenzie rose from the bed. It was hot inside the tiny chamber. No breeze blew, and the air was stifling. She went to her water bucket for a drink but found it empty. Grabbing her straw bonnet off a nail, she took the bucket and left the room.

In the yard, Mackenzie passed the water barrels that stood on pallets in the center of the yard. She knew from experience that the water in the barrels would be lukewarm and flat tasting by now. What she wanted was some cold water from the stream. Dropping her bonnet onto her head, she approached the fort gates. This time of day, they were often left open so that the men could hunt in the forest or exercise their mounts.

A soldier stopped her at the gate. "Can I help you?"

"The stream is straight ahead, isn't it?"

"Well, yes, yes it is, but—"

"But what?"

"But it's not safe for you to go there. If you want water, you can get it there." He pointed toward the center of the yard. The sow and her piglets were sleeping under the shade of the barrels.

"I want fresh water, and I want to walk. Is it or isn't it straight ahead?"

He lowered his musket to block her passing. "I'll have to get permission from the major before I can let you pass. His orders are strict about visitors."

"But I just saw Joshua Watkins pass through the gates not an hour ago."

"He was with a hunting party, and he is," the guard cleared his throat, "a man."

She gripped the bucket, controlling her irritation. "I just want to walk down to the stream and back."

"I'll still have to check with the major."

"I see." She smiled sweetly, changing tacks. "Well, go ahead."

"Now?"

"Of course. You go. I'll wait here." She fanned herself with her hand. "In the shade of the wall."

He stared at her in obvious indecision. "Well . . . all right. It won't take but a minute." He glanced at a soldier on the palisade above. "Clyde, can you come down and guard the gate? I gotta see Major Albertson."

"Be down directly."

Mackenzie smiled at the gate guard again and waved like a simpleton as he passed her. She waited until he was halfway across the yard and then walked out the gate, swinging her bucket on her arm.

Mackenzie entered the forest and immediately felt cooler. It was so damned hot inside the walls of the fort because no air could circulate. Only on the palisade wall could she catch her breath, but she was only permitted to walk there during the daylight hours. She'd spent four nights in the fort and on two of those nights, renegade Indian snipers fired muskets and flaming arrows over the walls. Apparently, on both nights, it was Fire Dancer's men who chased them off.

Her father and the major had paid her little mind when Mackenzie tried to question them as to why the Indians were shooting at them when they were in the midst of peace negotiations. Harry kept telling her that she didn't understand the Indians. Her father said nothing, except that she was to keep off the palisade walls after dusk, and away from any savages inside the walls. Even though they were Major Albertson's guests, he said they couldn't be trusted.

Mackenzie listened to the chatter of a towhee as she followed the path down toward the stream. She could already hear water bubbling over the rocks and she could imagine how cold and wet it would taste. Around a bend, she spotted the stream. It was narrow, perhaps only as wide as she was tall, but it appeared to be several feet deep in the center and the water was clear and fast moving.

She knelt on the bank and tossed down her bucket. With her hands she scooped up water and drank, sighing with pleasure. When she'd had her fill, she sat back on the bank, debating whether or not she should take off her boots and yarn stockings and wade in.

For a moment she watched a school of tadpoles zip in and

out of a hollow in the bank. When she touched her finger to the surface, to her delight, they came up to nibble on it.

Mackenzie scooped up a handful of water and brushed the back of her neck, letting the rivulets trickle down her neck.

Suddenly, she had an uncanny feeling that someone was watching her. She glanced over her shoulder, but saw only a squirrel shimmying up a tree trunk. She faced the stream, suspiciously checking left and right. Something didn't *feel* right.

"Guess I should get back," she said aloud to calm herself. She stood up and leaned over to fill her bucket with fresh water. An Indian with the long black hair stared back at her from a reflection on the surface of the stream. "Fire Dancer?" She turned, feeling a little ripple of excitement.

Her blood ran cold. It was an Indian, but not *him*. This one's face was painted in red and black stripes. He held some kind of hatchet with dangling feathers in the air. His black eyes were filled with hatred for her.

Mackenzie stood frozen, too frightened to move or cry out for help. *Sweet God, he's going to murder me in cold blood,* she thought wildly.

He lunged toward her.

"Papa!" she screamed in terror. She swung the only weapon she had, the wooden bucket filled with water.

The Indian yelped and lurched left as she struck his head, splashing them both with water. When he swung the hatchet at her, she screamed again. "Help!" She dropped to the ground and rolled out of the way of the shiny blade. The bucket flew from her hands. Covering her head to protect herself, she rolled onto her feet, ready to spring.

She cringed at the whoosh of an arrow slicing through the air, then glanced up at the Indian.

An arrow protruded from his chest. His eyes widened in shock as he fell straight back into the leaves, dead before he hit the ground.

Mackenzie scrambled to her feet, intent on reaching the fort's walls. A hand descended on her shoulder, holding her down.

"No!" she screamed, wrenching from the strong grip.

"*Mahtah,* Mack-en-zie."

She whipped around and raised her fist, ready to pummel her attacker. But he said her name . . .

"Fire Dancer?" she looked into the familiar bronze face. "Oh, sweet heaven, it's you," she panted, pressing her hand to her chest. Her heart raced so fast that she thought it would burst from her chest. "That Indian he . . . you . . ." She wiped at the hot tears that ran down her cheeks.

"You are all right?" he asked calmly, as if he killed a man every day of the week.

"Yes, I . . . I think so." She still couldn't catch her breath. She was shaking all over. "He . . . he didn't hurt me. Just sc . . . scared me half out of my wits."

"Get your water. You must go back to the fort." He studied the forest uneasily. "Hurry, Mack-en-zie."

She watched as he pressed his moccasin to the dead Indian's chest, and pulled out the arrow. It made a horrible crunching sound as the barbed tip tore through his flesh.

She pushed herself up out of the leaves. She stared at the dead man, unable to believe what had happened. "He . . . he was going to kill me! Why would one of your men—"

"My men?" Fire Dancer gave a derisive snort. He wiped the blood from the arrowhead on his bare thigh and thrust the arrow back into the deerhide quiver he wore on his back. "That is not my man! That is *Huron.*" He spat the word as if it was foul.

"Huron?" She picked up her bucket with shaking hands. There was blood on the bottom rim. The dead Indian's blood.

"*Huron. Iroquois.* Dogs. All the same. Get your water. Hurry."

She squatted on the bank to refill her bucket. She didn't really want the water now, but it was easier to fetch it than to argue. "So . . . so he's not one of your kind?"

"He is not one of *The People,* Lenape or Shawnee. Come." He signaled urgently. "You must go back. Now!"

With her bucket full of water, she ran down the path. Water sloshed against her legs. "So let me see if I understand. You're Shawnee, he's Iroquois, and Iroquois are bad?"

"This man is Shawnee of the Turtle Clan. The true *People*. He is Huron dog, an Iroquois dog."

"I understand," she said softly, catching sight of the fort through the trees. No one must have heard her scream. There was no unusual activity. "The Shawnee are good. The Huron are bad."

"Not all Shawnee are good. Not all Huron bad. Most are. But not all."

At the gates, Fire Dancer called in his native tongue to several Indians standing near some ponies. The men immediately drew weapons and slipped into the forest.

"Close the gates," Fire Dancer ordered as he strode into the fort with Mackenzie right behind him. He stopped just inside the walls. "You go inside." He turned away from her. "Close the gates!" he shouted again.

"We can't close them gates on your say-so." It was the same guard Mackenzie had outsmarted. "Hey, there you are. I wondered where you went. The major said you're not to go outside these gates. No way. No how."

"Close gates, *now*," Fire Dancer repeated.

"Yes," Mackenzie insisted, still so scared that her voice sounded strange to her. "You have to. Someone attacked me. A . . . a Huron."

The young man blinked. "Indians?" He raced for the gates. "Close the gates! Close the gates! Positions! Intruders!"

The fort yard exploded with activity. Men shouted and raced back and forth, passing off muskets, and rolling in kegs of powder. Dogs barked and howled. A musket went off accidentally. A string of curses followed.

Major Albertson burst through his door and out onto the plank walk. "What the hell's going on out here? Can't a man eat in peace?"

Fire Dancer laid his hand on her shoulder. "Go inside where you will be safe. Do not go to the stream without guards or a weapon. If you want water, or to bathe, this man will take you."

She nodded silently. His gaze held hers for a moment and there seemed something illicit about the way he looked at her

... maybe even the way she looked at him. Did he actually think she would bathe in the stream with him there? For some reason, the idea didn't seem as shocking as it should have.

"Thank you for saving my life," she whispered.

He nodded and turned away to cross the yard, the muscles of his thighs and calves flexing as he strode, the flap of his loinskin fluttering just below his buttocks.

"Mackenzie!" Franklin burst through another door, and raced toward her.

Mackenzie let go of the bucket and ran for her father. She had been brave long enough. Now all she wanted was to feel his arms around her and know she was safe. "Oh, Papa," she cried as he wrapped her in his arms that smelled comfortingly of oxen and wagon wheel grease. "You're not going to believe what happened!"

Mackenzie stepped off the plank walk into the mud the instant she spotted Mary emerge from the rear kitchen door. "Good morning, Mary." She smiled, trying to appear friendly, but not intimidating. Her father said she intimidated women with her manly ways—that was why she had no female friends.

Mary glanced up and nodded. She had a woven basket of wet laundry tucked under her arm. The young woman was barefoot and wearing an English-style red calico dress with the sleeves cut off at her shoulders.

"Need some help?"

Mary shook her head, avoiding eye contact.

"Oh, come on, hanging clothes is no fun alone." Mackenzie walked toward her. "And what are you going to do with the basket whilst you pin the clothes on the line? Drop it in the mud?" She grasped one side of the basket and tugged. Mary gave in after a little resistance.

The young Indian woman began to hang Major Albertson's shirts and stockings.

"I've been meaning to introduce myself for days," Mackenzie apologized. "I'm Mackenzie Daniels. I've come to paint

Major Albertson, Fire Dancer, and the French major, when he returns.''

Mary glanced up shyly. "You *paint* men?''

Mackenzie chuckled. "I paint likenesses of them on canvas. Portraits.''

For the first time Mary's gaze met Mackenzie's. "Likeness? This girl does not know the English, li-ke-ness.''

"A likeness. A picture.''

Mary shook her head, still not understanding.

Mackenzie thought for a moment, then pushed the laundry basket into Mary's hands. She picked up a charred stick that had been tossed into the yard.

"A por-trait,'' Mackenzie repeated as she picked up a board. It was the length and breadth of her hand. She looked up at Mary twice, sketching rapidly on the board with the charred wood. After a minute she raised it to show the Indian woman her efforts.

Mary's mouth opened, her eyes widened. *"Mahtah! Mah-tah!''* She shook her head violently as if frightened and reached out to smear the sketch of her face until there was nothing left but a pair of braids and a black smudge.

Mackenzie frowned in confusion. "I don't understand. It's just a picture.''

Mary walked away. "Likeness bad. No likeness, Mary.''

Unsure of what she'd done wrong, Mackenzie dropped the wood and ran back under the clothesline. "I'm sorry. I don't understand, but I'm sorry. I . . . I didn't mean to frighten you.''

"Mahtah, likeness,'' Mary repeated again. "Bad.''

Mackenzie sighed. Once again she'd stepped over some line of propriety, only this time, it seemed to be a cultural line. "Mary, I really am sorry. I was just trying to show you what I meant. What I do.''

Balancing the basket on her hip, Mary flung a shirt over the clothes line. "It is all right.'' She glanced up. "You only want be nice this woman. No?''

"Yes.'' Mackenzie smiled. "I was just trying to be nice. I . . . I was hoping you and I could be friends.''

Mary met her gaze with eyes nearly as black as Fire Dancer's.

She had a pretty face. She was young, perhaps even younger than Mackenzie had first guessed. *"Nee-tees.* Fre-end. Good. Other white women, not be friend to Mary. Spit on her."

"I'm sorry you've had bad experiences with other English women, but I want to be your friend. *Nee-tees,"* Mackenzie repeated. "A friend would be good for me, too. I don't have any friends here and I'm lonely," She hoped the girl understood at least part of what she was trying to say.

"This woman no have friend."

"You don't have a friend *either."*

Mary smiled, concentrating on her pronunciation. "Bad English. I do not have friend, *eith-er."*

"Very good!" Mackenzie laughed, touching the young woman on her shoulder. "You learn quickly."

Mary smiled and then stared intently at Mackenzie's ears.

Mackenzie touched one of the tiny silver pendant earrings she wore. "You like these?"

Mary's eyes shone. "Pretty." She touched her own lobes where there were holes, but no earrings.

"Here." Mackenzie pulled one from her ear and then the other. "Take them." She exchanged the earrings for the empty basket. "As a gift. I have others."

Mary stared at the earrings in her palm. "Gift? For this girl?" She looked at Mackenzie with tears in her eyes.

"Yes. A gift of friendship."

Mary slipped on one earring and then the other. She had the expression of a woman who had just been given the coffers of England. "A gift for this woman," she repeated in awe.

"So now it's definite. You and I are friends, yes?"

Mary smiled at Mackenzie as she reached for the basket. "Friends, yes." Then she looked away, shy again. "Must go. Get bread from oven. Major like bread not burned."

"I understand. I don't want to keep you from—"

"Nibeeshu Hongiis!" A harsh male voice startled them both.

Mackenzie looked up to see a fierce Indian warrior standing near the door to the kitchen. He was an ugly man with pox scars, distended earlobes, and a glistening silver ring in one nostril.

"Okonsa . . ." Mary lowered her head and hurried toward him.

Mackenzie remained under the clothesline, obscured by Harry's shirts, and watched the exchange. She didn't know who the Indian was, but she didn't like the way he spoke to Mary as he put one possessive arm on her shoulder and motioned for her to return to the kitchen outbuilding.

When Mackenzie pulled back one of the wet shirts to get a better look at the Indian, her movement caught his eye. He turned his head to stare at her, his gaze disturbing. There was something empty about the way he looked at her, empty and yet possessing at the same time.

He lowered his hand to cup his groin in some kind of strange masculine stance.

Insulted, Mackenzie turned away. When she dared to glance back at the door, he was gone.

Chapter Four

"You were looking for this man?"

"Oh!" Mackenzie spun around. Once again, she'd never heard him approach her. "Fire Dancer, you startled me."

"This man is sorry to scare Mack-en-zie."

She lifted a shoulder, the paint brush still held tightly in her fingers. "You didn't *scare* me, you just surprised me. I didn't hear you come up the steps." She was in her favorite place on the palisade, with the morning sun shining on her back.

He studied her sketch of Major Albertson and the color she'd just begun to apply. "Perhaps this man should not sneak like a heathen savage, no?"

She dropped her hand to her hip and met his gaze. "I didn't say that." She pointed, emphasizing each word with her finger. "You have never heard those words pass these lips, nor has anyone else!" It seemed so easy to talk to him now, as if more than the perilous moment with the Huron had passed between them.

He was silent for a moment, studying her face as if to assess the truth of her words. Then he nodded. "You are right. This man has not heard those words from your lips. I am sorry."

He was staring at her again, but his stares no longer made

her uncomfortable. She liked his attention. "You asked if I was looking for you. I wasn't, but since you're here—"

"This man meant yesterday. I saw you watching my horse from your window. I saw your eyes search the horizon for this man. You walked down to the stream, risked danger, looking for me."

Embarrassed to have been caught, she flushed and fumbling for words. Imagine, Mackenzie Daniels seeking out a man's company. A redman's, no less. And he was right. Going to the stream alone had been a dangerous, foolish thing to do. She'd tried to play the whole incident down when she told her father what had happened. But she and Fire Dancer knew the truth. Only she and Fire Dancer and the dead Huron knew how close she had come to being murdered. "I wasn't looking for you, except to know when you could sit for your portrait." She tried to sound businesslike and calm. "I'd really like to begin. Today."

Still he stared, as if he hadn't heard her at all.

Mackenzie tore her gaze from his. He made her uncomfortable. He made her want to look at him, not just at his face, but at his bare arms and legs, and his broad, bronze chest.

Mackenzie turned to face the major's portrait, her left shoulder to Fire Dancer. From the corner of her eye she saw him slowly reach out toward her. She thought to move, but couldn't, mesmerized by his hand and his slow, methodical movement. Her eyelids fluttered as his fingers brushed her cheek. Her heart beat too fast; she couldn't breathe evenly. She felt different inside.

"You say you feel no pre-ju-dice against this man or any other redman?" His words were like a whisper on the wind, so soft that she wondered if she only heard him in her head.

She concentrated on his words as his fingers stroked her cheek. "No. I do not."

"Then you would take a redman for your lover . . . your husband, for all of the eternity of the skies?"

His words evoked an image in her mind. She imagined herself locked in an embrace with Fire Dancer, their naked limbs tangled in bedlinens. She turned to face him head-on, hoping she wasn't blushing. "Of course not!"

He lowered his hand, a look of bemusement on his face. "Why not?"

"Well, because . . . because . . ." She grabbed her water cup off the camp stool, desperate to have something to do with her hands. Her father and the major had warned her that the Indians could be frank like this, not knowing which topics were proper to discuss and which weren't. "For . . . for the same reason I would not marry an Arab or . . . or a Chinaman. We are too dissimilar in our cultures. Our religions."

"You know of my re-li-gi-on?"

Mackenzie swished her brush in a tin cup of linseed oil. "A little. You worship trees and rocks and such. My father told me."

"Your father is good for colonist *manake,* but he is wrong."

She glanced up. "It wouldn't be the first time." She let out an exasperated sigh. "Why are you asking me these questions, anyway? In my culture, a man doesn't ask a woman he is unfamiliar with such personal questions."

"Then this man should become more fa-mil-i-ar with this woman?"

Was he flirting with her? She couldn't help but be flattered. Even if he was an Indian.

"Why don't you have a seat, and we can start your portrait?" She indicated the stool where Major Albertson had sat earlier in the week. "The morning sun won't last much longer, and then I'll have to change my position entirely."

He glanced at the stool with disdain. "This man did not come for the *manake* por-trait."

She dropped the cup and brush onto the stool, and turned to face him. "Then why did you come, sir?"

"To bring Mack-en-zie a gift."

She lowered her gaze, feeling badly that she'd snapped at him like that. "A gift? For me? I don't need a gift."

He drew a knife from a leather sheath on the waistband of his loincloth and turned the weapon so that the blade glistened in the hot sun. "A gift so that next time Hurons come, this man can save his arrow."

Mackenzie stepped forward, fascinated by the beauty of the simple fringed sheath and by the bone handle of the knife. "It's beautiful," she whispered. Her fingers glanced over his hands and lingered just a moment too long as she took the knife from him.

"Beautiful and deadly." He looked up. "Like Mack-en-zie, no?"

She smiled at him. "From you I would take that as a compliment."

"Because this man meant it as one. Wear the knife. It has been blessed. This man will sleep at night knowing you are safe, protected by the keen steel and the keen eyes of ancestors." As suddenly as he'd appeared, he walked away.

"Wait! Fire Dancer. The portrait." She ran after him as he descended the ladder. "I must know when you will sit for it."

He paused and looked up at her. "This man invites you and your father to his hearth to eat tomorrow night. The major and his officers will come. You will come?"

She didn't hesitate. "I suppose. Your hearth? What do you mean?"

"Outside the fort gates."

"Well, if Father's coming, yes. I accept."

He nodded as he reached the ground.

"I want to talk about this portrait with you!" she called as he disappeared around a rough hewn corner. "You can't just keep ignoring me, Fire Dancer. Do you hear me? I'll have this portrait!"

Mackenzie turned away, fingering the fringe of her new sheath. Something told her that talking to that man's back was like talking to a stump.

Mackenzie listened to the rhythmic beat of an Indian drum and the sweet notes of a flute as she washed up for supper in her room. She glanced outside her window to see fires blazing beyond the fort walls. So, that was where Fire Dancer and his men slept. Major Albertson had told her he refused the protection of the fort's mighty walls, but she hadn't realized his camp was so close.

The major was obviously annoyed by Fire Dancer's choice, but Mackenzie found it rather interesting. She understood the Shawnee's need for independence from the fort and all it stood for. She also understood his practicality. As hot as it was in her room, she'd prefer to sleep outside, too.

Mackenzie returned to her wash bowl, splashed water on her face and smoothed her hair back with her damp hands. Glancing in the hand mirror she'd hung on a nail on the wall, she wondered if Fire Dancer thought her attractive. She certainly looked nothing like the exotic Mary. Wouldn't Indian men only find Indian women handsome? "Why do you care?" she muttered to her reflection.

Checking the knife sheath she wore tied around her hips, she walked to the door, ready to go. She liked the feel of the weapon at her hip. It made her feel safe . . . confident.

She wore her leather skirt and her father's white shirt and over it, a tight blue waistcoat with embroidered flap pockets. Because of the heat, she had rolled up her sleeves. At home on the river, she'd never have dared show her elbows, but they were in the middle of the wilderness for heaven's sake. Surely propriety took a second seat to one's comfort.

Just as she was about to open her door, she heard light footsteps, then a hesitant knock.

"Yes?"

"It is Mary. *Ne-hee.* Mary!"

Mackenzie swung the door open with a smile. "What are you doing here? Aren't you going to the supper?"

Mary held out a small object wrapped in a square of red cloth. "This woman must go. I want to give gift to . . . to friend Mack-en-zie."

Mackenzie smiled. "Oh, you don't have to give me anything. I gave you the earrings because I wanted to, not because—"

"Take gift. You would shame Mary's face if you don't take gift."

Reluctantly, Mackenzie accepted the gift. "Well, thank you."

"This girl go now. Good night, friend."

Before Mackenzie could say another word, Mary retreated down the dark hallway, her footsteps echoing on the stairs.

Curious as to what the girl had brought her. Mackenzie lifted the red cloth, revealing a silver snuff box. It was old and battered, but very beautiful with curlicues and scroll work inscribed on the polished metal. *What an odd gift . . .*

The scent of tobacco was strong as she opened it, yet, it was empty inside, but for a tiny feather. Mackenzie smiled. It was a strange gift, but obviously heartfelt. She would have to make a point to thank Mary later.

Leaving the snuff box on the stool near the door, she blew out her candle and hurried from her room. She was anxious to see Fire Dancer, too anxious to contemplate Mary's strange gift.

Her father and Joshua were waiting for her at the bottom of the steps. Josh held a sputtering lamp to light the way. "Mary just pass through here?" she asked.

"That Indian girl? Aye," her father answered. "In quite a hurry. Never spoke."

Joshua snatched off his leather cocked hat. "G . . . good evenin', Mackenzie. You . . . you look very pretty tonight." Blushing, he looked away.

"Thank you. And you . . ." She peered at him more closely. "Heavens, did you bathe, Josh?" She sniffed the air, and her nose wasn't offended by his usual body odor. "Christmas coming early this year?"

"Oh, leave the boy be." Franklin dropped his arm over his daughter's shoulder. "A man has a right to pretty himself up occasionally, same as a woman."

"But God's teeth, Father, his hair is combed, too," she argued good-naturedly. "Do you think he means to find himself a bride out here? Maybe an Indian bride?" She gave a jump and a squeak as her father playfully slapped her on the hip.

"You're too hard on the boy." He glanced over his shoulder

at Josh. "And you, son, are too easy on her. You know she says these things to goad you."

Mackenzie chuckled. "I'm sorry, Josh. You do look handsome tonight. You just overwhelmed me."

"You know, daughter, these redskins bathe day and night. I've seen that Fire Dancer half a dozen times bathing in broad daylight at the stream."

She ducked as they stepped out onto the wooden walk. "He doesn't fear illness?"

"He tells me it keeps sickness away." Franklin chuckled. "As I've pointed out before, a little education could go a long way with these people. They don't seem to be stupid—just unknowing."

Mackenzie didn't say anything as she crossed the yard between her father and Joshua, circumnavigating the pigs and assorted garbage. She saw Fire Dancer's nephew, Tall Moccasin, seated on one of the water barrels, feeding some scraps to the sow and her piglets. Mackenzie waved and he returned the gesture.

As she crossed the compound, she realized that the sound of the flute still lingered in the air like the evening mist. She could feel the beat of the drum as readily as she could hear it. Her blood seemed to flow faster, her heart matching the rhythm.

The fort's gate was open, but the entrance was heavily guarded, as were the palisades. As she passed under the wall, she eyed the redcoat soldiers that fanned out in every direction. They looked to be prepared for Indian attack at any moment. It appeared no enlisted man would rest until the major and other officers were back inside the fort.

Major Albertson met them on the other side of the gates. "Franklin! Mackenzie! Watkins!" he called jovially.

Mackenzie could tell by the sound of his voice that he'd already partaken of the whiskey her father had brought with him. "Good evening, sir."

"Sir? Sir, is it, now?"

She smiled. "I was afraid you were still angry with me after the other day."

"Nonsense." He waved a meaty hand. "All forgotten. How

could I be angry with you? You're one of the few women I know—or men for that matter—who has the guts to stand up to me."

She smiled at him slyly. "Just as long as you weren't expecting an apology or worse yet, agreement."

Harry threw his head back and roared with laughter. "You certain you won't give me your daughter's hand in marriage, Franklin? I vow I'd not grow bored in my dotage with her for my bride."

Franklin glanced at Mackenzie, his face lit by the torches set in the ground by the Indians. "You know her well enough, Harry, to know I'll not be giving her hand to anyone. Who she weds will be up to her. Poor Josh is witness to that."

"Did you check the oxen tonight, Mr. Daniels?" Josh, interrupted, as he nervously looked toward the fort. "I forgot to check the animals."

"They'll be fine, Josh. We're suppose to be the guests of honor tonight."

"Nope. Nope." Joshua shook his head. "I might as well go back because I won't be able to think of anything else until I check them."

Franklin lifted his hand. "Whatever, boy."

"I'll be right back." He doffed his hat to Mackenzie and then hurried back toward the gate.

Mackenzie walked between her father and the major. "Expecting trouble tonight, Harry?" She indicated the soldiers pacing on the palisade high above them.

"Indeed not. But I thought I ought make a show to prevent it. I tried to convince that damned redskin Fire Dancer that we could be his guests inside the gates just as well as outside, but he'd not hear of it. Something about pigs and mud." He threw up his hand in exasperation. "Hell, I don't know what he was talking about."

Fire Dancer appeared magically before them as they walked into the broad circle of light cast from a huge central fire. He was dressed tonight in buckskin leggings and a sleeveless leather tunic decorated with elaborate quilling. From his left ear dangled a blue-green stone teardrop.

"This man thanks you for coming," he said formally. "Please come. Sit. Eat. Drink. Later we dance for you, honored guests."

Mackenzie watched the way the firelight played off his earring as her father and the major walked ahead of her.

"You like?" Fire Dancer asked as he touched his earlobe.

"It's beautiful. Where did you get it?"

"It comes from a place far from here, many moons walk into the setting sun. Over mountains and great streams."

"You've been there?"

"No. But others have. It was a gift from a friend many winters ago." He opened his arms to a place where deerhide mats had been spread out. "Sit and my men will serve."

Mackenzie sat beside her father on a deerhide on the ground, excited by all the strange sights, and sounds, and smells. To one side of the fire hung a deer carcass on a spit, sizzling as it roasted, filling the air with the heavenly scent of venison. Men milled about, carrying trenchers of food.

Though the musicians could not be seen, she could still hear their haunting tune. It was a party-like atmosphere, with everyone seeming to be in good spirits. For once, there seemed to be no distrust between the redmen and the king's soldiers.

Mackenzie accepted a bark trencher pressed into her hands and it was quickly filled with roasted red tubers sprinkled with raw sugar, steamed green beans, stewed squash, and baked mushrooms stuffed with tender bits of fish. She had grown so bored with the fort's typical fare of salted pork and beans that she enjoyed the meal immensely. The venison was hot and succulent and tasted so good that she had two portions. She was so full that she was certain she could eat no more, yet when she was brought shelled nuts and crunchy dried berries, she ate handfuls of those, too.

One of the officers rolled a keg of ale from the fort and tapped it and there were tin cups of ale for everyone. Whiskey bottles, purchased from her father, no doubt, were passed around between the redmen and the white. Some drank too much too quickly and the voices grew louder, the confusion more animated.

Mackenzie spotted Mary. The young Indian woman was with Lieutenant Allen. She was wearing his uniform cap and laughing with him. He touched her with a familiarity that made Mackenzie think they knew each other well.

"Harry?"

The Major leaned in front of Franklin, laughing at one of his officer's comments. "Dear?"

She kept her voice low. Her father rose and walked off into the darkness, perhaps in search of Joshua. "I see Allen is friendly with Mary."

Harry looked up, taking a swig of his ale. "Aye. Friendly enough it seems."

"And you allow that? Fraternizing, I mean."

He shrugged and grabbed a hunk of venison from an Indian holding a stick strung with meat. "The word passed to me by my superiors is that it's forbidden, but my superiors have comfortable quarters, plenty of food and white women to warm their beds back in London. They don't know what it's like here. We don't like it much, but the fact is that some of these men are going to take red wives. All through history, colonizing nations have done it."

"And what about them? Her?"

He looked at her blankly for a moment. "Oh, Mary. Hell, best thing that could happen to her, would be my guess. If she's smart, she'll hold out for a wedding ceremony with the circuit rider next time he passes through." He tipped his tin cup and nothing came out. "Hell, I need a refill. You?"

She shook her head, not caring for his insensitivity. "No, thank you." She watched as he trudged off, calling to one of his men in jest.

Mackenzie rose to her feet to stretch after her heavy meal. As she watched the soldiers and Indians, she lifted her hands over her head, arching her back. She tried not to look for *him* as she surveyed the crowd of rowdy men. Of course, he was busy as host, she told herself, and she had no idea as to the customs attached to such affairs. She searched the crowd, hoping to find an excuse to seek him out, or at least get closer to him. Maybe she could go over and thank Mary for the silver snuff box.

She sighed in frustration as the Indian brave with the nose ring grabbed Mary's hand to lead her away from the English officer and into the darkness.

The steady sound of the drum that had beat all night without pause suddenly grew louder and faster. Out of the darkness burst a dozen men dancing in a line that snaked into the circle of light and around the campfire. Mackenzie immediately recognized Fire Dancer, the tallest of the Shawnee, and the most impressive. He had removed his tunic to dance bare-chested like the other man, his body moving like hardened silk to the tattoo of the hollow drums.

The other Indians in the party began to gather around, singing in their native tongue, clapping their bronze hands, and stomping their feet. The redcoat soldiers joined in.

Mackenzie couldn't help but tap her boot under her skirt. She had never heard such tantalizing sounds nor seen men or women dance with such grace. Fire Dancer executed the same moves as his fellow dancers, but he stood out among them as a rose petal in a bowl of thorns. Every swing of his arms, every tap of his moccasined feet was smooth and fluid.

There was something about the music that made her heart pound to the same beat. Watching the half-naked men, watching Fire Dancer, made her breath ragged. She had never seen anything in her life so beautiful . . . so sexual . . . so masculine.

The drums pulsed louder, the beat more urgent as the men danced in a circle, drawing closer and closer to the fire then radiating outward. They swayed their arms and nodded their heads to the rhythm that seemed to come from them rather than the invisible drums. One of the braves danced so closely past her that he brushed her bare arm as he leapt by. Only then did she realize that she recognized him. It was the man with the nose ring who had been so harsh with Mary two days ago and had taken her into the trees only a few moments ago.

His gaze met hers as he danced by again and she remembered his lewd gesture. The next time he danced past her, she averted her gaze, fixing it instead on Fire Dancer. There was something about the one with the nose ring that made her wary. Something in her bones that told her she should steer clear of him.

The dance came to an end with the dancers on their knees, facing the fire, their bronze backs presented to their guests. The soldiers clapped with approval, shouting and passing more ale and whiskey.

Someone began to play a hornpipe and the men, both red and white, began to clap to the lively tune. Instinctively, Mackenzie lifted her leather skirt to tap her boots in the dust. When she realized the men were watching her, clapping and encouraging her, she danced toward the circle, her hands clasped tightly at her sides, her feet moving to the beat.

The Indians hooted and cried out in their strange language, seeming drunker than the soldiers. She whirled and twirled, counting her steps, pounding her feet to the jig. Out of no where, Fire Dancer appeared before her, also dancing. He imitated her steps, whirling and turning in the opposite direction that she did. His body was so close to hers that her boots touched his moccasins in the dirt, and yet he made no attempt to touch her. She wanted him to touch her.

The horn blower played faster and Mackenzie danced faster, caught up in the gaiety of the evening and the closeness of her dance partner. She couldn't take her eyes off him. There was something about him, about the forbidden that made her bold. As Mackenzie turned, drawing up her knees, dancing in a circle, she lifted her gaze to meet his.

"Mack-en-zie . . ." The men were too loud for her to hear his voice, but she saw his lips move, speaking her name.

"Fire Dancer," she whispered as his movements so matched hers that they seemed to move as one dancer joined by an invisible thread.

A musket shot sounded above the din of the soldiers. The hooting Indians hushed and the music stopped. Mackenzie spun around. "What's happening?" She stood on her tiptoes looking over Fire Dancer's shoulder at the clump of men blocking her view.

An Indian and a soldier burst through the crowd of men, falling to the ground near the fire, locked in a fist fight. One of the other soldiers shouted an obscenity and the Indian with the whiskey bottle hit him over the head with the flask.

Glass shattered everywhere and suddenly they were fighting, too. Mackenzie took a step back as an Indian wearing a soldier's coat drew a knife and one of the soldiers tried to knock it from his hand. The Indian nicked the soldier in the arm, bloodying his white sleeve. Another soldier tried to get between them and struck the knife from his hand with the barrel of a musket. Before Mackenzie knew what was happening, all the soldiers and Indians were fighting.

The merriment of laughing and clapping and dancing had suddenly turned into a brawl.

Fire Dancer grabbed her arm firmly. "No place for you here, Mack-en-zie. Come."

He was obviously angry, but his anger wasn't directed to her. She allowed him to lead her away from the fire and fighting men and toward the fort. "Where's my father? Do you see my father? He'll want to know I'm all right," she shouted above the din.

"Go to your room, Mackenzie. Lock the door. Too much whiskey. Too much ale," he said harshly. "This man should not have let his men drink the fire. Bad medicine for Shawnee. Bad for all redmen! In our village it is not allowed."

He stopped at the gate, calling to his nephew, sleeping in the middle of the yard against a water barrel. *"Niipoy! Buumska!* Come, Tall Moccasin! Take this woman into the fort. Keep her safe."

Tall Moccasin leaped up and ran across the muddy yard. *"Ah*, Uncle."

Fire Dancer grabbed her arm as Mackenzie started to walk away. He leaned against her, pressing his lips to her ear. "Leave your window open tonight," he breathed.

She stared into his black eyes. "Why? What do you want?"

"I would not harm you, Mack-en-zie. I would not take advantage of you as any man in this fort would."

For some reason she believed him. "Just talk?" she whispered. He was so close that she could feel the warmth of his skin. The thought of being alone with him tempted her, but she didn't want to make a mistake she would regret. She didn't want to put herself into a dangerous situation, not the way she was feeling tonight . . . about him. Harry had been right. Fire Dancer was dangerous, but not in the way he had meant. "Only talk, you promise?"

"This man swear by his mother's name." He touched his chest with a closed hand. "Only talk."

Before she could say another word, he was gone.

Slowly Mackenzie crossed the yard at Tall Moccasin's side. *Leave her window open? Did she dare?*

Chapter Five

Fire Dancer stood at the fort wall, staring upward in debate. It would only take him a few seconds to scale the wall undetected. Did he go? Did he follow his heart and take the risk to see her or did he let her go now, before it was too late? Fire Dancer didn't quite understand his attraction to the white woman, but he knew it was dangerous.

He turned and leaned his bare back against the wall, waiting for his burning desire to see her fade away. He stared into the darkness. The fire had died down to nothing but glowing coals. Still, the smell of the roasted venison hung in the air. Fireflies flickered in the trees. Somewhere he heard the rumble of one of his men's voice. Those who had had enough sense not to drink the Colonist's *manake* firewater were standing watch. The others were sleeping off the foul drink near the campfire.

None of his men or Major Albertson's soldiers had been seriously injured in the brawl, but Fire Dancer was upset by tonight's events. The British were a bad influence on his men. The drink was bad for redman's blood. He had warned them before they arrived. The firewater was not even permitted in their village, but he had let his men make their own choice in the end. For most of them, the choice was not a good one.

He wished that the French commander would return to Fort Belvadere so that the peace talks could continue and therefore come to some end. He was anxious to return to his village and escape from the stupid British *manake* and their filthy, decadent ways.

Fire Dancer glanced up at the fort wall again, then pressed his back to the wall as a soldier patrolling the palisade walked by high above his head. He liked Major Albertson. He was an honest man, but he was a fool if he thought these walls would keep out the Indians, Algonquian or Iroquois, if they chose to attack.

The soldier walked on and Fire Dancer glanced up again. Would it be a waste of his time to scale the wall? Would Mack-en-zie have barred her window? Would she be hiding beneath her blanket in fear, muttering to her beads as he had seen other white women do?

He smiled in the darkness. No. Not this Mack-en-zie. Most likely, she would be pacing at this very moment, trying to decide whether or not to unlock the window.

He had watched her dance tonight, and she had danced the English dance with him. He knew that she was attracted to him the same as he was attracted to her. When they danced, the differences between them had vanished. They were meaningless. If he held her in his arms, if he made love to her, he wondered, would it be the same?

Of course, that was just a fanciful thought. He had no place in his life for a white woman. When he married, it would be a proper Shawnee wedding. When he chose a wife, it would probably be the widow Laughing Woman from his village. He only wanted to see Mack-en-zie out of curiosity, to ease his boredom here beside this stinking fort.

Fire Dancer whistled softly between his teeth, signaling to his cousin, Okonsa, that he was in charge until Fire Dancer returned. His cousin whistled back from a copse of trees in the distance. Fire Dancer didn't like leaving Okonsa in command for long. The brave hated the British *manake* and he had a mean streak. But tonight it would safe enough. Most of the soldiers were as drunk as his own men.

Fire Dancer crept back to check the positions of the soldiers on the palisade and then picked up a rope he'd left coiled in the grass. Attached to the end of the rope was a rusty iron hook. It took Fire Dancer only two tosses to secure the rope on the top of the wall. Tugging it tightly, he scaled the wall in the time it took one of the soldiers on the palisade to light his pipe.

On the palisade walkway, Fire Dancer left the rope where it hung and crept along the shadows of the wall. The moon was dim tonight, casting off very little light. On the inner, western wall of the fort, he saw a slice of lantern light falling from a tiny, open window, a beacon in the darkness.

He smiled. So his Mackenzie, with her magical red hair, was not afraid of him.

When he reached the window, he whispered "Mack-en-zie . . ."

Her face appeared immediately in the window, blocking the lantern light. She looked slightly fearful. But he could see that, like him, she was curious.

"What do you want?" she whispered harshly, trying to cover her fear with impatience. "If they catch you here—"

"This man does not come to harm you. Only . . ." Why *had* he come? "Only to talk."

"Talk? A man wanting to talk with a woman? Talk of what?"

"Could this man come into your room? He swears by his mother's heart that he will not harm you."

"Come in?" She wrinkled her nose with its brown sun-speckles. "You can't fit through that window! It was built small enough so that a man can't fit through it."

Fire Dancer took her jumble of words as a yes, and stuck his head through the window. She climbed off the sleeping platform, backing away from him. He popped one shoulder diagonally through the small hole, then the other. The rest was easy. He tumbled onto the soft mat that smelled of her.

"If my father finds out you're here . . . If the major—"

"You wish this man to leave?" He crawled off the sleeping platform, bouncing to his feet. "Tell me to go and I will go."

She nibbled on her lower lip, studying him. Fire Dancer

stared back, letting her see the honesty in his eyes and his body language.

"You want to talk to me?" She frowned. "About what? Surely not about the fact that you've been avoiding coming for your portrait."

Now that he was here, he didn't really know what say. He just wanted to be near her. To see her face. But he knew the white woman wouldn't understand. He didn't quite understand himself. "This man . . . this man was thinking about what Mack-en-zie said about his people worshipping trees and rocks. This man does not like that you should think he prays to rocks. You do not know of me, and I do not know of you."

She crossed her arms over her soft breasts. "You care what I think of you? I don't understand."

He shrugged as he had seen her do so many times in the last few days. It was one of her gestures that fascinated him. "This man thinks that he could learn from you. Learn things to take back to his Shawnee and Lenape people." He looked down at his moccasins and then back up into her blue eyes. "Learn so that we will understand our enemies."

She laughed without humor. "You want me to tell you things so you can massacre us in our sleep?"

"No." He shook his head, not wanting her to misunderstand. "This man, this man's people, do not murder innocents. But the whites come whether we want them to come or no." He made a fist. "We must be ready. We must understand more of you . . . if we are to survive."

She ran her fingers through her bright red tresses that hung loose over her shoulders and for a moment he lost his line of thought. She wasn't beautiful the way Laughing Woman was beautiful, but Mackenzie was attractive in an exotic way. Her skin was so pale that it shone like moonlight. Her hair was the color of the red fox the English *manake* brought with them to hunt. Her eyes were as blue as the waters of the great bay of the Chesapeake. And her lips . . . her lips were as rosy as fresh strawberries picked in the springtime.

"I see," she finally said. "So we are enemies."

He said nothing as he watched her. She was a graceful

woman, powerful, like a doe. She moved with a confidence few women, even Shawnee women, possessed.

She uncovered the painting of Major Albertson. "What do you think?" She stood back to consider it, tucking the cloth behind her back.

He nodded. The moment he saw the likeness, he knew he had made the right decision. The picture was so real that it made the hair on the back of his neck stand up. Staring at the captain's face he could almost hear his laughter. He could smell his roanoke tobacco and the wool of his sweaty redcoat uniform. Fire Dancer turned away. "It looks like him."

She glanced at Fire Dancer. "Well, I would hope so. That *is* the point." She looked back at the portrait. "I'm anxious to get started on yours. I've already been toying with the red ochre. I want to get the color of your skin perfectly."

He walked to the silver looking glass that hung from a nail and ran his finger over the scrolled handle. He had known the conversation would turn to this matter again sooner or later. Perhaps it would just be better if he told her now. He watched her in the reflection in the mirror. "I will not have my portrait painted, Mack-en-zie."

"Why not? Look, if it's because I'm a woman, I—"

"No man or woman will paint this man's likeness."

She covered the captain's face again with the cloth and he was glad of it. It made him uncomfortable having the major stare at them like that and listen to their conversation.

"What do you mean?" she questioned. "Why not? That was the whole point of my coming. The army has commissioned the peace makers' portraits. If you come to a decision here, your face will hang in history as a great keeper of peace. You'll be famous!"

He gave a snort of derision. "Peace. How can there be peace? How can there ever be peace again now that you and yours have come?"

"And what's that supposed to mean?" She dropped her hand to her shapely hip. "You could learn something from us, you know, if you would just give us a chance."

He paced the tiny room. It was so hot in here that he didn't know how she slept. "Learn what? How to make whis-key? How to sell dark men and women? How to rape? How to murder children and take their scalps? These are the things my people are learning from yours."

She brushed her hair back again, damp at her temples from perspiration. "No! I'm not saying there haven't been bad influences, but there could be good ones, too. You could learn how to read and write. You could take Jesus Christ for your savior," she sputtered. "You could learn how to dress appropriately."

He glanced down at his favorite tunic with the porcupine quilling. He thought it was a handsome tunic. His mother had made it for him. "You do not like my clothing?"

She threw up a hand. "You're half naked, for heaven's sake."

"And this is bad?" He lifted a dark eyebrow, amused.

"It's . . . it's not that it's bad . . . it's just . . . just indecent."

"In-de-sent. I do not know this word. I do not know if my tunic is in-de-sent. This man does know that his tunic is not hot in the summer heat. It does not scratch his skin. It protects him from the burn of the sun and the sting of the wind and rain. This is in-de-sent?"

She let out an exasperated sigh. "It's not that your tunic isn't attractive on your body . . ."

He smiled as her cheeks turned red with embarrassment. He knew from experience that the light-skinned *manake* were ashamed of their bodies. They covered them up with as much hot, scratchy cloth as they could. When they made love, it was in the dark, under more scratchy cloth.

He thought for a moment. "I will give you a tunic and then you will see why it is what I wear. The women in my village do not wear tunics in the summer. Only loincloth. They are bare"—he searched for the correct word—"breast . . . bare breasted."

Her eyes grew round with shock, and then realizing he was trying to bait her, she turned away. "I really don't think we want to get into this tonight. Let's get back to the subject of the portrait. You say you won't let me paint it?"

He ran his hand over the white shirt that hung from a nail

near the door. It was hers. He remembered seeing her wear it. He crumpled the hem in his hand and brought it to his nose. It smelled of oil paints and forest flowers . . . like her.

She snatched the shirt off the hook and out of his hands. "Do you mind?"

He walked back toward the bed. The light-skinned *manake* were so possessive of their things. "You will not paint my face. No one will paint this man's face. It is bad medicine."

She took a step after him, the shirt balled in her hands. "What do you mean bad medicine?"

"It is not good to take away a piece of a man's soul and put it on cloth. Then you, too, possess the man's soul."

"Take away your soul?" It was obvious by her tone that she didn't understand. "It's just a picture. I wouldn't be taking anything from you."

He stepped on the sleeping rack to climb back through the window. "You will not paint this man."

"But I've been hired to paint you. You don't understand how important this is to me. It's my first commission, Fire Dancer. I can't fail."

"This man must go. Okonsa stands guard, but he is rash and impatient. If this man does not keep his eye on him, he would shoot his own brother for a Mohawk." He slipped out the tiny window as easily as he slipped in.

She followed him, lifting up her heavy skirt to climb onto the platform. "That's it? You're not going to let me paint you because you think I'll take your soul?"

Landing lightly on the palisade, he turned to look back in the window at her. The breeze on his back felt good. "This man does not expect this *manake* woman to understand. Only to accept what she is not capable of understanding."

"Oh, so now I'm stupid?"

"Good night, Mack-en-zie. Dream well. This man will." Already he was conjuring up memories of how she had danced with him tonight. They would lull him to sleep. "This man will come again another night if I can."

"Like hell!" she shouted after him in a harsh whisper. "You'll not find this window open again!"

* * *

Fire Dancer rappelled off the fort wall without making a sound. His feet hit the soft ground with a thump.

"And where you been, my friend? Surely not visiting my sister's mat, too?"

Fire Dancer recognized the voice immediately as his cousin's. Okonsa spoke in their native tongue.

"Cousin, you know I would not dishonor you in such a way." Fire Dancer pulled carefully on the rope until the hook came loose and tumbled down. "Little Weaver is a sister to me."

Okonsa laughed. "You forget she wishes for us to call her Mary. You forget she wears the stinking English clothes and does not bathe, as our mothers taught us. You forget she flirts with the white soldiers without shame on her face."

Fire Dancer coiled the rope around his arm. "She cares for the one called Allen."

"She cares for the baubles he gives her. She wants to be white and thinks he will make it so." He scowled. "As he could wash her of her red blood and the blood of her ancestors these three thousand winters."

Fire Dancer walked away from the fort wall. Okonsa followed.

"So tell this man," Okonsa continued. "Where have you been? Who do you seek behind the fort wall? Tell me not the white woman with the hair of fire."

Fire Dancer glared at his cousin.

"This man knew it." Okonsa cackled. "She is a fine bitch." He strutted, thrusting his hips and grasping the bulge of his loin cloth. "I would like to ride her as well."

Fire Dancer whipped around. "Do not go near her," he said with an edge of threat to his voice.

Okonsa took a step back. "You are very possessive, my cousin. She is white. She is nothing to us. Less than nothing. Bird crap on our feet. What does it matter to you?"

Fire Dancer tossed the rope onto the ground near the campfire. One of his men snored loudly. He could hear another vomiting. "This man warns you. Stay away from the one called Mack-en-zie."

"And what if she can not resist my charms?" Okonsa said in the native tongue of his Shawnee mother. "What if she prefers my grizzly rod to your squirrel?"

Fire Dancer turned on his cousin, losing his patience. "Did you hear this man?" He caught a fistful of his cousin's leather tunic. "Leave her be!"

Okonsa's black eyes met Fire Dancer's. "You claim her as yours, then?"

"I did not say that."

Okonsa nodded, as if all knowing. "This man will say no more of the matter."

Fire Dancer turned away. "This man must stand his watch. Get some sleep. We may be here longer than we expected, cousin. Still, the Frenchman does not come."

Okonsa ground the ball of his foot into the soft humus. "If you do not need me for a few days, cousin, I will take my men and go scouting."

Fire Dancer turned to his cousin. The dim moonlight fell across his face illuminating the silver nose ring. "Scouting for what?"

"Not really scouting." He picked the green tip of a twig and began cleaning his teeth. "One Ear and Battered Pot and some others, they grow bored. It would do them good to run, to hunt—"

"To find trouble?"

Okonsa gave Fire Dancer a look of complete innocence. "Cousin, you are forever distrustful of me and I know not why."

"You know why."

For a moment Okonsa could not look away. Then he tossed the twig. "Years ago. The past. Forgiven, forgotten."

"There have been other times, Okonsa. You and I do not hold the same standards. Your morals are not the same as those my mother, your mother's sister, taught us."

"I simply will not allow myself and those I care for to be trampled, to be dishonored . . . annihilated." This time it was he who turned away. ''We will not be gone long. Two nights, perhaps three.''

Fire Dancer watched his cousin strut away. Fire Dancer had considered leaving Okonsa home in the village where he would be less likely to cause trouble. But in the end, he'd brought him along, thinking it would be easier to keep an eye on him. Now he wondered if he had made the right decision.

Chapter Six

"Good morning, Father." Mackenzie walked into the officer's dining room. Her father was alone drinking a cup of tea and eating a thick slice of Mary's cornbread.

Outside, she could hear Harry shouting commands and the soldiers responding. She could hear their boots as they marched in six inches of mud, drilling as they did most mornings. Harry said it wasn't that they needed the practice, only that it was a way to diminish their boredom.

Mackenzie dropped her arm around her father's shoulder and gave him a quick peck on the cheek. She slid into Harry's vacant chair at the end of the table.

"Morning, daughter. You are just the one I wanted to see."

"Uh oh, that means I'm in trouble, right?" Another chipped china cup rested on the table, probably meant for Harry. She poured herself some tea, using his cup. "When I was a little girl you always used that phrase when I was in trouble."

"You're not a little girl anymore, Mackenzie," he answered seriously. "But that doesn't mean I've given up my responsibility to keep you safe. You'll be mine to care for until, God willing, I place you in the safety of your husband's care. Even then, you'll still be my daughter."

She dropped a lump of brown sugar into her tea and stirred it with her father's spoon. She had known this was coming. "I think I already know what you're going to say."

"Good. Then this won't take long."

She tasted her tea. It was so bitter that she added more sugar. At home they always had sweet, thick cream for their tea, but of course there were no cows here in the middle of the wilderness. She took another sip of the tea, and satisfied, reached for a slice of cornbread. She glanced up at her father. "Well? Go ahead. I'm ready for my berating."

"There'll be no berating. We're not talking about a county fair horse race you entered under a boy's name, or giggling during services, Mackenzie. We're talking about your life."

She sighed. "It was stupid to go to the stream alone the other day. I know that now. It won't happen again. I'll get an escort next time."

"That wasn't what I wanted to discuss. I know you have enough wits about you not to go to the stream alone again. I'm talking about last night."

Last night? She was afraid to make eye-contact with her father. Did he know Fire Dancer had come to her room? Sweet heavens, a redman could be hanged for such an offense. She concentrated on crumbling her bread, and tried to sound casual. *"Last night?"*

"Dancing with that heathen!" He slapped his hand on the table and the sugar tin jumped. "You ought to be ashamed of yourself!"

She took a bite of the bread, relieved her father didn't know just how far she'd gone against propriety with the Indian. "The dance? It was all in fun, Papa. The man with the pipe was playing, so I danced. I've done the same a hundred times in your tavern. I've danced with men I didn't know while *you* played your fiddle."

"It's not the same thing and you damned well know it." Her father's eyes reflected fear more than anger.

"No?" she said softly.

"No! You danced with *colonists* in my tavern!"

She licked her index finger and used it to pick crumbs off

the table. She licked the crumbs off her finger, taking her time to answer. Fire Dancer was like that. He took much longer to respond than was customary.

Franklin slurped his tea. "I take your silence as agreement that you erred in judgment."

She glanced at him over the rim of his tea cup. "It was completely innocent. He meant me no harm or disrespect."

"You may think so, but . . ." His tone softened. "But, Mackenzie, you don't know men as I do. Men can be crude creatures of urges rather than wits. And neither of us knows what goes on in minds of *their* kind."

"Fire Dancer has never been anything but respectful to me. For heaven's sake, Father, he saved my life! I can at least dance with the man."

"I am forever grateful for what he did and I told him so, but I still want you to stay away from him. And I want someone else with you when you work on his portrait. Me or Josh, or Harry. You shouldn't be alone with a man like him. He's dangerous. Unpredictable. Even Harry says so."

Suddenly depressed, she brushed the crumbs off her skirt. She'd come to Fort Belvadere with such high hopes. Nothing was working out as she thought it would. "He won't sit for the portrait, so there's no need to worry on that."

"Good. That's even better. I want you to finish up Harry's as quickly as you can. Hopefully, DuBois will be here within the fortnight, but if he isn't—"

She felt a sudden sense of panic. "We're going home?"

"I think it's best. Harry doesn't know what's going on with DuBois. He sends word he's been delayed again, but he could be preparing to attack us, for all we know."

Her chair scraped against the plank floor as she stood up. "But he's part of the peace negotiations. A man of honor wouldn't do such a thing."

"You're right. It's all probably perfectly innocent. I'm certain he was held up in one of his forts in New York, just as he says. But Harry is uncomfortable, so I'm uncomfortable. That Huron who tried to attack you wasn't alone. There have to be others out there."

Mackenzie lifted her cup to her lips and took a sip of tea. She knew what her father said made sense. It probably would be best if she avoided Fire Dancer altogether since he wouldn't sit for his portrait. Period. The job would be over. Period. Her first job would be a failure. Period.

"Mackenzie," her father said softly.

She slowly lifted her gaze to meet his. She knew he knew how important this commission had been to her.

He held out his hand to her. "I want to protect you. You're all I have in the world. You do understand, don't you?"

She took his hand and squeezed it. She did understand. Even though she wanted to do these portraits more than anything in the world, she knew that her father loved her and wanted what was best for her.

"All right, Papa." She kissed his rough hand. "I'll stay away from him."

"That's my girl." He rose from his chair and scooped up his leather cocked hat from the table. "I'm going to the stream to try my hand at fishing. Want to come?" He dropped the old hat onto his balding head. "Josh said he'd meet me there after he fed the oxen."

She rolled her eyes. "Josh."

"Mackenzie, I don't think you've really given him a chance. He's mad in love with you and he could take over the tavern and trading post when I get too old. He could care for you when I'm gone."

She groaned. "Please don't say that. I don't want to talk about it."

He turned toward the door. "Whether we talk about it or not, it's the truth. I'm nearly fifty-five, daughter, and I'm feeling my age in my bones. This trip made me realize that. I won't be here with you forever and these colonies are no place for a woman alone, especially with all the fighting. I'd feel better knowing Josh would be with you to care for you."

Mackenzie didn't answer. What was the point? As far as her father was concerned, a woman chose her husband by what he could provide. In her father's eyes, the fact that she could never love Joshua Watkins was inconsequential.

* * *

A few days later, late in the afternoon, Mackenzie wandered into the compound to find her father. She'd been working on Harry's portrait for hours. Past the point of actually needing him to sit, the portrait was coming together nicely. It was even better than she'd hoped, which, instead of encouraging her, frustrated her even more. A portrait of only one of the peace delegates was useless. Even if DuBois did arrive soon and she did finish his portrait, she still wouldn't have Fire Dancer's. Harry's superiors had specifically requested that the Indian Prince be included. Without it, she doubted they'd even pay her for the other two portraits.

Mackenzie rubbed her neck to relieve the tension as she made her way across the muddy yard toward the lean-to shed where her father locked up his supplies. Outside the door were stacks of wooden crates, some empty, some still containing goods he'd brought with him to sell. She spotted Tall Moccasin. He had taken to Franklin and could often be found nearby. Josh was there, too.

"Afternoon, Mackenzie." Josh swiped his hat off his head and nodded, trying to keep a bag of feed balanced on his shoulder at the same time. The Indian boy held a bag of equal size.

"Afternoon, Josh." She smiled and his face turned red with embarrassed delight. That was one of things she didn't like about him. He was like a puppy. She gave him the slightest encouragement and he was all excited. It was a smile, for bloody Mary's sake. She wasn't agreeing to wed or bed him.

"Well ... I.... I'm off to feed the oxen. Your father's inside."

She nodded as he passed by with Tall Moccasin behind him, both headed toward the paddock. Tall Moccasin nodded his head in greeting and grinned.

"What are you doing, Father?" She peered into the lean-to.

"Taking inventory," he said from the shadows of the building. "We've done well. Damned well. I've sold all the sugar and salt. Most of the tobacco, whiskey and ale, too."

Mackenzie leaned her back against the rough wall and tipped her face up to the bright sun, closing her eyes. She knew she shouldn't be out without her bonnet. She freckled so easily. But, despite its heat, she always found something revitalizing about the sun.

She opened her eyes at the sound of someone approaching through the mud, half-hoping it was *him*. She'd wondered when Fire Dancer would show his face, after pulling that trick the other night. For three nights she had waited at her window to see if he would come—so she could turn him away, of course. So far, she'd not seen him.

She frowned as the ugly, strutting one, Okonsa, came into view. Even when Mackenzie found out that he was Mary's brother, she didn't like him any better. He had mean eyes. He was crude and disrespectful to women, not just to her, but to Mary as well.

"Greetings, woman of beauty."

Still resting her back against the log lean-to, Mackenzie crossed her arms over her chest. "Can I help you?"

"This man thinks yes." His tone was suggestive as he crudely grabbed his man-parts.

This time, she didn't turn away. He did it to shock her and she knew it. What did she care if he liked to play with himself?

He chuckled at her lack of a reaction. "But this man come to barter with the father of the fire-haired woman. Later, you and Okonsa will talk of how you can help this man." He reached out to grasp a lock of her hair.

She jerked out of his way. It was different when Fire Dancer had touched her. He had never meant her any harm. She wasn't sure she could say the same about Okonsa.

"Father! You've got a customer." To busy herself while Okonsa was there, she lifted a quarter keg of ale onto her shoulder to carry it back into the lean-to. It wasn't heavy. She was used to hard work in her father's tavern.

Franklin Daniels appeared in the doorway, wearing a leather apron. He wiped the sweat from his brow with the back of his hand. "What can I do for you?"

The Indian lowered his voice. "This man comes for colonist *manake* firewater. Whis-key."

Franklin frowned. "Sorry. Can't help you."

Mackenzie walked back out of the lean-to and lifted another quarter keg onto her shoulder.

"Can't or will not?" the Indian with the nose ring demanded.

"I won't sell you any more whiskey."

"You have the whiskey and you will not sell it to this man?" The Indian took a threatening step toward Mackenzie's father.

Franklin didn't back down. "Not after that incident the other night. Redmen don't take well to liquor. You know it. I know it. One of these soldiers could have been killed in that brawl. One of your men could have been killed as well. It was a mistake for me to sell the whiskey to you in the first place."

"I have coin—English coin." Okonsa yanked a small red leather purse from the waist of his loinskin.

Mackenzie lowered the ale keg back to the ground. How curious it was that Okonsa carried a white woman's purse. It was dirty and stained, but very similar to the green one her father had bought for her last Christmas.

"I don't want your coin. I'll sell you tobacco. I have needles and cloth you can take back to your woman, but no whiskey." Franklin blocked the doorway, his legs spread wide. "I won't be responsible for any more fighting or injuries."

The Indian stared at her father with hatred in his eyes. "Do not make this mistake, white man." He shook his fist at him. "You do not want this man as enemy."

"You'll not threaten or bully me into changing my mind. I won't sell any more liquor to Indians. Not to your bunch, not to any others."

Okonsa's mouth twitched. He turned to Mackenzie. "Tell your father that he should sell whis-key to this man. There could come a time very soon when he might want this man for friend. To turn Okonsa away would be a great mistake."

Mackenzie lifted a brow. "He makes no mistake. He shouldn't sell you the whiskey. If it was mine, I wouldn't sell it to you, either. As for needing you as a friend, I think not."

He chuckled, speaking so softly that only she heard him.

"Ah, you have fire in your heart. This man can see why a man would be attracted to you."

Mackenzie leaned over and lifted the keg onto her shoulder again. Was he referring to Fire Dancer or himself? Just the thought of this man touching her made her skin crawl. "Come on, Father," she said hurriedly. "Let's get this stuff inside and locked up before it grows dark. You never know what thieves lurk about."

Okonsa only laughed and walked away.

She turned her back on him as he strode away, not wanting to look at him another second. Inside the lean-to, she heaved a sigh of relief. "Good job, Papa." She patted her father on the shoulder. "You stood up to him. You were right not to sell him whiskey again. Fire Dancer says it's bad medicine for his people. Okonsa never should have bought the first bottle from you. It's against the law in his village."

"You talked to Fire Dancer after I asked you to stay away from him?"

"Oh." She waved her hand. "That was what he said that night. You know, when he got me inside the fort safely after the fighting started."

Her father moved a crate of tobacco over to make room. "That Indian with the nose ring is bad medicine, if you ask me. The man scares me. I hope the hell DuBois makes it here soon, because I'm ready to go home."

Mackenzie felt a chill. Her father's words had a foreboding tone about them. Okonsa scared her, too. She considered speaking to Fire Dancer about him, but what would she say? He looked at her? He grabbed his groin? And Mackenzie knew that Fire Dancer considered him his own brother. She wouldn't feel right saying anything against his brother when she had no concrete evidence.

She glanced at her father. "Okonsa's bad medicine? I've never heard you talk that way before."

"I've got a bad feeling in my stomach, Mackenzie," He brushed the top of his balding head with his hand. "I just want to keep my scalp, that's all."

* * *

That night, when Mackenzie heard a tap, tap, tap on her shutter, she leaped out of bed, barefooted, in her thin, white sleeping gown. It had been so hot this week that she'd carefully pulled out the stitches on the sleeves and removed them.

She stood in the darkness and stared at the closed shutter, a sense of excitement making her heart flutter. She knew who it was, of course. A part of her wanted him to come. She lifted her hand to open the shutter, then drew back in indecision.

Fire Dancer excited her, but he made her feel vulnerable as well. When she was with him, she didn't seem to be completely in control of her thoughts and feelings, or even her own actions. And her father had told her to stay away from him.

She dropped to her knees on the bed, unlocked the shutter, and opened it a crack. "Go away."

"I must see you, Mack-en-zie. Let this man in."

"Go away. My father says I can't talk to you."

"What do *you* say, Mack-en-zie with hair of magic and a mind that speaks for itself?"

She ignored his enticement. "You won't sit for my portrait; why should I do anything for you?"

"Mack-en-zie, this man asks that you let him in. I will not harm you. You know that this man would never harm you. This man only wants to see you. To talk. It is lonely here so far from home."

She knew she should slam the shutter closed and lock it. Instead, she opened it a little farther so that she could see his face. His admission of loneliness struck a cord in her heart, and endeared him to her more. She was lonely, too. And only this man seemed to fill that loneliness.

"Give this man permission to enter," he pressed in a whisper. "It is what you want. It is what this man wants."

Her face was only inches from his "If I don't give you permission, will you come anyway?"

"This man will not." He stared into her eyes, the lamplight in her room casting light and shadows across his serious face.

Sweet heavens, but he was a handsome man, his face seemingly carved from a master's hand.

"This man wants . . . needs you."

"Need me?"

"Need . . . need to talk."

Mackenzie could feel herself trembling inside. He wanted to talk to her; he wanted to be with her. He wanted her. Other men had wanted her, but no one had ever made her feel like this.

Mackenzie rested her hand on the lock of the shutter and attempted to appear nonchalant. So did she let him in or not? She debated silently.

Mackenzie thought of the idea she'd been toying with all day. *If I'm going to go through with it,* she mused, *I need to see him, to study him. So why not let him in? He could talk and she could make the necessary observations.*

She knew she was making weak excuses, but she couldn't help herself. "All right," she whispered as she swung open the shutter. "But you leave when I tell you to leave. I swear by all that's holy, if you don't, I'll call for the guard that waits at the bottom of the stairs."

Fire Dancer climbed through the window.

Mackenzie took several steps back.

He sat on the edge of her bed and stared at her.

"Well," she said after a minute or two of silence. "You said you wanted to talk. Talk of what?"

He drew his thin, sensual lips back in a half-smile. "It does not matter what we speak of, really, does it, Mack-en-zie? It only matters that we speak. That we share the words that tumble in our heads." He crossed his arms over his bare chest. "This man wonders what thoughts are in your head. This man wonders of things about you."

"Things?" She took a seat on the camp stool an arm's length from him. They sat at eye-level. *A good way to study his face,* she told herself. "What things? I've never known a man to be interested in what a woman thought about anything."

"This man is not any man."

He stared at her with those black eyes of his and she was

unable to break the eye-contact. "No, you are not any man, are you?" she whispered.

Again that smile.

Mackenzie felt herself relax. He truly was interested in her, wasn't he? She laced her fingers and looped her hands over one knee. Her father was wrong. He wasn't dangerous. Only lonely. "So what would you like to know? My favorite food? The color of my last new gown?" She cut her eyes at him, an amused tone in her voice. "Why I won't marry Joshua Watkins, perhaps?"

He chuckled. "This man already knows why you will not marry the boy. You are not well suited. No, this man wants to know other things. Important things. Things that will tell this man what kind of woman you truly are."

Now she was intrigued. "Like what? Ask me a question. Any question."

He glanced away in thought. Then he looked back. "Name the men you have loved in your life, Mack-en-zie."

She rose off the stool and began to pace. "The men I have loved. What a strange question." She stroked her chin. "Hmmm. I love my father. I loved my grandfather very much." Her draped easel caught her attention. "He taught me to paint. He was schooled in Paris, you know." She pressed her lips together. "And I guess I love Harry—Major Albertson— because he's been so good to me all these years. And . . ."

Fire Dancer still sat on the edge of her cot, attentive as always. "And?"

She fiddled with a jar of paint that rested on the easel's shelf. "And Jack. He wasn't a man, just a boy. He was the cook's son." She smiled at his memory and felt a familiar ache. "I called him Jackie. He loved to fish. I used to take him fishing. The summer I was fourteen and he was seven he drowned in the river." The last word caught in her throat.

"This man is sorry you lost one you loved."

"Thank you." She smiled up at him. "Now my turn. If you can ask questions, so can—" She spotted a black snake slithering across the floor board in front of her and halted in mid-sentence.

Fire Dancer rose off the cot and made a hand sign in the motion of a slithering snake. *"Muneto."*

Mackenzie stood perfectly still as the snake, as long as she was tall, glided by. *"Muneto,"* she repeated.

Fire Dancer walked behind the snake, encouraging it to cross the floor and escape through a hole between two logs along the floor. "You fear *muneto,* Mack-en-zie who fights Huron with a bucket?"

She couldn't resist a smile at his teasing. She knew he was trying to ease her apprehension.

The snake disappeared through the wall.

"I . . . I'm not afraid of—" she imitated his hand-sign— *"muneto.* I just don't like them. Once when I was a child, four or five, I went out to the barn to feed the oxen. I put my hand into a feed crate to grab a handful of grain and the feed was alive with snakes." She couldn't repress a shudder. "I had nightmares for years."

He walked toward her. "This man will make a con-fess-i-ion."

"Oh?" Again she was intrigued. She had never met a man so honest and open about himself.

"When this man was a boy, I feared snakes." He chuckled. "Think of it, Mack-en-zie. Boy who is a prince. Boy who will grow to be great warrior and leader of his people. Shawnee boy who runs to his mother when he sees a snake."

She grinned.

"My brother-cousin Okonsa would tease me. Snakes on my sleeping mat. Snakes in my moccasins. Baby snake in my drinking cup."

"How cruel."

"He thought it was funny."

"Are . . ." she found herself lost in his gaze again. "Are you afraid of snakes now?"

He shook his head. "This man does not care for snakes in his cup, but no, I am not afraid. A wise man taught me not to be afraid. A man I wish you could meet." He caught her hand in his, and their fingers entwined.

Mackenzie felt light-headed. She was supposed to be studying the angles of Fire Dancer's face, the color of his skin, the shape of his ears. Instead, all she could do was stare at his lips and wish they would touch hers.

"Will you let me come again?"

"My father must not know." The warmth of his hand spread a warmth to her entire body. "He would take me away."

"This man will take care. I would not see you sent away."

"I know. I know, but if he even suspects . . ."

"We will not give him reason to suspect." He let go of her hand and walked to the cot where he stretched out on his side. "It is early, Mack-en-zie. And it is your turn to ask another question."

After that night, an odd, new relationship developed between Mackenzie and Fire Dancer.

During the day, she made a point to ignore him when she passed him in the fort yard. When they attended one of Major Albertson's suppers, she avoided him, remaining beside Josh and her father or their host.

Perhaps she avoided Fire Dancer out of a sense of guilt that she was disobeying her father, or perhaps she did it because she didn't trust herself. It was easier for her to ignore Fire Dancer in public than to talk to him without anyone suspecting the truth of her feelings for him, especially since she really didn't know what those feelings were.

Mackenzie told herself that she allowed Fire Dancer to come to her room at night so that she could study him. Night after night she let him in her window. He talked. She listened. Sometimes she talked and he listened. Sometimes they argued. Fire Dancer saw the British and French as nothing but a blight on his people. Mackenzie tried to convince him that they could all live in harmony, that the Shawnee and Lenape and the other tribes could learn from the white man. Fire Dancer only laughed and stretched out on her bed, his hands tucked behind his head, his half naked body gleaming in the lamplight. They talked until the middle of the early morning. Sometimes until the stars began to disappear and the sun began to show its first rays.

Then he left and she began painting.

Chapter Seven

Mackenzie leaned on the hitching rail, too busy watching through the open gate of the fort for a glimpse of Fire Dancer to pay attention to the conversation between her father and Major Albertson. For a full week, he'd secretly been coming every night to her tiny, dimly lit quarters. The more time she spent with him, the more time she wanted to spend with him. She experienced the strangest feelings when he was around. Her stomach was queasy whenever he was near, as if he made her ill, yet when he was gone, she missed him.

As agreed, they didn't converse in public at all. If they passed in the compound, they would cordially nod, avoiding eye-contact. If Fire Dancer was invited to Major Albertson's supper table, Mackenzie avoided him, staying close to her father and Joshua.

Because they only spoke at night in the privacy of her quarters, by day Mackenzie had to be content to watch him from afar. Twice this week, he had somehow managed to get into the fort during the day and leave a gift on her bed without being seen. Once it had been a shiny black stone, and another time, a wood carving of a bird no bigger than her thumbnail.

She kept both gifts safe in her traveling trunk along with the silver snuff box Mary had given her.

As Mackenzie searched for Fire Dancer among the men that milled about, she told herself that she searched for him because she was an artist and artists study their subjects. She studied him only because she was interested in portraying him as accurately as she could. She smiled at her own cleverness. And paint him she would.

Not seeing Fire Dancer, Mackenzie turned around and leaned back against the hitching rail. The Major was saying something about Major DuBois in a hushed tone. Was he coming? Was that what he'd said?

"So when you expecting him, Harry?" Her father puffed on his long-stemmed Dutch pipe. The smoke encircled his head and then drifted away in the still, hot afternoon air.

"The runner brought a message saying he'll be here in no more than a week, as long as he doesn't run into trouble."

"He's coming? The French major is finally coming?" Mackenzie interrupted unable to control her excitement. All she could think of was her success. With Harry's portrait done, she would paint DuBois, and then finish Fire Dancer's portrait.

"So says the half-breed runner he sent. Said DuBois was right as rain and anxious to return to the peace talks. I thought maybe the messenger had something to do with this morning's assignment." Mackenzie nodded in the direction of the palisade. Outside the wall most of the soldiers were lined up, spades in hand. She could hear the sound of their shovels as they dug.

"That?" Harry lifted his beefy hand and let it fall. "Just a precaution. I'm having them dig a trench so that the bulwark will be more difficult to climb."

Mackenzie turned to glance at the jagged walls. She knew first hand that the wall could be climbed. That was how Fire Dancer reached her each night. It hadn't occurred to her that they could be attacked by hostiles the same way. The hair on the back of neck prickled as she turned to face Harry again. "You're expecting trouble?" All she could think of was that if there was fighting, her father would take her away from the fort.

"A good leader always expects trouble." Harry plucked at his shaggy beard. "Don't worry that pretty red head of yours, Mackenzie. Truth is, I'm just giving the boys something to do."

Franklin spoke with his pipe clenched between his teeth. "What aren't you telling, Harry? You and I have known each other too long not to be honest with each other."

"Well . . ." Harry stalled. "Things happen out here. Isolated incidents."

"What? What happened?" Mackenzie half-whispered.

Harry made a point to study the cannon one of the soldiers was polishing on the palisade wall. "A patrol from another fort—only down the river a good day's ride from here—were ambushed."

Mackenzie's eyes widened. "By Indians?"

"Had to be." The Major grimaced. "They were all scalped and their livers were cut out."

Mackenzie swallowed the bile that rose in her throat. "But they wouldn't attack Fort Belvadere, would they? Not with the Shawnee delegation here. Not when you're trying to negotiate peace?"

"As I said, it was an isolated incident, Mackenzie. The redskins have got renegades the same as our army does and so do the French." He rested his hand on her shoulder. "No need to be afraid. We're as safe as the king's coffer. I've doubled the patrols and by week's end these boys will have that trench dug all the way around the fort."

Mackenzie watched Harry. "I'm not afraid. Honestly I'm not. I—"

"Major!" Lieutenant Burrow strode down the wooden walk, his polished boots tapping on the planks. "I must speak with you, sir." He halted and saluted.

Major Albertson returned the salute. "What is it now, Burrow? I told you what to do with Private Peters. A few days digging the new shit hole—pardon, Mackenzie—and he'll not sleep on duty again, Lieutenant."

The young man shook his head. "No, sir, it's not Peters. It's another matter."

"Yes, Lieutenant. Make it quick."

"It's about thievery, sir."

Mackenzie's attention was immediately tapped. Before Burrow said another word, she had a sneaking suspicion she knew what this was about.

"Thievery?" Albertson question gruffly.

"Yes, sir. Something has been stolen from me. From my personal affects."

"A thief among our men?" The major lifted his brow. "You know I won't tolerate thieving or taking the good Lord's name in vain. What's missing?"

"A snuff box, sir."

Mackenzie just stood there, barely hearing what the men said next. Of course, she knew where the snuff box was. It was in her room. She knew who stole it, too.

"Sterling silver and rather valuable," Burrow went on. "My father gave it to me before we set sail from Bristol. It was my grandfather's, sir, and of great sentimental merit."

Mackenzie felt a sense of rising panic. She had to do something before the soldiers found out what Mary had done.

"You certain you didn't misplace the thing?"

"No, sir, I—"

"Excuse me, gentlemen." She touched her hand to her forehead. "I've been foolish enough to misremember my bonnet again and now I fear my head aches."

The Lieutenant swept off his hat. "Are you in need of an escort to your quarters, mistress?" She must have appeared pale because he put out his hand as if he thought she might faint.

"Mackenzie?" Franklin took a step toward her.

"No. I'll be fine. Really." She lifted her hand to stop them. "I just think I need to lay down. Father. Major. Lieutenant." She gave a quick curtsy, bidding them good-bye, and then headed for the inside door. She had to talk to Fire Dancer. Quickly. He would know what to do about Mary.

A few minutes later, Mackenzie walked along the palisade walkway with her hands tucked behind her back, her bonnet tied neatly beneath her chin. Hopefully, to the soldiers, she appeared to be taking an afternoon stroll. She batted at a mosquito that buzzed around her head, and nodded cordially to a lieutenant seated on one of the cannons posted waist high on the corner guard tower.

"Afternoon, mistress."

She smiled at John Allen, the young man Mary was interested in. "Good afternoon, Lieutenant Allen."

Mackenzie swatted at another mosquito, slapping it dead on her shoulder. She peeled the insect off her homespun sleeve and flicked it off her finger. She passed two privates playing cards on the top of an empty ale keg. They nodded. All the while, Mackenzie searched her surroundings for Fire Dancer. His horse was inside the fort walls. Surely he was here somewhere, too.

Mackenzie made the turn on the wall, and headed back toward her room. She hoped her father and the major didn't notice her.

She groaned. Where could Fire Dancer be? Had he gone hunting, or fishing, or just wandered off as he often did?

Then she spotted him and checked to see if the guards were watching her. They weren't. She walked closer to the edge of the jagged wall. "Fire Dancer," she called softly. She glanced away innocently, just in case someone was watching her, then quickly back at him.

Fire Dancer broke off his conversation with another brave, and stared up at her with those black eyes that haunted her dreams.

"Mack-en-zie." His voice was so gentle on the wind that she barely heard him.

"I need to talk to you," she whispered loudly over the side. "Right now."

He said something in Shawnee to the other brave and the brave walked away.

Fire Dancer glanced up at the guard that walked on the palisade, his shadow casting a long, dark line on the grass far below. Fire Dancer's brow creased. "Now, Mack-en-zie? It is important?"

"Now." She stared off into the treetops, trying to appear

casual to anyone who watched her. It wouldn't be safe for Fire
Dancer to attempt to get inside the fort to her. It made more
sense that she go to him. "By the river. I'll be there as soon
as I can."

He nodded and walked away, crossing the soldier's shadow.

Mackenzie raced to her room and grabbed her water bucket.
Still a third full, she poured the water into her chipped wash-
basin. From the trunk on the floor, she took the silver snuff
box wrapped in red cloth, and shoved it through the slit in her
petticoats to the pocket she wore tied to her waist.

Shutting her door quietly behind her, she descended the stairs.
Instead of walking out the main door where her father and the
major probably still stood, she slipped into the main room
where they dined, then out the back door.

Fortunately, Mackenzie found the back gate of the fort open.
It had probably been left that way by the soldiers digging the
trench around the fort. Casually, she walked out the back gate,
swinging the bucket. Long ago she had learned that the best
way to get away with something was to pretend it was perfectly
normal.

"Afternoon, mistress. Afternoon, ma'am," several soldiers
called as she passed. She smiled and dipped a curtsy or two.
The men appeared so young and homesick. "Afternoon, gentlemen. It is indeed hot, isn't it?"

" 'Deed is," one replied.

" 'Deed so," the others echoed.

She walked along the trench they were digging, stepping in
the loose dirt that had yet to be hauled away. She could smell
the rich upturned soil and the scent of burning tobacco. Before
she reached the Indian's encampment, she cut left diagonally
across the forest toward the stream. She didn't look back over
her shoulder to see if anyone was watching her.

Mackenzie was concerned about Mary and the theft. She felt
terribly guilty. If Mary hadn't wanted to give her a gift, the
Indian woman would never have stolen from Burrow. Mackenzie didn't know what she should have done. Not accepted the
snuff box? Should she have understood the Lenape customs

well enough to know not to give the earrings to Mary without realizing she would have to return the favor?

All these things went through her mind as she walked deeper into the forest. But she also thought of Fire Dancer. She felt a trill of excitement. She liked the idea of being alone with him out here in his element rather than in the confines of her quarters. She liked the idea of being alone with him in the bright sunlight with no one but the bees and birds to hear and see them.

Mackenzie reached the stream. She saw no sign of anyone and immediately became a little uneasy. If Fire Dancer wasn't here, that meant she was alone and vulnerable again. She was disobeying her father's wishes and ignoring her own good sense. She tried not to think of the Huron who had attacked her or what could have happened. At least she had her dagger with her now. If need be, she could defend herself. She rested her hand on its hilt, fighting her uneasiness.

"Fire Dancer?" Her voice faded away until it was nothing but the breeze and the chirp of a katydid. She climbed up on a flat, brown rock chasing away a spotted lizard. She stared into the swaying trees and watched for any sign of Fire Dancer.

He'll be here any minute, silly goose, she chided herself. *There's nothing to be afraid of.*

It was cooler here by the stream and she discovered that if she turned her head just right, she could catch the breeze. It felt so good on her face that she closed her eyes for just a second.

"Mack-en-zie?"

She snapped her eyes open, startled. Of course she knew who it was immediately. "Leaping apes in hell!" She threw her arms up in frustration. "You did it to me again. How do you do that?"

Fire Dancer stood no more than a pace from her, staring earnestly into her face. His hands rested casually on his hips. He wore nothing but his fringed leather loin cloth, an open vest, and his moccasins. The only weapon he carried was a knife he wore on his hip. "It is easy, my Mack-en-zie. I walk with the forest, not against it." He held his hand out to her and helped her off the rock. "This man could teach you."

He didn't pull his hand away after she stepped down. Neither did she. Their hands just fell comfortably, their fingers locked as if they always held hands.

A strange electricity leapt between them. Mackenzie always felt it when he was near, but today it was different. It was stronger. She was more aware of her senses; the smell of the mossy river bed; the sound of not one species of bird, but several. All the colors of the forest appeared brighter, the leaves greener, the water more sparkling. And she was more aware of him and her own reaction to him. He had a woodsy scent that clung to him and made her dizzy. He smelled like the open forest, like rain . . . like a man.

"You needed this man?"

Needed him? It sounded so intimate coming from him. "Yes. I . . . I do. I need to tell you something. I . . . I need your help." Reluctantly, she released his warm, firm hand that was the same size as her own. She walked away, putting a little space between them. She couldn't think when he was touching her and she needed to be able to speak coherently.

Then the words just tumbled out. "Mary's done something terrible, Fire Dancer. But she did it for me." Mackenzie turned to face him, and wiped at the silly tears stinging her eyes, embarrassing her. She rarely cried. "I don't want her to be punished because of me. It was all my fault. I vow it was."

He put his arm around her and touched her on her bare forearm. It seemed so natural that he would comfort her. And the quiver of pleasure that leapt inside her when he touched her seemed natural, too.

"Do not have tears, Mack-en-zie." He touched her cheek gently with his thumb, wiping away a tear. "Tell this man, and this man will right the wrong for you, if he can."

She smiled. She had never felt comfortable being vulnerable or weak of spirit around any man, not even her father. But for once it felt good to lift the burden from her shoulders and place it on another's.

"Tell this man," Fire Dancer entreated. "And he will listen."

And Fire Dancer did listen, quietly and without interruption, comment or judgment on Mary or Mackenzie. For that she was grateful. For that, she could have kissed him.

Finished with her confession, she sat down on the rock and watched him pace. She wondered what he was thinking. Why was it taking him so long to say something? Anything. It always took the man so long to speak.

"Mack-en-zie?"

"Yes?"

"Did you bring the trinket?"

She nodded and shoved her hand into her pocket. "Here. It's right here." She offered the silver snuff box still wrapped in the red cloth.

"This man will take it and return it to the lieutenant's possessions." He took the box from her and dropped it into the leather pouch on his belt. "This man will move invisible through the fort. The lieutenant will think his God has returned it."

"I knew you would make it right. I don't want Mary to be punished. No telling what retribution Burrow might take if he knew she took it. I know he'd not understand why she did it." She watched Fire Dancer with eyes that were beginning to somehow see him differently. She felt so emotional today. *"You* understand why she did it, don't you, Fire Dancer?"

"This man understands." He shifted to stand in front of her. Because he was only an inch or so taller than her, he could look her eye to eye. "But this man is afraid for Mary. She wants to be English so much that she forgets where she comes from. She wants to make a friend in you so much that she would go against the laws of our people."

He was so close that her breath caught. She had this sudden, strong desire to reach out and touch that smooth, bronze chest. "What's the punishment for theft among your people?"

"Thieves are banished. Disowned by their families and their people. A thief must strike out on his own. He cannot live among the People with such shame and dishonor on his face."

"You won't tell will you? Not anyone?" She raised her chin. "Not her brother? He would be so angry with her." Then she did it. She raised her hand and placed it, not on his bare skin—she didn't dare—but on the leather vest.

''This man will not tell the secret, but I must speak to the one who calls herself Mary now. She is as a sister to this man. Raised in my mother's wigwam along with me and my sister and Okonsa.''

''You were raised as brother''—her voice twitched as his hand found her waist—''and sister?''

''*Ah*. Their father was killed in fighting when we were still young. Their mother . . .'' He sighed. ''This man does not wish to talk of it now.''

Mackenzie nodded. She could hear his easy, steady breathing. His hand felt so good on her waist. Other men had tried to touch her like this before, but she'd never wanted them to. Not like she wanted Fire Dancer to hold her now.

Fire Dancer's black-eyed gaze searched hers. ''This man would kiss you.''

Mackenzie swallowed against her fear and excitement. ''This woman would be kissed.''

As he tightened his grip on her waist, she let her eyelids fall shut. Mackenzie knew this was insane but she was dying for it. Just one kiss. *One taste of the forbidden fruit,* she wagered with God, *and I'll never do this again.*

His mouth moved so slowly toward hers that she had what seemed like seconds to think about it, to anticipate. When his mouth finally touched hers, it was a gentle caress, as if he was testing the waters. She felt none of the awkwardness she'd experienced the few times Joshua had attempted to kiss her.

Without thinking, she pressed her hand to his chest and brushed her fingertips against his bare skin. The heat of his warm skin penetrated her own flesh. His mouth felt so good against hers . . .

With slow, agonizing pleasure, he touched her lower lip with the tip of his tongue, then her upper lip.

She sighed. Or, heaven forbid, was it a moan? Her heart pounded. He tasted as nothing she had ever tasted before. Was this lust? Was it for this that men fought and ladies died for? She could believe it . . .

To her disappointment, he pulled away.

She opened her eyes. She had thought one kiss would be enough, but it wasn't. It wasn't.

Before she realized what she was doing, she leaned toward him again. She didn't know what made her so bold, but she had to feel his lips against hers just once more. This was it. Her first chance. Her last. Here. Now.

This time when their mouths met there was no hesitation—there was more of an urgency in how he touched her. Both knew this was by mutual consent. Instinctively, she parted her lips. She had never kissed a man open-mouthed before, but she wanted to. She wanted desperately to be possessed by this naked savage . . . and, shamefully, to possess him.

He pushed his tongue into her mouth; she was amazed by the sensation. The taste of him, the feel of his hard chest pressed against her breasts caught her unaware. She had never known it could be like this.

Suddenly her head was spinning. She touched her tongue to his. With one hand still around her waist, he cupped her chin, forcing his mouth against hers with just the right amount of pressure. Mackenzie strained to deepen the kiss, feeling a passion for this man she'd never known existed. She knew it was wrong, even as she explored the cool cavern of his mouth. But it seemed so right, this kissing. Him touching her.

The word *love* popped up in her head and it was as if a bucket of icy water had been splashed in her face. She pulled away, and stumbled backward, suddenly afraid. More afraid then she'd been the day the Indian had attacked her.

"I . . . I have to go. Someone will realize I'm missing." Mackenzie picked up her skirts and ran toward the fort, ignoring the lilting voice that called her name and tugged at her heart-strings.

Chapter Eight

Fire Dancer stood outside the log kitchen and listened to Little Weaver bang her tin pots and dishes. She had cleared away the officers' evening meal, making many trips from the dining room to the kitchen which was a log room separate from the main building. Now she stood inside her hot English kitchen washing the dishes in great wooden tubs. He could see her through the window. He walked in the back door. "Little Weaver." He spoke in their native Shawnee tongue.

She glanced up, then back at the soapy pewter plate in her wet hands. "Mary. This woman called Mary," she answered in English.

"For me, little sister," he replied in Shawnee, "you will always be Little Weaver. You are the woman with the sweet voice, the woman with hands that can make the English loom rattle and produce blankets too pretty for human eyes."

She stared at him with black eyes like Okonsa's. "I am Mary." Stubbornly, she continued to speak in carefully pronounced English. It was obvious she'd been taking speaking lessons from someone and Fire Dancer could guess who.

"The Shawnee girl you knew is gone. Little Weaver gone." She tapped her chest with her soapy hand. "Mary, Mary of the Fort Belvadere kitchen. John Allen's Mary, soon to be wife, this woman hopes.''

Fire Dancer leaned against the doorjamb and crossed his arms over his chest. It was hot and steamy inside the kitchen as in most other white man's rooms. He could still smell the scent of fried, salty bacon and scouring soap. He switched to English. ''This man did not come to argue over this woman's name. I came to speak of a greater matter.''

She dunked the plate into a tub of clear water and set it on a huge tree stump that served as her work table in the dirt-floor kitchen. ''Why do you come? My brother sent you to tell me I cannot speak to John Allen?'' She spoke with a fierce challenge. ''That I cannot choose the man to receive my affections?'' She grabbed another dirty plate. ''This woman is a widow. Her husband is dead and gone to the heavens.'' She waved her hand and soap suds flew. ''This woman is free to do what she wants.''

''The matter of the Englishman is between you and your brother—perhaps only between you and the soldier. I come to speak of a more serious matter.''

She began to scrub the pewter plate vigorously, keeping her eyes downcast.

Fire Dancer sighed, switching back to Shawnee. It was easier to express his feelings in his own language. ''Sister, I know what you did.''

Fear shone in her eyes.

''And this man understands why.''

Slowly, she lifted her gaze. Thankfully, he saw shame in her face. So at least she had not completely lost what lessons his mother had taught her.

''You took the lieutenant's trinket.''

''He had no need of it!'' she defended. ''He have many shiny boxes, buckles, beads!''

''That does not matter and you know it,'' Fire Dancer snapped.

Mary went on washing her dishes. She wiped at her teary eyes with the sleeve of her new blue and green calico English dress. A gift from the soldier, no doubt.

"This woman wanted to give her new friend, Mackenzie, a gift," Mary said softly in Shawnee. "And this woman had no gift to give."

"So you became a thief?"

Mary twisted her hands in her English skirt. "You do not understand, you Fire Dancer, who have always had whatever you wanted. You who have always been loved."

He took a step toward her, disturbed by her words. "You are loved, Little Weaver. You are loved by me and by our mother and our sister. Okonsa loves you more than any who walks this earth."

"Okonsa!" she spat. "He does not love this woman as sister. He only wishes to control her. To make her one of his cronies' squaws. To keep her in the village and never let her taste the English sugar, or choc-o-late, or see the pretty glass beads."

"He wants what is best for you, Little Weaver. It's all he's ever wanted. When you came to our village after your mother died, it was Okonsa who carried you on his back. It was Okonsa who got you to eat when our mother could not. It was Okonsa who bathed your face when the white man's small pox came."

She slapped a plate on top of another with a clang. "If Okonsa loved this woman, he would let her go. He would let her be John Allen's wife. He would let her go to Eng-land and live in a fine English stone house and drink tea from glass."

"John Allen has offered his heart to yours in marriage?"

She dried her hands on a ragged linen towel. "Not yet, but he will."

Fire Dancer rested his hands on his hips. "Little Weaver, we have strayed from our conversation. I came to speak of the theft. If the white soldiers had caught you, you could have been hanged until your death, or had your hand cut off. How will you enter the path of the heavens when you die, if you have no hand?"

She turned her back to him, still speaking in their native tongue. "I won't do it again."

"It should not have been done to begin with. You know better. It's not who you are, Little Weaver. You are not a thief."

"No?" She whipped around, her black braids swinging.

"Then who am I? The daughter of murdered ghosts? The sister of a brave who hates men for the color of their skin and nothing more? Who am I, but a woman doomed to grind corn in a cornhusk wigwam? I want more, Fire Dancer of the Thunder Sky. This woman will have more. If the Englishman, John Allen, will not give it to her, another white man will."

Fire Dancer ran his hand over his face. He didn't want to be here right now. He didn't want to deal with Little Weaver and her confusion of her own identity. All he wanted to do was see the woman with her bright red head. He wanted to hear her speak his name. He wanted to taste her lips again.

"The trinket has been returned without anyone's knowledge. I will not mention this incident to your brother."

"That is good because he would send me home to the village."

"As he should." He watched her walk across the room with a heavy pot in her hand. "As should I, if I could spare the escort for you."

"Do not trouble yourself with this woman again, Fire Dancer. She will not take what is not hers." She looked at him. "But do not send me home to Mother. Let me stay. Let me catch the white husband, if I can."

Fire Dancer nodded. "We will not speak of this matter of the trinket again. You may stay here until our party returns to our village, but if no marriage is made, this man must take you home. It is his duty to our mother."

She smiled, switching back to English. "John Allen says he loves this woman. He will marry me."

"This man hopes you are right, if that is what you truly want. I must go and find your brother. He is anxious to go elsewhere, but I will bid him stay. They say the French major approaches. We will begin our peace talks again and perhaps come to some conclusion without more bloodshed."

"Good night, Fire Dancer." She followed him to the door and kissed him on the cheek. "This woman thanks you for the goodness of your heart."

He slipped out the kitchen door and into the cover of darkness. Her sisterly kiss made him wish for one of another kind—

one as sweet as honeysuckle sprinkled with morning dew. A kiss of passion. Mack-en-zie's kiss.

Fire Dancer walked along the wall, keeping out of sight. He couldn't get Mackenzie out of his mind. At first, he had just been curious about her. He was fascinated by her wit, her intelligence, even her odd looks. He could think of nothing but her. It was almost as if she was beginning to possess a part of him. Fire Dancer knew that it was madness, but it was as if he was unable to control his logic when it came to her.

Right now he was concerned. She ran from him today after they had kissed under the tree boughs. Why, he was not sure. It was obvious to both of them that it was what she had wanted. He would see her tonight and know what was in her head. He had to.

Mackenzie chewed on the tip of her paintbrush. The sketching had gone so quickly that she had brought out her oil paints. She stared at the small portrait. The light of several stinking tallow candles illuminated the room.

Fire Dancer stared back at her.

The portrait was only two hands tall and one wide and easily hidden. That was why she had made the canvas so small. Fire Dancer would never find it in the room.

At first she had intended to paint just his bust, as she had with Major Albertson. But after she'd gotten the idea to paint him in secret, she realized she could not do him justice by merely painting his head. A full view would capture the subject more accurately.

So she had painted him standing proudly, dressed in his loincloth and quilled moccasins with the leather vest he was so proud of. Behind him she would eventually fill in trees and perhaps even part of the jagged palisade wall.

At first Mackenzie had felt guilty about painting Fire Dancer against his wishes. But that was all nonsense about possessing a man's soul, and if he were an educated man, he would know that. She was honestly doing him no harm. He would never know she had painted his likeness. He would leave the fort when the peace talks were over and then she would add his portrait to those of Major Albertson and Major DuBois to the crate to be transported to London. She would get her first commission payment and Fire Dancer would not be hurt in any way, real or imagined.

She leaned forward and added a stroke of black paint to his long, sleek hair. ''Take your soul, indeed,'' she muttered.

Mackenzie had worked all evening on the portrait, even excusing herself from supper. She suddenly had a burning desire to finish it. With Major DuBois riding for the fort, she'd be able to start his likeness next week. She told herself she had to spend as much time on Fire Dancer's portrait as possible, but in truth, she had skipped supper for fear of seeing him.

Mackenzie didn't know how she felt about their kiss today. Well, she did know how she felt. She smiled with giddy pleasure. She felt wonderful.

But her head was what she had to think with, not her emotions or the strange feelings coursing through her veins. The kiss had been the most wonderful thing that had happened to her. It was even better than the Christmas morning her grandfather had given her that first box of paints.

But of course the kiss could lead to nothing. She knew that. He was a heathen savage. She was a colonial woman with a life back on the Tidewater. It was pure sexual attraction, the devil's work. It was her desire to defy her father and Joshua, and the rules of common society that had prompted her to kiss him.

When she thought of it all logically, it made sense. She was just exercising a childish desire to rebel. And maybe she was just a little infatuated with her subject. Surely that happened sometimes to an artist. When an artist stared at a man's face, at his muscular, half-naked body, it was natural that she should think herself attracted to him.

Mackenzie added one more stroke with the black brush and then dropped it into a little can of linseed oil. She checked her pocket watch, one that had once been her grandfather's. It was nearly midnight. Would he come? She hoped not. She hoped so.

Mackenzie picked up the small canvas from the easel. If the

English government liked it, perhaps they would even commission her to paint a full-sized one. Perhaps she'd even get to go to England and work on it there, if she was lucky. The possibilities were endless.

Mackenzie kneeled on the floor and slid the portrait under her cot.

"Mack-en-zie . . ."

It was him.

She popped her head up. Her heart suddenly raced the way it had this afternoon at the stream. She wasn't ready for him yet. She wished she had a nightrail to cover herself. She hadn't prepared herself for what she would say to him. She scrambled to her feet and let the counterpane fall to cover the cot and what lay beneath it.

He climbed in through the window. "This man feared you would lock the window this night." He rolled over her cot and then instead of jumping up as he usually did, he stretched out on his side on the bed. He propped his head on his hand.

She turned away, wondering if it was really necessary that he display his body like that. After all, female or not, she was human and of the child bearing age. Even women had certain feelings . . . *down there*. She was discovering that pretty quickly.

"You do not speak for once, Mack-en-zie? Are you ill?"

She turned to face him, crossing her arms over her breasts, as if she could somehow isolate herself from him. Where were all those logical, reasonable thoughts now that he was here?

But instead of logic, all she could think of was their kiss, and wish that he would kiss her again. "I . . ." Without realizing it, she touched her lips with her fingertips; the memory of his mouth burned on hers. "I . . . I'm just tired, that's all."

"Come." He patted the cot. "Sit. Rest. This man will not stay long."

She stared at the place where his hand rested on her mother's patchwork counterpane.

"This man will not harm you," he said softly. "I would not touch . . . or kiss what is not offered."

This was her chance. If he was going to speak so frankly,

so could she. Now was a good time to bid him farewell. She could tell him to leave and not come back again. She could tell him her father was suspicious of him. She . . . she could tell him she was going to marry Josh . . .

She took the three steps to the cot and sat down. Her knees felt weak.

Without hesitation, he slipped his hand to the nape of neck and guided her mouth downward toward his.

She sighed as their lips met. "Fire Dancer," she breathed against his lips. "This . . . this isn't right." But as she spoke, she nipped his lower lip with her teeth. She pressed her mouth against his and slid her hand over his flat, hard stomach.

"There," he said as he raised his mouth from hers.

"There?" She stared down at him as she remained leaning over him, her hand still on his warm skin. "There what?"

"There. We both wanted to kiss. We could think of nothing else. Now we kissed. Now we can speak of what this is between us."

She took her hand from his waist and laid it in her lap. It was too tempting to touch him like that. It made her want to touch him elsewhere. "I don't know what you mean."

He laughed.

"What?" She couldn't help but smile. "Why are you laughing at me?"

"I laugh that you can deny what you feel. You whites, you are all alike in that way."

She crossed her arms on her lap, rubbing at the sienna paint drying on her thumb and forefinger. It was almost exactly the same shade as his skin. "I don't know what I feel, Fire Dancer." She rose from the cot to pace. "Honestly, I don't."

"It is not what we expected, this passion we feel. No, Mack-en-zie?"

"I would say not. I . . . I'm a colonial woman and you . . . you're . . . you're—"

"A savage?"

She ran her hand over her face and brushed the loose strands of hair back. She was spending too much time painting. She wasn't getting enough sleep. She was having a difficult time collecting the thoughts in her head. "I never called you a savage. It's only that we are so different, you and I."

He sat up. "This is true. This man knows all the reasons why he cannot come here at night in the darkness. The soldiers would hang this man, if they knew." He rose off the cot. "But this man cannot stop coming. He cannot stop thinking of Mack-en-zie," he reached out to touch the hair that fell over her shoulder, "and how she makes him feel inside." He touched his chest with his fist. "Here."

Mackenzie's gaze slid toward him, as if drawn magnetically. Everything she had grown up with and had been taught told her that this was wrong. Yet when he offered his arms, she stepped into them.

Fire Dancer wrapped his arms around her waist and drew her so close they were hip to hip. It was the most intimate position she'd ever been in with a man, and it amazed her how well they fit together.

"Mack-en-zie." He brushed the hair off her neck and kissed her there. "This man will talk to the British and French majors and then he will go home to his people."

"And I will go home with my father to the Chesapeake." Then she said what he hadn't. "And we will never see each other again."

He lowered his mouth again, kissing her harder. Mackenzie wrapped her arms around his neck, pulling him closer until their bodies molded as one. "I don't want you to go," she whispered. "I don't want to go."

He smiled sadly. "For this man's whole life he looks for a woman that makes his blood boil and his heart sing and what does he find? A white woman in a British fighting fort."

She rested her cheek on his shoulder. "It could never work. There is no compromise." She meant it as a statement, but a part of her saw it as a question. A remote possibility.

"No, Mack-en-zie. This man cannot join your world. I have a duty to my people. I would never fit in here. I would make you sad."

"And I cannot leave my father. I . . . couldn't be an Indian." She smiled sadly. "Imagine that."

He kissed the tip of her nose. "So, should this man go now? Should the good-byes be said now?" He stroked her bare shoulder and her breasts tingled beneath the linen sleeping gown. "Should we end what cannot be, now, before hearts break?"

Mackenzie couldn't believe this man was saying such things to her. Heartbreak? Was he trying to say that this was love they felt? Her father had always said that true love made no sense. Did true love also see no barriers of race or religion?

"Mack-en-zie?"

She knew he waited for an answer, but she had none. She just knew she didn't want him to leave her.

She drew back a little. "Can't we spend what time we have left like this?"

He stroked her cheek. "You do not want this man to go?"

She smiled up him. "Not now." She took his hand and led him toward her sleeping cot. "Right now, I'm so tired that I don't want to think about it." She plopped down on the edge of the bed. "I just want you to hold me."

He sat down beside her and slid his arm around her waist. "This man can do that for you, Mack-en-zie." He kissed her temple. "He only wishes that he could do more."

Chapter Nine

Okonsa stood outside the rear door of the kitchen resting his foot on the stone that served as a step. One stroke at a time, he leisurely shaved the bark off a stick with his long-bladed hunting knife.

He could hear his sister singing. Her voice made him smile. She had been so unhappy since the death of her husband, He-Whose-Name-Could-Not-Be-Spoken, Okonsa's best friend. She had hoped to have children by him. Instead he had been killed in a skirmish with the British.

The truth was that he'd been killed when their party had attacked the redcoat soldiers, but no one knew that. Everyone in the village thought the soldiers had attacked them. It was the way Okonsa wanted it. It was the only way to make the Shawnee of the Turtle Clan understand.

Okonsa heard Little Weaver approach the door. He stepped out of the way just before she threw a pan of dirty water onto the ground.

"You splash me, sister," he said in Shawnee.

She glanced at him and then clunked back into the kitchen in her leather shoes.

Okonsa hated to see her like this, working like a dog for the white swine. It made no sense to him. White men had killed her husband. White men had killed their father and had raped and tortured their mother. How could she want to be one of them?

He followed her into the kitchen that stank of lye soap and burnt animal fat. "This man came to tell you it is time you pack your sleeping mat."

She halted and faced him, the dishpan still in her arms. "What do you mean?"

"In Shawnee," he corrected. "The soldiers might hear us."

Reluctantly, she spoke in Shawnee. "You tell this woman she must go. Fire Dancer tells this woman we do not go yet. He waits for the Frenchmen. They will talk of peace again with Major Albertson."

Okonsa tucked his knife into its sheath and the stick into his belt to work on later. "There will be no peace. We do not go yet, but the time draws near. This man will come for you, sister, and we will leave this foul place."

Little Weaver set down the dishpan. "I will make ready. When you come for me, brother, I will follow."

He picked up a cold corn biscuit from the tree trunk table as he passed it on his way out the door. He had expected more of a fight out of her. This was good. Maybe she had spent enough time with the white men to know that she wanted no part of them. "This man must go away. Two days, maybe three. When he returns, we will go home." He hesitated at the door. "Only do not tell our brother, Fire Dancer." He grinned. "It will be a surprise."

"What will be this *surprise?*" Fire Dancer spoke the last word in lightly accented English.

Okonsa tried not to appear alarmed by his cousin's sudden appearance. He rearranged his testicles beneath his loin skin. "If I tell you of this surprise, it will not be a surprise." His gaze met Fire Dancer's and he grinned boyishly. "No?"

Fire Dancer made that face he always made when he was suspicious of Okonsa. "Why are you inside the fort walls, brother, now that darkness has fallen and the great gates are closed?"

Okonsa swaggered beside his cousin. Both men were careful to walk along the palisade fence inside the shadows so as not to be detected by the redcoats.

"I would ask you the same, Fire Dancer."

"I but look after my cousins."

Okonsa waved his finger. "I am not a boy any longer that you must follow me day and night."

"When we were boys, you found trouble when I did not follow you, Okonsa."

Okonsa ground his teeth. He was in a good mood and he would not let Fire Dancer ruin it. It was a strange relationship the two shared. Their mothers were sisters. When his parents died it was Fire Dancer's mother who took him and Little Weaver in and made them her own. Okonsa loved Fire Dancer for all that he was. And he hated him for all that he was.

"Battered Pot tells this man you, and he, and six others leave at dawn. I asked him where you go but he made no reply." Fire Dancer stopped beside the corner of one of the fort's outbuildings. This one held black powder and munitions. The door was locked with an iron padlock. "Where do you go, Okonsa?" Fire Dancer probed.

Okonsa shrugged and walked on. "Only hunting."

"He says you will be gone a sunset or two, perhaps three."

Okonsa nodded. He had learned long ago that the trick to lying was to believe in your own lies. "This is true, brother. The white *manake* have hunted this land until there is not a decent buck for a day's run. My men and I, we will bring back fresh meat. You can take some to the white woman, if you want." He felt a stiffening in his man rod at his mention of the red-haired woman. "Better yet. This man will take it to her himself," he baited.

Fire Dancer glanced at him, but would not take the worm. "We go home to the village soon. I think it will be better for all of us. Your head is too full of English things, the same as your sister's."

Okonsa stroked his scalp lock of hair thoughtfully. "You are wise to take our men and sister back to the village. This talk of peace is a waste of a man's breath." He slashed his hand in the air. "There will be no peace. If we don't kill them first, they will kill us. All of us. They will take our land. Our women. Our people will be broken. I say we kill them all now while they sleep."

"That is why the chief sent me and not you to these peace talks." Fire Dancer halted at the rope that dangled from the wall. "Go, Okonsa. Go back over the white fence before you are caught and we both are hanged from our gizzards."

"What? You do not come?" Okonsa mocked. "Do not tell this man you court the white woman with the fire hair."

"Good night, brother."

"Aieee!" Okonsa grinned. "You like her too, eh?" Then he frowned. "But this man had thought he might have her for himself. She is hot for me, you know."

"You think all maidens are hot for you." Fire Dancer slapped him lightly on his chest. "I told you. Stay away from Macken-zie."

"*Ah*, so you did. So I will." Okonsa winked. Long ago he had learned to say what others wanted him to. "Good night, brother. Sweet dreams."

"Good night," Fire Dancer answered. "Go carefully and do not get yourself into trouble that you cannot find your way out of."

"Me?" Okonsa grabbed the rope. "This man does not fear. You will rescue me, brother, should I stumble." His gaze hardened. "You always do."

Then he shimmied up the rope into the darkness and away from the man he wanted so desperately to be.

Mary pressed her hand to Lieutenant John Allen's bare, hairy chest as he rolled off her onto his back on the narrow cot. The only light in the kitchen came from the coals that still glowed in the stone fireplace. In the corner of the kitchen was where she slept, on this soldier's cot Major Albertson had given her.

Mary rolled onto her side and wiped the beads of sweat from her upper lip. It was hot inside the kitchen, too hot for sleeping or lovemaking, but John refused to go with her to the open forest. Something about *privacy,* he had said.

Mary draped her bare leg over John's legs and leaned to brush her breast against his arm.

He sighed and tucked his hand behind his head. "Ah, Mary, you're a sweet dear." He squeezed her breast. "As sweet as any dairy maid in Sussex."

She smiled, tracing a pattern with her finger on his sweaty chest. "You are stallion, John of my heart." She laughed huskily. Truth was, his man-stick was not particularly impressive, nor was his ability to please a woman on the sleeping mat. But that came with time in a relationship, didn't it? It had been so with her husband.

Mary rested her head on John's shoulder. She wished he would bathe more often. She had even tried to get him to swim in the stream one night with her, but he'd refused. She wrinkled her nose. All white men smelled, so she guessed she would get used to it, eventually. When she lived in England across the great ocean in a fine house she would be surrounded by smelly Englishmen and their women.

"John?"

He had closed his eyes. "Mary?"

"John, it is time we speak."

He didn't open his eyes. "Mmmhmmm."

"Soon the peace talks will be over. My brothers will go back to village." She waited for a response. She didn't get one. "John?" She pushed him with her hand.

He opened his eyes. They were as blue as the Father's sky. She liked his blue eyes.

"Did you hear this woman speak? I said, soon I will have to go."

"You don't think your brothers would allow you stay through my tour? I've only another six months in this Godforsaken wilderness and then it will be home I go. Home to Sussex and my mother's pudding."

"It would not be right for this woman to stay in the fort without her brothers. Not a woman unmarried."

He closed his eyes. "I'm sorry to hear that, love." He shifted in the bed, making himself more comfortable. "I'll miss you when you're gone."

The conversation was not going as Mary had hoped. She had hoped than when she told her soldier she had to leave, he would declare his eternal love for her and offer to wed her now. Tonight. Even a promise of hands would be enough to keep Okonsa and Fire Dancer from forcing her to return to their village.

She closed her eyes and then opened them again. "John."

His eyes were closed. "Mary, be a dear and allow me to sleep an hour, no more. My watch ends at two and it's necessary that I be on the palisade to turn over my duties to the next man."

"John." She punched his arm. "Did you hear what this woman said?"

When she punched him, his eyes flew open. "Ouch!" He rubbed his arm. "You said you were going back to your village. What else would you have me hear, wench?"

She lowered her gaze. "If you are going to wed this woman, it must be soon. Word must be sent to my mother."

He sat up instantly. "If I'm going to *what?*"

"W . . . wed this woman. Make to marry." She rose to her knees behind him and wrapped her arms around him. He jerked away from her and climbed off the bed.

"Marry you?" He picked up his dirty red uniform breeches from the floor and pulled them on with jerky movements. "Whatever gave you the notion I intended to wed you?"

The tone in his voice made Mary reach for the holey linen sheet on the edge of the camp cot and cover her nakedness. She wasn't ashamed of her body, but she was ashamed of herself. She realized she may have made a mistake. A terrible mistake. "You . . . you told this woman you love her. You say she is beautiful. You say she is your stars in your heaven."

He tucked his flaccid stick into his breeches and yanked on the laces. "I never said I was going to marry you." He laughed. "I never said any such thing."

She watched him as he dropped his white shirt over his head. "No. You did not say marry, but you said love. You . . . you take this woman's body to be yours. In my village, among my people, if you say love, if you accept a woman's gift of her flesh, a man marries the woman.''

"Well, this isn't the futtering village, and I am not one of your *people.*'' He stuffed his shirt into his breeches and reached for his redcoat, obviously in a hurry to get out. "I've already got a nag for a wife at home.''

She lowered her gaze. He hadn't told her he was married. All she could think of was the grass-mat floor of her mother's wigwam. She wanted to walk on the polished floor boards John had described. She wanted to see his mother's painted china. She wanted to see the orangery, even though she didn't know what one was. "John, this woman . . . this woman would be second wife.'' It wasn't what she had hoped for, being a man's number two wife. The Lenape didn't usually even approve of multiple marriages, except when they were made necessary by war or famine. But it would be worth being a less important wife, if only she could live in a stone and glass house. If only she could taste butter cake.

He propped his leg on an overturned bucket and rolled up his wool stockings. He had the strangest look in his eyes. "Second wife? You think I'm some heathen that I would defy God's law? You ignorant savage. We Englishmen do not take second wives.''

Savage. Heathen. She knew these words well. They were bad words. Hateful words. And they stung. "You do not take second wives?'' There were tears in her eyes. "But you do make love to women when your wife waits for you in your home?'' She wiped her runny nose with the back of her hand. "This woman thinks you are savage, John Allen.''

The soldier slapped her hard across her face. Mary closed her eyes and lifted her palm to her cheek. His strike smarted, but the pain was not nearly as great as the pain in her heart.

Mary sat on her knees, her eyes closed. She waited until she heard him go and then she laid back on the lumpy cot. Tears welled in her eyes, but they did not flow. She would not cry for herself, only for the baby that grew inside her.

* * *

Barefooted, Mackenzie hopped from one flat rock to the next. She laughed as she splashed cool water on her legs. It was a beautiful, hot afternoon. The sun shone, but the thick foliage of the trees shaded her from the burning rays. The forest was filled with insect and bird song and Mackenzie felt truly happy.

Everything was going so well for her. The portrait of Fire Dancer was nearly complete and she knew it was the best work she'd ever done.

Each night he came to her and told her stories of his people and their land. Major DuBois would be here within two or three days. Then she would paint him. She refused to think about what would happen then. She'd not think about going home and ruin her joy.

Mackenzie lifted her blue sprigged skirt to her knees and skipped to the next rock. Having forgone her corset weeks ago, she felt carefree and cool wearing only her shift, her father's shirt, and her skirt. The women at home would have been mortified. Mrs. Faye and Mrs. Canter would probably have fainted at the sight of her dressed like this. But it was so hot and Mackenzie was so far from civilization that it didn't matter.

Fire Dancer said the women in his village wore no corset, nor any bodice or shirt at all in the heat of the summer. Bare breasted, he said they were. What would Mrs. Faye and Mrs. Canter think of that? Compared to the Lenape woman, Mackenzie figured, she really wasn't so shocking, after all.

The sound of a musical note in the trees caught Mackenzie's attention. She saw nothing, but the sound of the sweet notes of a flute were unmistakable. Mackenzie smiled. She knew who played the pipe.

Fire Dancer was a romantic suitor beyond her expectations. He sang to her in his strange language. He played his bone flute for her. He brought gifts of shiny stones and bright feathers. Last night he had brought her a fistful of flowers he picked for her in the forest. Of course, he wasn't really a suitor. Mackenzie knew that, but it was fun to pretend.

She stood on her tiptoes on the rock and pirouetted in the direction of the sound of the music. "Fire Dancer?" She didn't call too loudly for fear one of the soldiers would hear her and come running. She sneaked out the back gate to come here, hoping Fire Dancer would follow her. Seeing him only in the wee hours of the night just wasn't enough anymore.

"Fire Dancer?" She jumped to another rock, and stepped into the water to wade toward the bank. The cold water made gooseflesh on her bare legs. "If you don't show yourself," she said to the trees, "I'll go back to the fort."

She climbed up the bank and turned, resting her hands on her hips. She could still hear the magical flute music. Each note was hollow and resonant. It was one of those tunes that made a strange ache in one's heart. It had to be a love song.

"Fire Dancer," she whispered. He was so close. Where was he? Then she noticed his bare legs swinging from a tree limb on the far side of the stream, the rest of his body obscured by the leaves.

"There you are," she called.

The music stopped and in one smooth motion he leaped from the tree onto the mossy bank. "The water feels good, *ah*?"

She smiled. "Yes. *Ah*," she pronounced, proud that she was picking up a few words of Shawnee.

He pointed upstream. "Not far from this place is a pool. You would go with me?" He held out his hand.

"You mean swimming?"

"Bathing. Swimming. It is much the same to this man." He still held out his hand, beckoning her.

The notion was shocking. Tempting. It was so damned hot and sticky today. Mackenzie could imagine the cold water trickling down her back. She could imagine washing her hair in the free-flowing water instead of with a pitcher of water and a pan in the kitchen.

Then, there was another matter to consider. Alone, they could touch, they could kiss. Mackenzie spent a lot of time these days thinking of kissing . . . thinking of what it would be like to experience even more intimacy . . .

Before she could change her mind, Mackenzie grabbed her

stockings and boots, dumped them into her dry water bucket and waded across the stream toward him. "You know, if my father catches us, he'll hang us both 'till we're dead, and that will be the end of the peace talks . . ."

"This man does not care to take his last breath at the end of a British *manake* rope." When they reached the far side of the stream, he took her hand in his. "But if this man must hang, then to hang beside you, Mackenzie, would make my heart sing."

She laughed. "You have a strange way with words, Fire Dancer. You compliment me by saying you'd like to share the noose with me." She laughed again, swinging her hand and his.

They walked along the stream bank for fifteen or twenty minutes. Mackenzie thought nothing of her father, or the fort, or even the portrait of Fire Dancer beneath her bed. She was living for the moment, today, and it was turning out to be one of the best days she'd ever had.

The terrain grew rockier as Fire Dancer led Mackenzie around a bend in the stream. The stream was wider here and the water ran deeper. She could tell by the movement on the surface of the water.

"This is the place this man likes to come when he wishes to leave the fort. This man rests here when he wishes not to think of fighting, or sickness, or the land he fears his people will lose."

Mackenzie set down her bucket and stared at the inviting swirl of water in the center of the stream. If she was going to do this, it had to be now. She couldn't be gone too long from the fort, or her father or Josh might realize she wasn't in her chamber.

Getting up her nerve to disrobe in front of Fire Dancer, Mackenzie unhooked her skirt and stepped out of it.

He stood behind her and said nothing.

She pulled her linen shirt over her head and let it float to the mossy ground. She knew he watched her. She knew how sheer her white shift must be in this bright sunlight. Slowly, she walked toward the water. She felt self-conscious, but not

enough to cover herself. It seemed that their relationship had
reached a point where ideas of right and wrong were no longer
so easily defined. Swimming, half-naked with Fire Dancer
seemed right. It was what he wanted, else why would he have
brought her? It was what she wanted, else she'd not have come.

Mackenzie heard him follow behind her.

She grasped the trunk of a sapling and stepped off the grassy
bank into the knee-deep water. She caught her breath as she
adjusted to the shock of the cold. The water moved behind her,
splashing her back as Fire Dancer approached. Nervous at the
thought of him so near, and feeling vulnerable, she plunged in
head-first.

Mackenzie came up for air in the center of the stream where
the water was waist-deep. Soaking wet, her shift clung to her
breasts. Her cold, hard nipples stuck out like raisins on an
oatmeal cookie. They couldn't be missed by man or beast.

Fire Dancer waded toward her, the muscles of his bare chest
rippling as he walked. He was a small, compact man compared
to many Englishmen she knew, but he gave off a sense of
power and confidence unlike any man she had ever known. As
she stared at his bare torso, she tried not to think about whether
or not he still wore his loin cloth.

She placed her hands over her breasts with a latent sense of
modesty and watched him wade through the water. He was so
graceful. He had such a presence about him. He truly was a
prince.

At two arms' length from her, he dove under the water with
a splash. Mackenzie covered her face and gave a squeal of
laughter. The water was so cold that it made her teeth chatter.

A second later he came up behind her. She was ready for
him. "Not so close." She splashed water at him playfully.

He tipped his head back and ran his hands from his forehead
back, over his hair. The water ran in rivulets from his sleek
black hair, over his shoulders, down his powerful arms.

"It is a good place?" He smiled.

She smiled back. *"Ah."*

They stood in the water, face to face and studied each other.
The same electricity that Mackenzie had felt in her room the

other night was here. It was so strong that she could feel it, smell it, taste it.

She wanted to taste him. She wanted to feel his wet skin beneath her fingertips. A part of her wanted to hide her nearly naked breasts from him, yet a part of her wanted to share them with him.

''Well, are you going to kiss me or not?'' The words popped out of her mouth before she had time to weigh the consequences. *This was why she had really come, wasn't it?* To make love, at least in some capacity.

He waded toward her. ''Only if you wish it, Mackenzie. This man would not take advantage of you. You are an innocent in the ways of men and women. Innocent of your own desires.''

She felt her cheeks color at his bluntness on this subject, although she didn't know why. He was blunt about the things that proper English men and women didn't speak of. Why should this be any different?

He brought his hands through the water and rested them on her hips. She leaned forward; her arms still covered her chest. When his lips touched hers, she raised her hands and slid them over his shoulders. The water was so cold. He was so warm.

Mackenzie kissed him once, twice, three times. Her tongue tangled with his in a frenzy of passion they equally shared. When he lifted his hand from her hip to move higher, she didn't stop him. This was what she wanted. It was what she had thought of when she lay alone on her cot at night, her own hands on her breasts. She had thought of his hands down *there*, even.

The wet material of her shirt was rough on her nipples. She could feel her breasts responding, even before he cupped one with his warm hand.

''Oh,'' she sighed. She closed her eyes and pressed her mouth to his collar bone.

Fire Dancer kissed her neck and nibbled at her earlobe. He stroked her nipple with the pad of his thumb. She didn't understand how it was connected to her breasts, but between her legs she felt a pulsing warmth.

Mackenzie smoothed her hands over his shoulders, his chest.

She loved the way his hard muscles felt beneath her hands. The cold water emphasized the heat of his sun-kissed skin beneath her fingertips.

She relaxed muscle by muscle. The caress of his hands made her sigh, made her moan. His touch made her want more. It made her want the world to be different. It made her wish that somehow she could be with this man forever. Mackenzie brushed her mouth against his and squeezed her eyes shut. She kissed him again and darted her tongue out to touch his.

Fire Dancer abruptly pulled away. He pressed a quick kiss to her mouth.

She opened her eyes to see the back of his head as he swam away. "Where are you going?" she called after him with disappointment. Her heart was pounding, her pulse still throbbing. "Is something wrong? Didn't you like it?

"I brought you to this place to swim, not to kiss. This man swims."

Understanding his meaning, she took a deep breath to calm herself. She was beginning to understand his Indian logic. He meant that he was afraid they were getting carried away with their emotion . . . with their feelings for each other.

He was right. Maybe it was time they cooled off, before they did something they might regret later. Mackenzie had enjoyed the touching and kissing, but she wasn't sure she was ready for anything more. To take that final step . . . to actually make love to Fire Dancer . . . there would be no way to turn back from that.

She dove into the water and joined him on the far side of the bank. They swam under water and above. They splashed each other. Once he lifted her and threw her high in the air. She landed in the center of the stream with a great splash and didn't surface until she had him firmly by the ankle and pulled him under.

Near the bank, Fire Dancer showed her how to catch minnows in her hands. He pointed out a turtle sleeping lazily on a warm rock in the sun on the far side of the stream. They kissed and laughed. They touched a little, but Fire Dancer seemed to understand her vulnerability. With some sense of honor she didn't comprehend, he took no advantage of her vulnerability, even though she half-hoped he would.

They must have swam for an hour, and then Mackenzie waded out and plopped herself in a sunny spot in the grass to dry her hair. She certainly couldn't go back to the fort looking like this.

Fire Dancer emerged behind her . . . naked as the day he was born.

Mackenzie's mouth dropped open. She should have looked away. But she couldn't. She knew full well what a man's parts looked like. It looked like something akin to a turtle without its shell, and she'd never found it particularly interesting before. But Fire Dancer's was the same bronze hue as the rest of his skin, and bigger than she'd expected.

He paid her no attention as she stared, but strode to where he had left his loin cloth and vest on a branch.

She swallowed the lump in her throat, feeling that warmth between her legs again. The warmth spread and became something of an ache. Her desire was so strong for him that she could almost taste it. Strangely, Mackenzie felt enlightened. So was this how God had meant it to be between a man and woman.

He turned his back to her and retrieved his clothing, the muscles of his taut buttocks rippling as he stepped into the loin cloth and tied it on. She was disappointed that he had covered himself, but a little relieved as well.

He walked over to her and she laid back in the grass and closed her eyes against the brightness of the sun. She knew she left nothing to his imagination as to what her body looked like. The wet, white shift clung to every curve.

Fire Dancer tossed his knife on the grass and stretched out beside her. He turned his head so that she could see into his eyes. They kissed and she closed her eyes again. Every nerve ending in her body tingled. The nearness of him warmed her skin. She wanted to raise up on her elbow and kiss him again, but she didn't. She didn't because she was afraid she'd not be able to stop herself. She was afraid she would hand this savage heathen her maidenhead right here under the open sky. She was afraid she would enjoy every moment of it. Maybe that was what she wanted, all along, deep down, for him to take the initiative. Why else would she lie here nearly naked?

Fire Dancer slipped his arm under her and cradled her against him. She rested her cheek on his broad, still damp, shoulder. He laid his hand on her rib cage, but made no attempt to stroke her.

"This man knows what we both want, Mack-en-zie. But it would not be right. I have no right. I cannot take you as my wife. I cannot take you as my lover."

A strange sense of disappointment came upon Mackenzie and she closed her eyes, afraid she might tear up. What was wrong with her? Of course, he was right. They couldn't make love. What if she became with child? Not even Josh Watkins would take a woman tainted by an Indian's seed.

She snuggled against Fire Dancer, wishing somehow that things could be different. "You're right," she whispered when she trusted herself to think. "I want you. I can feel it from the tips of my toes." She wiggled her toes. "To the top of my head." She kept her eyes closed so that she wouldn't have to meet his gaze. "But her maidenhead is the only thing a woman has to give to her husband. I doubt that I will ever marry." *Now that I have met you,* she thought. "But if I do, I must have that gift to give my husband on our wedding night."

"This man understands the wisdom of your words." He kissed her again. It was a gentle kiss not of passion, but of understanding and respect.

"I'm tired," Mackenzie sighed. It was so comfortable here in the grass under the hot sun, with her Indian's arms wrapped around her. Before she realized it, Mackenzie drifted off to sleep.

"Mack-en-zie."

Mackenzie felt someone shake her.

"Mack-en-zie, you must wake."

Her eyes flew open and she sat up, disoriented. They were still on the stream bank, but the sun was lower in the sky. She must have fallen asleep.

Fire Dancer strode toward a tree to retrieve his vest and belt, his knife clutched in his hand. "Hurry. You must dress."

Mackenzie jumped up. Her shift was dry but wrinkled. Her hair was a mess of dry tangles. How long had she slept? She grabbed her skirt. "What's wrong?"

He strapped on his belt and pulled a knife the length of his forearm from its sheath. "The fort. Trouble . . ."

Chapter Ten

"What's going on?" Mackenzie burst into the dining hall that also served as Major Albertson's office. "They closed the gates! I had to call up to get someone to let me in." She pushed back a lock of hair. In a hurry to appear presentable, she'd pulled her tangled hair back with a ribbon and stuck her straw bonnet on top of her head. "Well, Harry?"

He was very pale, his skin like milk glass, his lips drawn in a thin line. He stared at something on the table, so preoccupied that he didn't appear to have heard her.

There were others in the room—her father and Joshua, Lieutenant Burrow, Mary's John, and a few she didn't know by name. There was also a very young soldier in a tattered, bloody uniform. He appeared as if he'd been fighting. They all stared at the object on the dining table that was covered with a stained Indian blanket.

Mackenzie studied the men in the room, then the bundle, then the men again. They were all pale. They acted as if they'd all just swallowed a crumb of spoiled meat and were about to be ill.

Something was wrong. Very wrong. She could taste the metallic edge of fear in the air. Now she was afraid. "Papa?"

Franklin pointed to the door. "Joshua, take Mackenzie to her quarters. Now."

Joshua walked toward her, making a great effort to avoid the dining table.

Mackenzie stared at the blanket. It was stained with something dark. Blood?

"Papa, what is it?" When her father didn't answer her immediately, she turned to the major. "Harry? Please." She glanced back at bundle on the table. She couldn't take her eyes off it. "Papa? Someone, please tell me what's happened."

"Joshua!" Franklin snapped. "I said get her the hell out of here!"

Mackenzie had never seen her father so rattled. Sweat beaded on his balding head and his hand trembled as he motioned to Josh.

She pushed Joshua away as he grasped her arm. "I'm not leaving until someone tells me what the bloody hell is going on." She stepped toward the table. "And what pray tell is that?"

"Don't, Mackenzie." Her father spoke so softly that she stopped in mid-stride.

"Don't," echoed Harry.

"No," said another.

Mackenzie stared at the thing on the table. It *was* blood on the blanket. She saw it now. Perhaps she just imagined it, but she thought she could smell the sweet, sticky smell of it. Gooseflesh rose on her arms. There was the stench of something rancid in the air.

"Papa, please. I—"

The door swung open behind her. The solders saw who it was before she did and lifted their swords and muskets.

It was Fire Dancer, and she was glad to see him. Surely he would tell her what was happening.

"Where the futtering hell have you been?" Major Albertson's voice boomed as he crossed the plank floor.

Mackenzie didn't know what to do. Only *she* knew where he'd been. Only she knew what they had almost done. She felt no shame, or guilt, only apprehension for the man she feared she loved.

Fire Dancer's gaze met hers and she read his warning. *Do not speak of what passed between us,* his black eyes told her. *Or we will both suffer the consequences.*

She didn't speak. Instead, she leaped into action and stepped between her Shawnee brave and the major. "Just wait one minute. I was here first and I want to know what's going on. What in heaven's name is that on the table?"

Harry stared at Fire Dancer with a hatred that surprised her. "Ask the Indian why he'll not say where he's been."

Mackenzie turned sideways so that she could see both men. "Fire Dancer?" she said softly.

Fire Dancer stared at the Indian blanket on the table. When he moved toward it, the soldiers all tightened their grips on their weapons.

They were afraid of him. *Why?*

"Mackenzie!" Harry reached out to shield her eyes as Fire Dancer yanked the Indian blanket off the thing on the table.

Too late.

For a moment Mackenzie thought she would retch. Tears filled her eyes and she swallowed against the acidic bile that rose in her throat.

A head.

A decapitated head.

The fair-haired, blond-mustached thing was ghostly white and covered with bloody gore. She didn't recognize the face, but she feared she knew who it was.

She turned her back to it. She refused to swoon. This wasn't the time or the place to be a weak female.

"I'm sorry you had to see that," Harry said, a gentleness in his voice.

For a second it seemed as if it was only the two of them in the room. Everything else was swirling around her. "DuBois?" She whispered, not trusting her voice yet.

"Aye." Harry sounded tired and old beyond his forty-odd years. "And I want to know why the hell this happened!" he shouted at Fire Dancer.

Mackenzie turned back, her aversion to the head not as strong as her desire to follow what was happening, and how Fire Dancer was involved. Obviously Harry thought her brave knew something.

Fire Dancer carefully covered the head with the blanket and made some kind of sign with his hand, whispering something in Shawnee. "The body must be found for proper burial."

In the midst of the horror, Mackenzie was touched by his respect for the dead.

"Did you hear me, redskin?" Harry confronted Fire Dancer. "I want to know how the hell this happened and what you had to do with it."

"You do not think I would do this, Major Albertson, man I call friend?" Fire Dancer's voice was strong and confident.

"What the Christ am I supposed to think?" Harry spat. "They were massacred. All of them. All of them, but that poor boy who had to witness it, and then carry the head. You know why he had to do it? Because if he didn't they said they'd find him and torture him to death."

Fire Dancer gazed at the young soldier in the bloody coat. He looked back at DuBois's head. "The blanket is Huron."

"It's Indian. That's what I know! You were gone all day. That's what I know. You had something to do with this outrage. That's what I know." Harry wiped his hand across the back of his mouth. "Seize him!"

Five or six of the officers vaulted to do their major's bidding. Fire Dancer dove for the door, but there were too many soldiers and they were on him in an instant. They hit him over the head with their musket butts and yanked his head by his hair. Fire Dancer fell to his knees under the attack.

"Wait! Wait!" Mackenzie screamed. She tried to reach Fire Dancer, but Harry grabbed her arm and pulled her back roughly.

"He didn't have anything to do with DuBois!" she shouted. She shoved Harry right back. "He couldn't have. He was with me."

"She's lying!" Burrows grabbed Fire Dancer's arms and

jerked them behind him. He tied them together with leather straps.

Harry held her arms down at her sides so tightly that it hurt. "Stay out of this Mackenzie." He spoke through gritted teeth. "You'll not have your way on this one."

She struggled to escape Harry's iron grip. "You've got to listen to me. Where is that reason you pride yourself upon, Harry? He was with me. I swear it. Down by the stream. I can take you there and show you—"

"Franklin. Get your daughter out of here. The heat's gotten to her head. Get her out before she says something she'll regret."

"Let's go." Franklin grabbed both of her arms, his strength surprising. He had never been so rough with her.

Hot tears ran down Mackenzie's cheeks. A few hours ago she had been so happy. Life had been so perfect. "Please, Father. Listen to me."

"You can't defend the Indian at the sake of your reputation," Franklin snapped. He pushed her toward the door. "You can't lie for him."

"I'm not." She fought the sob that rose in her throat. She didn't know what had happened to DuBois or who had attacked his party, but she knew Fire Dancer had nothing to do with it. "Please listen to me. Harry's making a mistake. Fire Dancer wouldn't do that. He wouldn't murder a man in cold blood."

"Mackenzie!" Franklin shook her. "Shut your mouth."

When she refused to walk, her father half-carried her, half-dragged her out of the dining room. The last glance she caught of Fire Dancer was that of him on his knees, his head bowed. Blood gushed from a gash on his temple.

"Fire Dancer!" she cried. "I won't let them do this to you! I swear I won't."

"Go, Mack-en-zie," he called to her. "Do what your father wishes."

"Shut up!" Burrow kicked Fire Dancer in the stomach.

Mackenzie screamed.

"K`daholel," she heard Fire Dancer say as her father dragged her from the room. "K`daholel, Mack-en-zie."

* * *

"You can't do this to me, Papa!" Mackenzie stumbled as he pushed her into her room.

"Have you lost your mind?" her father ranted. His face was bright red. "Declaring such a thing in public! Do you want to ruin me as well as yourself? What man do you think would have you if he knew you had been alone with that savage? Even for a few moments?"

Tears ran down Mackenzie's face. She pushed herself off the plank floor with her palms. She was so afraid, so confused. "I don't want any other man," she whispered. "Only him."

"Tomorrow we leave this place." Franklin brushed back the thinning hair that fell forward over his forehead. He acted as if he had never heard her shocking declaration. "You've been here too long. I knew it wasn't a good idea. The sun and the isolation have touched your head."

"There's nothing wrong with my head, Father! I'm not lying to cover for him. We really were together. All afternoon. For hours."

"I don't want to hear it!" He threw up his hands and backed out of the room. "Tomorrow we leave this place. Tonight you stay here. I'm sorry, Mackenzie, but I'll have to bar the door from outside."

"Father!"

"It's the only way I can protect you. Josh will stand guard. If you need anything, he'll get it for you."

Mackenzie attempted to grab the knob, but her father slammed the door shut before she could reach it. "No!" she screamed furiously as she heard a loud thump hit the door. When she tried to open it, the knob turned, but the door wouldn't open. He'd blocked it with something.

"Father!" she screamed as she pounded on the door with her fists. "You can't do this to me! I can't believe you would do this!"

There was silence on the other side of the door for a moment and then she heard her father's voice again. He sounded as if he were crying. "I'm sorry, Mackenzie," he whispered. "I only do this because I . . . I . . .'' Then she heard nothing but his footsteps as he walked away.

Mackenzie fought another sob of frustration, as she pressed her back to the door and slid to the floor in a flood of tears. She brought her hands to her face and she shook in fury. She had to stop Harry and the soldiers. She'd been at the fort long enough to know how the English dealt with the Indians. There would be no trial. They would hang him. And she wouldn't let that happen to Fire Dancer. She couldn't. She couldn't because she loved him. She knew that now.

Fire Dancer struggled toward consciousness. It was difficult, as if he was swimming through mud. All around him he felt an oppressive darkness. His head pounded so hard that his eyeballs ached. He could smell his own blood.

His thoughts drifted. He was probably going to die. He knew that. The soldiers would not seek out the Hurons who murdered their French major. The British army was terrified. He could see it in their eyes. He felt it in their arms and legs as they struck and kicked him.

They needed someone to blame for the murders of the Frenchmen . . . anyone. It was poor luck for Fire Dancer, nothing more nothing less. He was the best choice. He was the most likely culprit in their clouded eyes.

A man never knew when his time to die would come, so he had to always be prepared. Fire Dancer felt his head roll as he fought to hold it upright. He was ready to die. At least he had been a few days ago, a few weeks ago . . . Now there was something that nagged at his resolve. Someone.

Mack-en-zie.

He wasn't ready to die because of Mackenzie. All along he had told himself that he would enjoy her company while he remained at the fort. When his duty to his people was done here, he would return home to them and leave the red-haired woman behind. But something had changed. When had it happened? His mind churned as he fought to recall the details.

When they had talked of making love this afternoon and

agreed it was not right, he had still intended to return to the village alone. Now as he stood here, tied to a pole, he could think of nothing but her. When her gaze had met his in the English dining room, they had shone with a bright light. A light meant only for him. It was the light of love that he knew a man saw only once in his lifetime . . . if he was lucky.

That changed everything. It did not matter that he was Shawnee and she was colonial *manake*. It did not matter that his mother expected him to take Laughing Woman as his wife. What mattered was Mackenzie. How the great *Tapalamawatah* would resolve this, he didn't know. All he knew was that it was not his time to join with his ancestors in the heavens.

Fire Dancer attempted to open his eyes. He felt dizzy and light-headed. His entire body ached. He would have slumped forward, but the leather bindings that bit into his wrists and calves prevented it.

Mackenzie. He could not die and leave her. He would not. He had told her he loved her. He had called out the words in his native tongue. He remembered now. Then the soldiers had beat him . . . beat him until he succumbed to the pain and lost consciousness.

"Mack-en-zie . . ." He whispered her name on his split, blood-caked lips. "*K˘ dolholel,* Mack-en-zie. This man loves you." Speaking the words aloud made him stronger.

He managed to open one eye. Then the other. It was dark and he was inside a small, enclosed building. It smelled of odd smells—sugar, tobacco, whiskey. Where was he?

Fire Dancer tried to clear his head, forcing himself to concentrate. He had to see Mackenzie. He had to ask her if it really was love that he had seen in her blue eyes. But first he had to escape.

Fire Dancer focused on his surroundings, and realized he was inside one of the small dependencies built in the fort yard, one used for storage. He breathed deeply, trying to think. He had to be inside the lean-to Mackenzie's father stored his goods in. It had a lock.

The soldiers had tied him to this support beam and locked him in for good measure. Was there a guard? His first impulse was to call out. If there was a guard, surely he would answer, either by shouting back or perhaps coming inside to club him again.

No. It would be better if the English didn't know he had regained consciousness. It was better if they did not anticipate his escape.

Fire Dancer tried to move his hands that were tied behind his back. The bindings were so tight that his fingers tingled. He pressed his spine against the rough, wooden pole and tried to move his feet.

Lieutenant Burrow had done an excellent job of tying up his prisoner. Fire Dancer blinked; the blood in his eyes stung. *An excellent job.* Of course, the lieutenant was an Indian hater. After the incident with Tall Moccasin he had made it plain to Fire Dancer that they were enemies.

So now what? Fire Dancer thought. *Okonsa?* His cousin would set him free out of family duty. He would probably like nothing more than the excuse to kill a few white men. But Okonsa wasn't expected back until tomorrow. Tomorrow might be too late.

Fire Dancer closed his eyes. What did he do now? Pray? It was the answer his mother said always worked. He sighed. "So I give myself up to you, Great Father."

The words were no sooner out of his mouth than he heard a noise behind him. A noise like wood scraping against wood.

"Father?" *Had the great spirit come for him?*

"Hssst," came a voice. "It is not the Great Father, but a small man."

Fire Dancer grinned and then winced. His lips were so cracked and bruised that it hurt to smile. "Tall Moccasin, nephew of my heart?" he called softly in Algonquian. It was too good to be believed. Was he hallucinating?

The wood scraped again, and as if by a holy man's magic, the boy appeared before Fire Dancer. "Hsst, Uncle. We must hurry. There is an English guard, but he has gone to take a piss." Tall Moccasin spoke half in English, half in Shawnee.

Fire Dancer sighed in relief as the boy cut the bindings at

his wrists. He still felt woozy, as if he wasn't quite in control of his mind or body. "How did you get in?"

Tall Moccasin knelt and cut the leather at Fire Dancer's ankles. "Through the door in the wall my Uncle Okonsa cut so that he could steal the white man's supplies."

The thought that Okonsa was stealing, even from the white men, concerned Fire Dancer, but this was neither the time nor the place to consider it. "You are a most clever young man." Fire Dancer tousled the boy's hair. Then he gripped the pole as he swayed slightly.

Tall Moccasin slipped his knife into his sheath and reached up to grab Fire Dancer by his arm. "Are you all right, Uncle? Should I bring another man over the fort wall to help you?"

"No." Fire Dancer pushed back his hair on his blood-caked forehead. "You did the right thing to come alone. Now show this man how you slipped in under the noses of the British."

Tall Moccasin led Fire Dancer to the rear of the lean-to. Moonlight shone in through a square hole at the bottom of the log wall, just the right size for a man to pass though.

"You see. Easy enough." Tall Moccasin dropped on all fours and crawled through the hole.

Fire Dancer followed. Once outside, with the night breeze on his face, he felt better. Keeping directly behind the boy, he followed him to the wall. When his hand brushed against the rough bark of the palisade wall, he grasped Tall Moccasin's shoulders and turned the boy to face him. "Listen. You must find your aunt, Little Weaver, and take her over the wall. We must flee before the soldier *manake* know I have escaped, else all our lives are in danger."

Tall Moccasin nodded bravely. "This man will escort his aunt over the wall and into the safety of forest."

"Good. You know the place we said we must meet if ever there was trouble."

The boy nodded. "I will take my aunt there and wait for you, Uncle. But what of the horses? Most of our horses are inside the fort."

Fire Dancer smiled in the darkness. He was so proud of his sister's son. "We cannot worry over the horses. They are not important compared to the lives of men. Go and may God protect you.''

''You do not come with me?''

Fire Dancer thought before he answered. The smartest thing for him to do would be to flee. There was nothing here for him. The peace talks had obviously come to an end. Nothing could come of seeing Mackenzie again. To try and see her, he would be taking great risk. Just over the fort wall lay freedom and life. Here inside the fort walls, he would find only pain and death. Still, he had to see her once more.

Fire Dancer's gaze met Tall Moccasin's. ''I will come right behind you.''

''But why do you not come now, Uncle? You are in great danger. You must escape. They said they would hang you even if the major did not give the word. I heard the one called Burrow say so.''

''Give me your knife, Tall Moccasin, and do as this man tells you.'' He accepted the knife the boy offered and staring up in the direction of the single window lit by candlelight. ''I will catch up to you and Little Weaver. First I must see someone.''

Chapter Eleven

Mackenzie ripped off her linen shirt and threw it on the floor. It was so hot that she couldn't think; she couldn't breathe. Still fuming, she stepped out of her sprigged calico skirt. She kicked off her boots and peeled off her yarn stockings. That was better. Wearing nothing but her sleeveless cotton shift, she could at least breathe a little easier.

She stepped over her boots in the middle of the floor and paced. She couldn't beleive her father had done this to her. He'd locked her up as if she were a madwoman when all she'd done was try to defend the man she suspected . . . no, the man she *knew* she loved.

The thought of Fire Dancer brought tears to her eyes. How could Harry have allowed the soldiers to treat him so cruelly? She had always had such a great respect for Harry and that respect was gone. How could men be so brutal to other human beings just because their skin color was different? Even her father and Joshua had stood there and permitted the beating to take place without offering a word of protest.

Mackenzie impatiently wiped her tears away. Crying would do neither her nor Fire Dancer any good. If she was to help him, she'd have to come up with a plan—and quickly. Her father insisted they were leaving in the morning, and from the look in his eyes, she knew she wouldn't be able to stall him even a few hours.

"Oh, Fire Dancer," she whispered to the hot room. "I'm so sorry this had to happen. I'm so sorry I didn't make love with you when I had the chance."

Just thinking about the way he had kissed her at the stream today, about the way he had touched her, made her warm and queasy in the pit of her stomach. *So this was what desire is,* she thought. But it wasn't just desire. It was love she felt for the man so different from herself. A true love that didn't recognize those differences. She walked to her camp cot and knelt. From beneath the bed she slid out the painting of Fire Dancer. It was nearly done and ready to have the background painted in. It was the most perfect piece of work she had ever done in her life. It was the piece artists waited for an entire lifetime to achieve.

With a bittersweet smile, she traced the outline of his face with her finger. The oil paint was still tacky in places. Closing her eyes, she could see his face laughing, smiling, teasing.

"I have to get out of here. I have to set you free," she said aloud. She dropped the portrait on the bed. As she rose off the floor she glanced at the window. Of course! Fire Dancer had slipped in and out of the window many times. She was the same size as he. Surely she could—

Mackenzie heard a sound outside the window and froze. Was someone outside? Could it be . . . No, impossible, and yet . . .

Mackenzie bounced up onto the cot. As an afterthought, she tossed the corner of the counterpane over the portrait. She yanked the shutter open, trying not to make any noise. Joshua slept on the other side of the door. She had heard his snoring earlier. She pressed her face to the open window. "Fire Dancer?"

"Mack-en-zie?"

Mackenzie put her hand to her heart. "Oh, thank God, you're safe," she whispered. "Where are you? I can't see you."

His face appeared before hers. In the darkness she couldn't really see him, but she knew it was him. She recognized the scent of his hair and skin, the sound of his voice, the feel of his breath on her cheek.

"Let this man in," he said softly. "There is not much time, woman of my heart."

Mackenzie backed off the bed and watched Fire Dancer miraculously appear through the window. He tumbled onto her bed and she flung herself into his arms.

"Oh, Fire Dancer, I was so afraid for you. I—" She stopped in mid-sentence, horrified by what she saw. It was Fire Dancer, and yet it was not. His face had been beaten so brutally that it was misshapen. His lips were swollen and split in several places. He was covered with blood, in his hair, on his face, down his arms.

"Oh," she whispered, smoothing his tangled, blood-sticky, hair. "Oh, what have they done to you?"

"Shhh," he murmured. He pulled her into his arms on the bed. "It's all right, *kitehi.*" He kissed her forehead. "It is not so bad as it looks."

She touched his face gently with her hands. She feared she would hurt him, but she needed to prove to herself that it really was him. She stared into his black eyes, eyes that said he loved her. "How did you get away?" she whispered. "Why are you here? You have to go! You have to run! If they catch you—"

He pressed his finger to her lips. "Shhhhh, my heart. There is probably a soldier outside your door. We must speak softly."

She nodded, her face only inches from his. "My father left Joshua to guard my door, but he's asleep." She went on faster than before. "They've locked me in. We leave in the morning. My father wants to take me far from here, but I don't want to go." She was crying again. "I don't want to leave you, even though I know I must."

He caught one of her tears with his fingertip. "Do not cry, Mack-en-zie. I came only to say good-bye, not to make you cry."

She threw her arms around his neck and hugged him tightly. "You didn't tell me how you got away."

"Tall Moccasin."

She pulled back a little. "Tall Moccasin?"

"The soldiers had tied me to a pole inside the shed where your father keeps his supplies. My cousin, Okonsa, had been stealing from him through a hole he cut in the wall."

Mackenzie wasn't surprised, so she said nothing, letting him go on.

"Tall Moccasin came through the hole in the wall and set me free. He was very brave. He waits for me now in the forest." Fire Dancer added gently, "This man must go."

"No." She choked back a sob. She had never been the hysterical type, but she felt as if her world was coming to an end. She knew he couldn't stay. She knew she couldn't go. The tragedy of their situation made her heartsick.

"This man is sorry, but I must go. If the soldiers find me, they will not give me a chance to escape again."

"I know," she whispered as she stared into his eyes. "At least let me wash the blood from your face. Will you allow me to do that?"

Fire Dancer glanced at the window as if it beckoned. "Mack-en-zie . . ."

"Please." She jumped up off the bed and ran to the water bucket. She hurried back to him with fresh water and a small, clean linen towel. She knelt in front of him on the floor. "Just a few more minutes."

He trapped her between his knees. "Just a few more moments," he agreed, brushing a stray lock of hair off her cheek.

Mackenzie procured the washrag from the bucket and squeezed it. Water ran between her fingers. As gently as she could, she dabbed at the blood-encrusted gouge that ran from the center of his forehead to his right temple.

Fire Dancer's eyes drifted shut and he rested his hands on her hips.

She rinsed the bloody rag again and again, wiping away the blood and perhaps a little of the sting of his wounds. As she washed his face and neck, and bare shoulders, his hand drifted over her body, caressing her through the sheer cotton of her shift.

"Mack-en-zie," he whispered, his eyes still closed.

"Fire Dancer." She kissed him gently on his mouth that was still damp from the washrag.

"This man will never forget you." He kissed her back, harder, and pulled her closer.

"Never," she answered, lost in the moment.

He drew her onto his lap and slipped his hand beneath her shift. She made no protest. All she wanted was him. In the desperation of the moment, she wanted nothing but to touch him, to be touched.

They kissed again and again. Her hot tears mingled with the water on his face. He laid her back on her bed and she sighed and moaned with pleasure, reveling in the feel of his body pressed against hers. Their mouths met; their tongues twisted in one last, hopeless union.

His hands burned a path on her bare skin.

Somehow her shift became rolled up around her waist, but she didn't care. Any sense of modesty she might have felt in the past was gone. All that mattered was Fire Dancer and the pulses of pleasure that surged through her veins.

Fire Dancer kissed the valley between her breasts and pushed her shift up farther. Mackenzie guided his head with her hands. She needed to feel the touch of his mouth on her breast. She groaned with pleasure when his tongue skimmed over her puckered nipple. Instinctively, she arched her back and pressed her hips to his. With nothing but his leather loinskin between his body and hers, she felt his heat as he lowered over her. His hands touched her; his mouth taunted her.

He kissed her breasts. He sucked with his mouth and licked with his tongue. Her breasts swelled and tingled as her nipples grew harder and more sensitive. Between her thighs she ached. When he lowered his hand over her belly to the bed of red curls, she jerked in surprise.

"Shhh," he whispered in her ear. "This is what you want, heart of my heart?"

"Yes, yes," she whispered. She took his hand and guided it back to the damp place. "It's what I want." She opened her eyes, staring into his. "I'll never love another like this. It's my gift to you. All I have to give."

He kissed her tenderly, the kiss not of a lover, but of a beloved. Then he lowered his body over hers. He pressed flesh against flesh, his hard muscles against her soft, feminine curves.

He stroked between her thighs with his experienced hand. Instinctively, she moved against his fingers. She rubbed and twisted. He brought his mouth to hers and their tongues twisted in an ancient dance of love. At some point he had removed his loin cloth so that she felt his manhood hard and stiff against her bare thigh. She caressed his back and his firm, bare buttocks.

Oddly, Mackenzie was not afraid. Even though she knew little more than the basic mechanics of joining, she felt no hesitation. This was what she wanted. She kissed him again and again, breathless, feeling so hopeless and yet so joyful with each stroke, each caress.

I'll never love again like this, she kept saying over and over in her head.

She parted her thighs. The ache inside her had grown so strong that she could think of nothing but release. She wasn't even sure how she would find that release; all she knew was that she needed him inside her.

"Mack-en-zie . . ." He whispered her name in that way that only he spoke it.

She felt him probing and she lifted her hips. With the aid of one hand, he slipped slowly inside her.

Mackenzie moaned. It felt so good. The word *sin* bounced around in her head. To fornicate with an Indian—she would be tainted forever if anyone ever found out. But how could anything that felt so right, so loving, be a sin?

She parted her thighs further and he slipped in deeper. This was so different than she had been lead to believe. There was no pain, only a sense of relief . . . and perfect pleasure. So perfect.

Inside her, he began to move. He seemed to know just what she wanted, needed, even when she herself didn't understand.

His strokes came faster . . . harder. She panted, lifting her hips to meet his in a rhythm she instinctively matched.

Perspiration covered her. She could smell the scent of their lovemaking in the close room.

She increased the pace of the stroke. There was something she reached for, something—

Without warning, her world exploded in a surge of unbelievable pleasure and contracting muscles. "Oh," she moaned. "Oh . . ."

He covered his mouth with hers so that her cries of ecstasy were only murmurs. He moved once more inside her, twice, as she rode the last waves of fulfillment. He thrust once more, hard. She took him deeply. He moaned and fell against her.

After a moment Fire Dancer rolled off her, onto his side on the edge of the bed and cradled her in his arm. He was still panting. "This man . . . is . . . sorry," he whispered, kissing her damp temple.

Her eyes fluttered open. Her heart still pounded. Her breath still came in short bursts. "Sorry? Sorry for what?" she whispered, amazed that the sounds of their lovemaking had not brought down the entire fort.

"Sorry that this man did not last longer." He had an embarrassed grin on his face. "I was in too great a hurry. I did not see to your pleasure as a lover should."

She giggled and pressed her lips to his bruised ones. "Didn't see to my pleasure? I've never felt anything so wonderful! No one ever told me there was any pleasure for a woman." She slid her hand over his side. "Because my mother was dead, my father had our cook tell me of the relations between a man and a woman. Mostly she mumbled about bees pollinating. All I really got was that it was a wife's duty to her husband. Something to be tolerated." She smiled wickedly. "She said nothing to prepare me for the pleasure I felt, I can assure you."

He smoothed her damp hair with the palm of his hand. "Among my people, a man is expected to pleasure his woman more than once in a night. To do less would shame him."

Mackenzie laid her head back on his shoulder, closing her eyes. Her body still pulsed with tiny shivers of pleasure. She knew Fire Dancer had to leave her, but she was satisfied that at least once in her life she had experienced real love. That it had been Fire Dancer who gave it to her. She wanted to savor every second of the feeling. She wanted to carry it with her forever.

"Fire Dancer," she whispered. She didn't know exactly what she wanted to say, but she wanted him to know how she felt about him. What he meant to her in her heart. "I—"

"Shhhh. Do not speak of what there are no words for. This man must return to his people. You must go home with your father where you will be safe—" He stretched out his leg on the bed and struck something hard. "Ouch. What trap do you lay for me on your sleeping mat, woman?"

In an instant Mackenzie realized what he had hit. It was the portrait! She had completely forgotten about it. She'd left it on the bed and they'd made love with it at their feet.

She remember an instant too late.

He sat up and reached beneath the twisted counterpane.

Mackenzie rose on her knees, shoving her shift down over her bare hips.

Fire Dancer gazed at his portrait and his face turned black with rage. "What is this?" he demanded.

"Shhhhh." She tried to snatch the portrait from him. "You'll wake Joshua and then we'll both be done for!"

He leapt from the bed, naked. He stared at the small painting. "I told you, you could not paint me."

"I'm sorry." She started to cry. "I . . . I meant no harm to you. I only—"

"Silence!" he hissed. "Don't you understand what you've done?"

She rose off the bed, shocked that Fire Dancer could be so angry with her. For heaven's sake, he'd just made love with her. How could he—

"Do you understand?" he repeated through clenched teeth.

The look on his face, the fury in his black eyes, made her realize that she did not understand. "No. No, I don't." She fought back a sob. She truly was sorry.

"You captured a part of my soul, white woman. You have taken a part of me."

"No. I haven't. That's ridiculous." She tried to grasp the painting but she couldn't get it from him.

"You painted my likeness and you took a part of me. You captured my heart falsely."

"I didn't. That's absurd. But . . . but we . . . we can just destroy it. Burn it."

"No!" He ground his teeth. "We cannot destroy it without destroying the one called Fire Dancer of the Thunder Sky." Tucking the painting beneath his arm, he jerked his loin skin off the floor and tied it on, quickly adding the knife and sheath. "Clothe yourself! You go with me."

Mackenzie was terrified. This man who shouted at her and talked of captured souls was not the gentle man she had fallen in love with. She began to back up toward the door. This man . . . this man was a stranger. This man was some kind of beast. A savage. And she was afraid.

With a scream, Mackenzie threw herself against the door. "Josh! Josh!" she hollered.

"Are you mad?" Fire Dancer grabbed her roughly by the arm and dragged her toward the bed.

He was serious. He meant to take her away. To kidnap her.

"Mackenzie!" Josh Watkins shouted in panic from the other side of the door. He rattled the bar that locked her in.

"Josh! Josh, help me. He's kidnapping me."

"Mackenzie?" Josh flung open the door and stumbled inside. He tried to take aim with his musket.

Fire Dancer took one look at Joshua and let go of Mackenzie, flinging her backwards. She fell back onto the bed just as Josh raised his weapon.

"No!" Mackenzie screamed. She didn't want Fire Dancer to kidnap her, but she didn't want him dead, either. Without thought of her own well-being, she hurled herself in front of the man she had just made love with. At the same instant Josh's musket exploded with sound and smoke.

Chapter Twelve

Fire Dancer flung out his arms to catch Mackenzie as she fell. The portrait hit the plank floor and slid away. *"Mahtah,"* he cried. He dropped on one knee to break her fall.

She landed in his arms, her eyes closed as if she were sleeping peacefully. A sense of panic ripped through Fire Dancer's chest as he frantically pushed her hair from her face. "Look what you have done!" he shouted in rage. "You have killed her!"

"No. No." The man with the sandy hair retreated. The musket fell from his hands with a clatter.

"Mack-en-zie, Mack-en-zie, *lenowaiwee.*" Fire Dancer lifted her and her head fell back. Her magical hair draped over his knees in a curtain of red tresses. The curls at her temple were still damp from their lovemaking in the hot room. He pushed back her hair to see a bloody gouge on her temple. The idiot had shot her in the head, but the musket ball had not penetrated her skull, only grazed it.

Fire Dancer pressed his mouth to hers in a fevered kiss. She still drew breath . . . She was unconscious, but alive. *Tapalamawatah* willing, she would wake, given time.

Outside, Fire Dancer heard the soldiers call to arms. Men

shouted. Doors slammed. Joshua's gunfire had alerted them. They would be here any moment.

Fire Dancer lifted Mackenzie as gently as he could to his shoulder and ran for the door. He ignored Joshua who cowered in the corner of the room. More boy than man, he was not worth Fire Dancer's time.

As Fire Dancer darted out of the room, he swiped his portrait off the floor. To lose it now, would mean certain death.

Fire Dancer burst through the doorway. He could hear feet pounding on the stairway.

"Mackenzie! Mackenzie!" Franklin Daniels called. "I'm coming, honey. Papa's coming."

Fire Dancer raced back into the room. He climbed up onto the bed with Mackenzie still in his arms. Could he pull her through the window? There was only one way to find out. He bent her knees so that she knelt and let her slump forward. Unconscious, she was as limp as a cloth doll.

Fire Dancer lowered himself through the window, feet first. He caught her below the armpits as he squeezed through the window.

He groaned under the strain of her slack weight. If he let go of her now, he would have to climb back through the window to get her. There wasn't time for that.

"Mackenzie!" Franklin Daniels cried, more urgently than before.

Fire Dancer couldn't see him, but he had to be at the door by now. Fire Dancer concentrated on getting Mackenzie out the window. He gritted his teeth and heaved with every ounce of strength he could muster.

"What the fiery hell are you doing?" hollered Daniels, obviously inside the room. "You can't take her! You can't take my daughter."

With one surge of power, Fire Dancer snatched her out the window. He fell on his backside, cushioning her fall with his body. As he hit the timber walkway, he heard the frame of the portrait tucked in his loincloth snap. It didn't matter. All that mattered was that the canvas remain intact.

"Bring her back, do you hear me?" Daniels shouted through

the window. "Get up, Josh! Get up and go, boy. We have to
stop that savage before he carries her off into the forest! We'll
have to go around!"

Fire Dancer heard the two men retreat and knew that they
headed down the stairs and out of the building so that they
could reach him on the bulwark. The delay gave him precious
minutes.

He bounded to his feet and lifted Mackenzie onto his shoulder
again. She was still unconscious.

He would have to repel down the wall. It would be too far
for him to jump with her in his arms.

As he started for the wall, a flaming arrow flew toward
him, passing over his head. The missile struck the wall of
Mackenzie's room and set the bark of the logs on fire.

Attack? Who was attacking?

Without warning, the air rained with flaming arrows. He
heard a burst of war cries. Muskets roared in response, and all
at once the air filled with smoke and the stench of black powder
and the cries of men. A canon belched in retaliation for the
arrows. Men appeared on the bulwark and scattered in opposite
directions. No one noticed Fire Dancer in the darkness and the
chaos.

He hugged Mackenzie against his body. Now he not only
had to escape the soldiers, but the warring redmen below. He
pressed a fevered kiss to her temple. "This man will not let
you die," he whispered. "No matter what you have done to
me, I will see you live."

Fire Dancer hurried along the wall, cursing himself for not
bringing a rope. He could have gotten one from Tall Moccasin.
How would he ever get Mackenzie down off the wall now?
Did he dare try to make it down the ladder and out the back
gate?

"Stop there," a familiar voice challenged from behind.

Fire Dancer felt like a fool. He had become too caught up
in his emotions. He had let his guard fall and the father approach.

Slowly Fire Dancer turned to face Franklin Daniels. Fire
Dancer held Mackenzie cradled in his arms, her head flung
back, her long hair dragging the ground.

"Put 'er down." Daniels held his musket pointed directly at him.

"You would not take the risk of shooting your daughter," Fire Dancer challenged.

"I will if I have to. I'd rather see her dead than raped by one of your kind."

The man was barefooted and dressed in a white night shirt stuffed into open breeches. A pistol protruded from the waistband. His bald head reflected the light of the spreading blaze. All around the two men musket fire cracked in the night. The smoke had thickened and choked them both.

Fire Dancer stared at the father. The man spoke in earnest. He thought Fire Dancer was going to harm her.

"I'll make you a deal." Franklin waved the musket. "Put 'er down and I'll let ye go. I'll let ye go right over that wall in thanks. I don't want you. Only my girl."

Fire Dancer could see the man's tears on his cheeks.

Fire Dancer tried to sum up his position. He was backed against a wall, surrounded by musket fire and soldiers. There was an unknown enemy on the other side of the wall. What did he do now?

He didn't care about himself, but he was concerned that Mackenzie might be further injured.

On impulse, he made the decision to put her down without knowing what he would do next. Could he really leave her behind and try to save himself? Yet, if he lost her, he lost that part of his soul she had taken when she painted him. Would it weaken him so that he could not make it home? Where was a holy man when he needed him?

Fire Dancer saw no good choice.

He stared through the darkness at the father. "I will put her down if you give this man your word. On your honor, on your mother's heart, you will not harm this man if he gives you your daughter."

Franklin nodded. "On my honor."

Fire Dancer felt his heart tearing inside his chest. How would he know if she was all right? What would he do without her? All would be lost, but she would live.

Slowly he lowered Mackenzie's unconscious body to the log walkway, all the while breathing deeply, trying to place the scent of her hair in some special corner of his mind. He brushed the hair from her cheek one last time, then straightened to face Daniels.

Fire Dancer wasn't sure what happened next. How did he know the father would fire? Instinct. Franklin Daniels moved slightly. Fire Dancer drew his knife. Daniels fired the musket point blank. Fire Dancer reacted as any warrior would, knowing the musket ball would reach him before the knife struck its target. He threw the knife in self-defense and dodged right.

The musket ball missed.

The knife did not.

Franklin Daniels dropped to his knees. The musket fell from his hands. His eyes were wide with surprise. His fingers gripped the hilt of the knife that protruded from the left side of his upper chest. He made a strange noise and then fell forward, dead before he hit the palisade.

Fire Dancer stood frozen, staring at the body. He had killed Mackenzie's father. Yet what choice had there been? The man had lied. And if the musket ball hadn't hit Fire Dancer, surely the ball from the pistol in Daniel's breeches would have struck home. Self-defense.

Fire Dancer looked at Mackenzie lying limp. She was not a small woman, but lying unconscious, she seemed small and helpless. He had to take her with him. Fate had laid the path.

Fire Dancer retrieved his knife from the father's chest. He closed the man's eyes and whispered a prayer. He blew the words toward heaven. Then he turned his back on the man who had betrayed the code of honor, and hoisted Mackenzie onto his shoulder.

"Hey! There's another one!" Fire Dancer heard a soldier shout amidst the musket fire and Indian war cries. "Kill him! Kill 'im. The red bastard's got Miss Daniels."

Fire Dancer ran to the edge of the wall and looked down. A musket ball whistled by, too close for comfort. The grass on the far side of the trench loomed far below. The drop was nearly the height of three men. He could have done it easily without Mackenzie, but would his legs hold with her added weight, or would they snap?

"Get the bastard!"

Another musket ball whizzed by.

Fire Dancer glanced up into the skies. "Your will, Father," he mumbled in the tongue of his ancestors, then leapt into the air.

Major Albertson strode through the center of the compound, attempting to survey the damage and set some order to the chaos of the night. "Out of my way." He gave the sow a kick on her rump and she squealed and darted between the water barrels.

Dawn had finally come. The Indians had retreated and the fort was still standing. Most of the fires had been put out. He swept his hat off his head and wiped the sweat from his brow. It was already hot and barely seven in the morning.

"O'Donaho!" he shouted.

"Sir." The private ran behind his major, trying to catch up.

"I want you to round up the officers and have them meet me in the dining hall."

"Sir, there ain't no dining hall left." The boy indicated a pile of smoldering rubble with his pointed chin.

Harry stared at the charred timbers for a moment. He'd known the main building of the fort had burned to the ground, thanks to the Indian's pitch arrows. He'd forgotten, yet made no apologies. A man's mind worked strangely after a redskin attack. "The kitchen is standing. Tell 'em to meet me there in one hour and be ready to report. I want numbers. Deaths, injuries. And I want to know where we stand on ammunition. The munitions shed blew straight to hell or heaven, I don't know which. All we've got is what the men have on their persons."

O'Donaho saluted. His hat was gone. His red uniform was torn and filthy, but the boy was in one piece. Harry was thankful for that.

"That all, sir?" O'Donaho held the salute.

"Aye. Go on with you. I'm going up on the wall to survey the damage from there."

"Yes, Major." The young man lowered his salute and took off at a run.

Only then did Harry realize that the private was wearing only one boot. "And Charlie . . ."

The private whipped around. "Sir?"

"Get a boot on that other foot else it'll rot in this mud."

"I lost my boot, sir. Can't find it."

"Get it off one of the dead men," Harry answered grimly. "They won't be needing it."

Harry turned and walked away. He knew he'd shocked the boy, but what could he do for these green soldiers? He couldn't wipe their asses all the time. They had to grow up someday. An attack like this usually did it. The new soldiers either died in attacks or they lived and gained the experience to survive the next one. It was like that in war.

Harry climbed the nearest ladder onto the walkway. From up here he could survey the damage better. He tucked his hands behind his back as if he was out for a morning stroll in Hyde Park. The wall was missing a chunk up by the front gate. He would have that rebuilt today. There were a couple more places where posts would have to be replaced, but otherwise the walls had held. On the other hand, the inside of the fort had been decimated. Only three buildings still stood: the kitchen, the shed the Indian bastard had escaped from, and the shithouse. He sniggered at the irony of it.

Harry stopped suddenly on the walkway and stared out into the treetops. Here was where Mackenzie had painted his portrait. Here was the best morning sunlight, she had said.

Mackenzie . . .

Harry felt tears well in his eyes and he rubbed at them. "Damned smoke," he muttered.

How had it happened? How had he let it happen? When he received the report that an Indian had carried her unconscious over the wall he'd been unable to send men after them. The attack was still underway. By the time the fighting stopped, it was too late. The bastard was long gone.

The soldier who witnessed the kidnapping couldn't identify the kidnapper, but Harry knew who it was. He had seen the way the Shawnee Prince had looked at Mackenzie. His regret now was that he hadn't killed the savage then. But no, he had behaved diplomatically, as his superiors in Boston had insisted. Hell, he was the one who had insisted on hiring a female artist to paint the portraits. He'd done it for selfish reasons. He knew how much she would appreciate the chance. And it was an opportunity to see her.

Harry kicked a charred stick and then realized it was the handle of a paint brush.

Mackenzie was gone.

And Franklin? His dear friend—dead of a knife wound in the heart. Harry had pieced together what the soldiers told him with the obvious evidence. It proved that all Franklin had tried to do was save his daughter. He'd even managed to fire his weapon after the redskin inflicted the mortal wound.

Harry turned away from the sunny place on the wall. He couldn't think about Mackenzie now. She was probably dead. God, he hoped so. Dead was better for a woman than being held captive by savages. He'd send out a few men to look for her body, but unfortunately, that would be all he could do. Right now, his duty was to the men here in the fort, and to his king. He had to call for reinforcements and repair the fort. Maybe then he could send out patrols.

Harry tugged on his red beard, his eyes tearing up again. She was gone. He knew it. Every man here knew it. The sooner he accepted the fact, the sooner he could focus on rebuilding this fort. Mackenzie Daniels was dead. Mackenzie . . . the only woman he had ever loved.

Chapter Thirteen

Mackenzie couldn't open her eyes or move her limbs. She felt as if she was floating in a warm, dark place. There was no pain, only a detached numbness. She wasn't afraid, but she was confused. The sounds and smells around her were unfamiliar. Where was she? Home? No. Fort Belvadere? No. Something pungent burned in the air. There were gentle voices, yet she had no understanding of the language.

She felt as if she were in a bizarre dream.

Kindly hands brushed her hair and washed her body. They fed her broth and gave her cool, sweetened water. A woman sang softly as she moved about. And then there was the bone flute. At times it seemed to go on for hours. That was the one thing she recognized and took comfort in.

Fire Dancer. She couldn't remember clearly who he was or how she knew him. All that mattered was that he was there, touching her, kissing her, whispering words she didn't understand.

The melody of the flute kept her from drifting away from this place. Fire Dancer's touch prevented her from falling into the deep sleep that tempted her so. She wanted him and she refused to let go of this little piece of him.

''Mack-en-zie, Mack-en-zie,'' a voice whispered. ''Will you not come back to this man?''

It was *his* voice. He held her hand, squeezed it, and then let it fall.

Mackenzie wanted desperately to get his attention. ''Don't go,'' she cried in her head.

He slipped away. A woman spoke softly. Though Mackenzie didn't understand the words, she knew they were meant to comfort Fire Dancer. It wasn't fair. Mackenzie wanted to be the one to comfort him. She didn't know why he sounded so sad, but she wanted to be the one to ease his suffering. If she could have, she would have played the bone flute for him.

Mackenzie sifted through her drifting thoughts. It occurred to her that Fire Dancer's sadness had something to do with her. It was her fault he was unhappy. Was it because she was sleeping and couldn't wake up?

She fought with every ounce of strength she could muster to call out to him. *Fire Dancer.*

No one heard her because his name was only in her head. She hadn't actually spoken the words. She tried again. ''Fire Dancer . . .''

This time she could have sworn she heard a voice . . . her own voice, throaty and ragged. ''Fire Dancer.''

''N⌐ thathah, weel la kahlawee. She speaks.'' It was the woman's voice.

Mackenzie heard someone kneel beside her. Was she on the ground? No, but very close . . . on some sort of platform, nestled in furs.

''Mack-en-zie, *kitehi?*''

''Fire Dancer?'' She tried to open her eyes. The dream drifted away and her head hurt. Fuzzy images appeared before her eyes. Baskets. Strings of dried herbs and flowers hung from rafters overhead. She could smell a pungent burning scent strongly . . . and she could smell him.

She blinked, afraid. She felt as if she'd been drugged with laudanum, like that time when she'd been ill as a child. ''Fire Dancer, where am I?'' she croaked.

He squeezed her hand and his face appeared above hers. Just the sight of his handsome smile calmed her.

"It is all right, my heart. You are safe, here in my village with me."

Dizziness was making her sick to her stomach. She closed her eyes. "The ... the fort. Why ... how did I get here?"

He paused a moment. "You do not remember? This man brought you here. It has been many days since we were at Belvadere. A fortnight by your count."

Pieces of memories drifted back like parts of a wooden puzzle and fell into place. She remembered making love with Fire Dancer. Then the portrait ... the way he had shouted at her like a madman. She remembered screaming for help, afraid of him. Josh had burst through the door. He was going to shoot Fire Dancer. She felt the same sense of the panic she'd experienced then and she gripped Fire Dancer's hand tighter. She remembered jumping between them and nothing after that.

Mackenzie opened her eyes again. "You kidnapped me," she said softly. It was an accusation.

"The fort was under attack. Hurons. You had been injured. Shot by the white man's musket. This man brought you here to let you heal."

If her memory served her correctly, he had already made the decision to kidnap her before he knew anything of Hurons, before she'd been shot, prompting her to scream for Josh. It was all because of that stupid portrait she'd painted. Fire Dancer had been so angry with her. "The portrait, where is it?"

"Here. Safe."

So it was because of the portrait that she was here. Mackenzie wasn't sure how she felt about all this. She was too confused. Her head hurt too badly. She rubbed her forehead with the heel of her hand. "You say I was shot? Josh shot me?"

"The boy-man was afraid. He did not mean to injure you. He meant to save you from me."

Even in her state of confusion she noticed he was defending Josh. "Where did he hit me?"

Fire Dancer released her hand and indicated her left temple. His touch was like the brush of a butterfly's wing. "Here."

''It doesn't hurt.'' It was difficult to keep her eyes open. She let them drift shut. ''Well it does, but not there. All over. I feel like someone ran over me with their ox cart.''

''The musket ball did not enter the skull. It only cracked it.'' He took her hand again. ''It was not your day to die, Mack-en-zie.''

She fought the pain and opened her eyes. ''But it was my day to be kidnapped.'' She couldn't help herself. The words just came out.

He released her hand, his face was devoid of emotion. ''Laughing Woman will see to your needs. This man must speak to the holy man, now that I know you will live. He will know what must be done with you, *kitehi.*''

His tone was ominous. Mackenzie felt that creeping sense of fear again. She knew from the way he looked at her that he was still angry with her about the portrait.

She squeezed her eyes shut, afraid she was going to cry. Why was Fire Dancer the only man who could make her feel vulnerable?

''Soup, Mack-en-sie?''

Mackenzie opened her eyes to see a beautiful Indian woman. Fire Dancer was gone. It was the same woman who had been here with her from the beginning. She recognized her tender voice. Only now she was speaking English in the same lilting manner that Fire Dancer did.

''Mack-en-sie, you must eat so that you will be strong again.''

Mackenzie gazed up at the woman. ''I've done a terrible thing,'' she whispered. ''I didn't understand. I painted him. He really thinks I've stolen a part of his soul. I didn't mean to harm him, only to finish the task I'd been hired for.'' As she babbled she realized how ridiculous she must sound. She wasn't even sure the woman understood that much English.

''Shhhhh,'' the Indian woman comforted. She knelt beside the sleeping platform and set down the hollow gourd soup bowl. She brushed the hair off Mackenzie's forehead and touched her as a mother would soothe a sick child. ''Do not worry over

Fire Dancer of the Thunder Sky. He is a man of honor, above all.''

''But he's so angry with me. He took me from my father.'' She opened her eyes wider, suddenly remembering her father. Her head pounded so hard that she had to close her eyes and lay her head back again. ''My father. He must be worried sick. I have to let him know I'm all right. I have to—''

''Shhhhh,'' the Shawnee woman whispered. ''Do not let yourself worry. Nothing happens that there is not reason for. No one will hurt you here. Take some of the good turtle soup I have made you and then sleep. Sleep will take away the pain in your head and in your heart.''

''I . . . I'm not hungry.'' But then Mackenzie smelled the soup that the woman was holding right under her nose.

''One bite and this woman will leave you to sleep.''

Mackenzie opened her mouth. She *was* hungry. She slurped the soup from the wooden spoon. She had another spoonful, then another. When a little of the broth dribbled down her chin, the woman wiped it with a soft cloth.

When Mackenzie had consumed half of the gourd bowl of soup, she laid her head back. ''Thank you. You have been too kind.''

The woman set the bowl on the floor and busied herself rearranging the neckroll under Mackenzie's head. ''I would do anything for Fire Dancer.''

Mackenzie glanced at the woman through half-closed eyes. ''Are you his sister?''

The woman smiled and shook her head. Tiny silver bells in her ears tinkled as she moved. ''No. I am not a sister. I am Laughing Woman.'' She rose. ''Now sleep. When you wake you will feel better.''

Mackenzie had so many questions. Laughing Woman? Fire Dancer had not mentioned her. Who was she? And who was this holy man he had just spoken of. What did this holy man have to do with Mackenzie?

Her head hurt so much that it was hard to think, but easy to give in to her exhaustion. She let go of her fears and drifted off to sleep.

Fire Dancer stood outside the holy man's wigwam, preparing himself for their meeting. He was so relieved to see Mackenzie awake and well that it was difficult for him to turn his attention away from his emotions.

Now that he knew she would live, he had to speak with Snake Man. Snake Man would know what to do with her, how to punish her for her crime. He would know what to do with the painting. He would know how to recapture the part of his soul she had taken.

Fire Dancer's thoughts wandered. He should have stayed away from Mackenzie and none of this would have happened. He felt guilty about the death of her father, not because he had been wrong, but because it would hurt Mackenzie. He didn't hold himself responsible for Franklin Daniels' death. The man had chosen his own path of dishonor by firing when he had sworn he would not. But the white *manake* were strange about such matters. Fire Dancer knew that Mackenzie would not understand. That was why he hadn't told her . . . not yet. First she had to gain back her strength.

Fire Dancer tugged at the single braid he wore down his back. Then what? Nothing was turning out as it should have. He had intended to return to the village and marry Laughing Woman. Now what would he do? He did not feel passion for Laughing Woman. Loving Mackenzie had made that all too clear to him in his mind.

Laughing Woman was a good choice for a wife to the chief's son. She was a proper Shawnee woman. A holy man's granddaughter. Fire Dancer cared deeply for her twin toddlers who had no father who walked this earth. But he felt no burning passion for Laughing Woman and now that he had held the flame-haired beauty in his arms, he knew he never would.

Fire Dancer stared up at the moon that hung brightly in the sky. He was angry at Mackenzie, as angry as he had even been at anyone, even Okonsa. He had trusted her and she had betrayed that trust. Perhaps he truly didn't love her at all. What if it was merely her sorcery at work? What if the act of her painting his portrait had made him feel this way toward her.

If it was magic, though, it was strong magic.

"Do you come in, or do you stand outside all night, son of chief?" The gravelly voice spoke from beyond the doorflap of the wigwam.

Fire Dancer grinned. How did the old man know he was there? He lifted the doorflap and stepped inside. He spoke in the tongue of his ancestors. "Snake Man, you honor me by this invitation."

"Sit. Sit. This man makes tea."

The wigwam was comfortably familiar to Fire Dancer. He had been coming here since he was a small boy. When he was a child, the hundreds of shedded snake skins hanging from the wigwam rafters had been scary. The live snakes that slivered through the rushes on the floor had been terrifying.

Fire Dancer stepped over a striped green snake that moved sinuously over one of his moccasins. As an adult, he simply accepted the holy man's fascination with his totem.

He took the mat the old man pointed to. "I have missed your tea, Snake Man. It will be good to feel it in my belly." The woven floor mats moved, alive with snakes; black ones, brown ones, green ones. There were short snakes, long snakes, snakes with forked tongues, snakes that hissed, and snakes that slept curled in baskets about the wigwam.

Fire Dancer wondered what Mackenzie's reaction to the holy man's pets would be. Would she be afraid? Would he be able to calm her fears as he had that night in her sleeping chamber?

The old man made a smacking sound with his toothless gums. "Bring me sugar?" He offered his palm across the banked coals of the fire pit.

Fire Dancer pushed aside his thoughts of Mackenzie as he reached into his leather pouch and pulled out a small lump of brown sugar wrapped in paper. He could not think of her now, not in such an emotional way. It might hide the truth. "This man would not forget your taste for the English sugar."

The holy man took the sugar and sniffed it. Then he gave it

a lick, as if testing to be certain Fire Dancer hadn't cheated him. Satisfied, Snake Man dropped the sugar into a little basket to the left of him.

The old man's aim always amazed Fire Dancer. How did he know where the basket was without feeling for it? He'd been blind from birth. One could even move the sugar basket as Okonsa had once done as a boy's practical joke. Yet Snake Man had made the drop accurately; he always did.

Fire Dancer watched as the holy man lifted the English kettle off the hot coals and poured the boiling water into a porcelain tea pot painted with green vines and yellow roses. It had been a gift from Fire Dancer years ago. With the water poured and the tea left to steep, Snake Man returned the kettle to the coals and retrieved two mismatched teacups from behind his back. He set them on a flat rock between his folded, withered legs.

"You come for this man's advice?" Snake Man's raspy, but strong voice broke the silence.

"Yes. This man comes for your wisdom, holy man. This man has found himself in great trouble."

Snake Man held up his finger for Fire Dancer to wait with his story. The old man poured the tea and handed Fire Dancer the first cup. Then he took the lump of sugar from the sugar basket and scraped off a little into his tea cup with a long thumbnail. He did not offer any of the sugar to Fire Dancer. He never did.

Fire Dancer waited patiently for the shaman to blow on his hot tea and slurp it loudly. The old warrior made that smacking sound between his gums again. Satisfied, he set down his cup.

"Now this old man is ready to listen. Come, come, do not be shy. Tell Snake Man what troubles your heart and I will see if I can ease your pain."

Fire Dancer took a sip of the bitter, dark tea and set down his cup. Out of respect for the holy man's totem, he waited for a black snake as thick as his wrist to creep over his thighs and slither away under the sleeping platform. Then he began to relate the story of how he met the red-haired English woman and what she did to him.

Snake Man listened patiently as he always had, asking a

question occasionally, clarifying Fire Dancer's statements. He
asked about details that seemed inconsequential to Fire Dancer.
But Fire Dancer told the holy man everything, trusting him
unconditionally. He even confessed that he had made love to
the white woman.

Finally, the tale complete, Fire Dancer sighed and took a sip
of his now-cold tea. Relating the events had tired him. He
didn't know how he could have been so blind as to not have
seen what Mackenzie was doing to him. She had lured him
with her beauty and her laughter. She had made him, a Shawnee
warrior, vulnerable. She had made him want her, and then she
had taken a part him that perhaps he could never regain.

Snake Man sat so quietly, breathing so evenly without making a sound that Fire Dancer wondered if he had drifted off to
sleep. There was no way to tell with those milky white eyes
of his that never blinked.

Finally the old man gave a nod of acknowledgement. "This
is bad, indeed. Worse than I had thought."

Fire Dancer watched a snake drink from a shallow water
dish left out for just that purpose. "It is indeed serious, holy
man of my mother's people. That is why I came to you. I do
not understand such matters of the soul."

"Did you speak to the chief?"

"It was the chief who said wait until we see if the woman
lives and then come to you."

"Our chief is wise.

Fire Dancer grimaced. "Indeed."

"So, now that the white woman lives, now that you have
this *por-trait*,"—he said the word in English—"you ask this
man for advice."

"I truly do not know what to do, Snake Man. It is my belief
that she possesses a part of me. My thoughts are always with
her thoughts now. I cannot eat nor drink nor sleep without
thinking of her. I feel as if a part of me is gone when I am not
with her. This man has seen and experienced many frightening
things in this world, but never one as frightening as this."

The old man stared straight ahead with those eerie white
eyeballs of his. "You understand that by coming to me, Fire

Dancer, you give up your choosing of a solution. The decision is mine.''

"*Ah* "

"The decision is mine no matter how cruel you may think it. You must understand that my job is to save you, son of chief, not concern myself with the woman, or even with you personally."

Fire Dancer felt a tightening in his throat. Magic or not, he loved Mackenzie. The idea of seeing her come to harm—he stared straight ahead at the holy man. Fire Dancer knew that his own life or that of Mackenzie's was not as important as the life of the village, nor that of their tribe. For a white woman to possess a Shawnee warrior's soul could mean greater disaster than one could imagine. Someday, Fire Dancer might be chief if the Council so wished it. The life of the Shawnee might depend upon him. "*Ah*," Fire Dancer said softly. "This man understands that the decision is yours."

"And you will abide by that decision without argument," Snake Man intoned. A shiny black snake with coral strips rested on his lap. He stroked it.

"*Ah*. This man will accept without question. You are a wise man, our holy man. Only you can know what is right in matters such as these."

"Go then." Snake Man flipped his wrist in dismissal. "This man with think. He will pray. Maybe he will even dance. Bring the white thief here tomorrow at the setting of the sun and I will pass my judgment."

Fire Dancer stood at the wigwam door. Snake skins from above brushed his hair. "*Ah*, Snake Man. This man thanks you for your wisdom." He stepped out into the darkness with a heavy heart.

Chapter Fourteen

Mackenzie lay perfectly still on the sleeping mat and stared up at the woven baskets and strings of herbs that hung over her head. It was dark, except for the glow of light from a fire pit.

Where am I? she wondered, her mind still fuzzy. Then she remembered. *With Fire Dancer. He kidnapped me and brought me here.*

But where was *here?*

She studied the dome roof with its sapling rafters and corn-husk shingles. It was some kind of hut. In the center of the roof moonlight shone through a hole that allowed smoke from the firepit to escape.

This had to be the Shawnee's living quarters. Fire Dancer said he'd brought her to his village. Was this his own personal home? Was she sleeping in his bed?

Mackenzie pushed up on her elbows. Her head still hurt, but the sharp, blinding pain had receded to a dull ache. She took a deep breath, waiting for the dizziness to pass. She could feel her pulse pounding in her temples, but she needed to get up and stretch. Her muscles ached from lying so long in one position. A fortnight, Fire Dancer had said. Two entire weeks gone from her life. That was hard to believe.

She swung her legs over the side of the sleeping platform and perched on the edge. As she waited for the next wave of dizziness to pass, she studied her surroundings. The bed was made of smoothed pine logs with a leather pad that acted like a hammock. Assorted furs softened the sleeping platform even more.

Despite the crudeness of the circular hut, it had a safe, comfortable feel about it. It was cool and airy inside, not hot and stuffy like her room in the fort. She dug in her memory for the word Fire Dancer had used when he'd told her of his village and the homes they lived in. *Wigwam,* that was the word. This was a wigwam.

There was no furniture, just the baskets of dried foods hanging from the rafters, and larger baskets lining the walls. It was difficult to see in the semi-darkness what was inside the floor baskets, but it looked like some held furs and leathers, while others contained dried corn and tubers. Clean, dry mats woven of grass covered the floor. Near the firepit there were flat rocks, used for cooking, no doubt. Near the door she spotted something on the floor. A blanket? She rose slowly from the sleeping platform.

It moved. *Definitely not a blanket. A person?*

Standing, she felt as if the floor was rushing up beneath her. She grabbed one of the ceiling supports to steady herself. "Fire Dancer, is . . . is that you?"

He was on his feet quickly. "Mack-en-zie, you should not be up." He crossed the wigwam, which could not have been more than ten feet across from the door to the sleeping platform.

His hand felt cool and reassuring in hers. She held onto it, still feeling shaky . . . and afraid. She had nothing to cling to in this strange place but her own inner strength . . . and him. "I . . . I wanted to get a drink and . . ." She was embarrassed to say she needed to relieve herself. "I wanted to go out."

Still holding her hand, he put his arm around her waist and walked with her toward the door. "I will take you as far as the edge of the woods line."

She was thankful he understood her meaning. "That would be good. Thank you." She looked up at him shyly. "And thank you for taking care of me. I didn't want you to think that I wasn't glad you helped me. I mean you took me from the fort, but—"

"This man understands. We are both filled with emotions that tug us from two sides."

Outside, she and Fire Dancer walked between wigwams that all looked exactly the same—dome-shaped with holes cut in the eastern side for doors. Not a soul was about. From the position of the moon, she guessed it was around three o'clock in the morning. A cool breeze blew, chilling her. Somewhere an infant cried, but only for a second before he was hushed by a mother's arms.

Fire Dancer ran his hand up and down her bare arm in a soothing motion. "I want you to believe my words when I say this is as difficult for me as it is for you, Mack-en-zie."

When he brushed her arm, she realized it was bare. She looked down to see that her English clothes were gone. She was barefoot and wore nothing but a soft leather, sleeveless sheath. Delicate sea shells were sewn into the edging of the V-neck. The garment was unbelievably comfortable, like wearing nothing but her shift. She smiled to herself in the darkness. If only her father could see her now.

Her father.

Too wobbly to walk unassisted, she held tightly to Fire Dancer's hand. Surely her father was going mad with worry about her. She glanced at Fire Dancer's face. As usual, she could read no emotions there. She had to know about her father. About the fort. She had to know what Fire Dancer intended to do with her now that she was going to recover from the gunshot.

He stopped at the edge of the clearing where the wigwams stood and pointed into the trees. "There is a small path that leads into the woods for pri-va-cy."

"I'll be right back." She touched his bare forearm and felt a trill of excitement in her chest. It was the same excitement she had felt the night they'd made love. She lowered her hand

and walked away. *I guess I am feeling better,* she thought grimly.

She walked just out of his sight, did what she had to, and then hurried back toward the clearing where Fire Dancer waited patiently.

"You are all right, Mack-en-zie. You are not too tired to walk back?"

She laughed shakily, accepting the support of his arm. "No. I'm fine." Actually, she was feeling better. The fresh air had cleared her head. Most of the dizziness was gone and she was ravenously hungry.

She walked beside him trying to think of some way to broach the subject of her father. Finally, she just blurted it out. "Fire Dancer, I need to send a message to my father. To . . . to let him know I'm all right. That I'm with you."

"I cannot allow you to do that. The soldiers must not know where the village is. They would follow the messenger. They would attack our village in retaliation for the attack on the fort."

The coolness in his tone surprised her. "But I thought you said it was Hurons."

"*Ah*. But you know it does not matter to the British army . . . or to the French. We are all the same to them. The Frenchmen will be looking for us, as well, because of DuBois."

She hugged herself against a sudden chill. "But that's so unfair."

He chuckled.

She grimaced at her own silliness. Of course, it was unfair. She'd spent enough time in the fort to know that the Indians were treated unfairly. "Anyway," she went on. "You can't keep me here. Not against my will."

She ducked her head and stepped inside as he lifted the leather flap of his wigwam.

"You forget, Mack-en-zie, that you brought this upon yourself. You painted this man's image against his will. I told you, you could not do it."

She walked across the floor mats to the sleeping platform and sat down, trying to keep her temper. She was a stranger in a strange place. Fire Dancer was her only ally . . . and perhaps her enemy as well. "I understand that you're angry with me, but—"

"You do not understand." His voice was sharp as he strode to the fire pit and lit a blade of dry grass. He lit a lantern that hung from the rafters.

Mackenzie lowered her gaze to her folded hands. Her head was beginning to hurt again. "I said I was sorry," she said through clenched teeth.

"It does not solve my problem, Mack-en-zie." He brought her a gourd ladle of water.

She was tempted to refuse it. He had no right to kidnap her. He had no right to keep her from her father. That she cared for him so much made it hard, though. Nothing was cut and dried. She didn't want to be here . . . but she did. A part of her wanted to be with him, even if that meant being away from her father. Yet she didn't want to be here against her will. She would not remain here.

She felt guilty for painting the picture. He was right. She was wrong. Even if she didn't understand his reasons for not wanting his portrait painted, she should have respected his wishes. But was punishment really necessary? Obviously, she still didn't understand the Shawnee.

"So just how can we solve your problem?" she asked, camouflaging her fear with anger. She snatched the gourd ladle from his hand and a little water spilled onto her bare leg. "I assume we're speaking of this problem of my possessing your soul."

He walked away from her. "You make light of that which you do not understand."

"You're right." She sipped the water. "I don't understand. Englishmen have been painting portraits for hundreds of years." She glanced up at him. "You think all those people are missing parts of their souls?"

"This man cannot speak for the English. Nothing about the English *manake* makes sense to me. All I know is what my mother taught me and what her mother taught her." He placed his closed fist over his heart. "I know that you should not have taken that part of me."

Finished with the water, she tossed the ladle into the bucket that stood against the wall. She noticed that the portrait of him hung from one of the rafters. The frame was broken, but the canvas was in good condition. She was tempted to take the damned thing down and toss it onto the glowing coals in the firepit.

"How do we solve this so I can go home?" Her voice was beginning to sound hoarse. Her head was pounding harder. She didn't want to fight with Fire Dancer. She wanted him to hold her. To comfort her.

He pushed a little wooden bowl into her hands. "This man does not know. That is part of the reason I brought you here. Our shaman, Snake Man, understands matters of the soul. I have already spoken to him. He will tell me what must be done." He tapped the rim of the bowl. "Eat. It will give you strength."

She tasted a little of the crumbly stuff. It was sweetened with dried berries and they were delicious. "Shaman? What is that?"

He thought before he answered. "He is a holy man. A man who stands between us and the spiritual world. He has been gifted by *Tapalamawatah*—God. He guides my people in that which they do not understand."

She gave a small, humorless laugh. "And this man is going to tell you what to do with me?" She could feel that sense of fear creeping up on her again. "Like . . . like what?"

"Let us not speak of this again tonight. Eat. Then sleep. I will stay with you the night, Mack-en-zie."

She didn't like the way he looked at her. For once she could read his emotions and it scared her.

Fire Dancer was afraid.

She set down the bowl, rose and walked to him. He stood stoic, his gaze locked with hers. She lifted her hands and rested them on his broad, bare shoulders. "Fire Dancer . . . he . . . he wouldn't hurt me, would he? I mean you . . . your people, they don't do sacrifices like the Powhatan, do they? Harry told me

he Powhatan Indians in Virginia Colony murder people for
eligious reasons.'' She searched his gaze. ''Tell me, you
wouldn't let anyone hurt me.''

In his eyes she could see that he was torn. She knew he
oved the Shawnee. ''Mack-en-zie, heart of my heart. This man
does not know what solution the Snake Man will offer.'' He
pulled her tighter against his chest as if he thought he could
hug her hard enough to make her a part of him. ''This man
has agreed to what Snake Man says.''

Mackenzie rested her head on his shoulder, fighting tears. It
felt so good to be held by him. She was so confused by her
feelings for the man. The night they had made love she had
known she loved him, that she had always loved him in her
heart of hearts. Then he had taken her from the fort and from
her father. He accused her of heinous crimes she didn't understand. Now he was allowing some old medicine man to deter-
mine her fate. She should hate Fire Dancer for what he was
doing to her. So why didn't she?

Mackenzie buried her face in his silky, black hair that smelled
of the pine forest.

She shook her head, still trying to comprehend what was
happening. ''I don't understand. How can you agree to something when you don't know what it is?''

''Mack-en-zie. It is not my life nor even yours that this man
must think of. Our chief reminded me of my responsibilities
to my people. Not just to my village, but to all Shawnee. I am
what you would call ''prince''. Some day I will become chief
of my village, leader of my clan.''

Her lower lip trembled. ''You won't let them hurt me. You
won't let them kill me,'' she said fiercely. ''No matter what
you say now, I know in my heart you wouldn't let them.'' She
leaned back to meet his gaze. ''I wouldn't let anyone harm
you. No matter what I had to do.''

He smoothed her hair and she rested her cheek on his bare
chest where she could hear his heartbeat.

''Let us wait and see what the Snake Man says, Mack-en-
zie.'' He kissed her forehead. ''Now you must sleep. You must
be strong for whatever tomorrow will bring.''

Mackenzie's head was so full of thoughts that nothing made
sense. Fire Dancer was right. She needed sleep. She was in no
immediate danger. What she had to do was rest and prepare
herself for whatever might come . . . whatever she might have
to do to get away from here. Of course to flee meant leaving
Fire Dancer . . . forever.

Mackenzie bit down on her lowering lip, fighting waves of
desperation. What frightened her most was that her fear of
losing Fire Dancer was greater than her fear of whatever sentence Snake Man might decree.

She smoothed his cheek with her palm. "Will you sleep with
me? Hold me, Fire Dancer?"

He took her hand and led her to the sleeping platform.
"Among my people a man does not sleep the night with a
woman unless they have made their commitment before the
great God and all his people." He slid into the bed and put
out his arms for her. "But tonight I will hold you, *kitehi.*"

She climbed onto the narrow bed beside him and pressed
her back to him, allowing him to curl his arm around her waist.
"Wed, you mean?" She gave a little laugh. The thought was
ridiculous, an impossibility . . . wasn't it? She closed her eyes
and was asleep before Fire Dancer had formed a reply.

Fire Dancer rose at dawn and spoke his prayers to the rising
sun as he did each day. Afterward, he gathered a few supplies
from his wigwam and went outside to prepare a meal for Mackenzie. He knew she would be hungry when she woke.

Fire Dancer started a fire in front of his wigwam and fetched
water to boil for corn mush. A cool, fall breeze blew a cleansing
breath over the Shawnee wigwams. The village began to stir.
Women walked back and forth from the stream retrieving water.
Men checked the horses. Some prepared for an early morning
hunting trip. Other men sat outside their wigwams and con-
versed with their wives, taking a quiet moment for themselves
before their children rose.

It felt so good to Fire Dancer to be home. He had missed
the smell of corn cakes baking on hot rocks. He'd missed the

laughter of the young maidens, and the comforting wisdom of the older men and women.

"Good morning, brother,"

Fire Dancer glanced up to see Okonsa, dressed for the forest, with several weapons tied on his belt. "Good morning, n`tha-thah." He spoke in the tongue of their ancestors. "I see you go scouting this day."

"Ah`. This man has volunteered for extra duty." Okonsa adjusted his nose ring. "Since our return from the fort with the white woman, our own women have feared the British manake will find us and massacre us in our sleep. Our chief has doubled the patrols."

Fire Dancer didn't like his reference to Mackenzie. The tension between the Shawnee and the French and British had been increasing for months. Mackenzie was not solely responsible for the villagers' fear.

He pulled an ear of corn from a basket and began to shuck it. "This man brought the woman here because he had to. You agreed with me. Remember?"

Okonsa's manner changed abruptly, his accusing tone gone in the flutter of a sparrow's wings. "I make no accusation, brother," he said innocently, touching his chest with a closed fist. "You were right to bring her here, so that Snake Man could tell you what to do. Only a holy man could know the strength of her power over you."

"Ah`, you speak the truth." Fire Dancer reached for another ear of corn, feeling guilty that he had been so quick to jump to the conclusion that Okonsa was against him. Ever since their return from the fort, he had been supportive. Fire Dancer liked to think that the change in the Shawnee's political situation had matured Okonsa. Okonsa seemed to be making an honest attempt to find his place among their people.

"I have defended your decision to the others," Okonsa continued. "I go scouting to help you. To protect you and the others I love."

"This man is grateful for you, brother, and for your friendship these days." Fire Dancer smiled. "I say this honestly."

Okonsa scuffed his moccasin in the dry dirt. "Our sister tells me the fire-haired woman is awake. She says Snake Man will give you his decision tonight. Is this true or merely women's gossip?''

"Our sister speaks the truth." Fire Dancer shelled another ear of corn. "The entire village will gather tonight at the communal fire to hear the holy man's words."

Okonsa nodded. "Give Mack-en-zie this man's good wishes. Tell her I am pleased she is alive and well."

Fire Dancer smiled genuinely. "Thank you. I will."

Okonsa imitated a salute. "This man goes. I will see you tonight at the great campfire, brother. I will be there for you."

"Tread carefully and safely." Fire Dancer waved a good-bye and watched his cousin stride away.

Okonsa's new attitude gave Fire Dancer hope for his cousin's future. Okonsa had been of a concern to him ever since they had reached adulthood. Okonsa had never seemed to fully recover from his parents' murders. Maybe he had finally accepted the path of his fate and theirs.

A short time later Fire Dancer heard his name spoken again. He glanced up from the corn kernels he ground. "Gentle Bear." He grinned. He had not had much time to spend with his good friend since his return to the village. Bear had been his best friend since they were children. "It is good to see you."

"Good to see you, *n`thatha*." Gentle Bear squatted across the firepit from Fire Dancer and lowered his massive body onto a grass mat. "This man had hoped he could find you alone."

"You want to speak?" Fire Dancer gestured. "My hearth is open. This man has always been here for you. Speak.

"It is not me I have concern for, friend. It is you. Laughing Woman tells me the white woman you took captive will live."

Fire Dancer poured ground corn into a gourd mixing bowl. "I did not exactly take her captive."

"No? She came of free will, shot through the head?" Gentle Bear raised a bushy eyebrow. "Hmmph. She is a strong woman, indeed."

"You do not know the circumstances. I am sorry I have not had time to talk with you."

"No. I only hear what Okonsa says, and you and I both

know he is not to be believed. What I do know is that you brought a white woman to our village and she sleeps in your wigwam with you. You understand, friend, that some women are willing to share a husband, but Laughing Woman is not. I only speak these words because this man is concerned for what would be best for you and our people.''

Fire Dancer sighed as he twisted the stone pestle and ground more corn on the mortar between his feet. "I have not spoken to Laughing Woman on this matter.''

"She cared for the white woman for you, not for the white woman.''

"Laughing Woman is a good soul. This man has always known he could count on her friendship.''

"I think it is more than friendship she feels for you. She will be hurt by your relationship with the white woman with the flaming hair—whatever that relationship is . . .''

Fire Dancer glanced away, trying to keep his emotions in check. Only with Gentle Bear could he share his vulnerability. It had always been that way, since they were boys. "I did not mean to fall in love with a white woman, Cub." He used his affectionate name for his friend, a name that had caused many a busted lip in their early years. "By the time I realized I was under her spell, it was too late.''

"Love is not an emotion we have control over, Fire Dancer." He picked up a handful of dirt and filtered it through his fingers. "And what is done is done and cannot be changed. Who is to say what is fate? Perhaps you were never meant to marry Laughing Woman. Perhaps this white woman is your true mate. Marry her and make her one of us.''

"The chief would never approve, even if I so wished such a union.''

Gentle Bear held up a meaty finger. "Ah, but the mother. How would she feel about her son finally taking a wife and giving her grandchildren?''

Fire Dancer ground the corn kernels faster. He did not want to consider impossibilities. Of course, he couldn't marry Mackenzie. Shawnee princes did not marry white women. He would not allow himself to daydream of that which could never be.

"Do we have to talk of this now? This man has more pressing concerns than finding a suitable wife."

Gentle Bear tossed a piece of firewood onto the fire. "*Ah*ˋ, the likeness the white woman painted. Little Weaver told me. They say the Snake Man will make a decision on the proper form of reprisal. Perhaps you will not have to make the choice between women. Perhaps it will be done for you."

Fire Dancer dumped more ground corn into the mixing bowl. "It is not just my own trouble that concerns me." He pounded the stone pestle harder. "After the Huron attack on the French delegate and then the fort, I fear the entire village is in danger. I feel at least partially responsible. And . . ." He paused. "And there is the matter of Okonsa."

"*Ah*ˋ, Okonsa." Gentle Bear nodded. He and Okonsa were as much enemies as he and Fire Dancer were friends. "What of Okonsa? He has been pleasant since his return. Helpful. So friendly it scares this man."

"He seems to be trying to fit in, to take responsibility, doesn't he?"

"What is your concern? Perhaps a man can change." Gentle Bear shrugged his massive shoulders. "It is hard for this man to believe Okonsa could change, but stranger things have happened in this forest, no?"

Fire Dancer chose to ignore his last remark. "The circumstances of the attack on the Frenchman DuBois were suspicious, as was the attack on the British fort. Okonsa was gone when the Frenchman was ambushed. He appeared as if by magic when the Hurons attacked the fort. I am suspicious and yet I feel guilty for my suspicion. Okonsa has done wrong things in the past, but he has never threatened such harm to our people. I cannot believe he would do such a deed."

Gentle Bear took his time to answer. "It is a serious accusation to say you think your cousin might have played some part in the attacks. You were sent as peace negotiators. If Okonsa was a part of the attack, it would be the same as an attack upon his own people."

"*Ah*ˋ," Fire Dancer said. "This is why I am hesitant to speak with Okonsa about what happened . . . or to speak to anyone else. I think I am better to watch him and wait. A poison snake always shows his fangs eventually, does he not?''

Gentle Bear rose. "He does. You are wise to wait and watch, friend. And I will watch as well. Who knows? Perhaps he is innocent. This man must go see to his wife and son, but we will speak later, friend.''

"Later, Cub.''

"And Fire Dancer . . .''

Fire Dancer glanced up. *"Ah ?''*

"I think you can stop grinding now. You have enough cornmeal there to make mush for the entire village.''

Fire Dancer frowned into the mixing bowl. He'd been so intent on the conversation that he hadn't paid attention to what he was doing. The bowl was filled to overflowing.

Gentle Bear burst into laughter and walked away.

Fire Dancer had the good sense to laugh with him.

4 BESTSELLING HISTORICAL ROMANCES BY YOUR FAVORITE AUTHORS CAN BE YOURS, FREE!

Kensington Choice brings you historical romances by your favorite bestselling authors including Janelle Taylor, Shannon Drake, Rosanne Bittner, Jo Beverley, and Georgina Gentry, just to name a few! Each book is filled with passion, adventure and the excitement of bygone times!

To introduce you to this great club which is part of Zebra Home Subscription Service, we'd like to send you your first 4 bestselling historical romances, absolutely free! And once you get these 4 free books to savor at home, we'll rush you the next 4 brand-new books at the lowest prices available, as soon as they are published.

The way the club works is that after your initial FREE shipment, you will get our 4 newest bestselling historical romances delivered to your

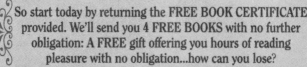

doorstep each month at the preferred subscriber's rate of only $4.20 per book, a savings of up to $8.16 per month (since these titles sell in bookstores for $4.99-$6.99)! All books are sent on a 10-day free examination basis and there is no minimum number of books to buy. (A postage and handling charge of $1.50 is added to each

shipment.) Plus as a regular subscriber, you'll receive our FREE monthly newsletter, *Zebra/Pinnacle Romance News*, which features author profiles, subscriber benefits, book previews and more!

 So start today by returning the FREE BOOK CERTIFICATE provided. We'll send you 4 FREE BOOKS with no further obligation: A FREE gift offering you hours of reading pleasure with no obligation...how can you lose?

*We have 4 FREE BOOKS for you
as your introduction to
KENSINGTON CHOICE!
To get your FREE BOOKS, worth
up to $24.96, mail the card below.*

FREE BOOK CERTIFICATE

Yes! Please send me 4 Kensington Choice (the best of Zebra and Pinnacle Books) Historical Romances without cost or obligation (worth up to $24.96). As a Kensington Choice subscriber, I will then receive 4 brand-new romances to preview each month for 10 days FREE. I can return any books I decide not to keep and owe nothing. The publisher's prices for Kensington Choice romances range from $4.99-$6.99, but as a preferred subscriber I will get these books for only $4.20 per book or $16.80 for all four titles. There is no minimum number of books to buy and I may cancel my subscription at any time. A $1.50 postage and handling charge is added to each shipment. No matter what I decide to do, my first 4 books are mine to keep, absolutely FREE!

Name _____

Address _____ Apt. _____

City _____ State _____ Zip _____

Telephone ( ) _____

Signature _____

(If under 18, parent or guardian must sign)

Subscription subject to acceptance. Terms and prices subject to change.

KC1197

AFFIX
STAMP
HERE

KENSINGTON CHOICE
Zebra Home Subscription Service, Inc.
120 Brighton Road
P.O.Box 5214
Clifton, NJ 07015-5214

Chapter Fifteen

Mackenzie awakened to find herself alone. She sat up and rubbed her eyes. The first thing she noticed was that Fire Dancer had moved his portrait. It now hung from a rafter too high off the floor for her to reach.

She slid off the sleep platform. How did he know her so well? Obviously, he suspected she might attempt to destroy the portrait, otherwise why else would he have moved it?

She yawned and smoothed her doeskin dress, fascinated by the fact that leather didn't wrinkle. "Fire Dancer?" she called softly. She glanced around the empty wigwam.

Outside, she heard people laughing and talking. She could hear children's merry voices. A dog barked. From inside the wigwam, the Shawnee village sounded like any small town along the Chesapeake Bay.

Hesitantly, Mackenzie walked to the door. Half-expecting a guard, she lifted the flap and peered outside. Three stark-naked boys raced past her, squealing with laughter as they kicked a leather ball. A naked girl busied herself hanging a doll's cradleboard on a tree branch. Fire Dancer had told Mackenzie that in the heat of the summer Shawnee children wore no clothing, but she still found it startling.

To her right, Mackenzie spotted a woman her own age bathing a baby in a bark tub. Straight ahead, between the next two wigwams, identical to Fire Dancer's, two adolescent boys were digging a hole. What Mackenzie saw seemed harmless enough so she stepped out into the bright sunlight.

Surrounded by forest, the village was situated between a ridge of mountains in the distance to the left and another to the right. Nothing looked familiar. The terrain was rockier and the air smelled different. How far had Fire Dancer brought her? In all of his talk of his village back at the fort, he had never once indicated where it was.

Mackenzie noted that the heat of the summer had vanished. The air smelled not of fresh grass, but of drying leaves. It wasn't cold yet, but the air was cooler. Of course if she'd been unconscious two weeks, than it was nearly the first of October. Summer had left while she had slept.

"Mack-en-zie. This man feared you had fallen into the great sleep again." Fire Dancer appeared at her side and took her hand. "Are you hungry? This man prepared food."

She wondered how a man could kidnap a woman and then treat her with such courtesy and attentiveness. It probably made perfect sense to him. "I am hungry."

He led her to an open cook fire in front of his wigwam. "Sit." He indicated a grass mat similar to the ones that covered the floor inside the wigwam. "This man will bring you food."

Mackenzie sat cross-legged on the mat. The warm sun shone on her face and a light breeze blew her hair. "It's really not necessary that you serve me. I can get my own."

He brought her a wooden bowl of what appeared to be corn mush. On the top, he sprinkled precious sugar. He handed her a crude wooden spoon. "Eat. Today is an important day for both of us, Mack-en-zie. We must have our strength."

Skeptical, she tasted the mush, but found it to her liking. She took one bite and then another. "Today the holy man tells you what must be done with me?"

"*Ah*. At dusk, we go before him. Now I must join the chief. There are decisions that will be made. The English will be looking for you. The French will be looking for me and my men. My people must decide if we will prepare to fight or if we will move our village.'' She glanced up at him over the rim of the wooden bowl. ''You could let me go,'' she said casually.

''Point me in the direction of the fort. I'll find my way on my own. I would never tell anyone where to find you. You know I wouldn't.''

He face remained stoic. ''You understand that I cannot do that, Mack-en-zie.''

She set down the bowl. ''Fire Dancer—'' she lowered her voice—''you wouldn't have to tell anyone. You could make it look like I simply escaped. I could—''

He made no attempt to keep their conversation private. ''This man does not have time to speak of this. I must go, but Laughing Woman will come. She will take you to the stream to bathe. Stay with her until I return from Council.''

She crossed her arms over her chest stubbornly. ''You can't make me stay.''

He turned to walk away, then turned back to her. ''This man will warn you. Do not try to escape when Laughing Woman takes you to the stream. There are braves who guard the village. They have my orders not to let you pass. If you try, this man will bind you to my lodge pole. Do you understand my words?''

She said nothing and refused to make eye contact. Be damned if she'd make such a promise. If she had chance to escape, she would.

''Mack-en-zie? You must give me your word, or I will bind you now.''

If she gave him her word, could she break it? Honesty meant so much to him that she wasn't sure she could disappoint him by lying or playing him false. She dragged her gaze from the ground to his solemn face. ''Yes, yes, yes,'' she snapped. ''I understand. I can't leave.''

With a nod, he walked off.

Mackenzie picked up her bowl and crammed a spoon of cornmush into her mouth. No one paid any attention to her. Although she was surrounded by Indian men and women, there seemed to be some sort of rule about privacy. Surely those who spoke any English at all had heard what just went on between her and Fire Dancer. Even those who only spoke Algonquian must have known they quarreled. Yet the Shawnee all looked away discreetly and concentrated on their domestic tasks.

Mackenzie had eaten half of the delicious corn mush when she saw Laughing Woman walk toward her. A little boy and a little girl hung on her hands. The naked children were twins and could not have been more that two years old.

"It is good I see you awake," Laughing Woman called. Her smile lit up her face and she was strikingly beautiful.

"Th . . . thank you."

"You have feel good?"

Mackenzie couldn't resist a smile. Laughing Woman's speech was difficult to follow, but Mackenzie quickly got the hang of it. "You speak English, too? Fire Dancer said he learned English from a Jesuit priest, but how do you come to speak it?"

The Indian woman released both children and the babies toddled off in pursuit of an orange butterfly. "Our chief think it is good to know the words of the enemy." She bit down on her lower lip. "This woman did not mean to hurt. I do not call you enemy. You are friend to our Fire Dancer and no enemy to this woman."

Mackenzie grinned, thankful for her consideration. "It's all right. Really. Considering what happened back at the fort, I can't honestly tell you who's on whose side anymore."

Laughing Woman nodded and began to clean up the breakfast dishes. "This woman understand." She tilted her head one way and then the other in an exaggerated motion. "Men say friend, women say enemy. Women no see as easy as the men. This woman wish there was no enemy. Only friend."

"Exactly," Mackenzie agreed.

Laughing Woman chuckled as she sifted a big bowl filled with ground corn. "Look. This woman let Fire Dancer cook his mush one time and he grind enough corn for whole winter."

Mackenzie chuckled with her. It was funny that Fire Dancer would grind so much corn. The woman's words also made her curious. What was her relationship with Fire Dancer? She felt a strange tightness in her chest. Was she jealous of this beautiful Indian woman? "Do you usually cook his meals?" she asked casually.

Laughing Woman met Mackenzie's gaze. "This woman cooks when he *la-lowe* her. She make him loin cloth, soap. Laughing Woman have no man to care for." She smiled, as if reminiscing. "Like make Fire Dancer smile."

So a relationship did exist between Laughing Woman and Fire Dancer, but just how intimate, Mackenzie couldn't deduce. Fire Dancer said there were no servants among his people, so she couldn't be his maid. She wasn't his sister. Who was she? She didn't feel right asking Laughing Woman, but she made a mental note to ask Fire Dancer later.

Finished with her breakfast, Mackenzie accepted a gourd of cold water. "Are those your children?" she asked, making conversation.

The Indian Woman turned to watch the little boy and girl now chasing each other around Fire Dancer's Wigwam. "*Ah*. When *waiseeyah* die, this woman have no one but babies in belly." She touched her flat abdomen. "Gift from *Tapalama-watah.*"

Mackenzie guessed that she spoke of her husband by her tone of voice. So the children had been born after her husband's death. *How sad*, she thought. "You must miss him very much."

"*Ah.*" she knelt to wash Mackenzie's bowl in a bark bucket of water. "Not good be sad. My *Waiseeyah* go to great sky." She pointed upward with a wet hand.

"*Why-see-ya,*" Mackenzie repeated. "Is that the word for husband?"

Laughing Woman chewed on her bottom lip in thought. "This woman not know English word. *Waiseeyah.*" She tapped her heart. "Love of Laughing Woman." She pointed to the children. "Father."

Mackenzie nodded. "Husband," She repeated. "That's got to be it. *Waiseeyah.*"

"*Hus-band,*" Laughing Woman mimicked.

The two women smiled at each, both pleased by their ability

to tackle the language differences and learn something in the process.

"May I help you with cleaning?" Mackenzie asked. "Maybe doing something with all that corn meal?"

Laughing Woman's eyes twinkled with amusement. *"Mahtah.* You were sick from head. You must rest. Get strong. This woman can clean up bowls. Then I think we pick the berries."

As the Indian woman spoke, Mackenzie got the strange feeling that someone watched her, but when she looked around, she saw no one.

"You think you strong to walk in field and pick berries?" Laughing Woman asked.

"I think the sunshine would do me good." Mackenzie smiled. "I—" She spotted Okonsa standing behind a tree, beyond the next wigwam, staring directly at her. He gave her an arrogant grin and grasped his groin in his usual suggestive gesture. This time he lifted one black eyebrow in invitation.

Mackenzie's first impulse was to shout something at him. Who did he think he was that he could be so obscene to her? She gritted her teeth. She bet he'd not behave thusly in front of Fire Dancer.

"Mack-en-sie? Mack-en-sie?"

Mackenzie shifted her gaze back to Laughing Woman. "Yes?"

Laughing Woman's face was etched with concern. "You feel sick?" She knelt and felt her forehead. "Have need of rest?"

Mackenzie looked back toward the tree. Okonsa was gone. She shuddered. *"Mahtah,* I'm fine. I'd love to pick berries with you and your children." She didn't mention Okonsa to Laughing Woman because what would she say? That he'd looked at her?

"You want bathe after pick berries, *ah` ?"* Laughing Woman rose. "Fire Dancer say take Mack-en-sie bathe with Laughing Woman and babies." Her gaze met Mackenzie's and she tapped her cheekbone. "He say no let white woman out of eyes."

Mackenzie rose slowly. She still felt a little dizzy when she moved too quickly. So Laughing Woman had been sent to look after her, but also to guard her. "It would be nice to bathe."

She pushed her dirty hair off her cheek. "And I'll not try to escape. I'd not put you danger of Fire Dancer's wrath."

Laughing Woman didn't appear to understand.

Mackenzie rephrased her words. "I won't run. I wouldn't want Fire Dancer to be mad at you."

The Indian woman caught her daughter by the hand and reached for her son, speaking to them rapidly in Shawnee. She turned her attention back to Mackenzie. "Fire Dancer keep you here Shawnee village, you no want?"

Mackenzie gave a sigh. "He took me from the fort, from my father. I have to go home. I want to go home."

Laughing Woman thought for a moment before she replied. "Fire Dancer have good reason keep you, even if you no understand." She turned away, leading the children. "Even if this woman no understand."

Tall Moccasin crept through the grass on his hands and knees, keeping his head low, moving it one way and then the other in an attempt to imitate the bobcat. He wished he had made himself a tail to sway. How could he ever convince Snake Man that his totem was the bobcat, if he couldn't imagine that tail? He would have to try harder. He would have to concentrate on becoming the bobcat.

Tall Moccasin, the bobcat, heard the sound of flowing water. He slinked out onto the flat, hot rocks of the streambed and lowered his head to drink, lapping the cold water with his fuzzy tongue.

He knew he should get back to the village-den. He had strayed too far and his mother cat would be angry with him.

Tall Moccasin lifted his head and water dribbled down his chin. He tried to slurp it up with his tongue. Staring straight ahead, he noticed a cylinder of smoke curling in the air. He wiggled his cat nose. The smoke had a strange, unrecognizable stench. Who would be in the forest burning a fire this time of day?

Tall Moccasin glanced over his shoulder in the direction of

the village. He felt torn between returning home before he was missed, and searching out the source of the smoke.

After a moment's hesitation, he crawled across the shallow streambed, still on all fours. It was in a bobcat's nature to investigate, wasn't it?

Tall Moccasin heard a man's voice on the wind. The man sang and talked. The voice sounded familiar. Tall Moccasin crept between the trees of the forest, ignoring the prick of dry pine needles and angry nettles on his palms and knees. His cat-curiosity had the best of him now.

The voice grew clearer as Tall Moccasin drew closer to the source of the stinking smoke. Laughter echoed in the trees. Scary laughter.

"Perfect. Perfect," the man said in Shawnee. "This one will work well. Only a few more prizes and this man will have a coat for the winter."

Tall Moccasin sat back on his heels behind a patch of poke-berry plants and parted the leaves. His eyes widened. Uncle Okonsa? He made the stinking smoke and laughed like a crazy man? What was he doing? Tall Moccasin watched in fascination.

His uncle was drying a hide of some sort over a small, open fire. But what kind of animal hide it was, Tall Moccasin couldn't tell. It wasn't squirrel or rabbit and it was too small to be deer or fox. The hide was thin and circular in shape. It looked as if it had been scraped, but there were still patches of dark, bristly hair.

Okonsa had stretched the hides on circular hoops and placed the hoops on a rack above the fire.

Tall Moccasin wrinkled his nose. It sure did stink. He guessed he should make his uncle aware of his presence. It was rude to sneak up on an adult. Uncle Fire Dancer had told him that time and time again. Even young bobcats did not sneak up on their family members.

Tall Moccasin started to get to his feet when he heard Uncle Okonsa talking again. . . . Talking to himself in Shawnee.

"Perfect . . . perfect. This man thanks you for your contribution to my English *manake* coat. It will be beautiful, the envy of the next great clan gathering, no?'' He laughed that strange laugh and picked up one of the hoops that dried over the fire. He took a handful of what looked like bear grease and rubbed it on the skin.

"This man is sorry he did not take some of your friends' as well," he said to the hide. "I could make a coat for my cousin Fire Dancer. But this man could not remain and fight once he lead the Hurons in. The Shawnee had to escape from the fort before you sent for reinforcements. It is like that in battle, isn't it?''

Tall Moccasin's brow creased. What was his uncle talking about? Did he speak of the fighting at Fort Belvadere from where they had come? What did he mean, he lead the Hurons?

The boy knew his uncle had been involved in the fighting. Once the Shawnee delegation was far enough from the fort to consider themselves safe, they had stopped and regrouped. Tall Moccasin had seen Uncle Fire Dancer corner his brother and ask Okonsa how he became involved in the fighting with the Hurons and the soldiers. Okonsa was supposed to be off hunting.

Uncle Okonsa had said Fire Dancer was lucky he had appeared when he did, otherwise the Shawnee delegation might not have escaped.

There had been so much confusion that night with the cannons booming and the crazy Hurons running everywhere, that Uncle Okonsa probably did have to fight to get away. But his uncle's words now did not sound like those of a man who had retreated from fighting. It sounded as if he had been in on the attack. But surely Uncle Okonsa would not have joined stinking Hurons to attack the fort.

Okonsa returned the hoop to the drying rack and picked up another loose skin from the ground. This one had long hair on it . . . blond hair.

Tall Moccasin felt a sudden chill. Hair? Blond hair . . . not fur? It couldn't be possible. Uncle Okonsa would not take a scalp. It was a barbaric practice and not permitted in their village. Such a desecration of a human body—even the enemy's body—was forbidden.

And yet Tall Moccasin had learned to believe what he saw

and smelled. He would have to tell Uncle Fire Dancer. He dropped flat on his belly. He was no longer the bobcat. He was just a scared Shawnee boy and he wanted his mother. He turned on his belly to slink away. His foot hit one of the pokeberry plants and a dove eating berries spooked and fluttered off.

Tall Moccasin held his breath, fearing he had given away his hiding spot. He waited a long second and then another. With his back to his uncle he couldn't see where he was. Uncle Okonsa must not have noticed the dove. Tall Moccasin leaped to his feet to make his escape.

A hand clamped down on his shoulder and the boy couldn't resist a cry of terror.

"Spy," his uncle accused in their native tongue. "I will kill you for spying on me." He held a skinning knife to Tall Moccasin's throat, the same blade he had used to scrape blond hair from the scalp.

"You took scalps!" Tall Moccasin accused, so frightened that he shook. "Our law does not allow you to take scalps. You have so many!"

"Silence," Okonsa bellowed as he held Tall Moccasin by the neckline of his leather vest, the knife point still held to his Adam's apple. "You do not know what you speak of. I take no scalps."

"Those . . . those are scalps with hair on them." Tall Moccasin's lower lip trembled. "This boy saw them with his own eyes."

"This boy's eyes deceive him." Okonsa stared with a crazed wide-eyed glare. "Wrong. Wrong. Wrong. Do you understand?"

The tip of the knife nicked Tall Moccasin's throat and he felt the warm wetness of his own blood. "I do not understand. Let me go. Let me go to my uncle Fire Dancer." He struggled, truly afraid. Uncle Okonsa had gone mad or was possessed by some evil demon. Why else would he behave like this?

Okonsa held tightly to his vest so that Tall Moccasin couldn't wiggle out of it. "You will not repeat what you thought you saw, because you are wrong. Do you hear me? My brother does not have time for a boy's foolish lies. If you tell such lies the flame-haired woman will not want me." He shook Tall Moccasin. "She wants me, you know. She is hot for this man."

Tall Moccasin ceased to struggle. What was Uncle Okonsa saying? None of it made any sense. Surely he didn't think Tall Moccasin so stupid that he didn't know a human scalp when he saw one. He stared up at his uncle, unsure of what to do. He was too far from the village to call for help.

"You will not speak of this incident, boy. Else it might be your scalp that is lost." His uncle raised the knife from his throat to Tall Moccasin's hairline.

Suddenly it became clear to Tall Moccasin. His uncle was saying "Tell and die."

Tall Moccasin began to shake all over. "Yes, Uncle," he whispered.

Okonsa lowered the knife and smiled. "That is a good boy. Now go back to your mama. Soon it will be dark and the families will gather. We have been summoned by our holy man."

The moment Okonsa let go of Tall Moccasin's vest, the boy dropped and rolled. He hit the grass and came up running. He ran until his lungs were bursting, until he smelled the smoke of his mother's cookfire.

Chapter Sixteen

Mackenzie sat on the edge of the sleeping platform and combed out her hair with a brush made of porcupine needles. The brush was a gift from Laughing Woman, as was the dress she wore.

Mackenzie stopped brushing her damp hair to finger the fringe of the leather dress. It was a long-sleeved sheath made of soft, white doeskin with fringe hanging off the shoulder seams and hem. There were tiny sea shells tied on the ends of the fringe that made a chiming sound when she walked. There were matching leggings for colder weather, Laughing Woman had explained. Those were folded neatly and placed in a basket beneath Fire Dancer's sleeping platform.

Laughing Woman had taken Mackenzie with her and her toddlers to pick berries after Mackenzie had finished her breakfast. Then she had taken her to a bathing area at the stream nearby where they had joined other women and children. Despite the language barrier and Mackenzie's apprehension concerning her position in the village, it had been an enjoyable afternoon. The children were curious. The women were friendly.

Mackenzie met Fire Dancer's sister Bird Song, Tall Moccasin's mother, and several pretty cousins. Bird Song had made a point, in broken English, to thank Mackenzie for saving her son's life from the soldiers at Fort Belvadere. The afternoon had ended with all of the women bathing naked in the stream and washing each other's hair. Laughing Woman had made Mackenzie a gift of the white dress after the women had returned to the village, damp and wrapped in soft leather hides.

Mackenzie resumed brushing her hair. It was late afternoon now, and she'd not seen Fire Dancer all day. He had said they would see the holy man at dusk. The waiting was beginning to wear on her nerves. What possible way would the holy man punish her for painting Fire Dancer? Would she be whipped? Tied to a pole and starved? Would they try to burn her at the stake?

Mackenzie had seriously considered attempting to escape, but Fire Dancer had not exaggerated when he said there were numerous guards along the perimeter of the village. Mackenzie had spotted at least four braves patrolling only an hour ago when she'd returned from the stream. Okonsa had been one of them. She guessed there were more guards that she couldn't see.

And if she did run, where would she go? She knew which way was east and west, but because she'd been unconscious when Fire Dancer brought her here, she had no idea in what direction the village lay in relation to the fort.

Her instinct told her that this was not the time to attempt an escape, not when Fire Dancer expected it. Besides, surely her father was searching for her. Mackenzie knew Major Albertson didn't know where the village was, but perhaps if they searched long and hard enough they would find her. Then it wouldn't be up to the holy man or Fire Dancer what became of her.

She glanced up at the portrait of Fire Dancer hanging high above her head in the rafters of the wigwam. He still appeared as handsome to her as he had the first day she'd met him in Fort Belvadere's muddy yard. In truth, he was even more handsome, now that she knew him . . . now that she loved him.

Despite her fear and confusion, she knew she did love him. The realization had come the night he'd climbed through her window, beaten and battered by the soldiers. The night they had first made love. She sighed. When she thought back over the events that had led to their lovemaking, she had to wonder if she had always loved him.

Because of the love they shared, she knew in her heart that he wouldn't allow anyone to harm her, even if he didn't realize it. She studied the portrait. His black eyes, a difficult feature to capture in any model, were perfect, alive with his strength and depth of character. She wished he was here now, to hold her hand, to calm her fears.

She glanced up at the sound of someone entering Fire Dancer's wigwam. The last of daylight spilled into the wigwam. It was him. Once again, he knew when she needed him most.

Feeling the need to occupy her hands, she picked up her brush and began to run it through her long hair.

"Mack-en-zie, this man's sees that Laughing Woman has taken good care of you." He let the flap fall and it was once again semi-dark. The only light that illuminated the wigwam came from the hole in the ceiling.

"She . . . yes." Mackenzie didn't know what to say to him. Did she declare her undying love or tell him how furious she was that he had put her in this position? A part of her wanted to scream and pound him with her fists. A part of her wanted to run into his arms.

Fire Dancer shimmied up the center support post, grabbed his portrait, and brought it down with him.

"We bathed in the stream," she finished lamely as she watched him. "She gave me this beautiful dress."

Fire Dancer set the portrait by the doorway and approached her. "This man must speak to you before we meet with the holy man. There is something I must tell you." He pulled a pair of moccasins from the waistband of his loin skin and placed them on the sleeping platform beside her. His gaze fixed on her, he clasped her hand and pulled her to her feet. He had an odd, almost guilty, look on his face. Then his gaze swept over her garb and his expression changed to one of concern.

"What?" The seashells on the leather fringe rang like tiny silver bells. "You don't like the dress on me?"

"*Mahtah.* It is not that." He still held her hand tightly. "The dress is beautiful. You are beautiful, only . . ."

"Only what?"

"It is a garment for special occasions. Laughing Woman should not have given you her special dress."

"What kind of special occasions do you mean?" She stood in front of him. It seemed only natural that she place her hand on the bare spot at the opening of his porcupine-quilled vest.

"Weddings, naming ceremonies . . . funerals."

Mackenzie took in a sharp breath. Was that fear she heard in Fire Dancer's voice? "He . . . Snake Man, he wouldn't really try to have me—"

Fire Dancer pressed his finger to her lips silencing her. "Do not speak of it. It would be bad luck so close to dusk and the time we must face our holy man."

"But he's not my holy man," she protested firmly. "I asked for no part of this." Then her gaze met his and she knew what he was thinking. "Until I painted your portrait."

"*Ah`.*"

"*Ah`,*" she whispered.

He rested his hands on her waist and stared directly into her eyes. Mackenzie brushed her palm across his bare chest beneath the leather vest and a trill of excitement pulsed through her veins. Her head was filled with images of Fire Dancer touching her, kissing her. In reaction, her breasts tingled and her nipples grew hard beneath the doeskin. She knew she was mad to think of such things. What kind of wanton woman was she that someone might hand down a death sentence to her and all she could think of was lying with a savage?

She felt another shiver of pleasure as Fire Dancer brushed the nape of her neck with his hand. When he leaned to take her mouth with his, she put up no resistance.

"No matter what happens," he whispered. "This man will love you until the sands of time run out."

Mackenzie sighed. That was the most beautiful thing anyone had ever said to her. She slipped her hands around his neck and kissed him again. "How did this happen?" she murmured.

He touched her, his hand skimming over the doeskin dress,

sending waves of pleasure through her. "This man does not know. I did not intend to love you or to take your body."

She leaned her head back so that he could kiss the pulse of her throat. "You did not take me. I gave myself freely because . . ." She didn't know why it was so hard to say. "Because I love you, Fire Dancer."

He smiled. "Those are words that fill this man with hope." He sat down on the edge of the sleeping platform and pulled her onto his lap. "Though for what, I do not know. I do not know what path has been chosen for us."

Mackenzie didn't know anything about fate. She didn't even know if she believed in it. She couldn't think about it now. Her thoughts were too jumbled, her emotions too overwrought. What seemed to matter at this moment was Fire Dancer and her love for him, no matter what was about to happen.

She sat on his lap facing him, her legs straddling him. Outside, someone began to beat a drum, the rhythm so slow that each beat seemed to be the last. Just when she didn't expect another, it came. The anticipation made her breathless. "Do . . . do we have to go soon?"

"Ah." He took a handful of her hair, brought it to his nose and breathed deeply, inhaling the scent of her. "The holy man instructs that you and I must come together and bring the portrait. The entire village will join us along with our chief. We will meet at the center village fire as the sun sets over the tree tops."

His whispered words sent shivers down her spine. She was afraid. Perhaps it was her fear that heightened every sensation she felt. Each time he touched her she trembled.

She brushed her lips against his smooth cheek, upward to the lobe of his ear. "How soon?"

His mouth touched her cheek. "Soon."

Without realizing it, Mackenzie ground her hips against his. The bulge of his loincloth felt so good against her groin. "So soon that we could not . . ." Not knowing a word to use, she let her voice fade.

He chuckled huskily, drawing her closely, lifting beneath her. It was so dark inside the wigwam now that she could only see the outline of his face. "You would have this man after what he has done to you?"

She wrapped her arms around his neck, nipping at his lower lip with her teeth. "Call me mad as May butter," she breathed, raggedly. "It's all I can think of."

He caught the hem of the precious white dress and lifted it so that it bunched around her waist. The air felt cool on her bare buttocks.

She moaned as he crushed his mouth hard against hers. He caressed her bare bottom with his hands and kneaded the sensitive flesh. Her tongue twisted with his in a slow, delicious dance of love and lust.

Did she dare make love with Fire Dancer here in the middle of his village? Outside the cornhusk walls she could hear the drum pounding; she could hear men and women's voices and the sounds of their moccasined feet as they passed. They were headed toward the central campfire . . . waiting for her and for Fire Dancer.

Mackenzie's heart pounded. Her breath came in short gasps as she caught the feminine scent of her desire for Fire Dancer.

She wanted him. It made no sense, but she wanted him, anyway.

She ground her hips against his. Boldly she reached down to untie his loincloth.

As her fingers found the warm, hardening flesh of his manhood, she wondered wildly if there was some truth to the concept of possession of the soul. Only it was Mackenzie that felt as if she was possessed by his man, and not the other way around.

"Mack-en-zie . . ." He groaned in her ear and gripped her hips tighter.

She felt the length of his shaft in her hand and marveled at the delicate softness of his skin and the pleasure he found in her touch. The notion that she could give as much pleasure to him as he had given to her excited her.

He buried his face between her breasts. Through the doeskin she felt her nipples puckering with pleasure. He tugged on the leather ties at the neckline and the dress fell open to her waist.

She sighed with pleasure as he slipped his hand inside the dress
and cupped her bare breast.

She stroked him again and again and he grew longer . . .
thicker in her hand.

"Mack-en-zie . . . Mack-en-zie," he murmured as he chafed
her nipple with the pad of his thumb. "You truly do possess
me, woman of my heart."

She smiled at his sweet words. It was completely dark in
the wigwam now. The last rays of the sun no longer shone
through the hole in the roof. Surely it was time they joined
the others, yet joining here in the darkness was all she could
think of.

Mackenzie's breath came in short pants. The beat of the drum
was faster now, pounding urgently in her ears. Her heartbeat
matched the rhythm. All she could think of was her compelling
need to feel him inside her. She attempted to slide off his lap
to lie on the bed, but he stopped her.

"*Mahtah,*" he crooned. "Do not leave me in such need. Sit
here, *kitehi.*"

Her eyes widened. "Here?" she whispered.

"*Ah*. There are many ways for a man and woman to share
their love. This man will show you. It will be pleasure for us
both, I promise."

Trusting him completely, she lifted up on her tiptoes and
allowed him to guide her. With one hand, he found the source
of her desires already wet with want of him. Without a fumble,
he guided his shaft inside her.

Mackenzie moaned in surprise. It felt different this way, but
good . . . so good.

She slipped her hands around his neck. He encircled her hips
with his arms. By rising and lowering on her toes she discovered
that she could control the rhythm of their lovemaking.

Up and down she stroked. Sweat beaded above her upper
lip. Her breath came faster. She thrust faster, matching her pace
to his breathing. His breath quickened and she slowed down.
His breath came more evenly and she stroked faster.

He groaned with pleasure, calling her name, caressing her
back and bare bottom. Soon she could no longer move only to

give him pleasure. Her own desire had become too strong, too overpowering. The urge to drive faster, take him deeper was too intense.

He caught her hands and they laced their fingers together. "Fire Dancer." She called his name with wild abandon, unaware that someone might hear her cries of pleasure.

Her world suddenly burst into a thousand shards of bright light, each twinkle a shudder of pleasure. She felt Fire Dancer's entire body stiffen beneath her and with one last thrust he released his seed into her with a groan of relief.

For a long moment Mackenzie sat perfectly still on his lap, riding the last waves of sensation. Outside she could hear the drums again. Men were chanting. There were no individual sounds, only the drums and the haunting voices.

"We must go, Mack-en-zie," he said, his voice still husky from their lovemaking.

She smoothed the silky black hair on the crown of his head. "This woman knows," she answered simply.

She climbed off his lap and pushed down her dress. She wished he would light a lamp so that she could see his face. It was so dark inside the wigwam that she couldn't see his face.

She heard him stand and search for his loin cloth on the sleeping platform. With a smile, she reached into the bed furs and held it out to him. He made a motion to take it from her with his hand that trembled.

She was touched that she could affect him in such a way. "No," she said softly, pushing his hands away. "Let me." She had watched him do it before. She knew how it tied. She needed no light to see. As she wrapped the soft leather around his bare buttocks and tucked in his manhood, she felt a strange sense of closeness with him she'd not felt before. This closeness was comfortable.

She gave the knot she tied at his hip a pat for good measure. "Done." She glanced up. "There was something you wanted to tell me when you came in?"

"I . . ." He wiped his damp forehead with his hand. "It is nothing. This is not the time." He reached behind her to the sleeping mat. "This man brought you a gift. Moccasins. Sit and I will put them on you."

They both looked toward the door at the sound of the door flap moving. It was Laughing Woman. Mackenzie felt flustered. What if she had come in only a few moments before? Mackenzie would have been mortified to have been caught in the act . . . and sitting on his lap for heaven's sake.

"It is time you come to the great fire," Laughing Woman said simply. "Snake Man and chief wait."

Mackenzie could feel her cheeks burning with embarrassment. She couldn't see Laughing Woman's face and yet she got the impression that the woman knew what they had been doing. Before Mackenzie could say anything the flap fell and she was gone.

"Fire Dancer, who is she?"

He turned to her. "She is Laughing Woman, of course."

"No. Who is she? To you." She felt a tightening in her throat. "Is that what you came to tell me? Please say she's not your wife."

"Laughing Woman is not my wife. This man would not have been free to make love with you if he had a wife. Now sit and let me place the moccasins on your feet."

She sat down and dangled her bare feet over the edge of the bed. "Where did you get them?" Even in the darkness she could see that the moccasins were made of white doeskin like her dress.

Each touch a caress, he slid her foot gently into the buttery leather. "My mother's wigwam."

She stared at his bowed head. Her woman's sense of intuition told her he did not give the whole truth. "They were meant for Laughing Woman, weren't they?" It was a question, not an accusation.

He tied the moccasin tight on her foot and reached for the other. "This is not the time to speak of this matter, Mack-en-zie. We must turn our thoughts to that which is more important." He tied the other moccasin and took her hand, raising her off the bed. "Come. We must go."

Mackenzie swallowed against her fear and took her place at

Fire Dancer's side. He picked up the portrait and carried it as they stepped out of the privacy of the wigwam and into the unknown.

Joshua Watkins warmed his hands over the open camp fire in the center of the fort compound. It was late at night and a chilling breeze blew through the treetops. All around him soldiers patrolled the palisade walls.

Josh cleared his throat. "You have to let me go, Major, with or without soldiers. I'm not under your command. You can't make me stay."

Major Albertson stood directly across the campfire and puffed on his long-stemmed Dutch pipe. "It's not because I don't want you to go, boy." He sounded worn out. "It's not because I don't want to find her, but you're young and you're inexperienced."

"Not as young as I was two weeks ago."

Albertson gazed at Josh, the firelight flickering across his face. "Guess you're right on that one. An Indian attack does that to a man. Some it strengthens, others it breaks down. It broke Lieutenant Allen. I sent him home to England babbling about his mother's pudding. You . . ." With his boot, he scuffed the dirt that had finally dried in the yard. "I've seen you grow up fast. I've seen you act like a man. You've been a great help to me these last few days since the attack. More of a help than some of my officers."

Josh hooked his thumbs into the waistband of his wool breeches. "I gotta go, Harry. Her father's dead. It's my place to find her." *And I was the one that shot her,* he thought. "To make sure she really is all right."

Josh hadn't told anyone what had happened that night. He was too embarrassed, too horrified by his own actions, his own stupidity, to confess.

Albertson sighed and scratched his beard. "Hell, Josh." He sounded choked up. "I hate to be the one to say this but, you know she's got to be de—"

"Don't say it," Josh warned. He kept his voice low, but he

wanted the major to know he meant what he said. Mackenzie couldn't have died from the gunshot wound he inflicted. It could only have been a graze. There'd been no blood. "She's not dead. I know Mackenzie. She's a survivor. She'd do whatever she had to live."

Albertson groaned. "If I can accept the fact, you can. Josh, you don't know these redskins like I do. They'd not give her a chance to escape. They—"

"With all due respect, there's no need for us to be gettin' into this discussion again, Major." Josh stared across the campfire at him. "I'm going out looking for her. I've found a half-breed scout willing to lead me. He knows where the Hurons and the Shawnee winter. He thinks he can help me find her."

"For a price."

"Aye, for a price. But hell, I got Mr. Daniels' money. I got his tavern and trading post back on the Chesapeake now." Josh fought the tears that stung the backs of his eyeballs. "But without Mackenzie, without my woman, I got nothin'." He wiped his runny nose with the sleeve of his coat. It was a coat Mackenzie had patched for him just last winter. "You understand what I'm saying?"

"I understand. Hell, I wish I could go with you." He looked away. "But facts are facts and my first responsibility is to my men. Without reinforcements, I can't send any soldiers with you. I just can't." He put out his hand. "If you wait another week or so, maybe the fresh troops will arrive. Maybe—"

"With all due respect, I can't wait, sir. Winter is coming in fast. The first snow will fly soon." Josh held out his hand in goodwill. "I gotta go now before it's too late."

Major Albertson took his hand and clasped it tightly. "Good luck. I hope to hell you find her. I really do."

Josh released the major's hand, tipped his hat and walked away from the campfire. "Don't you worry. I will. I will because I know Mackenzie's countin' on me."

Chapter Seventeen

Mackenzie was so afraid as she walked past the empty wigwams that her feet were numb in her new white moccasins. But the drums called, and she walked beside Fire Dancer, her chin high, her back straight.

No one, man or woman, red or white, would call her a coward. In the remote possibility that she would die at the hands of the Shawnee, she knew she had led a good life, better than most. She had a father that cared for her and a man who loved her. No one could take that away from her. Not Laughing Woman, not Fire Dancer's father, the chief, not even the holy Snake Man. If she went to her grave tonight, it would be with the thought that she had truly lived because she had loved.

Not that she would give up without a fight . . .

"You must not speak at the communal fire," Fire Dancer whispered, breaking her reverie. "It is not your place."

"I'm just supposed to stand there and let some snake person hand down my sentence?"

"It must be approved by the chief."

She gripped his arm. She had not met the chief or Fire Dancer's mother yet. "But he would not see me harmed, would he? Because I'm your . . . I'm your woman." She wished she could see into his eyes. They had never defined their relationship. They hadn't had a chance. "I *am* your woman, right?"

Fire Dancer patted her hand that gripped his arm so tightly. "You are my woman. This man is your man. Sometimes we must allow ourselves to be swept down the path of the unknown. We must trust fate and the great *Tapalamawatah.*"

She stepped easier beside him. *Fire Dancer's woman.* She wasn't sure exactly what that meant, but it gave her strength to keep walking.

Ahead a huge campfire blazed. More than a hundred men, women, and children gathered around the circle of bright light. All black eyes were focused on her and Fire Dancer.

Mackenzie sucked in a strangled breath, fighting the sense of panic in her chest. "Fire Dancer wouldn't let me die," she repeated beneath her breath like a chant. "He won't. He loves me."

Fire Dancer released her arm and walked ahead. Mackenzie fell in behind him, sensing her role.

The circle of men and women parted and allowed Fire Dancer and Mackenzie to enter the inner circle. The drums beat in a frenzied crescendo. The men shouted words she didn't understand.

An old man, his face wrinkled by time, stood close to the blazing fire. Two long white braids framed his sunken cheeks and a snake made a stole around his shoulders. Another snake coiled on the ground at the old man's feet, and yet another protruded from a leather bag he wore on his shoulder.

Mackenzie feared she would stumble. It hadn't occurred to her that the man might bring his damned snakes with him.

Fire Dancer caught her eye and made the hand sign for the word snake. She could have sworn she saw a teasing smile on his face.

The gesture was enough to calm her nerves and strengthen her resolve. It was a private joke between them. Only she knew that he had once feared snakes. She made the hand sign at her side in response. He gave a slight nod and returned his attention to the holy man.

The drums stopped and the voices abruptly ceased. No one

moved; not a child peeped. There was only silence and the crackling of the fire.

Fire Dancer walked to Snake Man. He nodded in obvious reverence and said something in Shawnee. The old man responded. Next Fire Dancer spoke to the middle-aged woman standing proudly beside the holy man.

Who was she? She seemed too young for Snake Man's wife. Perhaps she was his daughter or his assistant, Mackenzie surmised.

The woman, dressed in a dyed red doeskin dress very similar to the one Mackenzie wore, nodded regally to Fire Dancer, then to Mackenzie.

Mackenzie nodded, but did not smile because the woman did not smile. She wondered where the chief, Fire Dancer's father, was.

Fire Dancer switched to English. "Greetings, oh great chief and holy man of the Shawnee."

Chief? Mackenzie was confused. Snake Man wasn't the chief; he was the holy man. Did that mean that this woman was the chief? How was that possible? A woman? Where was Fire Dancer's father? Mackenzie thought he was the chief.

The old man lifted his jutting chin in Fire Dancer's direction but made no indication he saw Mackenzie.

The woman smiled. It was Fire Dancer's smile.

Mackenzie stared at her. This had to be his mother.

"Greetings, Mack-en-zie of the Brit-ish," the woman said in a loud, capable voice. "I am *M^ shwahwee Wahkochathee,* of the turtle clan of the Shawnee. Red Fox in your Ing-lish *manake* words."

"Greetings, Red Fox," Mackenzie replied, relieved she was able to respond sensibly. "This woman would thank you for your care during my illness."

The old woman's black-eyed gaze did not stray. She watched Mackenzie closely. "It was not I who cared for you, but my son—"

So she *was* Fire Dancer's mother . . .

" . . . and Laughing Woman," Red Fox finished.

Mackenzie did not break eye contact. "This woman understands,'' she responded in the formal Shawnee manner, ''but this woman still thanks you. Without your approval, I would think I would not have been permitted to enter the village, and your son would not have been permitted to care for me as well as he has.''

A smile tugged on the corner of Red Fox's mouth as her gaze swept from Mackenzie to her son and back to Mackenzie again. ''Fire Dancer of the Thunder Sky was right when he spoke of you, Mack-en-zie.'' The chief raised her hand, dismissing Mackenzie with a turn of her wrist. ''Let us begin. *Muneto Eelenee.*''

Everyone's attention once again focused on the holy man. Mackenzie tried not to look at the snake that slithered at his feet or the one wrapped around his neck that flickered its forked tongue.

The old man barked something in Shawnee.

''Ah`.'' Fire Dancer offered the portrait of himself he carried under his arm.

The holy man took the portrait with shaky hands and leaned it against a large rock at his feet. He produced a bleached white turtle shell rattle from his leather snake bag and shook it, chanting in the ancient language. His sing-song voice rose into the treetops with the wisps of smoke.

Fire Dancer took one step back so that he stood beside Mackenzie.

The old man danced around the snake and the portrait on the ground, with tiny, rehearsed steps. He chanted and shook his rattle. The drums picked up the beat and the Indians clapped.

Mackenzie was overwhelmed by sounds of the Shawnee. She had no idea what the old man was saying. Fire Dancer listened intently.

Mackenzie whispered in Fire Dancer's ear. ''What is he saying?''

''Hsst. He tells a story. Silence!''

Mackenzie had a nearly uncontrollable urge to run. She felt as if she was being propelled through the air with no way to govern the speed or destination. She knew that what the old man was saying had something to do with her. She just didn't know what.

The chanting and dancing went on for a few minutes until the music came to a sudden halt. The Indians all raised their fists in a shout and fell silent.

Mackenzie watched Fire Dancer, wishing she could read his thoughts. What was happening?

The Snake Man raised the turtle rattle over his head, gave it one more shake, and spoke rapidly.

Mackenzie had learned a few Shawnee words from Fire Dancer and from Laughing Woman, but Snake Man spoke so rapidly that she had no idea what he was saying.

Fire Dancer pulled his lips back in a taut grimace. *"Mahtah."*

Mackenzie spotted movement in the crowd and heard a woman cry out in angst. Laughing Woman bolted from the circle of light, her cheeks wet with tears, and disappeared into the darkness.

Mackenzie wanted to go after her and comfort her. Laughing Woman had been so good to her. Mackenzie knew that she had something to do with Laughing Woman's tears. It had something to do with what the Snake Man had said and what Fire Dancer protested.

Mackenzie whipped back around and faced the holy man. He still chanted in Shawnee. Fire Dancer stood with his legs spread, his arms crossed over his partially bare chest. He set his jaw in anger.

What was the sentence? Were they going to kill her? Was that why Laughing Woman had fled? Was this really funeral attire Mackenzie wore?

Mackenzie stepped forward. She'd not stand quietly behind Fire Dancer while some old man with a snake around his neck issued a death warrant. "What is it?" she demanded of Fire Dancer. When he didn't respond immediately, she grabbed his muscular forearm.

The crowd gasped in unison.

"I said, what the blessed bloody hell is going on here?" Mackenzie shouted. "Does he want to kill me?"

"It is not death he sentences you to," Fire Dancer said, his voice grave. "It is marriage."

Mackenzie felt nothing but numbness. "M . . . marriage? To you?"

Fire Dancer did not meet her gaze. "*Ah*. Our holy man says that if part of a man's soul must be possessed by a woman, it is best if he be possessed by his wife."

Mackenzie took a stumbling step backward. She heard Fire Dancer's words, yet she couldn't believe them. Surely this snake man couldn't force Fire Dancer to marry her. She was in complete shock . . . but at the same time she felt a crushing sense of disappointment. Fire Dancer was agitated. He obviously didn't want to marry her.

"I . . . I won't marry him," Mackenzie said. She took a step back from the holy man and Red Fox. If Fire Dancer didn't want to marry her, she certainly wasn't going to marry him. "You can't make me. I . . . I'm a Christian." All she could think of was that she wanted to turn and run. Run and keep running. "I'm a citizen of the British empire. I . . . I have rights."

Fire Dancer grabbed her arm and pulled her back toward him. "Silence. I told you, you must not speak. This holy man has the right to issue a death warrant. Don't you understand?" His black-eyed gaze met hers and the look in his eyes told her he was serious. She really could have died.

"Fire Dancer," she whispered. "This . . . this isn't what you want, is it? You don't really want me to be your wife."

"This man—"

A man's loud voice interrupted Fire Dancer. "*Muneto Eekwaiwah!*" Okonsa broke away from the circle of men and women. He said something else in Shawnee.

Mackenzie, in confusion, looked to Fire Dancer for interpretation.

"Okonsa says he protests the marriage," Fire Dancer whispered. He still held her tightly against him. "He says we cannot force you to marry me. He says it will only cause more trouble between the Shawnee and the British."

Snake Man barked something at Okonsa.

Red Fox chimed in.

Okonsa answered in short, abrupt sentences.

Red Fox spoke again, and Okonsa lowered his gaze.

Fire Dancer glanced at Mackenzie. She shook with a mixture of fear, anger, anguish. "What? What's going on?"

"Our mother tells Okonsa to be silent. He may not interfere. My mother declares this a spiritual matter rather than a political one. It is not the village's decision, it is Snake Man's."

Snake Man picked up his snake from the ground, draped it around his neck, and wobbled away.

The crowd broke up and the men and women began to mill about. They all spoke at once in their native tongue.

Mackenzie stared in skepticism as the old man wandered off into the darkness, muttering to himself. "That's it," she whispered. "No discussion?"

Fire Dancer released her arm. "It would be so bad to become this man's wife?"

She could have sworn she heard distress in his tone. "Well, no . . . Yes . . . I . . ." She didn't know what to say. He'd caught her completely off guard. A moment ago he acted as if he didn't want to marry her and now . . . "Fire Dancer . . ." She gazed into his black eyes. "This should be between you and me. They can't force me to marry you or anyone else."

"No? Is that not what your people do all the time? You wed off your daughters to men they have never met? Men who will never love them and care for them?"

Mackenzie was so rattled by Snake Man's edict that she couldn't think clearly. She was making such a mess of everything. "That . . . that's different."

He lifted a haughty black eyebrow. He was angry with her, and she didn't know why.

"How?" he demanded.

"Colonial women are married off to colonial men, not—"

"Savages?" he cut in.

She had hurt his feelings and she didn't mean to. "Fire Dancer—"

"Greeting, daughter to be," Red Fox interrupted. She smiled proudly as if her son had just been betrothed to the king's daughter. "It will be good to have you as a daughter. Better that you will make this woman a grandmother again. My grandson, Tall Moccasin, grows to be such a man that he does not have time for old women."

Mackenzie didn't know how to respond. She hadn't expected Red Fox to be pleased by the thought of her son marrying a white woman. "Th . . . thank you. I . . . I didn't realize that you were chief. Fire Dancer didn't tell me. I thought he meant that his father was chief."

"His father, chief?" She tipped back her head and laughed. "He-Whose-Name-Cannot-Be-Spoken was a good man but not a chief man." She touched Mackenzie's sleeve. "Come to this woman's wigwam tomorrow. We will speak. This woman would like to know the woman who will make her son happy." With a smile, Red Fox walked off.

Mackenzie faced Fire Dancer. She felt like she was hurling through space again. "Can't we talk about this?"

He took her arm, none-too-gently. "The holy man has spoken. You will have to accept your marriage to this *savage.*"

She shoved his arm away angrily. "I never said that. I love you."

The walked through the village, past wigwams. Some of the Shawnee watched them with interest.

He stared straight ahead and spoke softly in English. "But you do not want to marry me?"

"I . . ." She exhaled. He acted like he didn't want to marry her, and yet, he seemed hurt by the idea that she might not want to marry him. The man made no sense. "I don't know what I want. Don't you understand?"

He raised the doorflap to his wigwam for her. "This man is trying to understand."

She ducked in and he followed. He lit an oil lamp. It glowed softly, casting shadows across his face. A cricket chirped under the bed.

She stood in the center of the wigwam, her arms wrapped around her waist. "I need some time to think about this." Her head was so full of thoughts, her chest so tight with emotions that she had a difficult time finding anything to say that made sense.

"The shaman can't just tell me to marry you. You . . . you didn't even ask me. And—" she lifted her hand weakly "—what about Laughing Woman?" She dropped it to her hip. "The idea of you marrying me obviously upset her. Why?"

He crouched at the firepit and fed the red coals slivers of wood. "This man probably would have married her."

He said it so calmly that for a moment she stared at him in disbelief. "What? She was your betrothed?" she sputtered.

"*Mahtah.* It was not official, but everyone knew we would probably wed."

"Including Laughing Woman?"

"*Ah.*"

Mackenzie paced. She fought twinges of jealousy, but mostly she felt badly for Laughing Woman. The woman had been so kind to Mackenzie. Surely she suspected what was between Mackenzie and Fire Dancer. When she walked into his wigwam earlier, there must have been no doubt. Mackenzie felt an overwhelming sense of guilt. She had stolen another woman's man.

"Why didn't you tell me back at the fort?" Mackenzie demanded angrily. The anger gave her something to hold onto. It made it easier for her to keep her thoughts rational.

"Would it have mattered?" He stood. "Would you have loved this man any less because he was promised to another?"

"I'd never have let myself fall in love with you!" she shouted. Unwelcome tears sprung in her eyes. "I hate you." She grabbed her hairbrush off the sleeping platform. "I hate you for what you've done to me."

He walked to the door.

She hurled the brush at him. "I wish I'd never laid eyes on you."

The brush glanced off his back, and he left the wigwam without another word.

Mackenzie regretted her foolish reaction immediately. She dropped to her knees and buried her arms and face in the furs piled on the sleep platform. Tears welled up in great sobs. No one had ever told her it would be so hard to love someone so deeply.

Fire Dancer stepped out of his wigwam and crouched outside the door, lowering his head to his hands. He was so frustrated by his own turmoil that he didn't know how to deal with Mackenzie's. He knew she loved him as surely as he knew the hairbrush had been flung in fear and anger. But the fact that she hadn't immediately consented to marrying him still hurt.

She didn't want to marry. She said she loved him . . . but not enough to love him forever?

Fire Dancer felt like a fool. Here he was, a Shawnee prince, a warrior, a man who would be chief someday, and he was nearly in tears over a woman. He loved her so much. He didn't like the idea of being told to wed, either, but if a man had to wed, why not wed the woman of his passions? Secretly, perhaps, he had hoped for this sentence all along. Then the decision could be made for him.

But Mackenzie didn't want him—not enough to join him and his life. Did he love her enough to leave his people? It wasn't that simple. He could not leave the Shawnee now. The war was escalating. The Shawnee council was about to choose sides between the French and the British. His mother's people needed him. He could not abandon them, not even for love.

Fire Dancer stood and exhaled slowly. He drew a cleansing breath. Snake Man had spoken. He would marry the fire-haired white woman. It was the only way to keep his soul intact. Mackenzie would come around. He had only to give her time to accept him as her husband. Who else was there for her? She had said herself that she had never loved a man as she loved him. Certainly she had not loved the towheaded Josh Watkins.

But she had loved her father . . .

Fire Dancer stared up into the dark sky. Why hadn't he told her when she'd awakened last night that her father was dead? Why hadn't he told her this evening when he went to his wigwam to tell her?

Because he didn't want hurt her. Because he wanted her to

grow strong. He wanted her to be happy. He wanted her to love him. She would hate him if she knew he was responsible for her father's death. What chance would they have at a good marriage then? Fire Dancer understood the anger she felt for him at this moment. He could deal with her anger. But hate? Could he survive her hatred or would his heart shrink in his chest? Would he perish?

With a heavy heart, Fire Dancer strode through the village. Most of the men and women had retired for the evening. A few gathered at the home firepits for a last smoke of a pipe, or to talk of the day's events. He spoke to no one as he walked, his gazed fixed on a wigwam near the far side of the village. If there was to be any hope for this marriage Snake Man had commanded, there was someone he had to speak with first.

Fire Dancer halted at the wigwam Laughing Woman and her children shared with Mary. Before he had a chance to speak, a soft voice came from inside.

"This woman wondered how long it would be before you came."

Fire Dancer stepped inside the open door. "I must speak with you, Laughing Woman."

She smiled. "I know. Let me say good night to my babies and then I will serve you drink at my hearth."

Fire Dancer stood in the shadows and watched as Laughing Woman knelt at a sleeping platform. She spoke gently to her toddlers, covering them with a sleeping fur. She kissed each one and wished them happy dreams.

Fire Dancer felt a sense of sadness. Laughing Woman would have a made a good wife. She would have been a good mother to their children. She was a good mother. He wished desperately that he had felt passion for her. If he had, he would have married her before he left for the peace negotiations at Belvadere. But there, again, was that path of fate Snake Man had spoken of. It was clear that the marriage between them had never been meant to be. Her children tucked into bed, Laughing Woman crossed the wigwam. She placed her hand gently on his arm. "Let us go outside, friend. My sassafras tea seeps for us."

Outside, at her firepit, Laughing Woman had already set out

two gourd cups. A clay pot of tea rested on a rock near the coals where it would stay warm.

He watched her. She was so beautiful, so exquisite with her thick ropes of black braids and proper black eyes. But they were not blue. And they were not Mack-en-zie's . . . and they did not make his heart sing. "You did expect me, didn't you," he asked.

"*Ah*'." She sat cross-legged on a grass mat. "Sit, rest, Fire Dancer. It has been a long day for you." She poured him a cup of tea. "You know it is not necessary that you come here."

He accepted the cup. "But it is. I came to apologize."

"It is this woman who should apologize. I should not have made a spectacle of myself at the communal fire tonight. I should not have dishonored you or myself by acting like a foolish maiden."

"That was my fault, not yours. The holy man's words took you by surprise." He took a sip, choosing his words carefully. "Before I left, there was an understanding between you and me, Laughing Woman."

"Or at least between your mother and my grandfather, eh?" She laughed.

He smiled, pleased that she could find humor in their situation. He certainly couldn't. "*Ah*'." His drew his lips down in a frown. "But this man led you to believe he would wed you. I led you to believe I would care for you and your children." He raised his chin so that his gaze met hers across the campfire. "This man honestly intended to do so."

"But then you met the white woman with hair the color of flame."

He glanced away. "I met her and I did not use the common sense my mother gave me. I could not resist my attraction to her, though she was forbidden. And as my punishment, she now possesses a part of my soul I cannot regain."

She stared over the rim of her cup. "You truly believe that?"

"*Ah*'. It is true. When I am away from her, I cannot think. I do not feel like myself. We are so different, and yet I am only whole at her side." He shook his head. "It is a terrible thing."

Laughing Woman smiled as if she was an old woman of great wisdom. *"Ah',* love is." She reached across the campfire and took his cup from him. "Now go. Return to your woman and be whole. Do not worry for this woman. I can care for myself."

He rose. "This man is truly sorry for what pain he has caused you."

She didn't get up. "This woman would have married you because you are a good man, Fire Dancer, and you would have been a good father to my children. But I would never have loved you as this woman loved her husband, so it is better this way, I think."

Her smile was infectious. He felt better. He had come here to comfort Laughing Woman, and instead she had comforted him. "Good night," he said as he walked away.

"Good night," she called. "But you go the wrong way, Fire Dancer. Your wigwam is that way." She pointed.

He turned back to her. "This man will spend the night with his brother and allow the white woman to calm her anger. Besides, I have much to do. It is just come to me that I must give her a peace offering and I know what it must be."

Laughing Woman waved and Fire Dancer walked off in the direction of Okonsa's wigwam. For the first time in many weeks, he felt a bright sense of hope in his heart.

Chapter Eighteen

Mackenzie woke to the silence and chill of the morning. Fire Dancer had not returned to the wigwam last night as she hoped and she'd slept restlessly.

She swung her legs over the edge of the sleeping platform, and dragged a sleeping fur with her. The fire had burned to embers and she was cold. She retrieved firewood from a neat pile near the door and carefully fed twigs, then larger pieces of wood to build up the fire.

Sometime in the middle night as she had lain on her back, she had considered going out to search for Fire Dancer. He had to be somewhere in the village. Where could he have gone? His mother's wigwam? Okonsa's? She bit down on her lower lip, not wanting to think the worst. Laughing Woman's?

No. She thought not. It wasn't in his character.

The flames of the fire radiated a soothing heat and Mackenzie extended her hands to warm herself. Last night she'd had a lot of time to think. Fire Dancer said they must wed. It was that or death for her. She had tried to imagine what it would be like to be married to him, to call him husband.

The idea of sleeping each night in Fire Dancer's arms warmed her all over. She tingled with pleasure at the thought of them making love whenever they wanted. But it hurt her deeply that he had not said he *wanted* to marry her. There had been no words of love from him last night, only talk of Snake Man's decree.

Could she make Fire Dancer want to marry her? Could she make him love her enough?

The next question was, did she want to marry him? Could she live like an Indian? Could she become one of the Shawnee? Deep down she knew that would be their only chance at making a marriage. Even if Fire Dancer was willing to try to live on the Chesapeake with her, it would never work. He belonged here in the open forest far from store fronts and rutted roads. Was this were she belonged? Was this her fate?

She thought of her father. She missed him, but she didn't miss her home in the tavern. She didn't miss the life she had led on the Chesapeake. She only missed her painting.

"Mack-en-sie?"

Mackenzie recognized the voice. "Laughing Woman?"

"May this woman come?"

Mackenzie hurried around the fire pit to push open the door flap. "Oh, I'm so glad you're here. I wanted to find you last night, only . . ." She backed up, allowing the woman entrance. "Only I didn't know where to look and I was afraid that if I tried to leave, Fire Dancer . . . someone might think I was trying to escape."

Laughing Women knelt at the firepit, her back to Mackenzie, and placed two clay pots on rocks near the flames. From a small basket, she extracted two fried corncakes and placed them on another rock. "Why you want come to me?"

Mackenzie stood near the door, the deer hide around her shoulders. "I wanted to tell you how sorry I was."

"Sorry?" Laughing Woman rose and dug through various baskets along the wall. "Why sorry? You marry good man. He make nice babies."

Mackenzie felt the heat of her blush. It seemed all Shawnee were blunt with sexual matters. "I wanted to tell you how sorry I was that I . . . I took him."

Laughing Woman glanced up, a wooden trencher in one

hand, a spoon in the other. "Take Fire Dancer? Take where? He take you to Shawnee village, *ah*?" She laughed at her own joke.

Mackenzie couldn't resist a smile. "No, you know what I'm trying to say. I'm sorry that you were going to marry him and I took his affections." This was so hard to explain with the language barrier. "I took his love."

Laughing Woman returned to the fire, signaling for Mackenzie to join her. "Ahhhh." She nodded. "This woman have understand." She patted a mat she covered with a fur. "Sit."

Mackenzie did as she was told.

"You cannot take a woman's man. You cannot take man's heart," she explained. "Fire Dancer of the Thunder Sky give his heart to white *manake*. Mack-en-sie give heart to Shawnee prince."

"I didn't mean for it to happen," Mackenzie confessed. "I wasn't even supposed to speak to him. My father forbade it."

"This woman understand." Laughing Woman placed a corn cake on the trencher and poured maple syrup from one of the small clay pots over it. "Your father say not talk. You catch Shawnee prince with spell of paint." She pushed the wooden plate into Mackenzie's hands with a wink. "Smart woman."

"*Mahtah.*" Mackenzie swept her hair back with her hand. "I didn't understand the part about taking his soul. I wanted to paint him so desperately that I ignored his wishes. I never meant for any of this to happen. He loved you, Laughing Woman."

Her smiling face grew serious. "*Mahtah.*" She took Mackenzie's hand in her small one. "Fire Dancer never love this woman, only like. Laughing Woman never love Fire Dancer, only like. Ad-mire. Laughing woman loved hus-band. Husband dead." She closed her eyes and hugged herself. "Only mem-mor-ies." She opened her eyes again. "Fate bring you and Fire Dancer of Thunder Sky to-geth-er. Fate and paintbrush, understand?"

Mackenzie smiled. "I understand. So you're not angry. I thought you were when you left the fire last night."

Laughing Woman hung her head. "Bad manners. Like Fire

Dancer very so much. Thought he make good husband. This woman feel dis-poin . . .'' Her pretty brow creased. ''What is the word—sorry it would not happen?''

''Disappointment?'' Mackenzie took a bite of the sugared corn cake. It was delicious. ''You were disappointed that Snake Man said Fire Dancer had to marry me?''

''*Ah*ˋ. Dis-ppoint-ment first. Then happy.'' She smiled with exaggeration. ''Happy Fire Dancer happy.''

Mackenzie gave a little laugh. ''Oh, I don't know about that. He didn't seem too pleased to me. He likes sleeping with me well enough, but I don't think it ever occurred to him to marry me.'' She licked the maple syrup from the spoon. ''You know, a white *manake* woman rather than a proper Shawnee woman like you.''

Laughing Woman patted Mackenzie's knee. ''Love is hard for man, even Shawnee man. Give him days. Give him kisses. Make nice. He will want to marry white woman with red hair. Fire Dancer have much love in his heart for his Mack-en-sie, just afraid.''

''You think so?'' Mackenzie looked up hopefully. It was hard to believe Fire Dancer could be afraid of anything. But she could understand fearing love. She was afraid of the intensity of her love for him. ''You really think he loves me?''

''*Ah*ˋ, much.'' She rose. ''Here.'' She tapped her left breast with her fist. ''Much fierce love.'' She waved. ''All will be right, Mack-en-sie. Will see.''

''Wait, where are you going? Can't you stay?''

''No. Have much sorry. Babies hungry. You come this woman's wigwam later. I teach you make corn cakes and stew rabbit to warm Shawnee prince's stomach and heart, yes?''

''Thank you. I will. And thank you for the breakfast.'' Mackenzie took the other corncake. ''It's delicious.''

As Laughing Woman left the wigwam, Fire Dancer entered carrying a leather sack over his shoulder. The doorflap fell behind him and he stood there obviously feeling awkward.

Mackenzie stared at her plate. ''Good morning,'' she said softly.

The tension in the air was as stiff as the bristle of a horsehair paintbrush.

"Good morning," he answered, thin lipped.

So he's not come to talk, she thought wryly. *He's come to stand and look at me.*

But that was unfair. He had made the effort to return to the wigwam. It was her place to make the effort to discuss last night. "I waited for you." She pushed a bite of corncake around her plate. "Last night. You never returned."

"This man went to Okonsa's lodge."

"I wanted to . . . um . . . tell you I was sorry. I shouldn't have thrown the hairbrush at you. It was childish. And I said things I didn't really mean. I don't hate you. I could never hate you. It's just that . . ." She dropped the spoon onto the plate and it clattered. " . . . That I'm very confused right now about how I feel about all this." She swept her arm indicating the wigwam, meaning the village and the Shawnee.

"Confused about your love for me?"

She forced herself to meet his gaze. "No. Not that. I know I love you. I'm just not sure it would work—a marriage between us, I mean. You and I are so different, Fire Dancer. We come from such different worlds."

He knelt beside her. "This man understands." He tapped his temple. "Here this man has many questions. He does not know many answers." His black-eyed gaze locked with hers. "I only know this man loves this woman greatly."

She touched his hand. She wasn't ready to throw herself into his arms, or agree to the marriage yet, but she had an intense desire to comfort him. "That's very sweet of you to say. You know men do not often speak of love among my people. It's not that they don't love, only that they don't know how to express it."

He slipped his hand out from under hers and pulled the leather bag off his shoulder. "This man does not speak well of his feelings, but I can express my love in other ways, Macken-zie." He thrust the flat bag into her arms. "For you, *kitehi.*"

"For me? What is it?" From inside she pulled out two supple

white skins completely void of any hair. She glanced up at him questioningly.

"Look deeper," he urged, obviously pleased with himself.

She dug her hand into the bag and came up with three small red clay pots corked with wooden lids.

"Look again." His black eyes sparkled. "There is one thing more."

This time she brought a hand carved wooden stick with trimmed horsehair bristles tied on the end. "A brush?" she breathed. She glanced up. "You made me a paintbrush?"

He opened one of the clay pots and tipped it to show her what was inside. "See—paint. You must experiment with the colors and the amount of oils. This color came from ink berries." He dipped his finger into the paint and brushed a streak of purple color across the back of his hand. "It is pretty, is it not, Mack-en-zie?"

Paints and a brush. Fire Dancer understood her love for painting. A lump rose in her throat. It was a gift that touched her heart because she knew that it had come from his heart. Her eyes brimmed with silly tears of happiness. "I don't know what to say, but thank you."

"This man has no way to get canvas now, but the hides would be very good, I think, stretched over birch frames. I could make frames this winter, if you would allow me."

"I can't believe you did this for me," she whispered. "You made the brush, the paint, all for me, even after what I did with my paints?"

"It was wrong for you to paint this man's face, but you did not do it to harm me. You did not understand the way of the Shawnee."

"No, I didn't. And I thought because I didn't believe, it meant it wasn't true. The idea that one person could possess a part of another person seemed so absurd." She lifted one shoulder in a shrug. "Now I'm not so sure." She brushed the back of her hand across his cheek and down the solid line of his jaw. "I certainly feel as if you possess a part of me right now, Fire Dancer."

He lifted her hand to his lips and kissed it. "A council

meeting has been called." He released her. "The French have sent a messenger. There are some in my village who would join with them."

She glanced up, recognizing the concern in his voice. "You mean against the British?"

"*Ah*."

"They would do that?"

He caught a lock of bright hair and twirled it around his finger. "*Ah*, if it is what they believe would be best for Shawnee."

She held one of the tiny paint pots tightly in her fingers. "I'm English. That would make me the enemy, Fire Dancer."

"No. If you married me, we would make you Shawnee. You would forever be protected by my mother's name."

A sigh settled in her throat. Mackenzie didn't understand these matters. How could she be Shawnee simply by them saying so. It made so little sense . . ."

He squeezed her hand. "I must meet with my mother before council begins."

Mackenzie placed the precious painting supplies one by one back in the beaded bag. "Your mother the chief, you mean?"

He pressed his hands to his powerful thighs and rose. "I am sorry I did not explain that it was my mother who was chief. This man did not really consider that you would not understand it was she who ruled our people. My father is dead."

"I'm sorry."

"He died last winter of a *manake* illness. It has not been long and it is not good to speak of the dead so soon after their spirits have risen."

"I understand." She walked to the door with him. The seashells on her dress made a musical sound as she walked. "I was just surprised that a woman could be a chief. Colonial women don't rule anything but their households."

He frowned, obviously puzzled. "White *manake*, they make no sense. Why would a woman not be chief if she is most qualified?"

Mackenzie laughed. She had a lot to learn about the Shawnee if she was going to try to become one of them, wasn't she? "Why indeed," she agreed with a grin.

At the doorway he brushed his lips against hers in a gentle, husbandly kiss. "Tonight I will come here when the Council meeting is over and we will talk." He squeezed her hand. "The holy man says that we must marry, but he does not decree happiness. That must be up to you and to me, my beautiful maid with hair of flames and a temper to match."

He met and held her gaze for what seemed a sweet eternity, then strode away.

Fire Dancer sat cross-legged beside his mother and listened as he watched the smoke of the center fire curl upward toward the hole in the ceiling, then disappear into the darkness of the night. Torches burned inside the communal wigwam. The stench of the bear grease mingled with smell of the herbs that smoked in Snake Man's incense pot.

The council meeting was not going as well as Fire Dancer had hoped. The entire village had been here for hours talking . . . arguing. An hour ago he'd had to break up a fist fight between two braves twice his own age.

The French had sent a messenger by way of a half-breed Mohawk scout. Fire Dancer didn't like the scout and he didn't trust him. He said the French did not hold him accountable for the attack and murder of Major DuBois. They had found the guilty Huron party and strung them all up by their necks until they were dead.

Okonsa and many of the men and women of the village felt that because the English believed it was the Shawnee who had attacked Belvadere, the Shawnee had no choice but to join with the French. It was Okonsa who led the group bent on siding with the French.

Fire Dancer argued that he could speak with Major Albertson and explain that it had been the same Hurons who had attacked the British fort. His men had only fought to defend themselves and to escape. Albertson was a reasonable, intelligent man. He had means of gaining information from the French side. He could easily confirm that it was a Huron war party that had murdered DuBois and had attacked Fort Belvadere.

But Okonsa would not hear of it. He felt that the French were offering their protection for very little in return other than the Shawnee's word of support. Many of the other villagers agreed. They feared that because of the attack on Fort Belvadere, the British could not be trusted, that, at some point they would seek revenge.

Fire Dancer attempted to listen patiently to another of Okonsa's diatribes. His cousin strutted back and forth speaking with a loud voice and exaggerated gestures. Tonight he had an aura about him that made him handsome as well as charming. He spoke with such confidence that Fire Dancer could understand why some of the frightened Shawnee could so easily be persuaded by his words.

"*Neekeyah,*" Fire Dancer whispered to his mother, "Okonsa repeats himself again and again."

"Silence." She glared. "Each man and woman has a right to speak his or her thoughts at council. You know that."

Fire Dancer groaned. "But he monopolizes the conversation."

"Hsst." She patted her son's knee. "Above all else, a good chief is a good listener. You will sit on my blanket one day, son, and you must prepare yourself for that time."

Fire Dancer knew his mother was right. She usually was. He picked up his water skin and took a long pull. He was tired and he was hungry. He wanted to be with Mackenzie, not here with this unrest.

Okonsa finally sounded as if he was winding down his argument. Fire Dancer raised his index finger to be recognized.

"I am not done, brother," Okonsa said, his tone so polite it was insincere.

"You are done, son," Red Fox spoke up. "Sit. You have made this woman a winter older listening to your prattle."

Okonsa took his seat beside Battered Pot and the other men who followed him. He did not dare go against the chief at a council meeting, even if she was his surrogate mother.

"You wish to speak, Fire Dancer of the Thunder Sky?"

Fire Dancer stood. "If I may, great chief."

She snapped her fingers. "Make it quick."

The council broke up into softly spoken conversations as was appropriate when a new speaker was called. It gave the speaker a moment to prepare and the council members a moment to comment to those sitting near them.

Fire Dancer took a deep breath, as he gazed from one face to the next. These were the men and women he had grown up with, the men and women he had loved since he was a child. They were not just his neighbors. They were his brothers and sisters, and mothers and fathers, and grandparents. They were also his race and it was for his race that he was most concerned.

Fire Dancer raised his hand and the chatter ceased immediately. "As our chief suggested, I will make this short and it will be my final words for the night. You already know my feelings on this matter. I do not think it is time to choose sides between the French and the British. If this decision was solely up to me, I would wait out the winter like a fox in his hole and see what blows in on the spring breeze."

"So fearful to make a decision he would make no decision at all," scoffed Okonsa.

Fire Dancer gazed at his cousin. "Listen to my brother's words. He speaks out of anger . . . out of his desire to seek revenge for the deaths of his parents so many years ago. We all know that he wants to kill Englishmen because it was Englishmen who murdered his mother and father."

"It is not true," Okonsa defended. "I want what is best for the Shawnee. To fight with the French is best."

Fire Dancer ignored his cousin's rude interruption. "I do not mean to say that my brother's intentions are meant to be harmful. My question is, would you listen to man who makes his decisions with his emotions rather than his head?"

"Ha! Look who calls the cardinal red! You do not want to fight the British because you take a Colonial woman to your sleeping mat."

"That is enough, Okonsa," Red Fox barked.

Okonsa lowered his gaze apologetically. "I am sorry for my rudeness, brother. Go on with your words."

Fire Dancer tucked his hands behind his back. "I do not

want to join with the French, my beloved friends, not because I do not want to fight the British, but because I think it is unwise that we join in this conflict at all.'' He paused to let his words sink in before continuing. "I love you all as I would love my brother or sister, or mother or father or grandparents so I say this in respect. You do not understand the white men as I do. Perhaps it is because part of my spirit is possessed by a white woman, I do not know. What I do know is that English or French, they are the same in that the one thing that drives them above all else—'' he made a fist ''—their desire to possess land.''

A murmur rippled among the council members.

Fire Dancer continued. "We know that land belongs only to the mother earth and the father in the sky, but they do not. They exchange wampum for soil, and if a man does not leave that soil, they will murder him for it. That is what this fighting between the French and British is about. Who possesses land— land that we have loved and protected for more years than the generations can count, brothers and sisters.''

Fire Dancer now had their attention with his passionate words. He only hoped that they would understand. "Do you not see? No matter which side wins, we will lose. We will lose this land we stand on now . . . and we will lose our lives . . . the lives of our sons and daughters.''

"So what do you say?'' asked his shy sister, Song Bird. "Do we lie down and die brother?''

"No.'' He thrust out his jaw. "We have two choices, perhaps three. If you want to fight, we could unite as redmen, Shawnee, Cherokee, Lenape, Huron, Mohawk, Menomineee, and send the white men back into the ocean they came from.'' He sighed. "Or, we could move west to the land of our teepee cousins where no white men yet sets foot.''

"Our third choice?'' Song Bird asked.

"Learn to live beside the white. Share the land. Lose a part of ourselves and our culture, but save our people.''

Okonsa clutched his chest. "Brother, such a dramatic speech. I am touched.'' He let his hands fall. "Touched, but not convinced.''

Fire Dancer took his place beside his mother. "I have nothing more to say. You know my thoughts. You also know that I am loyal to the Shawnee and I will follow the path they choose as is my place."

Red Fox stroked her son's head with affection before turning her attention back to the council. "We have heard the arguments. Let us take the vote and be done. I pass a basket. Take the stick given to you when you entered this lodge and cast your vote. A half stick votes we join the French. A whole stick votes we choose no side yet."

The chief handed the basket to her left. Slowly it was passed around the circle. Fire Dancer closed his eyes and tried not to listen for the sound of breaking sticks. All too soon the basket came to him and with a quick prayer he dropped in his whole stick.

It took Red Fox only a minute to turn around to the blanket behind her and count the sticks. "It is decided," she said solemnly, as she turned back to face her people. "The vote was very close, which is disturbing. Only one vote made the final decision."

Everyone stared at Red Fox, silent in anticipation.

Red Fox sighed and when she spoke she sounded older than she had only moments before. "It has been decided that we will place our alliance in the hands of the Frenchmen."

There was a great cheer from Okonsa's side of the council circle. Everyone began talking at once.

Fire Dancer felt his heart fall in his chest. It was the wrong decision.

"Our war council will meet with the Mohawk delegate tomorrow," Red Fox said above the din. "We will compose a reply to the French and state our terms at that time." She rose and lifted her hands above her head. "Go in peace, brothers and sisters, until we meet again."

The crowd immediately dispersed as everyone separated into groups to talk of the decision. The feeling of doom in Fire Dancer's chest was so tight that he couldn't breathe. He didn't want to speak to anyone, only to get out of the council lodge and into the fresh night air. He kissed his mother good night and strode for the door.

Just when Fire Dancer thought he'd made his escape undetected, Okonsa grabbed his arm. "Ah hah, you flee."

Fire Dancer halted. He was not in the mood for Okonsa's games. "I do not flee. The meeting is over. I have matters to attend to if the war council meets tomorrow." Fire Dancer lead the war council. "We must send messages to our sister villages as well as a missive to the French."

Okonsa stroked his scalp lock. "I do not want you to take what I said here tonight personally. I do not attack you, brother."

Fire Dancer gazed into Okonsa's black eyes. Okonsa's words were honorable, and yet Fire Dancer was suspicious. He could feel the heat of Okonsa's hate for the British. "I do not take your words to heart, brother. I am only concerned for their wisdom."

Okonsa gripped Fire Dancer's shoulder. "All will be well, you will see. You would be better to turn your thoughts to your own hearth. I hear that your wife-to-be is not pleased with your impending marriage." He cupped his testicles beneath his loincloth and re-adjusted them. "Perhaps her affections lie elsewhere, eh?" He laughed and walked away, surrounded by men who had no doubt cast a short stick in the vote.

Fire Dancer walked into the starry night, but instead of heading toward his wigwam, he walked toward the stream. On the one hand he felt a need to feel Mackenzie's arms around him. On the other, he did not want to be near her when he was in such a foul mood. He needed some time to think and cool his anger.

Not far from the place where the Shawnee bathed, Fire Dancer found his favorite sitting rock. This was where he liked to come when he needed to think. He climbed up on the rock, folded his legs beneath him and leaned his back against a tree. The warmth of the day's sun still radiated from the granite. It was peaceful here with the chirp of the night insects, the rustle of falling leaves, and the gurgle of the water.

A twig snapped behind Fire Dancer and he slid his hand to his knife. ''Who goes there?'' he called softly in Shawnee. All he could think of was that the British had found the village and they were all about to die.

Chapter Nineteen

Fire Dancer rose, the moonlight reflecting off the blade of his skinning knife. He stared into the darkness and silently chastised himself for allowing someone to get so near to him undetected. What kind of Shawnee warrior was he? Before he had gone to Fort Belvadere, before he had met Mackenzie, this would never have happened. He had grown soft.

"Identify yourself," he said quietly in Shawnee.

"Fire Dancer?"

He recognized the voice immediately and relaxed his arm, lowering the knife against his thigh. "Mack-en-zie? What do you do here so late at night without escort? Do you understand the danger—" He stepped around the tree to find her standing in the moonlight . . . the knife he had given her drawn.

He smiled. She was a vision of beauty in her doeskin dress with the dangling seashells and a fur tied around her shoulders for warmth. She had braided two strips of her long red hair and tied them with leather straps as was the Shawnee custom. She wore his gift-moccasins.

Fire Dancer's chest swelled with pride. Her skin was not red. She was not born of a line of Shawnee who had walked this land for more than three thousand years ... but she had the heart of a Shawnee. Here was where she belonged.

"You can sheathe your knife," he said with a grin. "I will not harm you, I swear it." He raised his hands in surrender. "I am yours to do with as you please."

She laughed as she slid the knife into its sheath on her waist. "The scary thing is, I believe I'd have used it if you'd been one of those Hurons."

He caught one of her braids and give it a tug. "This man believes you would." She fixed her green-eyed gaze on him. "Laughing Woman told me I might find you here."

"Ah, on my rock." He climbed back up on the granite slab and patted the place beside him. "Will you join this man?" He offered his hand to assist her.

She climbed up beside him and rested her head beside his against the tree trunk. "Laughing Woman also told me what the council decided." She slipped her hand into his. "Which makes what is between us more difficult."

"*Ah.*" Her warm hand comforted him. "I believe it is the wrong choice, but it is the village's decision. Do you understand this man's words?"

She squeezed his hand. "I understand, Fire Dancer. It's not necessarily your choice to fight us ... the British. And I don't blame you." She sighed. "Hell's bells, none of this makes any sense to me any more. Choosing sides, fighting over land. The English, my people, came here and took what belonged to you. The French did the same. Now they fight over which patches of land belong to whom, when you and I both know it belongs to neither." She rested her head on his shoulder. "I can't blame your people for siding with the French, Fire Dancer. I won't."

He took her hand and raised it to his lips. It was peaceful here in the forest. It felt so good to sit beside Mackenzie and feel the heat of her body beside his.

This would be a good time to tell her about her father, he thought. *About what happened and why.* He glanced sideways at her beautiful face with its speckled sun spots and vibrant green eyes. He loved her so deeply that he despised the idea of hurting her, even indirectly. But the truth had to be told—

"Fire Dancer?" She interrupted his thoughts before he had a chance to speak.

"Yes?"

"Tell me the truth. Do you want to marry me? I mean do you really want me to be your wife, or are you just willing to have me because it's best for the village?"

Fire Dancer thought for a moment before he replied because he wanted to answer honestly. If Mackenzie had the courage to ask this question, he had to have the courage to answer. Of course, he already knew deep in his heart what that answer was. "If this man could make a choice of the woman he would live the rest of his days with, the woman who would give him the gift of a child, *Tapalamawatah* willing, it would be Mack-en-zie Daniels of the English *manake*. If this man could have one person to love and be loved by, it would be you."

She smiled that smile that made his heart sing. "Fire Dancer of the Thunder Sky, did you just ask me to marry you?"

"No."

Her brow creased. "No?"

He climbed over her and leaped off the rock. He went down on one knee, as he would to honor a great chief or Shaman, and took her hand and lowered his head submissively. The moonlight fell across her face in a halo of gold.

"Mack-en-zie, *now* this man humbly asks you to wed him. Will you allow our hearts, our souls, our bodies to be bound forever more, not just in this life but in the life hereafter? This man begs you—be his wife ..."

Still seated on the rock, she clasped his hand and pulled him to his feet. She laced her fingers through his and stared at him, her eyes shining with tears. "I'll be your wife," she whispered.

Fire Dancer wrapped her in his arms and kissed her hair, her forehead, her cheekbones, the tip of her nose. His heart sang with joy. Mackenzie would be his wife. She loved him. With her love, he could fight the British, if he had to. He could fight the world.

Mackenzie returned his kisses, her hand warm on his bare chest beneath his vest. She nuzzled his neck and all thoughts of discussing her father's death blew away with the falling leaves. Now was not the time, he told himself as he lowered her to the mossy bank. His need to possess her burgeoned beneath his leggings. She was so happy they were to be wed. How could he ruin that happiness?

Tomorrow, he would tell her . . . or if not tomorrow, the next day.

Two weeks later, on a warm fall morning, Mackenzie sat on her knees in the rear of the dugout and dragged her fingers through the spray as the boat cut smoothly through the water. The sun shone brightly on Fire Dancer's bare back. With each stroke the muscles of his powerful shoulders and biceps flexed and the dugout canoe gained a length on the river.

Married, Mackenzie thought as she watched Fire Dancer paddle. *I'm married to an Indian.* The extraordinary thing was that it didn't seem so extraordinary. It seemed right. When Mackenzie looked back on her life it was as if every moment up until now had been directed toward this event . . . toward him.

The wedding this morning had been simple and poignant. Mackenzie had dressed in her white doeskin dress and Fire Dancer had looked so handsome in his white tunic embellished with sea shells and porcupine quilling, his hair flowing freely down his back. The sight of him had brought tears to her eyes. Who could have thought a groom in knee-moccasins could have been so striking?

The entire village had gathered to witness the ceremony that took place just as the sun rose over the mountain ridge to the east. Snake Dancer had performed the ceremony in Shawnee to the beat of a single drum. He bound Mackenzie and Fire Dancer's hands together with a beaded holy cloth. Fire Dancer had explained in a whisper that the binding of the cloth symbolized the binding of their souls. Now she had a right to possess a part of him.

With a few waves of a turtle shell incense-pot the ceremony was over and under God's clear sky, Mackenzie was bound in marriage to Fire Dancer forever.

Mackenzie had feared that, without a vicar, she wouldn't feel truly married, but as the holy man had chanted his words and Fire Dancer had gazed into her eyes, Mackenzie had known in her heart that the marriage would always be true. In the name of God, before his mother and the entire village Fire Dancer had vowed to care for and love her. With a solitary *ah`*, Mackenzie had vowed the same. What difference was there between that and being wed by a circuit rider in her father's public room?

"*Penno`*, look." Fire Dancer interrupted Mackenzie's dreamy thoughts. "There." He pointed.

She spotted a doe and her twins drinking water at the riverbank. As the dugout swept by, the deer glanced up. When Mackenzie turned in the canoe, they were drinking water again.

"They were beautiful," she said softly, hating to break the peaceful sounds of the river by her human voice.

"They were beautiful." Fire Dancer glanced at her over his bronze shoulder, the paddle poised over the resplendent water. "As are you, *nee wah.*"

Wife. He called her wife. She was learning the Shawnee language quickly. "*Wai see yah,*" she answered with a smile. Husband.

He pursed his lips and kissed the air, a kiss meant for her. Then he turned to face forward again and sliced the water with the paddle.

They rode down the river for more than two hours. Fire Dancer pointed out animals to her as the dugout glided downstream as much a part of the river as the otters or the mud turtles. There were foxes and deer, squirrels and even a wildcat. The air was filled with birds and fluttering fall leaves. It was a magical morning. Mackenzie and Fire Dancer talked some, but mostly, they enjoyed each other's silent company and the beauty of the day.

When the sun rose directly overhead Fire Dancer angled his canoe toward the western bank. "If I was a proper husband," he said, "if it was not a time of war, this man would take you on a long trip down the river. We would spend time alone together in the forest, making love under the treetops and gathering flowers. We would visit other villages and share our joy with our neighbors and cousins.''

''It's all right,'' she assured him. ''Just one night alone with you away from the village and all your concerns is enough for me.'' She stroked his bare arm, marveling at the iron-hard muscles. ''There will be plenty of time later. A lifetime.''

''*Ah`*, lifetime, Mack-en-zie.''

He pulled the paddle through the water and lifted it high as they rode up the muddy bank, onto the grass. Jumping out, he dragged the dugout farther out of the water and then put his arm out to her.

Mackenzie took his hand to jump out, but he swept her feet out from under her and lifted her in his powerful arms. She laughed and looped her arms around his neck. ''Is it the Shawnee way for a man to carry his wife everywhere?'' she asked, pressing a kiss to his lips.

Still holding her in his arms, he yanked a deerskin from the bottom of the dugout and climbed the bank. ''It is the Shawnee way that a man should make love to his wife at least three times on their wedding day.'' He kissed her mouth. ''Look the sun rises high in the sky. This man has fallen in his duty to his wife.''

She giggled, already feeling the heat of her desire for him pulsing in her veins. ''Three times, eh?'' She nuzzled his neck. ''Then I supposed we should begin our work.''

Under the canopy of a weeping willow tree he lowered her to her feet and spread out the deerskin. ''I have thought of nothing since I woke this morning,'' he whispered in her ear, ''but of touching you.'' He ran his hands over her arms, down her hips and inward to her thighs. ''Smelling you.'' He buried his face in her hair and breathed deeply. ''Tasting you.''

His tongue flicked out to tickle Mackenzie's lower lip and she sighed with pleasure. ''Me, too,'' she whispered. ''There I was standing before your mother listening to the solemn words of the holy man and all I could think of was . . .'' She blushed and whispered in his ear.

He chuckled, his breath husky with desire. ''This man will have to teach you the Shawnee word for that.''

She gazed into his ebony eyes, their laughter mingling. "I suppose you will."

He teased her lower lip with his tongue, taunting her, making her want to kiss him. Then at last his mouth met hers, his lips parted, and their tongues twisted open-mouthed.

He kissed her until she was breathless and then he kissed her again. "Will you be warm enough or should this man get another skin?" He lowered her in his arms to the bed of deerskin and soft grass beneath it.

"I think I'll be warm enough without it." She smoothed his cheek with her hand and kissed him. As their lips met she felt his hand glance over her hip and down her thigh.

The canopy of tree limbs overhead seemed to spin in the gleaming sunshine as Fire Dancer stroked her. He took his time, undressing her slowly as he caressed her arms, her legs, her face. The chill of the fall air made goose bumps on Mackenzie's skin but it only seemed to heighten the feel of his hot, wet mouth on her hot, damp flesh.

As they rolled on the deerhide blanket she couldn't help thinking of what her wedding day would have been at home. If she'd married Josh, she'd have worn a stiff new gown and married under her father's roof. There would have been no white doeskin dress or the rising sun. The consummation of the marriage would have taken place in her own rope bed beneath the eaves on the third floor attic of her father's tavern. There would have been no open skies, no bird song, no breeze.

Mackenzie rolled on top of Fire Dancer and sat up. He had removed her dress and moccasins, but she still wore her leggings. Sitting on his lap, barebreasted while he lay beneath her gave her an odd sense of power. She caught his hands with her own and pinned them to the ground. Slowly, her gaze locked with his, she lowered her head until her lips met the nub of his male nipple.

Fire Dancer's nipple immediately puckered and he moaned. A sensual laugh bubbled from her throat as she took his nipple between her teeth and tugged gently just as he had done to her only a moment before.

He ran his fingers through her loose hair and moaned. Mackenzie licked his nipple and dragged her tongue across his bare chest to the other. She could feel him growing hard beneath her, the evidence of his desire feeding her own.

Mackenzie tugged on his nipple with her lips and then moved downward, painting imaginary lines with the tip of her tongue on his warm, sun-baked skin.

"*Kitehi,*" he whispered.

She kissed his ribs and the flat plane of his stomach, dipping her tongue into his navel. "What does it mean?" she whispered. "*Kitehi?*"

"*Kitehi* . . . my heart . . . my soul."

"It's beautiful," she breathed as she lowered her head to kiss the tender flesh just above the waistband of his loincloth.

Fire Dancer groaned and stopped her. "Not yet, my love."

"*Mahtah?*" She lifted one eyebrow teasingly.

"No."

Before Mackenzie realized what he was doing, he grabbed her shoulders and flipped her over onto her back. She struggled, laughing and pushing him as he climbed on top of her, bare skin against bare skin. "There is something I have thought of all morning," he whispered in her ear. His tongue flickered out to tease her lobe. "A taste as sweet as honey, as magical as a holy man's powders."

Their mouths met and she threaded her fingers through his hair, massaging his scalp. She loved the way his long hair tickled her when it fell across her breasts. "Here in the light of day?" she murmured.

He sat up and tugged at the leather ties of her leggings. "Where better to see the fire of those red curls?"

Fire Dancer slipped his hands beneath the doeskin leggings and Mackenzie let her eyes drift shut. There was nothing better on this earth than the feel of his touch.

She arched her back and lifted her hips to meet his fingers. He yanked the leather leggings down and she give a kick helping him. Despite the chill of the autumn breeze, she felt only the warmth of his touch and her own building desire.

She moaned as his fingers found the warm, damp folds of her womanhood. He always knew how to touch her just right, how to stroke her until she cried out with want of him. She ground her hips against his hand and when he lowered his head, she wound her fingers through his hair, guiding him.

The first sweep of his tongue took her breath away.

No matter how many times he touched her like this, she would never cease to be amazed by the depth of the pleasure. The rustle of the trees and the bird song faded, until she heard nothing but the sound of his breathing and her own moans of pleasure.

Again and again, he brought her to the precipice of ultimate ecstasy only to draw her back. She laughed, she cried a tear or two . . . she had never been so happy. Finally, when every inch of her flesh ached for him, they joined as one. Once, twice, three times he lead her over the cliff before he finally drove home and collapsed beside her.

In the early afternoon sun, he covered them both with a soft deerhide and they slept. When Mackenzie woke, he was gone, but she found him on the bank fishing. They shared a late lunch of blackened fish, honeyed corn cakes and icy river water and then went for a walk.

As evening fell, Fire Dancer prepared for the night. Mackenzie sat on a rock and sketched the tree line and the riverbank with a charred stick on flat white rock. He built up the campfire and fashioned a shelter from saplings and some of the animal hides they carried in their canoe.

"It is very good," he said as he leaned over her shoulder to wrap her in an otter cape.

She glanced up. "It's all right, but it doesn't feel right." She glanced back at the sketch. "I guess I'm just a portraitist at heart."

He kissed the top of her head and walked away. "This man is certain you will find a way to meet the needs of your heart and those of the Shawnee."

She watched him toss a piece wood onto the campfire where a squirrel sizzled on a spit. "That's an odd thing to say. What do you mean?"

He squatted and turned the squirrel spit. "You do not think *Tapalamawatah* brought you here only for me, do you?"

She nodded. It was that fate thing again. "You think I'm here because I can do something for your people? What could that be?"

He lifted one shoulder. "This man does not pretend to understand all the Father intends for his children. I only play my part and my part was to bring you here . . . and to love you."

She smiled bittersweetly. Her father would be shocked by her marriage to Fire Dancer, but she couldn't help thinking he would be happy for her because she was so happy. She wanted to send him a message telling him of the marriage, but she decided not to bring the subject up tonight. Not when they were getting along so well. She didn't want to spoil the tranquillity of their night alone. There would be plenty of time for the argument she knew was coming, when they returned to the village.

Mackenzie put down her sketching and walked to Fire Dancer who still crouched by the fire. She wrapped her arms around his neck and leaned over to kiss his cheek. "How long before supper is ready?"

"A while longer."

She smiled mischievously. "Didn't you say that a man and a woman should make love at least three times on their wedding day?"

He caught her hand in his and kissed each fingertip. *"Ah ."*

"Well, we've only done it once," she purred. "And surely you want to rest in between."

With a chuckle he grabbed her by the shoulders and wrestled her to the ground, rolling on top of her. He tickled her stomach and she squealed with laughter, and purred again as he lowered his face to the valley between her breasts.

Chapter Twenty

Mackenzie stirred the venison stew with a bark-stripped stick to prevent it from burning. For a week after she and Fire Dancer returned from their night alone on the river, friends and family members had brought them meals. It was so that they would have more time to spend together in the sleeping mat, Laughing Woman had explained with a twinkle in her eyes.

Tonight's meal was the first Mackenzie would prepare for her new husband and she was nervous. It wasn't that she didn't know how to cook; she'd been preparing meals for her father's tavern guests since she was old enough to leash the spit dog. But tonight she prepared a meal Shawnee style, over an open firepit, with heated, flat rocks for griddles, sticks for spoons, gourds for ladles, and one battered, tin cooking pot.

Fire Dancer had offered to take the responsibility, even though it fell to the Shawnee women. After all, he'd explained, he'd been cooking for himself for many years. But Mackenzie wanted to show her commitment to adjusting to his way of life. So far, she was pleased with her efforts.

She altered a venison stew recipe she'd used at home in the tavern. The Shawnee had no potatoes, but they grew a long tuber very similar to the potato. She'd added fresh peas and several pinches of piquant herbs that hung from the rafters over their sleeping platform. In a clay dish she baked squash, and for dessert she'd made flat corn cakes dimpled with dried wild strawberries.

Fire Dancer had gone to meet with the men of the war council and a delegation of French soldiers who had arrived in the camp this morning. Apparently, from what Mackenzie could gather, the alliance was to be made.

Mackenzie stirred the stew again and checked the bucket to be sure there was fresh water to drink. Nervously, she walked around the wigwam, straightening a basket here and there, rearranging the furs on the sleeping platform. At the makeshift easel Fire Dancer built for her, she adjusted the scrap of linen she used for a cover cloth to keep the still wet paint from attracting dust. Not that the painting was anything worth preserving. She was trying her hand at still life. Beneath the linen cloth was a half-completed painting of an ear of corn, a feather, and a quilled moccasin. She had managed a good copy of the articles, but there was no life in them. Of course there wasn't; they were inanimate objects. And life was what she painted. Or at least she used to . . .

Mackenzie pushed back an unruly hair and refused to feel sorry for herself. She'd made a choice to honor the Shawnee traditions and she would grow from that choice.

She glanced at the door, wondering for the dozenth time where Fire Dancer was. She'd spent half the day preparing for his return, and not just at the hearth. She'd bathed, washed her hair, and plaited it in a thick braid down her back. She wore a new long-sleeved dress with a rabbit fur stole attached at the shoulders. In her ears, she wore new shell earrings Mary had given her as a wedding gift.

At the stream Mackenzie had talked with Mary for a long time. Mackenzie was worried about her. She just didn't seem like herself. Although she was genuinely pleased with Mackenzie's marriage to her cousin, all she talked of was returning to a fort, if not a British fort, then a French one. She was quite excited at the prospect of the alliance between the Shawnee and the French because she saw it as an opportunity for her to find a white man to marry. The woman simply no longer wanted to be Shawnee.

Mackenzie's heart ached for her but she didn't know how to comfort her friend. She hoped she could bring up the subject with Fire Dancer tonight.

Mackenzie knelt on the grass mat floor to rearrange a bark crate of wooden and hollow gourd cooking utensils and containers—wedding gifts from the Shawnee. So far, her days in the village had been pleasant. She had feared she might become bored with the Shawnee's simple way of life, but that wasn't the case at all.

The women included her in their everyday tasks, while teaching her their ways. Together, they picked the last of the fall crops, and dried fruits and meats. They packed food in underground storage pits. They sewed winter garments and made toys for their children.

Again and again, as she performed her daily tasks, her artist's eye saw opportunities to paint the men, women, and children of the village. But of course she couldn't paint them because it was forbidden. She sighed. That left her with nothing but ears of corn and moccasins to paint.

Mackenzie walked back to the open fire to stir her stew again. As she knelt, something beneath the sleeping platform caught her eye.

On one knee, she scooped up Laughing Woman's daughter's rag doll. The leather-bodied black horse-hair doll immediately brought a smile to her lips. It was a beautiful doll with a doeskin dress and beaded moccasins. It was a doll that would have been the envy of any little girl on the Chesapeake . . . except that it had no face.

No face . . .

Hearing Fire Dancer's voice outside the wigwam, she ran to the door. She'd not seen him all day and had missed him more than she realized. The doll still in her hand, she threw her arms around his neck as he entered the wigwam. "I've been waiting for you."

"This man is sorry. The day was long." He shrugged off his outer buckskin tunic and hung it on a birch hook suspended from the ceiling. "We still have much to decide. The French want us to send a dozen men. The council disagrees as to whether or not we can send them."

She caressed his arm, her cheeks growing warm with the nearness of him. "Wait for our meal and we can sit down and you can tell me everything." She glanced at the doll in her hands. "First I have a question."

He pushed a lock of dark hair from his face and sat cross-legged at their hearth. "Yes, my heart?"

"Why doesn't this doll have a face?" She held up the toddler's toy. "Does it have something to do with souls, like in my portraits?"

He stuck his finger in the stew pot and fished out a chunk of venison. "Yes. No images of faces are allowed, not even on toys." He popped the meat into his mouth. "Mmmm, *ohwe-sah*. Ex-cel-lent."

She stared at the doll's face, clinging to a thread of excitement. "Does that mean that I could paint the Shawnee if I don't paint their faces?"

He glanced up in thought. "This man does not see why not."

She hugged the doll to her chest, delighted with her idea. "I could paint scenes. Domestic scenes here in the village. I see so many that touch my heart. Snake Man playing in the dirt with his grandson. Mary weaving on her loom. The young boys braiding the ponies' manes." She swung around one of the support beams. "I could paint you with your head bowed in prayer as the morning sun rises over the mountain."

He smiled. "This man told you that you would find a way to use your paints. I am pleased that you are pleased." He snitched another piece of meat. "Did this man tell you Okonsa comes to share our meal?"

"No. *This man* did not." She tossed the doll onto the sleeping platform, her good mood slipping away. They'd had had only two disagreements since their marriage over a week ago, and both had concerned his cousin.

The brave made her uncomfortable, and she didn't know how to explain it to Fire Dancer. He had not threatened her in any way. He barely spoke to her, but he often watched her from a distance with a strange look on his face. No matter where she went, to the river, to the bean field, to the wigwam Mary shared with Laughing Woman, he just *happened* to be there.

Earlier in the week Mackenzie had met Okonsa on the path to the stream. She had tried to pass him with a customary Shawnee greeting, but he backed her against a tree and quizzed her on her satisfaction of Fire Dancer's sexual performance as a husband. Mackenzie understood by now that the Shawnee looked differently at human bodies and natural acts than the English, but Okonsa's comments were not casual as Laughing Woman or Red Fox's were. Mackenzie's instincts told her Okonsa was dangerous.

Mackenzie had tried to talk with Fire Dancer about his cousin, but Fire Dancer didn't really listen to what she was saying. He insisted that his cousin had made some poor choices in the past, but he was honestly trying to change. He said he felt that he had to give him a chance.

Mackenzie walked to the dish basket and jerked three wooden trenchers out, one at a time. "You know how I feel about Okonsa."

"You have expressed your feelings, wife. But I do not understand. He has done nothing to harm you. When I brought you unconscious from the fort, he carried one end of the litter. When Snake Man ordered our marriage, only Okonsa spoke for you against it."

Mackenzie groaned with frustration as she dropped one clattering plate on top of the next. "I know all that, but I still don't trust him. It's something about his eyes."

"His eyes?" Fire Dancer arched a black brow. "This man does not understand, *his eyes.* If Okonsa demonstrates that he is trying to become a responsible brave of this village, we must support him. I do not say that he has not made mistakes in the past, wife. Only that if he is trying, we must believe in him."

Mackenzie should have known better than to broach this subject again. It was as if Fire Dancer thought that if he believed Okonsa was changing, it would make it so. She stared into the reed basket, the trenchers balanced on her knees. "It's our first real meal together. I wanted to be alone with you,'' she said, trying not to sound too disappointed.

He walked up behind her and massaged her shoulders. "This man understands, Mack-en-zie, but Okonsa eats alone each night. He is my brother, so he is your brother now. It is only right that we should offer our hearth in hospitality. We've plenty of food to share."

She brushed past him. "It's not the food, Fire Dancer." She grabbed the pot of baked squash and burned her finger. "Ouch! Damn it."

He knelt beside her and patiently took the trenchers from her. He clasped her hand and tenderly put her burnt finger in his mouth. The cool, wetness soothed her.

"This man is sorry that he asked Okonsa to our meal without asking you first. I have never had a wife before, and this man is slow to learn the rules." He looked into her eyes with that black-eyed gaze of his that made her heart melt. "I will not do it again."

Mackenzie sighed. She loved him so much. How could she argue with him over a silly thing like feeding his cousin a plate of stew? She wrapped her arms around his neck and rested her head on his shoulder. "It's all right. I've never had a husband, either. It will take time for us to learn how this marriage business works." She kissed his cheek, offering a reticent smile. "I'm sorry I snapped at you. Send your brother home early and I'll make it up to you." She winked.

His husky laughter filled the cozy wigwam as she returned to the task of preparing supper.

Mary sat on the edge of her sleeping platform and opened the crude wooden box where she kept her white *manake* treasures. Laughing Woman had taken the children to have breakfast with her grandfather so Mary had the wigwam they shared all to herself.

Mary pulled a silver thimble from the box, a red ribbon, a green ribbon, a yellow one. One by one she spread her treasures on the bearskin blanket. She had a silver salt spoon and two shoe buckles she would wear some day on heeled leather shoes. There was a pewter-handled toothbrush, a bone hair pin, and three silver sewing needles. Mary's most prized possessions, her bell earrings given to her by Mackenzie, dangled from her earlobes.

Laughing Woman said that the Shawnee had agreed to the alliance. Only a few days before the war council, led by Fire Dancer, had made the final pact. There were French soldiers in the village now. It was official and the village would be expected to provide men for scouts. They might even be asked to provide escorts to a fort somewhere. If one of the braves in the village was headed for a French fort, she was going with him.

With a sigh, Mary returned her treasures to their box. She didn't understand how Mackenzie could be so content here after the exciting life she had led at her father's tavern.

Mary was bored in the village, bored with her weaving, bored with the talk of illness and child-raising, bored with her clay pots and wooden spoons that still looked like sticks to her. She yearned for the life of the white woman with her starched white mob caps and her heeled, calfskin shoes. She yearned for that life for the child she carried.

Absently, she ran her hand over her stomach that was beginning to swell. Soon others would realize she was pregnant. She already guessed that Laughing Woman knew. She was just being polite and waiting for Mary to confess.

It wasn't that Mary feared condemnation from the villagers. Hers would not be the first child born out of wedlock among them. There was no stigma to being born to an unwed mother because there was no illegitimacy among the Shawnee. A child belonged to his or her mother's family, and who the father had been was insignificant. But it mattered to Mary that the child would not have a father and that she would have no husband to help her raise the infant. Mary didn't want her baby to sleep in a cradleboard hanging from a rafter. She wanted him to be in a wooden cradle like the one she'd once seen in a settler's house.

"Little Weaver?" Okonsa's voice broke the silence of Mary's contemplation.

"I am here, brother," she said without much encouragement. She wasn't up to visiting with her brother. He was the one person she knew would be angry and unforgiving about the baby, not because she carried it, but because it was half white,.

Okonsa stepped into the wigwam and let the door flap fall behind him. "This man came to say good-bye. I travel with the French to their fort in the north."

Mary jumped up, nearly upsetting her treasure box. "You go to a fort? Oh, take me with you!"

Okonsa frowned and adjusted his testicles beneath his fringed legging. "I will not."

She clasped her hands together. "Please. This woman begs of you. Allow me to—"

"*Mahtah.*" He sliced his hand through the air. "This man has decided his sister will no longer associate with white men. It has given you crazy ideas." He spotted the box on her sleeping platform and gave it a shove. "These shiny baubles, they make you crazy."

Mary's precious keepsakes scattered across the floor.

"No," she cried, fighting tears. "I want to be with the white men." She dropped on all fours to gather her trinkets. "I want to be one of them. To marry a white man."

"How dare you say such words!" He shook his fist, but kept his voice quiet so that anyone passing the wigwam would not hear him. "You mock the memory of our mother and father with your words."

"I do not say I wanted to marry the men who killed our parents, only that I want to live in a pretty house and drink tea from china." Tears streamed down her face. "Is that so wrong?"

"You were too young to remember the attack." Okonsa's black eyes glimmered strangely as he stared ahead, his eyes unfocused. "You do not know what they did . . . they did to . . . her . . . to him."

Mary dropped a handful of ribbons into her box and grabbed up the thimble. "You must forgive or at least forget what happened to our parents. That is done with. You cannot change it and you cannot continue to blame those who are not to blame."

"I do not have to forgive," he said through clenched teeth. His nose ring glimmered in the sunlight that poured through the hole in the roof. "And you will not wed a white man, if I have to kill you to keep you from him."

"It is what I want," she shouted, defying him. "It's what I want for my baby."

"For your what, you say?" Okonsa hissed like one of Snake Man's pets. "Your what?"

Mary sniffed, wiping her nose with sleeve. "My baby. My baby who will be half-white," she flung.

Okonsa drew back his foot and kicked her in the abdomen. Mary had no time to react, no time to protect herself as she reeled backward from the blow.

She clutched her stomach and cried out in pain. How could Okonsa do this to her? Okonsa her brother. . . . Okonsa who loved her?

Okonsa dropped to his knees beside her in a second. "This man is sorry. So sorry." He grabbed her hands and pulled her upright. He smoothed her hair and wiped at her wet cheeks, tears running down his own face. "This man did not mean to lose his temper. I am so sorry." He peered into her face, looking much like a little boy who had caused mischief. "Are you all right, dear sister?"

Mary felt numb for a moment. She couldn't catch her breath. "I . . ."

A contraction gripped her middle and doubled her over. "Oh . . ." she cried. "I think . . ." She saw the blood that pooled beneath her and she cried out again, in fear this time. She felt faint. The wigwam was spinning. Her head was spinning.

"Little Weaver," Okonsa sobbed. Tears ran down his cheeks as he gripped her hand. "You are all right. Tell this man you are all right."

"Laughing Woman," Mary whispered, staring at her own bloody hands. Another contraction gripped her and she gritted her teeth to keep from moaning. ''Find her. Baby . . . save my baby . . .''

Okonsa leaped up and dashed out of the wigwam. Mary leaned against her sleeping platform, fighting tears. Why would Okonsa do such a horrible thing to her? He had always had a temper, but he had never harmed anyone. Fire Dancer would be furious. He would have her brother banished for such a crime.

It wouldn't be fair . . . it wouldn't be right . . .

Mary heard Laughing Woman's voice shouting to someone else outside. A moment later she appeared at Mary's side, on her knees.

''What happened?'' Laughing Woman asked. She hugged Mary before she parted her legs to examine her.

Mary glanced over her shoulder to meet her brother's gaze. Maybe this was her fault. She had made Okonsa angry. He hadn't really meant to harm her or her baby. He'd just lost his temper.

Mary's gaze fluttered to Laughing Woman. ''I . . . I fell.'' She tried to laugh. ''Silly . . . silly me, I wanted to put my trinket in a basket hanging from the rafter.''

''Get me rags from the basket, Okonsa,'' Laughing Woman ordered, pointing. ''Hurry.''

Okonsa hurried to follow her bidding.

Laughing Woman wiped Mary's sweaty forehead with her cool palm. ''Someone said they thought they heard you and Okonsa arguing,'' she said softly.

Mary's eyes grew wide.

Okonsa knelt beside the two women. ''Fighting?'' He gave a little laugh. ''My sister and I were not arguing, were we?''

''N . . . no.'' Mary couldn't tear her gaze from his. ''We weren't fighting. Just a disagreement. I wasn't paying attention to what I was doing because I was talking with my brother. I . . . I slipped.''

Okonsa passed the rags to Laughing Woman. ''She slipped,'' he echoed. ''My poor, dear sister.''

''It's going to be all right,'' Laughing Woman said, trying

to staunch the bleeding. "You may lose the baby, but there can be others."

Mary closed her eyes and let the pain wash through her. The contractions were coming regularly now. She was going to have the baby. Of course it was too soon. The wee soul could not survive.

Laughing Woman talked softly to Okonsa. Mary couldn't understand what they were saying. She sent Okonsa for medicinal herbs and for Mackenzie.

Mary fought back a sob as she rode the wave of another contraction. She didn't know why she had lied to Laughing Woman about what happened. She told herself it was to protect her brother. It was just an accident. He hadn't meant to harm her. That's why she lied. That and because she was afraid of him . . .

Chapter Twenty-One

Mackenzie rested her head in the crook of Fire Dancer's arm, relaxing in the afterglow of their lovemaking. He had been gone three days on a scouting trip for the French and she'd missed him dearly. Lately she'd been so emotional. Anything could bring a tear to her eyes. She had cried buckets over Mary's miscarriage.

Mackenzie had done nothing but worry over Fire Dancer since the moment he'd left the village. It didn't matter that he was only scouting, and he was not supposed to engage with the enemy even if he saw them. She was so afraid he would be injured or killed should there be fighting. It had been one thing for her to reason that she could not be upset with him for joining his village on the side of the French, but now that it was a reality, she was having a difficult time dealing with it.

Mackenzie rolled onto her side and snuggled against Fire Dancer, her back to him. The wind blew outside, howling at the eaves of the wigwam, but inside a birchwood fire blazed, keeping the room warm and snug. "Did you run into any Englishman on your patrol?" she asked, trying to sound casual. She still hoped she could somehow get a message to her father, just so that he would know she was safe.

"I did not," he answered sleepily.

"But if you did . . . meet someone." She traced an imaginary line along his forearm. "Would there be any way you could send a message to my father at Fort Belvadere so he knows I'm alive?"

"You know this man cannot contact the English Fort. If the French knew, we could all be murdered as traitors."

She breathed wistfully. "I know. I just feel so guilty. I sleep here warm and safe in my husband's arms and my father thinks I've been kidnapped or killed."

He kissed her bare shoulder. "Do not worry for your father, Mack-en-zie. He knows that you are well cared for and that you are happy."

"He knows?" She rolled over to face him. "You contacted him? Why didn't you tell me?"

"I did not con-tact him, but he knows."

She wrinkled her nose. "That doesn't make any sense. More Shawnee magic?"

He touched his bare chest above his left nipple. "Heart magic. He knows here."

She sighed and rolled back onto her side. "I wish I could believe you were right," she whispered, snuggling down again.

"I am. Sleep, wife." He pulled her tighter against his chest and cupped her breast.

"Careful." She placed her hand over his. "They're tender."

"Tender?" He kissed her neck. "This man is sorry. Perhaps you should see Laughing Woman for an herb tea. As the grand-daughter of a Shaman, she has a way with medicines."

"I'll be all right. I must have bruised myself or something silly like that." She closed her eyes.

Mackenzie loved this time at night just before they both fell asleep. No mattered how tired he was, or how concerned he was about the war, Fire Dancer always held her in his arms. Often, they made love as they had tonight, but sometimes he just held her close. He never fell asleep before telling her first that he loved her. It had become their ritual.

"Mack-en-zie." His voice was as cozy as their bearskin blanket.

"Fire Dancer?"

"This man loves you."

"How much?" she whispered as she always did.

"As the moon loves the stars."

Mackenzie felt his body relax against her as he drifted off to sleep. She couldn't help thinking about what a good life she had found here among the Shawnee, even if it was bittersweet. She knew she might not ever see her father again. But perhaps if not for the sadness, Mackenzie wouldn't be able to fully appreciate the joy.

By the flickering light of the firepit, she studied her draped easel. She had painted two village scenes and was working on a third. Secretly she had begun a new project. It would be a surprise for Fire Dancer.

Mackenzie closed her eyes. Fire Dancer's breathing was deep and rhythmic. She wondered how she had ever slept without the sound of his breathing, the feel of his naked body pressed against hers. If only these moments could last forever.

Josh lowered his head against the driving wind and pulled his wool hat down further over his ears. His hands were so numb that he could barely feel the leather reins in his hands.

He walked his horse because the terrain was too rough, the forest too dense. Of course that was nothing new. He'd spent most of the last six weeks leading his mount through the woods.

"We head right at the pass," Robert Red Shirt called over his shoulder, his voice carried on the wind.

Josh glanced up. It had begun to flurry. Snowflakes danced in the dreary sky and stung his eyes. He nodded.

Robert had been an excellent choice for a companion on this trek. A man of all trades, he worked as a guide, a trapper and a trader. He was friendly and personable. He knew the woods of Penn's colony well and knew the inhabitants even better. Hiring the half-breed hadn't been cheap, but Josh reckoned he was worth every shilling. In six weeks, they'd visited more than a dozen Indian villages in the vicinity of Fort Belvadere.

Some were Shawnee, others Delaware, and even a few Iroquois that had strayed south.

Some of the Indians were British allies, some French allies, others neutral, but they all welcomed Robert into their lodges. They fed him and Josh, gave them a warm place to sleep and traded for supplies. The only thing they refused to supply was information. Oh, everyone had heard of the Shawnee called Fire Dancer. He had an honorable reputation. Apparently, he was a sort of hero. Everyone had met him, knew him, but oddly, no one knew where his village lay. One brave who admitted he'd been to the village, couldn't recall its location, even when Robert cornered him with a knife.

The redskins were a tight-lipped bunch. Everyone considered everyone else their "cousins", even when they weren't from the same tribe. Josh felt like he was hitting brick wall after brick wall. No one knew anything of a white captive with red hair. Major Albertson's words kept echoing in his head. He said Mackenzie was long dead by now. Killed by Josh's own musket, perhaps? No, he couldn't believe it. He wouldn't. Mackenzie was alive.

Josh didn't blame the major for not sending out any soldiers after those initial sweeps of the area. Albertson had a duty to his men and to the army. He couldn't go off half-cocked through the forest when he barely had enough troops to maintain Belvadere through the winter.

But Josh wasn't ready to give up on Mackenzie. Not yet. Something told him she was still alive. Maybe it was because he knew her and knew that she was a survivor. Maybe it was because he loved her ever since they were kids fishing in the river.

It didn't matter to Josh that she didn't love him. He'd accepted that fact long ago. Her spirit was too wild and his was too tame. She was too passionate. He was too impassive. That didn't stop him from loving her or caring for her. In place of her father, Josh saw it as his duty to find Mackenzie and to kill the red bastard who kidnapped her. No matter what the heathen had done to her, Josh would take her home to the

Chesapeake. He didn't care if she was sullied. He'd marry her and he'd love her the rest of his life.

Josh tripped on a dead vine and grabbed his horse's neck to keep from stumbling.

"You all right?" Robert Red Shirt halted.

Josh waved his hand covered by a thin leather riding glove. "Fine. Keep moving," he shouted into the wind. "We have a good hour of daylight left before we have to set camp."

Robert nodded and trudged on, his Dutch pipe leaving a trail of smoke behind him.

Josh looped his horse's reins over his arm and rubbed his hands together. Next Indian village they reached, he'd have to see if someone could sell him a pair of fur mittens. It was cold here in the mountains, far colder than on the Chesapeake for late October. Robert said they only had a few more weeks and then they would have to head back to the fort for the winter. After winter passed, if they hadn't found Mackenzie, it would be up to Josh if he wanted to hire Robert again.

Josh didn't want to think that far ahead. He wanted to believe he would find Mackenzie . . . perhaps even at the next village.

Tall Moccasin sat on the stream bank and jiggled his fishing line. The west wind blew and whistled overhead and he snuggled deeper into his hooded, leather tunic. His mother had told him not to leave their wigwam without his fur wrap. He wished he'd listened to her.

But Tall Moccasin was on a mission and Shawnee braves on missions didn't have to listen to their mothers. He jiggled the fishing line again, hoping to attract the attention of a fish that wasn't too cold to come to the surface. Tall Moccasin was scouting . . . actually he was trailing.

Ever since Tall Moccasin had seen Uncle Okonsa drying those scalps, Tall Moccasin had been watching him. He'd been too afraid to tell anyone what his crazy uncle had said and done that day, but felt an obligation to the village to keep an eye on Okonsa. After all, someone had to.

There was something not right about Aunt Little Weaver's

accident, and he feared his uncle had more to do with it than
he or his aunt admitted. Tall Moccasin had heard his aunt and
uncle arguing that day. Then he'd heard Aunt Little Weaver
cry out in pain. Without actually being inside the wigwam,
there was no way Tall Moccasin could say Little Weaver hadn't
fallen, but he was suspicious. Uncle Okonsa's words had been
vicious. He had shouted at her for being pregnant. That was
when she supposedly fell and her tiny baby died.

After the funeral, when the little bundle had been laid to rest
in a burial pit, Tall Moccasin had tried to talk to his aunt about
what happened. All Little Weaver had said, though, was that
he ought to mind his own business and stay away from Uncle
Okonsa.

But how could Tall Moccasin do that? Where would his
sense of duty be? He was such a coward that he was afraid to
tell Uncle Fire Dancer what Uncle Okonsa had said and done
the day with the scalps. But secretly, Tall Moccasin could
protect his family and the village. He could protect them by
keeping an eye on Okonsa. So far, his uncle hadn't noticed
him.

Tall Moccasin smiled to himself as he swished the wooden
fishing lure through the chilling water. He was a good scout.
Uncle Fire Dancer had taught him well. Tall Moccasin could
move through the forest undetected. He could stand near a
wigwam and look like he was playing with a leather ball, when
actually he was listening to every word that passed inside the
wigwam. He could sneak into Uncle Okonsa's lodge, pick
through his possessions, and sneak out again without being
seen.

Tall Moccasin spent hours watching Uncle Okonsa watch
Mackenzie. It seemed to be his favorite pastime. He followed
her to the river when she bathed. He followed her to the fields.
He watched her when she cooked on her outside hearth. One
night Tall Moccasin even caught Uncle Okonsa listening outside the wigwam as Mackenzie and Uncle Fire Dancer made
love.

Tall Moccasin wrinkled his nose. When his father was alive,
his father and mother had done that kissing and touching stuff.

His father had explained that it was what married people did and that it was rude to listen or to watch. There was many a night Tall Moccasin remembered falling asleep to the sound of his parents making those loving noises. It had always comforted him. Knowing that his mother and father loved each other had made him feel loved.

Tall Moccasin spotted movement in the woods upstream. Uncle Okonsa had been there all morning with his friends burning out a new dugout canoe. His uncle separated from the group and crossed the stream, jumping from rock to rock.

Tall Moccasin pulled up his fishing line and wrapped it carefully around a smooth pine stick. Whistling to himself, he tucked the fishing line into the bag he wore on his belt. He tried to act casual so that if Battered Pot or one of his uncle's other friends saw him, they would just think he was a boy out fishing.

Tall Moccasin crossed the stream further down, skipping across the rocks like he was playing.

Where was Uncle Okonsa going?

A few yards into the forest on the far side of the stream, Tall Moccasin spotted Gentle Bear sitting on a limb, keeping watch over the village.

Tall Moccasin waved a greeting and smiled.

"Where do you go, Tall Moccasin?" Gentle Bear asked in their native tongue.

Tall Moccasin ducked under the branch wondering how it held his great weight. "Out to check my rabbit snares."

Gentle Bear glanced north. "You would be better to bring your snares in closer to your mother's hearth. We are at war, you must remember. It is dangerous for cubs to stray far from the den."

Tall Moccasin wrinkled his nose. "I'm big enough to take care of myself." He thrust out his chest proudly. "When spring comes, Snake Man says I will receive my totem."

"Go with you, then, but do not linger in the forest. If you see anything out of place, come back to the village, do you understand this man?" Gentle Bear asked.

"Ah^." Tall Moccasin gave another wave. He would have to hurry if he was going to catch up with Okonsa.

Tall Moccasin ran through the forest and veered to the right, hoping he would cross his uncle's path. Where was he going in the middle of the day? Not hunting. He carried no bow. Not scouting. He carried no pack. Any man who left the village for more than an hour carried a pack in case he was stranded from the village.

Tall Moccasin came upon a dry, shattered leaf on the elk path he followed. Studying it more closely, he found a moccasin print, still damp at the very edges. It was Uncle Okonsa's print.

With a grin, Tall Moccasin hurried on. As he walked, he listened to the sounds of the forest. He heard the trees rustling in the wind. He heard squirrels chatter. Something big rubbed its back on a tree trunk. Tall Moccasin stopped and sniffed the air. Luckily he smelled no bear . . . it had to be an elk or a deer. He walked on.

Further down the path, a chipmunk dropped an acorn and another chipmunk grabbed it and ran. Tall Moccasin chuckled and stopped to watch their antics. Soon all the small animals would retreat for the winter and the forest would be silent until the coming of spring. Tall Moccasin was looking as forward to spring as he thought those chipmunks were.

Tall Moccasin passed under an elm tree and realized he had lost his uncle's tracks. He stopped and spun around and stared at the ground. Had Uncle Okonsa strayed off the path? Tall Moccasin walked back down the elk path. He was good at tracking, especially if a man wasn't trying to hide the signs.

A sound in the tree startled Tall Moccasin and he fumbled to unsheathe his knife. Someone leaped from the tree overhead.

Uncle Okonsa.

"You follow me," Okonsa accused.

Tall Moccasin's lower lip trembled. He did not return his knife to its sheath. "I . . . I do not, Uncle. I . . . I search for my rabbit snares. I . . . I guess I lost them."

"Liar!" Uncle Okonsa's hand snaked out and he smacked Tall Moccasin hard across the face.

Tears welled in Tall Moccasin's eyes. No one had ever struck him before. The Shawnee did not hit their children.

Tall Moccasin touched his palm to his stinging cheek. "You should not have done that, Uncle."

"How long have you been following me, you little dog turd?" Okonsa took a step toward Tall Moccasin.

Tall Moccasin took a step back. "I . . . I wasn't—"

"Don't lie to me." Okonsa's hand flew so fast that Tall Moccasin didn't have time to react. He tried to duck, but Okonsa hit him hard on his temple and struck his eye.

Tall Moccasin didn't make a sound, but it took a second for his vision to clear. The side of his face throbbed with pain. He was afraid, but he didn't know what to do. Did he try to run? Did he call out in the hopes that he wasn't too far from Gentle Bear to be heard?

"I asked you a question," Okonsa barked harshly. He raised his hand to strike Tall Moccasin again.

"N . . . not long. I wasn't really following you. I only wanted to see . . ."

"See what?"

"Where you were going without a bow or a pack."

Okonsa's black eyes narrowed dangerously. His nose ring glimmered in the sunlight. "You have been following me, turd. The other night when I was in the sweat house." He pointed accusingly. "It was you I heard outside."

Tall Moccasin took a step backward and shook his head. "No. No it wasn't me," he lied. "I . . . I was in my mother's lodge. I'm not allowed out after it grows dark. I was with my mother."

"Liar!"

This time Okonsa struck him so hard that Tall Moccasin fell backward. Tall Moccasin felt his feet crumble under him and he lashed out wildly with his hunting knife. As he fell back, he heard his uncle grunt in pain. Tall Moccasin must have nicked him with his knife.

Tall Moccasin hit the ground hard and balled himself up to try to roll away. His Uncle kicked him in the stomach and Tall Moccasin lost the grip on his knife.

Tall Moccasin was ashamed of the tears that ran down his cheeks. "I'm sorry, I'm sorry," he cried. "I . . . I won't do it again. D . . . don't hit me again. I won't tell . . . please Uncle . . ."

Tall Moccasin saw his uncle's face leering over him. He saw his balled fist come toward him. He felt the blow to his head and the explosion of pain . . . and then he felt nothing but coldness seep around him.

Chapter Twenty-Two

"Nthathah?"

Mackenzie heard a woman's urgent voice outside her door.

"Nthathah?" came the voice again.

Mackenzie's Shawnee was improving every day. It sounded like Fire Dancer's sister. She called for her brother.

"Bird Song?" Mackenzie raised the doorflap to discover her standing in the dark, her hands clutched nervously. "Come in. What's wrong?" She followed the older woman.

"This woman have need of brother."

"I can find him for you." Mackenzie touched her with her paint-stained fingertips. She'd been working on a portrait when she heard Bird Song outside her door. "Please tell me what's wrong. Is Little Weaver all right? She's not bleeding again, is she?"

Bird Song laid her palm against her cheek. "Not Little Weaver. It . . . it probably nothing." She shook her head and attempted a smile. "Tall Moccasin he . . ." She opened her arms. "No find him. He no come home."

"He's missing?" Mackenzie felt a surge of panic in her chest. In the last few weeks Fire Dancer's family had become her family. His people had become her people. "How long has he been gone?'' She grabbed the doeskin wrap she'd fashioned into a hooded cloak. "Who saw him last?"

"He went fishing. Noon day. No come home for supper. No come home for dark. *Neekweethah* always come home dark, no worry his mother."

Mackenzie threw her cloak over her shoulders and grabbed Song Bird's hand. "I'm sure he's here somewhere. In someone else's wigwam, mayhap?" She led her out of the wigwam, intent on finding Fire Dancer. He would know what to do and where to look.

Bird Song shook her head. "No. No wigwam. This woman ask. No one see him but Gentle Bear. Gentle Bear see him in the forest noon day. Not again."

Mackenzie hurried across the compound, between the wigwams. Fire Dancer said he was going to see his brother who was headed out on a scouting trip for the French. Mackenzie had been so relieved that Fire Dancer wasn't going, that she'd sent him off with a pot of candied carrots for Okonsa.

Mackenzie reached Okonsa's wigwam. "Fire Dancer?"

"*Ah`*," Fire Dancer called from inside.

Mackenzie didn't wait for an invitation. All she could think of was that Tall Moccasin was out in the cold, dark forest somewhere, injured or lost. She pushed through the door and pulled Bird Song along with her. "Fire Dancer, you—"

She halted inside the doorway and glanced up. A shiver crawled up her spine She'd never been inside her brother-in-law's wigwam before.

The wigwam was darker than hers, or any other she'd ever been inside. Strips of bark hung from the vaulted ceilings and filled the room with the distinctive, pungent aroma of cedar. From the ceiling, between the strips of bark, hung British-made goods. It was the strangest thing Mackenzie had ever seen.

The natural air flow caused by the heat of the fire and the cold of the night air that seeped through the chimney hole made the trinkets swing. The effect was haunting. There were silver-handled toothbrushes, fringed epaulettes, pewter hand mirrors, barrettes, purses, even a mob cap. All the objects swung eerily overhead.

"Mack-en-zie, what is wrong?"

Fire Dancer's face appeared before hers. She held tightly to Song Bird's hand. "Tall Moccasin . . ." she said, dragging her gaze from the objects. ". . . is missing. Bird Song can't find him anywhere."

"You have checked the other wigwams and the stream?" Fire Dancer questioned his sister.

"Ah`." For Mackenzie's benefit, she spoke English. "Look everywhere. Call his name." She gripped Mackenzie's hand. "Have fear in my heart, brother. Son would not stay away from home so late. He would not scare his mother this way."

"This man will search for him." Okonsa thrust out his chest. "He is nearby. Only playing boy's games. His Uncle Okonsa will find him."

Mackenzie focused on her husband and ignored Okonsa and his ghostly treasures. "I think we should form search parties. Gentle Bear was the last to see him at noon."

"This woman will look for son."

"No." Mackenzie squeezed Song Bird's hand gently. "You should wait by your hearth. If the boy comes home on his own, he'll want his mother." In the back of Mackenzie's mind, she thought, *if we find his body killed by an animal or murdered by English soldiers, I wouldn't want you to see him.*

"Mack-en-zie is right." Fire Dancer grabbed his otter skin cape off a hook and tossed it over his shoulders.

Mackenzie knew he was thinking the same things as she.

"Okonsa," Fire Dancer ordered. "Gather men and make torches. This man will organize search parties. We will meet at the stream."

Mackenzie hurried into the darkness, anxious to be out of Okonsa's wigwam. "I'll take Song Bird back to her wigwam and gather the women. Perhaps Snake Man can watch over the young children."

Fire Dancer clasped her arm and lowered his voice. "This man would feel better if you stayed with Song Bird. We do not yet know if danger lurks in our forest. If there are British soldiers . . ." His voice faded.

Mackenzie's gaze met his. She was touched that he was so

fearful of leaving her. "No man is going to take me from here against my will," she reassured him as she rubbed his arm. "This is Tall Moccasin we're talking about. We need every able-bodied adult we can find to look for him. Mary isn't well enough to trek through the forest yet. I'll have her stay with Song Bird."

Fire Dancer opened his mouth to protest, but Mackenzie didn't give him a chance. "Hurry," she whispered and gave him a nudging. Then she took Song Bird by the arm and led her across the compound.

By the time Mackenzie reached the stream with a dozen women wrapped in cloaks, Fire Dancer was pairing men and women off to form as many search parties as possible. No one would leave the village alone or without a weapon. They would sweep the area around the village, walking within voice-distance of each other. As a precaution, Fire Dancer doubled the guards around the village. There had been no signs of redcoat soldiers nearby, but he would not leave the village unprotected even for the sake of his nephew.

"Those are your instructions," Fire Dancer said in Shawnee. "You know where each of you must search. Get your torch from Okonsa and move out. Call out if you see or hear anything suspicious."

The crowd of Shawnee dispersed, their faces solemn. When one woman's child was missing, he became everyone's child and they all felt Song Bird's fear and pain.

Fire Dancer signaled to Mackenzie. "If you must aid in the search, you'll come with me."

Mackenzie grabbed a torch and passed it to him. "I must." They crossed the stream on the stepping rocks, her arm linked through his. "I must because I'm one of you now. Tall Moccasin is as much my nephew as he is yours."

Fire Dancer patted her arm. "This man is sorry. I did not mean to push you away." The flame of the spitting torch illuminated his sober face. "This man is only concerned for your safety. I would not lose you now, Mack-en-zie. I cannot."

"I understand." It was a tender moment between them. His

simple words made her understand the depth of the love between man and wife, a love that saw beyond skin color or politics.

She walked beside Fire Dancer, and kept her eyes open for any sign of the boy. Around her, she heard sounds of the Shawnee walking through the forest and calling Tall Moccasin's name.

"I have never been in your brother's wigwam," Mackenzie said as she snuggled deeper into her doeskin cloak. "I found the hanging trinkets disturbing." She searched for any expression the torch illuminated on his face. "Don't you?"

He gave a noncommittal shrug. "His sister collects English objects. It is harmless."

"That's different. Mary keeps her things in a box, and they were gifts. Okonsa . . . his wigwam is like some sort of madman's shrine. Mary wants to be English. He hates Englishmen."

"He does not hate you."

Mackenzie wasn't so sure about that. She wondered if Okonsa's preoccupation with her really was due to hate and even he himself didn't realize it. But this wasn't the time to discuss the matter with Fire Dancer. "Where does Okonsa get all those British *manake* things."

"This man does not know." He tapped a bush with a stick. "Trades for them, I suppose."

She gave a shudder. "And what's the purpose of the bark strips hanging everywhere?"

"Shawnee medicine. It protects the man from the evil spirits of the objects, of the white *manake* who owned the objects."

Mackenzie frowned and ducked beneath a low-hanging branch. Her husband was as an intelligent a man as any colonist she'd ever known, but when it came to his brother, he had little sense. He saw what he wanted to see, believed what he wanted to believe.

"How far should we go?" she asked, changing the subject. She knew from experience that there was no point in questioning him about Okonsa. If he saw anything wrong with his brother's *collection,* he'd not admit it.

It was beginning to snow. Fluffy white flakes fell on her cloak. Mackenzie knew that the snow would make it more difficult to find any signs of Tall Moccasin, but she felt no need to say so. So often, she and Fire Dancer had the same thoughts.

"We must walk to the fork oak and then turn back."

Mackenzie heard the echoes of the villagers as they called to the lost boy.

"Do you think we'll find him?" she asked softly. She needed Fire Dancer's assurance.

"This man does not know." He grimaced. "What I know is that I must pray to the Father, *Tapalamawatah* . . . and keep looking."

Mackenzie woke beside Song Bird's hearth and stretched her stiff muscles. Song Bird and Mary still slept. Mackenzie fed the dying coals a few sticks and left the wigwam to search for her husband. It was dawn. The snow had covered the ground in a thin, white blanket that sparkled in the first rays of sunlight.

She trudged across the compound, her heart heavy. They had not found Tall Moccasin and sometime after midnight, Fire Dancer had suspended the search. They would begin looking for him again this morning.

Mackenzie found Fire Dancer and Okonsa at her hearth.

"Good morning, wife." Fire Dancer kissed her on the lips. Intuitively knowing her need to be comforted, he hugged her before he returned to his mat beside the fire.

"Could this woman make you men something to eat?" Out of respect for Fire Dancer, she included Okonsa.

"No, thank you, sister." Okonsa stretched and reached down to adjust his testicles inside his leggings.

Mackenzie paid him no mind. She had become so used to his fixation, that she actually found it funny. "You are certain, brother? This woman has rabbit she can fry up and oat mush."

"No. Many thanks, but I cannot. My men and I must leave. The French are expecting scouts. If we do not come to them, they will come to us and your husband does not want them here." He shrugged into a deerhide mantle decorated with red slashes of paint that looked like blood. "This man would rather stay and search for his nephew, but our War Chief is insistent. He says I must go and, of course, I must do what our War Chief says.''

Fire Dancer walked his brother to the door. ''Take care, *Neetahnathah*. Do not be too trusting of our allies.''

''We are safe enough, He-who-worries-too-much,'' Okonsa said. ''We but scout. We've not been involved in a skirmish yet. Our warriors are growing fat and lazy.''

Fire Dancer clapped him on the back. ''Take care the same. I will expect you in seven nights. If you do not return or send word, I will come looking for you.''

''Good-bye, sister. Have care while I am gone.'' Okonsa winked at her, but Fire Dancer didn't see it.

''Farewell,'' she responded formally. Inside, she was seething. It was easy for her to see through his polite words and declarations, even if her husband could not. Okonsa didn't want to stay and look for the boy. He wanted to be off on one of his scouting trips. He wanted to fight the British, not just scout for the French. He wanted blood.

Fire Dancer returned to the hearth, his face etched with fatigue and worry.

Mackenzie placed a tin pot of water on the coals to boil and knelt behind him. She massaged his broad shoulders. ''Tall Moccasin is not nearby, is he?'' she asked gently. ''Else we would have found him last night.''

''This man does not understand.'' He made a fist in frustration. ''Even if the boy was dead, we would find his body. How can there be no trace? It is as if he vanished.''

''Do you think he could have been kidnapped . . .'' She hesitated to say it. ''. . . by the British soldiers—maybe because of me?''

He shook his head no. ''No one has come looking for you here. Redcoat *manake* leave a trail any Shawnee child could follow. They have not been here.''

She peered into his face, wishing there was some way she could comfort him. ''But the snow, it could have covered soldiers' tracks, right?''

''*Ah*, the snow would make following signs harder, but not

impossible.'' He lowered his hands to his sides in a helpless gesture. ''I walked the forest all night. There are no signs. He is just gone.''

Mackenzie kissed the top of his head and rose to prepare a hot meal. ''I'll feed you and then you can take men and search the area for anything we might have missed last night in the dark. There must be something out there to tell us what happened.''

''We will look. This man wants you to remain in village and keep the women busy. Give my sister, Song Bird, work so that she will not spend her hours weeping.''

''I'll do whatever I can to help her. I'll look after the women. You and the men just keep looking.''

The portrait on the easel near their sleeping platform caught Mackenzie's eye. The nearly complete painting was of three boys kneeling in the grass beside a wigwam, each of their faces turned so that all one could see was their inky black hair. They were playing a game with clay marbles. One of the boys in the portrait was Tall Moccasin.

The days blew by like the last leaves of the trees that sheltered the village. Snow fell and the Shawnee settled in for the winter. After a week of searching, Fire Dancer finally gave up the hunt for Tall Moccasin. Now all Song Bird had left of her son was a few of his possessions and the dismal hope that he might return to her someday.

Mackenzie kept occupied with her portraits of the Shawnee and tried to keep from thinking too much about Tall Moccasin. She loved the boy and it was hard to imagine he was gone. It was the Shawnee way that gave her strength.

Mackenzie had been surprised that there was very little mourning for Tall Moccasin, even from his mother. The Shawnee's strong religious beliefs sustained them in times of tragedy and encouraged them to find joy, even after sorrow. Song Bird had explained to Mackenzie, that *Tapalamawatah* cares for all his people. If her son still lived and had been kidnapped or lost, God watched over him. If he had be killed by man or beast, he was now being rocked in the arms of the Great Father.

"I wish you didn't have to go," Mackenzie said as she packed Fire Dancer's leather bag for his scouting expedition with the French. "Your mother says a storm blows in. We're expecting a lot of snow."

Fire Dancer sat on the edge of their sleeping platform restringing his bow. "I must go. The French have kept their bargain. We have not seen any signs of redcoat soldiers. We must keep our side of the pact and provide scouts."

Mackenzie dropped a leather pouch of pemmican into his bag. The mixture of dried meat and berries she'd made herself would sustain Fire Dancer when he could not stop to make a campfire and cook meat. "I understand the logic. That doesn't mean I want you to go." She stuffed an extra pair of mittens into the bag. She felt on the verge of tears and she didn't know why. "Couldn't you send someone else in your place?"

"We must all take our turn, *kitehi*. You know that."

She smiled and sniffed. She loved it when he called her that. *My heart.* She was his heart, and he was hers.

"Mack-en-zie, you are crying. Why?"

She wiped her eyes. "I ... I don't know. I just ..." She exhaled. "I don't want you to go. I don't want you to leave me."

He walked to her and held out his arms. She allowed him to pull her close.

"This man is not leaving you," he said gently. He kissed her forehead. "This man but goes scouting." He grasped her shoulders and gazed into her eyes. "Are you well? Yesterday you cried because you burned the venison."

She gave a small laugh. "I don't know what's wrong. I just don't feel like myself."

He kissed her soundly on the lips. "This man must go. The others wait. They will tease me and say that I cannot leave my wife's sleeping mat. But I will send Laughing Woman. She is a healer and knows of women's illnesses. Speak to her. Perhaps she can give you an herbal tea."

Mackenzie clung to him. She felt foolish. "I'm sure it's nothing. Go. I'll see you in a few days."

"Do you want me to stay until you speak with Laughing Woman?"

She forced a smile. "No. Really. I'm all right. Go." She threaded her fingers through his long hair and kissed him passionately. It was a kiss she hoped would entreat him to hurry home.

Fire Dancer grabbed his pack. "Good-bye, wife. This man loves you."

She followed him to the door. "How much?"

"As the fishes love the great ocean."

She kissed her fingertip and blew the kiss to him. Then he was gone.

Mid-afternoon, Laughing Woman entered Mackenzie's wigwam. Mackenzie was working on Fire Dancer's original painting.

Laughing Woman studied it carefully. "This is good, Macken-zie. Much, very good. I feel the strength of the man. I feel his honor."

Mackenzie stood back beside the Indian woman. "It's still good, isn't it? Even with the alterations?"

"Much good." Laughing Woman placed a pan of water on the coals to heat for tea. "Your husband came to me on his way out of the village. He say you not feel good. Say you cry and not know why."

Mackenzie laid down her brush and joined Laughing Woman at the hearth. "I don't know what's wrong with me. I feel so strange."

"Mmm hmmmm." Laughing Woman sprinkled herbs into the heating water. "Tell this woman sym-toms."

Mackenzie sat crossed-legged on the grass mat she had covered with deerhide for the winter. The wind howled and the snow blew outside, but inside, the wigwam was cozy and warm. "I don't know. I've been emotional. I'm not a crier, but now I cry all the time. And I'm hungry. And I'm tired. Yesterday I slept half the day away." She brushed her hand across her bosom. "And I'm sore."

Laughing Woman smiled. "Your moon cycle. Does it come?"

That seemed like an odd question to Mackenzie. "My bleeding?" She thought for a moment. "No, I guess it hasn't. Not since I joined the village. I thought perhaps because of my head injury . . ." Her eyes widened. Now she really felt like a fool. "You don't suppose?"

Laughing Woman beamed. "Yes, this woman suppose you have papoose on the hearth." She slapped her thigh and laughed heartily at her own joke.

Mackenzie lowered her face to her hands. She was in shock. *A baby?* And she was embarrassed. How could she not have known she was pregnant? "I feel stupid," she confessed. "It . . . it never occurred to me that I might . . . might be with child."

"It is all right. This woman does not laugh at you." Laughing Woman rubbed her shoulder. "This is a happy time for you, for your husband, for all of us."

"It just never occurred to me," Mackenzie said in numb disbelief. "My . . . my mother died when I was very young. Our cook told me about my woman's bleeding because my father was too embarrassed. She wasn't very helpful. She never told me the symptoms of pregnancy. I never knew a pregnant woman."

Mackenzie's mind whirled and she glanced up nervously. "I don't know how to take care of a baby. How will I—"

Laughing Woman pushed a cup of tea into her hand. "Do not worry. When I place your daughter or your son in your arms, you will know how to care for him or her. We will all help, women and men of the village. It is why we live together as we do. To share our knowledge."

Mackenzie held the cup in her trembling hands. She was so happy. So scared. She and Fire Dancer had never discussed children at any length. She knew he wanted them, but now?

"It is the Shawnee tradition," Laughing Woman explained, "that our women do not tell of a child until its little soul is formed. Do you know when our prince make baby inside you?"

Mackenzie shook her head. "I don't know. It could have been as long as three moons ago."

"Better to wait another moon, not tell anyone. Not Fire

Dancer. He has much to worry. He does not need to worry about what only *Tapalamawatah* can care for.''

"You're right." Mackenzie sighed with relief. This would give her time to get used to the idea. "I'll wait to tell Fire Dancer." Her unsteady gaze met Laughing Woman's. "I don't know how he'll react, anyway."

Laughing Woman covered Mackenzie's hand with hers. "Do not have worry. Drink and be happy. You will give your husband the most best gift a woman can give." She laid her hand on Mackenzie's flat stomach. "Gift of your womb. Of your heart."

Mackenzie smiled over the rim of the cup and took a sip of the soothing tea. Laughing Woman was right. She and Fire Dancer were going to have child and everything was going to be fine.

A shout outside the wigwam startled Mackenzie. She couldn't translate the Shawnee.

Laughing Woman bolted up, her smile falling from her face. Mackenzie grabbed her friend's hand. "What is it?"

"Intruders," Laughing Woman cried as she ran for the door. "Grab your weapon. "It is Englishmen."

Chapter Twenty-Three

"My children," Laughing Woman lamented. "This woman must go to her children. Pro-tect them."

Mackenzie seized the precious wheel-lock musket Fire Dancer left her. She knew it was primed and loaded because she'd done it herself last night.

"Go," Mackenzie told Laughing Woman calmly. "I'm behind you. Go to the children."

The two women burst out of the wigwam and raced across the snowy compound. A single musket cracked in the cold, fresh air.

Women and children ran through the village. The men who'd remained behind from the French scouting expedition sprinted through the snow with bows and spears and a few old rifles.

"How many?" Mackenzie asked Gentle Bear as they crossed paths.

"This man have not know," he shouted as he ran. "Take cover of wigwam."

Before they reached the wigwam Mary and Laughing Woman shared, Mackenzie heard Laughing Woman's children crying. "They're here. Go inside. I'll guard the door," Mackenzie ordered.

Laughing Woman lifted the doorflap and Mackenzie caught a glimpse of Mary huddled on a sleeping platform holding the toddlers in her arms. The flap fell and Mackenzie swung around, the rifle cradled in her arms. No one would bring harm to her family as long as she breathed. Laughing Woman and her children were Mackenzie's family. Mary was her family. She'd die protecting them.

"How many soldiers?" Mackenzie called out to a Shawnee woman who passed by.

"Do not know. Not soldiers. White men. Down by stream."

Every nerve in Mackenzie's body crackled with dread as she waited, her musket in her hand.

What if her father had found her? What if they were coming for her? What would she say? How would she tell her father she could not leave . . . that she had married a redman and now carried his child? How could she tell him that she was now more Shawnee than English? A minute passed and Mackenzie didn't hear any more gunshots. She fought with indecision. Did she remain here to protect the woman and children or did she go to the stream to see who the intruders were? If it was her father, she didn't want him injured.

"Laughing Woman," Mackenzie called, making her choice. "I'm going to the stream to see what's happening. Stay inside. Have a weapon ready."

Mary burst through the door. "This woman go with you. See the Englishmen."

Mackenzie knew there was no sense in arguing with her. "All right, but stay behind me, Mary. If I say run, you run. Understand this woman's words?"

"*Ah* ." Mary fell in behind her.

Mackenzie followed the path, along with other villagers, to the stream. Obviously there was no army attack. Who were the intruders?

At the streambank, Mackenzie spotted Gentle Bear holding a musket on a man in a coon-skin cap dressed in bear hides. He had black hair and medium toned skin—a half-breed probably. Mackenzie didn't know him.

She approached the crowd of Shawnee men and women and

her gaze fixed on the ground. Someone had been shot. The
Indians stood in a ring around him, all talking at once. A pale-
skinned man's hand lay in the snow . . . spotted with blood.

Not my father, Mackenzie prayed. It didn't look like her
father's hand. It wasn't broad enough. She pushed through the
crowd. "Who—" She halted.

Josh? It was Josh Watkins.

"Josh!" she hollered. She pushed her musket in someone's
hands and dropped to her knees. He was unconscious, his face
as pale as the snow he lay in. An arrow protruded from his left
shoulder. The shaft had been feathered by a Shawnee; the style
was unmistakable.

"What happened?" Mackenzie demanded as she checked
for a pulse at his neck. His heart still beat. Blood oozed from
the arrow wound.

"Our guards catched these men try to sneak into village,"
Gentle Bear said, still holding his weapon on the man that
looked to be a trapper.

"Don't shoot. Don't shoot me," the man said, holding his
hands high. "We didn't mean harm. I am Robert Red Shirt.
We . . . we're just lookin' for a woman. Lookin' for his
woman." His gaze met Mackenzie's. "A white woman with
red hair."

"If you meant no harm," Mackenzie stated, "who the hell
shot the musket? How did Josh get hit with an arrow? Our men
don't shoot unprovoked."

"Watkins got scared, I guess. I told him not to fire. The
Indian spooked him and the musket went off. He wasn't aimin'
at nothing. I swear by the virgin he wasn't."

Mackenzie wished Robert Red Shirt wouldn't stare at her
like that. She knew that he knew he'd found who he was looking
for. She glanced back at Josh and spoke in broken Shawnee.
"Someone help me get him to a wigwam." She backed up as
two of the men grasped Josh's arms and legs.

"Mine is closest," Mary offered, hovering over Josh's limp
body. "Bring him to my wigwam."

They passed Mackenzie and hastened up the path, back to
the village.

"What are you going to do with him?" Mackenzie asked Gentle Bear, indicating the trapper with a nod of her head.

The crowd broke up. Some of the Indians followed the men carrying Josh. Others walked toward the village on their own. A handful of men and women remained behind to glare at Robert Red Shirt.

"This man have not know." Gentle Bear poked the half-breed with the barrel of his musket. "Maybe cut off his balls and make tobacco pouch. *Ah*?"

Robert Red Shirt blanched.

The women giggled.

Mackenzie laid her hand on Gentle Bear's bulging forearm. "Tie him up. Give him food and water. Don't let anyone harm him. It's what Fire Dancer would do if he was here. After I talk to Josh, I want to talk to him."

"*Ah*, Mack-en-zie. You are wise like our Prince." Gentle Bear grinned as he switched to Shawnee. "You would make a good chief yourself someday."

Mackenzie laughed. It was becoming easier each day for her to understand their language and to speak it herself. At times, her thoughts came in Shawnee rather than English. "You are very funny," Mackenzie answered in his native tongue. "Now take him and put a guard on him. I'll come as soon as I can."

By the time Mackenzie reached Mary and Laughing Woman's wigwam, they had shooed everyone out.

Josh laid unconscious on Mary's sleeping platform. The arrow still projecting from his shoulder.

Mary cut his shirt open with a knife and began washing the wounded area with a hot, wet cloth.

"This is Josh Watkins, a friend of mine," Mackenzie said. "He came from Maryland to the fort with me, Laughing Woman. Can you help him?" She knelt beside Mary and brushed his matted blond hair off his forehead, surprised by the tenderness she felt for this man who she knew she could never love. She couldn't believe he had found her. It had been three months since Fire Dancer had taken her from Fort Belvadere. Had he searched for her all this time?

"Can you save him?" Mackenzie questioned.

"Is not so bad wound." Laughing Woman dug through a basket of herbs. "I pull out arrow. Kill bad spirit with hot tip. Make herb poultice. Man dancing around camp fire few days."

Mackenzie turned back to Josh as he rolled his head and groaned in pain.

Mackenzie clasped his filthy hand in hers. He was thin. His chest bared, she could count his ribs. Josh had always been slender, but never like this. He was starving.

"Josh," she whispered and squeezed his hand. "It's me, Mackenzie. Can you hear me?"

Mackenzie. He moved his lips to say her name, but no sound came out.

"That's right," she comforted him. "It's Mackenzie."

His eyelids fluttered open. "Mackenzie?"

"I'm here."

He swallowed. "Redskins. C . . . captured. Must save you from filthy redskins."

Laughing Woman stood behind Mackenzie. "You sure you want me save him?" she asked tartly.

"Yes," Mary cried passionately. "Save him. He doesn't know what he's saying. He's delirious. Help him, Laughing Woman." She peered up at her friend, her hands clasped. "Please. This woman begs you."

"Mackenzie?" Josh moaned.

"Josh," Mackenzie whispered. "Listen to me. You've been shot. These women are going to help you. Try to relax and save your strength." She squeezed his hand and let go.

He followed her with his gaze. Despite his pain, his eyes were filled with relief.

Mackenzie stepped back and Laughing Woman took her place beside Mary.

Mary clasped his hand and nodded. "Pull," she whispered.

Laughing Woman grasped the arrow shaft with both hands and yanked.

Josh hollered and rose off the bed. Mary pushed his chest and eased him back down. "Is all right," she crooned in English. "I'm here. Mary is here."

Laughing Woman took the bloody arrow and held the iron tip over the hot coals of the fire.

Mackenzie felt her stomach twist. She wasn't normally squeamish, but as Laughing Woman carried the glowing red arrow over to Josh, Mackenzie turned away.

"Hold him," Laughing Woman told Mary.

Mackenzie heard Josh scream and the sizzle of his burning flesh. She gagged as the smell of scorched skin filled the wigwam.

"Be right back," Mackenzie said and ran out of the wigwam.

Outside in the cold air, she caught her breath. She needed a minute and then she'd go back inside with Josh. She knew he was in capable hands. Laughing Woman knew as much about healing as any Colonial surgeon Mackenzie had ever known. And obviously Mary was taking it upon herself to care for him. That was good. It would gave her something to think about other than her dead baby.

Mackenzie breathed deeply, exhaling in frosty puffs.

"Mack-en-zie." Gentle Bear approached.

"Gentle Bear."

He pointed toward the wigwam. "He live?"

"*Ah`.*" She spoke slowly in Shawnee. "Laughing Woman cares for him. She says he'll survive."

He nodded and lifted his rabbit fur cloak off his shoulders and lowered it onto hers. "That is good . . . this man supposes."

Mackenzie dug her moccasin in the snow. She wished desperately that Fire Dancer was here right now. Josh's appearance scared her. It made her feel like her marriage and life as she now knew it was threatened. "Gentle Bear, the white men came for me. From the fort, this woman guesses."

"*Ah`.*"

She gazed out over the wigwams toward the mountain range to the west. Some of the Shawnee talked of moving west, far from the hand of the white man. The idea sounded good to Mackenzie right now. "This woman thinks we must add extra guards to the perimeter of the village. I will talk to the one who calls himself Robert Red Shirt and to Josh when he wakes. I will see if others come, but to be safe, we must be ready."

* * *

''Mackenzie?'' Josh called weakly.

''I'm here.'' She jumped up from the hearth where she was sharing a cup of tea with Laughing Woman and Mary. Laughing Woman's toddlers had been sent to spend a few nights with their grandfather.

Mackenzie knelt beside the sleeping platform and clasped his hand. ''I'm right here.''

He opened his eyes. ''Feel like ... like I've been hit by a cannon ball.''

She raised up on her knees to look into his eyes. ''A Shawnee arrow, actually.''

Slowly he reached up to give one of her red braids a swing. ''I found you. Harry said you were dead, but I knew you weren't. I knew it as well as I know my own name.'' His gaze locked with hers. ''I'm so sorry I shot you. I didn't mean to. I just—''

''It was just a graze,'' she interrupted. ''A scratch.'' She lifted her hair to show the small, healed scar. ''See. The scar you gave me on my calf with that pitchfork when we were ten was worse.''

He smiled at her joke, then sobered. ''I'm sorry the bastard carried you off. I should have stopped him. I should have—''

She lowered her lashes. ''His name is Fire Dancer and he's my husband now, Josh. You can't talk about him that way. Not to me.''

''Your ... your husband?'' He struggled to lift up on his elbows and flinched with pain. ''The savages made you marry him?''

''No,'' she answered him firmly. ''I married him because I love him.''

''A redskin?'' He stared at her with a look of shock and bewilderment. ''You married a bloody redskin of your own free will? Instead of me?''

''Are you listening to what I'm saying? I don't mean to hurt you, Josh, but I love him. I don't care what color his skin is. I love him,'' she repeated passionately.

For a moment, she thought Josh might cry. The hurt was written all over his face.

"You mean it, don't you?" he whispered.

"Ah`. We fell in love at the fort."

"But he kidnapped you!"

She rubbed his hand in hers. "He brought me here to save me after I was shot." *No need to tell him the whole portrait story now,* she thought. *It will only complicate matters. All he needs to know now is that I want to be here.* "I was unconscious for a fortnight. If I'd not been cared for by our medicine woman, the same woman who saved your life, I'd have died. Do you understand, Josh? I'd have *died* at the fort."

"You really love him?"

"I love him with all my heart. He and I were meant to be husband and wife. It was fate," she said as gently as she could.

He glanced at the cornhusk wall. "All these weeks I looked for you. I felt responsible for you because of your father."

"And I thank you for . . ." She tugged on his hand, a sinking feeling in her stomach. "My father? What about my father?"

Josh drew his lips together grimly. "There's no way to tell you but to tell you. He . . . he's dead, Mackenzie. Been dead."

A lump rose in her throat and a single tear slid down her cheek. She stared unseeing. *"Mahtah."*

"I'm sorry. I'm so sorry."

Her lower lip trembled. She could feel her heart breaking. Her father dead? How sad to no longer be a child . . . anyone's child. "How . . . how did he die?"

It took him a long time to answer, as if he had to recall. "The night you . . . you left. The whole fort was under attack. He was shot." This time he squeezed her hand. "I'm so sorry, Mackenzie."

She rubbed her nose with the back of her hand. "All this time I thought he was alive." She shook her head slowly in disbelief. "And he was dead."

"Part of the fort burned. Albertson lost a lot of men."

"And Harry?" she asked, still feeling numb all over.

"He's fine. He's good. He sent men to look for you after

the attack. Look for your body. He thought you were dead. Murdered by the savages.''

''It is good, you are awake,'' Mary interrupted as she knelt beside Josh. She took his hand in hers. ''What can this woman get you? Water? Food? This woman had corn much sweetened with maple syrup. It will make you strong again.''

Josh's gaze shifted from Mackenzie to Mary with interest. ''I . . . I'd like something to eat. That would be good. We didn't eat much on the trail.''

Mackenzie rose from the bed. Josh was in good hands with Mary. He didn't need Mackenzie.

Laughing Woman wrapped one arm around Mackenzie's back and gave her a squeeze. ''This woman is sorry your father is dead.''

''I just can't believe it.'' She sniffed. ''I thought he was alive all this time. I fretted that he was worried about me. And he was dead. Dead.''

Laughing Woman squeezed her in another hug. ''In the heavens, loved ones look down on us and watch us. Father of Mackenzie knew you were happy and safe.''

''That's what Fire Dancer said,'' Mackenzie whispered. ''He said the heart knows . . .''

''Mack-en-zie? Mack-en-zie?'' A familiar voice called her name from outside the wigwam.

''Fire Dancer?''

She threw herself into his arms. ''Oh, Fire Dancer. My father is dead.''

Fire Dancer closed his arms around his wife's waist and held her close. Over her shoulder, his black-eyed gaze met Josh's.

Chapter Twenty-Four

"I told her what happened," Josh said weakly.

"You told her?" Fire Dancer attempted to keep his voice temperate. Had Josh told her the truth? *He couldn't have, else she'd not be holding me so tightly.*

Mackenzie wiped the tears from her eyes. "He was killed in the fighting that night we left the fort. Josh said a lot of the soldiers were killed. The Hurons burned the fort."

Fire Dancer released Mackenzie with one arm, but held her with the other. He faced Josh. "Gentle Bears tells this man you tried to enter our village. You were shot as an intruder."

"I was trying to save Mackenzie," Josh answered. "I didn't know—" He glanced away. "That she stayed here of her own free will. That she married you." He said the last words with a tone of finality to his voice.

Fire Dancer pressed a kiss to Mackenzie's forehead. It felt so good to have her in his arms again. When the French had canceled the scouting expedition, he'd been relieved, and then he felt guilty. What kind of warrior had he become that all he wanted to do was sit at his hearth, smoke his pipe, and watch the sway of his wife's hips as she painted her pictures?

"This man would ask the women to leave this wigwam so

that I might speak to the white *manake*.'' Fire Dancer kissed
the top of Mackenzie's head. Her hair smelled as sweet as
clover honey. ''Wait for this man in our lodge,'' he whispered
to her, his voice full of promise. He kissed her again and
released her. He hated the emptiness he immediately felt inside.

Mackenzie, Mary and Laughing Woman took their leave,
allowing the two men privacy. Fire Dancer stood at the hearth
and warmed his hands. His chest was filled with mixed emotions. He was thankful that the young man had not told Mackenzie who was responsible for her father's death. Such words
should not come from anyone but himself. At the same time,
Fire Dancer felt immensely guilty. He had intended, from the
beginning, to confess to her, yet his confession had never come.
He'd made one excuse after another, but the truth was that he
hadn't wanted to tell her because he couldn't bear to lose her.
To lose her would break him.

''You did not tell my wife the truth,'' Fire Dancer said
quietly.

Josh rested flat on his back on the sleeping platform, his
hand on his bandaged wound. ''I told her the truth. Franklin
Daniels was killed in battle. I just didn't tell her the whole
truth.''

Fire Dancer turned his gaze to the boy that he knew loved
his wife. If Franklin Daniels had had his way it would have
been Josh who would have married Mackenzie, not Fire Dancer.
''But you did not tell my wife her father died by my hand.
Why?''

He lifted his good shoulder in a shrug. ''Hell, I don't know.
I should have told her.'' He stared at Mary's good luck ornament
that hung over the sleeping platform. ''But I couldn't. Didn't
see any point. You're married.'' He paused. ''She loves you.''

Fire Dancer walked to his side. ''I will care for her always,''
he said gratefully. ''Love her fiercely, always.''

''She wanted you, not me. I saw it the day we marched into
Fort Belvadere.'' Josh made no attempt to hide his disappointment. ''She never would have married me, even if you hadn't
come along.'' He shook his head. ''I just never thought she'd

o such a thing. This is even outrageous for Mackenzie. To
arry a sa—an Indian. Live with Indians."

"She is well-cared for. Well-loved among my people."

"I know. I can see it in her eyes. But living with redskins . . ."
le grimaced. "Is she safe?"

"She is safe."

Josh nodded. "As long as I know she's all right. If this is
hat she wants, guess I can . . . should go."

Fire Dancer felt a great sense of respect for the boy . . . the
an. "I will tell her the truth."

He snapped his head around. "Why? What will you accom-
lish? I saw what happened from the end of the palisade.
ranklin fired on you after you lowered your weapon—after
e swore he wouldn't."

"You do not think I should tell her? It was in self-defense."

Josh glanced at him. "Don't tell her. All you'll do is relieve
our own conscience. She doesn't need to know."

"This man wants to be honest with his wife, always. I expect
onesty from her. Marriage is based on honestly and trust
mong my people."

"So tell her if you want. I'm just sayin' what I would do."
osh closed his eyes and rubbed his wound. "Damn thing hurts.
ou think your medicine woman could give me more of that
ea? It makes the pain better than anything a surgeon's got."

Fire Dancer stood over Josh. He wanted to somehow express
is gratitude, but it was difficult. He considered Josh Watkins
is enemy. Or at least he had. "I will send our medicine woman
n, and my sister."

Josh smiled. "Your sister, Mary. She's sweet. She's been
o good to me. She sat up all night with me last night. She
ripped water into my mouth when I was too weak to drink."

"Mary is a good woman."

Josh closed his eyes. "Pretty, too."

Fire Dancer wondered if he imagined the man's interest in
is cousin. "I will send the women." Fire Dancer patted Josh's
ood shoulder awkwardly. "Thank you for not telling my
Mack-en-zie. This man will always be grateful to you."

Josh waved his hand as Fire Dancer left. "Just go to her. Comfort her. You're the one she needs."

A few days later Mackenzie entered her wigwam to find Fire Dancer standing at her easel staring at a painting. It was Fire Dancer's original portrait. In her haste to leave earlier, she must have forgotten to hide it.

She tucked her hands behind her back. "I . . . I wanted to surprise you when it was done." She lifted her hand lamely toward it. "I checked with Snake Man first. He said I'd not harm your soul or mine by altering it."

Fire Dancer dropped his arm over her shoulder. "It is good, Mack-en-zie."

She studied the painting proudly. She had altered Fire Dancer's stance slightly so that his head was turned, his face concealed by his long, thick black hair. Beside him, she had added a red-haired woman whose face was also concealed. Herself. In the portrait, their hands were linked. When their child was born, she already knew where she would add him or her to the painting.

"It is beautiful," he whispered. "The best you have painted." He turned toward her and hugged her. "This man is honored."

Mackenzie squeezed him tightly. Over his shoulder she studied the growing number of portraits that lined the wigwam walls. She loved painting the Shawnee. It gave her a purpose other than being Fire Dancer's wife. But what was she going to do with all the paintings? A few of the Shawnee had accepted portraits as gifts, but many were still too superstitious to do anything but admire them.

He kissed her and Mackenzie pressed her hips seductively to his. "Our guests will be here soon," she whispered in his ear. "I do not think there is time."

He flicked his tongue over her upper lip. "This man knows. He but makes a promise for later."

She giggled and kissed him again. They parted. "It was good of you to invite Josh to our evening meal." She stirred a pot of venison and corn soup. "I'm glad there are no hard feelings between you."

Fire Dancer sat beside the hearth to carve a pipe he was making for Snake Man. "He is a good loser." He grinned.

Mackenzie laughed and gave him a playful kick with the toe of her moccasin. "Have you noticed . . . Mary seems to be interested in Josh."

"She is *interested* in any white man."

"No, this is different." She shifted a clay pot of cornbread over the coals. "He likes her. Yesterday I saw them kissing behind the sweat house."

Fire Dancer's forehead furrowed. "Are you to become the matchmaker of our village? Perhaps you could find a mate for my brother, as well."

She ignored his comment. She was in too good a mood to ruin the evening by discussing Okonsa. "I'm serious. I see a possibility. Mary wants a white husband. Josh needs a mate. They're well-suited for one other."

Finally seeming to realize Mackenzie was serious, Fire Dancer glanced up from the rosewood pipe. "He would take Little Weaver as a wife, a redwoman, a woman who carried another man's child?"

"He's a good man, Fire Dancer. He just wasn't the right man for me. I think he'd make an excellent husband for Mary. Since I'm not returning to the Chesapeake, I'll be giving him my father's tavern. Mary could have a new gown every year, and a cupboard of china plates."

"This man would miss her if she left."

"But you want her to be happy, don't you?"

"*Ah*. She has been through so much. She deserves happiness if there is anyone on this earth that does."

Outside, Mackenzie heard Mary's laughter and the low rumble of Josh's voice.

"Here they come." Mackenzie met her guests at the door. "Josh. Mary. Robert." She stepped back to allow them entrance.

Fire Dancer formally greeted their guests and they all sat down for a meal of venison soup and corn bread with honey

Mackenzie had harvested herself. Afterward, the men sat back to smoke their pipes and nibble on nuts and dried berries. The women cleaned up the dishes.

As Mackenzie gathered the wooden trenchers and spoons it occurred to her that life on the Chesapeake was not as different from life here as she had once imagined. The Shawnee's homes were different, their language was different, the color of their skin was different, but people seemed to be universally the same. They laughed and cried about the same concerns. They made love, they argued. After supper, men smoked pipes and talked of livestock and hunting, and women cleaned dishes and gossiped.

"He is handsome, yes?" Mary whispered as she dipped a dirty dish into the wash bucket.

Mackenzie glanced over her shoulder at the three men in conversation. "My husband? *Ah`*, he is handsome."

Mary giggled and elbowed Mackenzie. "No."

It did Mackenzie's heart good to see Mary smiling again. "Robert Red Shirt?" She frowned. "I think he already has a wife."

Mary burst into another fit of nervous giggles. "Joshua. This woman thinks he likes me."

Mackenzie looked into Mary's eyes. "And why shouldn't he? You're an intelligent, caring, beautiful woman."

Mary lowered her gaze, blushing. "He makes me laugh. He knows I have been with other men besides my dead husband and he says he doesn't care."

Mackenzie's eyes twinkled. "He would make a good husband, would he not?"

Mary nibbled on her lower lip. "*Ah`*. He would, if he would have me."

"If he would have you?" Mackenzie rinsed a wooden spoon. "If you will have him, you mean."

Mary watched Josh wistfully. "This woman would make him a good wife. He says he will return to your father's tavern. This woman could cook and clean for the tavern. Make for suc-cess-ful man."

"I agree." Mackenzie glanced over her shoulder at the men again. "So all we have to do is convince him, right?"

The two women's gazes met and both laughed.

"What are you two laughing about?" Robert Red Shirt asked, rising. "Us, would be my guess. Women are like that."

Mackenzie dried her hands on a linen towel and passed it to Mary. "We would do no such thing, honored guest."

Robert Red Shirt stood with his hands on his hips and studied Mackenzie's portraits, one at a time. "These are very good," he said. "As good as the paintings this man has seen in galleries in France."

"You think so?" Mackenzie stood beside him.

"Yes." He turned to see the ones that hung on the wall behind him. "There are so many. What will you do with them all?"

"Well, they're not all finished. I paint in stages." She shrugged. "I don't know what I'm going to do with them. I paint because I must, not because I have something to do with them when I'm done."

His dark eyes narrowed. "This man would buy them from you, if you would be willing to sell them."

"Buy them?" Mackenzie gave a small laugh. "You would buy them? For what?"

"To sell. This man thinks there are ladies in Philadelphia that would grace their parlors with portraits of the *wild Indians.*"

Mackenzie lowered her hands to her hips speculatively. "You think so?" She glanced at Fire Dancer. "Do you hear what Robert Red Shirt says, husband? He wants to buy my paintings and sell them."

"You would be willing to sell them?" Fire Dancer walked over and stood beside her.

"All but a couple. Perhaps if the English saw portraits of how the Shawnee live, they would realize we're not as different as they think. Not as threatening."

"I could take them when I leave here. If they sell, I would come back for more in the spring."

"And you would pay me."

"English coin."

Mackenzie's mind was churning quickly. "Could I have goods, instead?"

"Goods?" Robert asked.

"You're a trader. Could I have cloth and needles instead? Wool, knives, silk thread. Supplies our village can use."

"This man could bring you supplies in the spring."

Mackenzie looped her arm through Fire Dancer's. She couldn't believe it. Someone was actually going to buy her paintings! "It's a deal. Pick any you like, except . . ." She released Fire Dancer's arm and walked to her easel. "This one of Fire Dancer and me, and that one." She pointed to the portrait of the boys playing marbles. The painting was all she had left of Tall Moccasin . . . it and her memories.

"If they sell like I think they will, I'll want more."

"I can paint more," she assured Robert, returning to her husband's side. "I'm going to be here a long time."

Fire Dancer's gaze locked onto hers and they kissed, oblivious to the others in the room.

Fire Dancer burst into the wigwam. "This man must go."

Mackenzie jumped up from her stool and dropped her brush. "What's wrong?"

Fire Dancer grabbed his travel bag and stuffed necessary items into it. "Okonsa returned with his men, but not all of them. Battered Pot and Sits Silently are dead."

"There was fighting? I thought you were only supposed to scout."

Fire Dancer grabbed his water skin and his extra pair of moccasins. "I go to the French fort. We did not agree to fight. We should not have had to fight."

Mackenzie touched his arm. "Please be careful."

"I must take Gentle Bear with me, but I gave instructions to Okonsa to watch over you. If you have any need, tell him. Do not stray from the camp. Send a boy for water."

Mackenzie didn't want Fire Dancer to go, but she didn't

voice her protest. She knew there was no point. "How long will you be gone?"

"This man does not know."

"You'll miss Josh and Mary's wedding. Josh was hoping they could leave in a few days if the weather breaks. He's anxious to get home."

"This man is sorry. It cannot be helped. I will say good-bye to my sister in case I do not return in time." He balled his fist angrily at his side. "I did not want to fight the English."

Mackenzie's heart ached for Fire Dancer's anguish. In the last few weeks she'd begun to understand how difficult it was to be a leader. Fire Dancer felt responsible for everyone in the village, yet he had to honor their decisions, even when he thought they were wrong.

Fire Dancer slung his pack over his back and reached for his snow shoes. "Give this man a kiss, wife."

She grasped his tunic and pressed her mouth hard against his. "I love you," she whispered, resolving not to cry. She was glad she hadn't told him about the baby yet. Fire Dancer had enough to worry about. He didn't need to be concerned about her and a child.

"You will be all right?"

She forced a smile. "Fine. I've the wedding preparations and I have to pack up the paintings Robert will take with him. He's going to escort Josh and Mary back to the Chesapeake."

Fire Dancer kissed her again and started for the door. "Good-bye, wife. This man loves you."

She grabbed one of the support beams and hung onto it for strength. "How much?" she whispered, not trusting her full voice.

"As the birch tree loves its bark."

The doorflap fell and Fire Dancer was gone.

Mackenzie stared at the door for a long a moment. "He's going to be all right," she said aloud to calm her fears. "He's a warrior. He knows how to fight if he must. He'll come home to me safely." She picked up her brush and dabbed it in the brown bark paint. "He has to."

* * *

That night Mackenzie turned in early. She was physically tired, and emotionally weary. She fell into a deep sleep, with the aide of one of Laughing Woman's herbal teas.

Sometime in the night, she was vaguely aware of Fire Dancer sliding into bed beside her. She snuggled against his warm nakedness and sighed. She was glad he was home. She always slept better with him beside her.

His hand grazed her breast and she recognized that he didn't smell right.

Somewhere in her sub-conscious, an alarm went off. Fire Dancer had gone to the French fort. How could he be here? The thought startled her and she jolted wide awake.

Mackenzie stiffened in horror. The man held her in his arms, his hand possessively on her breast. He was not Fire Dancer.

Chapter Twenty-Five

Mackenzie froze in horror.

The stranger nuzzled her neck, and panted in her ear.

She didn't know what to do.

The hand slipped between her breasts and moved lower.

Mackenzie reacted instantly. "Get off me," she shouted as she gave him a shove.

She pushed him so hard that he fell off the edge of her sleeping platform.

"It is all right, love. I will not harm you." The man's arms came through the darkness and she jerked out of his way.

She thought she recognized the voice. *It couldn't be . . .* "Okonsa?"

"Ah¬." He climbed back onto the bed.

Mackenzie pressed herself against the wall and slapped his hands away. "What are you doing here? Get out of my bed!"

"Shhh," he crooned. "It is all right, love. My brother said I should take care of you. I should give you what you need."

"I'll give you what you need, if you don't get the hell out of my bed," she threatened.

"Ah, my kitten, she has fangs. Is this what you like in love play?"

Mackenzie knew she mustn't panic. Okonsa's mind wasn't stable. She had to be careful how she handled him or she would truly be in danger. She drew a bearskin across her bare breasts to cover herself. There was scarcely enough light from the firepit to see the outline of his face.

"Okonsa, I don't know what gave you the idea I wanted you here, but you're wrong. Get out now, and I'll never mention this incident to anyone."

He slipped his hand beneath the fur and brushed her bare thigh with his fingertips. "It is all right, Mack-en-zie. Fire Dancer gave me permission—us permission. You no longer have to hide your desire for me."

She shoved his hand off again, wishing desperately her knife wasn't out of reach. His touch made her skin crawl. "I said get away from me." She gave him a kick, realizing that she protected not only herself, but her unborn child. Fire Dancer's child. "Get off my bed and get the bloody hell out of here."

"You know you are hot for me." He moved and she knew he caressed his groin. "Give me your hand and I will show how hot I am for you," he murmured.

Without thinking, Mackenzie slapped him across the face. The second she did it, she realized she'd made a mistake.

He slapped her back, hard across the mouth. So hard that her lower lip went numb and she felt a trickle of warm blood run down her cheek.

"You son of a bitch," she shouted. "You won't ruin my life like this!"

"Silence, or they will hear you."

She struck at him again, crazy with anger. "Get out, get out!"

"I said shut up, white bitch!"

He hit Mackenzie again and she tumbled off the end of the bed. On the way over the edge, she was vaguely aware that she struck her temple in the same place she'd been shot. She felt no pain, only a numbness that swallowed her up.

"Mack-en-zie? You are all right?"

She heard his voice as it were from a distance. She felt his touch as he gathered her into his arms and then everything dissolved into blackness.

"Mack-en-zie? Mack-en-zie?" Okonsa held his brother's wife in his arms and shook her gently. Her body was so soft; she smelled so good.

Tears ran down his cheeks and he buried his face in her hair. "This man is sorry. This man is sorry. I did not mean to hurt you. Only to love you." He shook her a little harder, anger bubbling up.

Her head bobbed lifelessly.

"Wake up, bitch, white woman. You did not fall that hard!"

Okonsa felt a suffocating sense of panic. It was the same panic he had felt in Mary's wigwam that day she fell. The same panic that had engulfed him when Tall Moccasin had accosted him on the trail.

Okonsa didn't know what to do. Fire Dancer would be angry with him if he knew Okonsa had hurt her, even accidentally. Okonsa did not want his cousin to be angry with him.

He stared at her pale-skinned face by the dim light of the glowing fire. He brushed a lock of red hair off her smooth cheek, trying to think.

I could kill her. Make it look like the Hurons had sneaked into the village and done the horrible deed. It had worked with the Frenchman.

He inhaled again and her honey-clover scent enveloped him.

But Okonsa didn't want to kill the white bitch. He loved her. He loved her because Fire Dancer did. He loved her because he loved Fire Dancer.

Pity she was white *manake*. He hated her for that.

A dog barked outside the wigwam and startled Okonsa. He had to do something quickly. She wasn't waking up.

Blood trickled from her temple. He licked his thumb and dabbed at the wound.

He could take her away . . . That was an idea!

Okonsa was tired of this village and of his cousin's cowardice, anyway. And he was tired of Fire Dancer always getting what he wanted. First it was the position of War Chief. Then his mother named him her successor as chief. Then he had gone to the fort and found himself a white woman whore to warm his bed.

Okonsa would take the white woman north. They could join one of the Iroquois tribes and truly be a part of the fighting. Up north he could have the white woman. He could control her as he had not been able to control those white men the day his mother had been murdered.

Okonsa stared at her bare breasts, her flat belly, the nest of curls at the apex of her thighs. He could smell her woman's scent. He knew she wanted him. It had been that way since the day they had met at the fort. He only needed to give her the opportunity and she would come to him. She would spread her white thighs and she would give herself to him.

Just thinking about it made Okonsa throb.

Gently, he lowered her to the floor. He didn't dare risk returning to his own wigwam so he would have to pack for their journey from what he could find here.

Okonsa tossed a piece of wood onto the firepit and the flames rose, casting brighter light. He found two leather bags and stuffed them full of supplies. He included a dress, leggings, and a pair of moccasins for Mack-en-zie.

The bags packed, he smoothed out a bearskin on the floor and added a doeskin blanket on top. He picked up the unconscious white woman and placed her on one side. He rolled her up so that her feet and head were covered. He checked to be certain she could breathe and then heaved her onto his shoulder.

Without anyone seeing him, Okonsa slipped out of the wigwam and into the darkness with Fire Dancer's wife.

Mackenzie felt the sensation of drifting downward and as her awareness sharpened, she realized she was being lowered to the ground. She jolted awake as panic seized her. Where was she? What was happening? Something was wrapped around her, encasing her from head to foot. Her face was covered, her arms pinned to her sides.

Her head was pounding. She felt like she couldn't breathe.

She remembered Okonsa. He'd hit her . . . knocked her off the sleeping platform.

Oh, God, he's kidnapped me. He's taken me from Fire Dancer.

Mackenzie's first impulse was to scream. But if Okonsa still had her . . . if he'd done this to her, she knew she had to remain calm. She had to protect herself and the child she carried.

Mackenzie wiggled. Perhaps he had left her for dead and she could escape the confines of the sleeping furs and run. But perhaps he was still here.

"Okonsa?" she said softly. Then again, "Okonsa?"

Mackenzie heard a sound and then felt hands on her body through the blankets.

"Mack-en-zie. Mack-en-zie, you are well?"

He unrolled the bearskin she was wrapped in and Mackenzie emerged from the cocoon, clutching the inner doeskin blanket. She was stark naked beneath it and it was cold.

They were somewhere in the forest, on a mountain ridge. The sky was gray as it was at first light in the winter.

"What have you done?" Mackenzie asked softly.

Okonsa tried to touch her forehead, but she pulled away. "Don't touch me," she threatened.

He drew back his hands and grinned like a school boy. "You are good. You are well, Mack-en-zie. This man knew you were not hurt."

"Okonsa, where are we? Where have you taken me?" She tried not to sound as if she were afraid. "Why have you taken me from our village?"

"Shhh, it is all right, my love." He pulled through a leather bag—one of Fire Dancer's bags—and extracted her dress, leggings, and moccasins. "Put these on and you will be warm. This man would make you tea but a fire would not be safe."

Mackenzie snatched the clothing from his hand and fumbled to dress under the cover of the blanket. It was cold outside and her skin puckered with goosebumps.

"You didn't answer my question," she snapped. "Why have you brought me here?"

"We will be together, you and I, Mack-en-zie. You do not

love my cousin. You did not want to marry him. I tried to save you from the marriage that night at the communal fire. Do you remember?''

Dressed, Mackenzie felt less vulnerable. She slipped her feet into her moccasins and laced them one at a time. She tried to stay calm and follow his line of thinking, no matter which way it wandered. "I remember. You defended me."

"This man should have offered to take you then. It was what you wanted. You wanted me."

She shook her head. She could play along some, but this was too far. "No, she answered firmly. "I never wanted you, Okonsa. Only Fire Dancer, only my husband, who will soon realize I'm gone."

He shook his head in agitated way. "No. *Mahtah. Mahtah.* He is gone. My brother cousin is gone with the French. He will not know for many days that the lovers have escaped."

Dressed, Mackenzie pulled the doeskin over her shoulders to protect herself against the wind. "We are not lovers, Okonsa. We never have been," she said rigidly. "And we never will be." She started to walk away. "Now take me home before anyone knows we're gone."

"Can't." He grabbed her arm roughly. "Can't go home to the village. Never. You are my woman now." He cupped his groin. "Okonsa's woman. You go with me, north." He pointed toward a steep mountain ridge.

She struggled to escape his iron grip. "Aren't you listening to me? I said I'm not yours. I'll never be yours. I want to go home. You have to take me home before you get yourself into greater trouble."

He held tightly to her arm, sinking his fingers into her flesh. "Listen to this man." He gave her a shake. "This man says you are mine."

"No. I'm Fire Dancer's wife. I love him. He loves me."

Okonsa cackled. "Loves you. My brother cousin, he does not love you. What man loves a woman and then kills her father?"

An eerie tingle of fear crept up Mackenzie's spine. What was this mad man's babble now? "What do you mean?" she demanded. "Fire Dancer didn't kill my father. He was killed in the fighting the night the Hurons attacked the fort. You remember the night. You conveniently showed up just in time to be in the thick of things."

Okonsa laughed like a child. "He did it. Fire Dancer killed the whis-key selling *manake* and then he took his daughter."

Of course Mackenzie didn't believe him. Fire Dancer wouldn't have harmed her father. Fire Dancer loved her—even then he had loved her. "I don't want to hear any more of your nonsense," she told Okonsa as she jerked her arm from his grip. "Now take me home. I'm not going anywhere with you."

His face hardened. "You will go with me," he threatened, "or—"

She thrust her face into his. She'd been through too much to find her happiness, and Fire Dancer and the Shawnee were her happiness. She'd not give them up. "Or what?" she demanded fiercely. "You'll what?"

His black eyes grew narrow and beady. "Or this man will kill you and throw you into the same mountain crevice where Tall Moccasin sleeps."

Mackenzie froze in fear. His words rang in her ears. She felt so light-headed that she feared she might pass out again. But she refused to give in to her terror . . . or to him. "You?" she whispered. "You kidnapped him? You murdered him?"

He gave her a shove northward. "Silence, woman." He grabbed the two bags and left the bearskin behind. "March and do not speak. I have heard enough of your white *manake* bitching."

"Gone? Gone where?" Fire Dancer stormed into his wigwam. Everything was in place. Mackenzie's paints were on the stool. Their portrait rested on the easel. Everything was neat and orderly. Nothing was out of place. Nothing missing . . . except his wife.

Laughing Woman followed him inside. She spoke softly in Shawnee. "This woman does not know. She was not here the morning after you left."

He spun around, numb. Had she found out about her father? Had Joshua told her the truth? He was overwhelmed with guilt. Even if she knew, surely she would have waited for him. He knew her too well to believe she would have left without a farewell, without a fight. "The morning after I left?" he repeated, Laughing Woman's words sinking in. "But that was more than seven days ago."

Laughing Woman folded her hands. *"Ah`."*

He refused to believe she left him. "Someone has taken her. English *manake*. Hurons. Frenchmen. I do not know who."

"There are things missing," Laughing Woman said. "This woman has looked through your belongings. I know what was here. Two bags are missing besides the one you took with you. Water skins are missing. Food probably. Two sleeping furs."

Fire Dancer shook his head in disbelief. His world was crumbling like an old clay pot. The French had changed their terms. Now they demanded the Shawnee fight with them. His wife was gone . . . His Mack-en-zie. She who possessed more of his soul than he did.

"There is more, my friend," Laughing Woman said gently.

Fire Dancer hesitated. Her tone made him not want to look at her or hear her words. "More?"

"Okonsa is missing."

His headed snapped up to glare at her. He felt as if he was falling . . . falling from the highest peak of the highest mountain. "You do not suggest she would—"

"Mahtah," she answered firmly. She grabbed his arm, forcing him to listen. "This woman does not sug-gest she went with him. Mack-en-sie would not even go to the stream with your cousin. She did not like him. She feared him."

What Laughing Woman said was true. Guilt washed over him. His wife had been afraid of his cousin. Again and again, she had tried to express her fear to Fire Dancer. He hadn't listened. He had been so sure that Okonsa was changing that he had been unwilling to hear her words.

"Okonsa has taken my wife." It was a statement, not a question. Fire Dancer knew in his heart of hearts that it was true. His cousin, who he had called brother, had betrayed him and for that he would kill him.

"*Ah*", this woman believes it is true. We heard nothing that night. He must have carried her out of the village as we slept."

Fire Dancer balled his fists in fury. "How could I have done this to her? I left her in his care."

"It will do her no good for you to chastise yourself," Laughing Woman said. "You must take action."

"I must speak with Joshua to be sure he knows nothing of her departure, and then I leave." Fire Dancer burst through the door, out into the morning sunshine. Snow sparkled off the mountains in the distance. "It will be hard to track Okonsa in the snow that has fallen." He stared northward. "But this man knows his cousin as well as he knows his own palm. I know which way the thief goes."

Laughing Woman handed him his pack and his musket. "You will find him. You will find her."

"*Ah*." Fire Dancer threw the pack over his back and strode away. "I am coming, Mack-en-zie," he murmured. "I come, *kitehi*."

Chapter Twenty-Six

Mackenzie sat on the floor and rested her cheek against the rough headboard of the bed she was tied to. It was late afternoon and the dark shadows cast across the un-planed floorboards were lengthening. Okonsa snored on the bed above her.

Mackenzie was cold, but she couldn't get up to throw a log on the fire in the crumbling stone fireplace. She wouldn't be able to rise until Okonsa woke and she wouldn't wake him if she was in danger of freezing solid. As long as he slept, he kept his filthy hands off her.

It had been nine days since Okonsa carried Mackenzie from the village. Nine days she had endured imprisonment. He had walked her over a mountain ridge and north through steep terrain. For two days, he dragged her through the mountains, and then a snowstorm had hit, and they'd taken shelter in this abandoned trapper's cabin.

Mackenzie stared at the log walls. It could barely be called a cabin; it was more of a shed. Wind and snow blew through the cracks and rodents fought Okonsa and Mackenzie for what little food they had left.

Mackenzie glanced up at Okonsa's sleeping form. He lay on

his back, his mouth wide open. He breathed deeply, snorted, and rolled over.

So far she'd been able to keep him at arm's length. He wanted to have sex with her, but somehow in his crazy head, he had the idea that she would come around to his way of thinking and give herself to him. He pawed at her breasts some. He had tried to kiss her several times, but so far she'd been lucky; his advances hadn't gotten out of hand. Tied up as she was, Mackenzie didn't know how she could defend herself if he made up his mind to rape her . . .

Mackenzie exhaled softly and closed her eyes. She was so tired that her eyeballs ached, but it was hard for her to sleep. She was so afraid of what Okonsa might do to her that she rarely closed her eyes for more than a few minutes. She was hungry, too. She slid her hand across her still-flat belly. She was worried about not getting enough food to eat. If she wasn't eating, she knew her baby wasn't, either.

"Oh, where are you, Fire Dancer?" she whispered to the cold, empty room.

She opened her eyes. She knew Fire Dancer would come for her. She knew he searched for her at this very moment. She could feel him near. All she had to do was to remain alive until he could reach her. Something poor Tall Moccasin had apparently been unable to do.

Mackenzie pushed thoughts of Tall Moccasin out of her head. If she thought about Tall Moccasin or about what Okonsa had said about Fire Dancer killing her father, she'd go as mad as Okonsa. Right now, she had to concentrate on staying alive.

She slipped her hand under the bed and pulled out a small piece of floorboard she'd manage to pry up from under the bed, then picked up her charcoal stick. With her wrists and ankles tied with leather thongs, it was difficult to maneuver, but she managed.

Mackenzie placed the floor board on her lap lengthwise and took up the burnt stick in her right hand. When Okonsa slept during the day, she sketched him. The portrait was full length. She dressed him in his hide mantel with the red streaks. She added feathers to his scalp lock and a glimmer to his nose ring that she had come to despise.

The sketch was quite good. Just looking at it made her shiver. Through her portrayal of the man, she could feel his madness . . . his anger. One could stare at the haunting charcoal eyes and know that he was dangerous.

Mackenzie didn't know what possessed her to sketch Okonsa while he slept. He'd probably kill her if he found out. She sketched it anyway . . . in defiance of his wishes.

Okonsa rolled over again and Mackenzie glanced up. He was waking. She shoved the board and writing stick under the bed.

He opened his eyes and yawned. When his gaze met hers he smiled that boyish grin of his and adjusted his testicles.

Mackenzie stared at him, her face expressionless.

"Ah, good rest," Okonsa said. He slid his feet over the side of the bed and rose. "It's cold in here." He rubbed his hands together as he crossed the uneven floor boards. "You should have woken this man, and I would have added fuel to the fire. This man does not want you to be cold, my love."

She watched him.

He tossed a log onto the fire and added another one. "Why do you not answer me? You do not talk and you make me lonely."

She said nothing.

He stood in the center of the twelve by twelve room, his hands planted on his hips. "This man does not understand your stubbornness. This was to be our time away from the others. Time to know each other."

She glared.

Okonsa lifted his foot and booted a broken chair across the room. It hit the wall and smashed into splintering pieces. "Speak to me! Tell this man what you want!"

"I want to go home to my husband," she said softly.

"Not that!" He walked toward her, his arms outstretched as he opened and closed his hands. "Something here. Something I can get you. Something that will make you happy."

"Fresh meat." She didn't know what made her say it. Survival instinct, she supposed. "We need fresh meat. The snow has stopped. We've eaten nothing but pemmican for days, and I'm hungry."

"The snow is deep outside. This man does not know what he can find."

"You are a great hunter," she said, stroking his ego. "This woman knows you can find a snow hare."

He thrust out his chest. "Your words are truth. This man is a great hunter, besides being a great warrior, and a great lover." He hit his chest with his closed fist. "This man will shoot a hare for his woman's evening meal."

He grabbed his outer cloak and bow at the door. "I will not be gone long."

Still seated on the floor, she lifted her bound wrists. "Could you untie me?"

"So you can escape?"

"How could this woman escape?" she asked innocently. For days, she'd been waiting for this chance. "The snow is deep and I do not know my way. I am not a hunter and a trapper as you are. I would be lost without you to guide me," she lied smoothly.

Truthfully, she'd paid careful attention to the direction they'd walked. She'd even left behind a few marks on trees to guide her home to the village, should she manage to escape.

He narrowed his black eyes. "If you tried to escape this man might kill you and throw you in the gully."

She knew he was trying to bully her, like he'd bullied Tall Moccasin probably. She wouldn't think about the boy. Not now. What mattered was getting away from here and saving her baby.

"I will not try to escape," she said. She forced the barest smile. "I could melt snow while you are gone. If you bring back a hare, I could stew it."

He rubbed his stomach. *"Ah`,* this man would like a meal made from his woman's hands."

She lifted her bound wrists. "Please?"

He hesitated, then came to her.

She turned her head away as he untied her wrists. Free, she rubbed them and tried to stimulate circulation.

His face was still close to hers.

"A kiss?" he asked.

She kept her face turned. "I think not . . . not now."

He drew back and grinned. "Yes? You say 'not now', which makes this man think you mean 'later'." He adjusted his testicles proudly. "A good meal in this woman's belly and he thinks she would look about this man with favor in her eyes."

Mackenzie sat on the edge of the rope bed and untied her ankles. "It will be dark soon, Okonsa. Go fetch the hare before you cannot see it bound in front of you."

Seeming reluctant, he walked out the door. "This man will return soon. You will be here when I return."

"Where else could I go in the middle of a snowstorm?"

The moment the door slammed shut, Mackenzie leaped up and into action. She grabbed one of the bags Okonsa stole from her wigwam and crammed necessities into it; the flint and steel box to light a fire, the remainder of the dried pemmican, a waterskin.

She dragged the doeskin blanket from her own wigwam off the bed and tossed it over her shoulders. She didn't know how long Okonsa would be gone, so she had to hurry. At the door she grabbed a pair of old snowshoes down off a peg on the wall. The last trapper who had lived here had left them behind. Hastily, she strapped them to her moccasins. They were a little large, but they would do.

Mackenzie threw the bag onto her back and stepped out of the cabin. Her heart fell when she discovered how deep the snow was. Even in the snowshoes, it would be slow-moving.

She spotted Okonsa tracks leading north. That was perfect. With any luck he would be gone an hour or two. By the time he reached the cabin and realized she was gone, she'd have a good lead on him.

She walked around the cabin, circumnavigating the yellow snow, evidence that Okonsa had been too lazy to walk far from the cabin. She tightened the bag's strap on her shoulder and lunged forward into the snow. Mackenzie half ran, half walked, fear and excitement pumping through her veins. All she could think of was escape. She panted hard, plowing through the drifts.

"Ah hah!"

Okonsa appeared from behind a sycamore tree and stepped into her path. "You think this man is stupid? Stupid white *manake!*" He bellowed furiously.

Mackenzie screamed and darted left, out of his grasp. She tried to run, but the snow had drifted too deep. Even in her snowshoes, she couldn't move. She fell headlong into the snow, screaming and flailing her arms.

When he grabbed her by the doeskin mantle, she kicked him hard and rolled out of the cloth, freeing herself.

"Come back!" he bellowed. "You will not escape! You are mine! Mine!"

"No," she screamed. "Fire Dancer's!"

He fell on top of her, crushing her into the frigid, crackling snow. "Mine!"

"Only Fire Dancer's," she defied, spitting snow from her mouth.

He rolled her onto her back and thrust his face into hers. "Then I will have you anyway!"

Mackenzie struggled furiously, but Okonsa was so much stronger. He yanked her out of the snow and half carried, half dragged her back along their beaten path to the cabin.

Inside the door, he threw her to the floor. As he walked toward her, he stripped off his clothing, strewing it on the floor.

Mackenzie crawled backward out of his way. *Don't panic. Don't panic,* she kept telling herself.

Okonsa flung off his cloak and his tunic, showing off his bare, tattooed chest.

"You can't do this," Mackenzie protested as she scrambled off the floor. "You can't rape me!"

He yanked on the leather laces of his leggings. "No?" he screamed, completely out of control. "This man cannot? What of those men so long ago? The redcoat *manake*. I said they could not rape." Tears rolled down his cheeks and he batted at them as he stalked her. "I said they could not rape this boy and they did anyway."

Mackenzie backed up against the table and stared in horror. Did Okonsa mean what he thought she meant? The . . . soldiers had raped him? Fire Dancer had never told her. She looked into Okonsa's eyes and realized Fire Dancer had not told her because he didn't know. No one knew. No one but Okonsa and the men . . . and now her.

"I'm sorry," she whispered, meaning it. She held out her hand to make him keep his distance. "This woman is so sorry for your pain."

"You do not care about my pain," he shouted. His nostrils flared. "No English-speaking *manake* cares for this man's pain. For any redman's pain." He reached into his leggings and pulled out his member.

For an instant Mackenzie froze and stared at it, swollen and veined in his hand.

He lunged at her.

She screamed as he pinned her against the table with the full weight of his muscular body. Her hands fell back on the table as he knocked the wind from her chest. Miraculously, one of her hands met with something cold and sharp.

His hunting knife. He'd left it on the table . . .

She grabbed the hilt of the knife. She was not helpless. She would never be helpless.

Okonsa yanked at the crotch of her leggings, his other hand still on his engorged rod.

Mackenzie raised the knife over her head. "Get off me," she threatened, "or I'll use it, I swear by the great *Tapalamawatah,* I will."

He burst into sick, hearty laughter. "You will use that on me?"

She held so tightly to the knife that she could feel her knuckles going numb. "I will."

He grabbed her arm and twisted it cruelly. She bit down on her lower lip to keep from crying in agony.

"Let go of it," he shouted in her face.

"I won't!"

"Let go!"

"Mahtah!"

He twisted her hand down to her side. She felt like the bones of her arm were breaking, but she didn't let go. The knife was her only chance, her baby's only chance.

He snapped her wrist to make her release the knife. To Mackenzie's surprise she heard Okonsa grunt with pain and she felt the knife sink into flesh. She gave it a hard twist upward and he screamed.

She shoved him backward with all her might and he fell off her.

Mackenzie darted away from the table as Okonsa reeled backward clutching his groin.

She stared in horror at the bloody knife in her hands. She watched it fall from her fingers and clatter across the uneven floor boards.

He fell and rolled onto his knees. "I will kill you for this," he groaned in pain. "This man will kill you."

"You will not."

Mackenzie looked up through a veil of tears to see who the voice came from.

"Fire Dancer?" His named croaked from her throat.

She couldn't believe it was him.

"Get back, Mack-en-zie," Fire Dancer ordered from the open doorway of the cabin. "Stand back so that this man can kill Okonsa."

Okonsa staggered to his feet, his hands and his leggings bloody. "Kill this man?" He threw his head back with that same crazy laughter. "You cannot kill this man who you call brother. You do not have the courage."

With one swift motion Okonsa dove for the hunting knife on the floor and came up with it clutched in his blood-sticky hands.

"Get back," Fire Dancer told Mackenzie.

She climbed up onto the bed. "He didn't hurt me," she told her husband. She didn't know why, but she felt sorry for Okonsa.

"That is good, brother," Fire Dancer said smoothly. "Then your death will be swift and merciful."

The two men drew closer to each other. As cagey as mountain cats, they bobbed and swayed, waiting for the other to make the first move. With a strength surely borne of his madness, Okonsa circled Fire Dancer, seemingly unaware of the blood that poured from his wound.

Okonsa took a stab at Fire Dancer, but cut nothing but air. Fire Dancer's blade nicked Okonsa's muscular forearm. The two men circled again.

Mackenzie covered her mouth with her hand to keep from crying out each time Okonsa lunged. She didn't want to distract Fire Dancer.

"Come, come," Fire Dancer dared. "Strike this man."

"You do not want to kill me, brother. You can forgive me for this," Okonsa said. Blood stained his legs and dripped onto the floor. "I did not take your wife. This man only *borrowed* her."

Fire Dancer lunged and cut a streak across Okonsa's bare chest.

Okonsa grunted with pain and bounded backward. Instead of retaliating, he spun around and leaped out the door into the snow.

Fire Dancer went after him.

"Be careful," Mackenzie screamed as Fire Dancer chased his cousin through the snow.

"Get back," Fire Dancer shouted to Mackenzie. "Lock yourself in the cabin."

Mackenzie waded through the snowdrifts after the two men. "Watch out, Fire Dancer," she yelled. "There's a cliff—"

Fire Dancer halted abruptly, and Mackenzie rushed up to meet him.

Okonsa tottered on the edge of the mountainside, his hands outspread, still oblivious to his crimson blood that dripped into the white snow. He had nowhere to go, no way to escape. He swayed on the edge of the deep precipice as if he were a tree in the wind.

"Brother!" Fire Dancer called.

Okonsa took one last look at Fire Dancer and Mackenzie, gave a war cry and hurled himself over the edge of the mountain cliff.

Mackenzie raced forward to grab Fire Dancer's arm. She stood beside him and watched in horror as his cousin hit the snowy mountainside. Okonsa's body bounced over jagged rocks like a child's discarded doll, his limbs flailing. He screamed once and his voice echoed through the treetops. Then she heard nothing but the sound of his tumbling body and the rain of falling stones. Finally his body met a cluster of saplings at the bottom of the ravine and came to a halt. It had to have been a three or four hundred foot drop.

Mackenzie and Fire Dancer stared at the bloody, naked body far below them. Okonsa did not move.

"We should go down," Mackenzie said as she clung desperately to Fire Dancer. "To be sure he is dead."

"No." He hugged her with one arm, his gaze fixed on his cousin's still body below. "No man could survive such a fall—not even Okonsa. It's so far down and it's almost dark."

"But the wolves are lean and hungry this winter," Mackenzie whispered, horrified by the thought. "They could—"

"Okonsa's dead." Fire Dancer sliced the cold mountain air angrily with one hand. "Let the wolves devour my cousin's betraying heart."

Tears ran down Mackenzie cheeks. She had remained strong as long as she could, but suddenly there was no strength left in her knees. She hated Okonsa, yet her tears were for him. "Hold me, husband" she whispered. Her gaze meeting his. "Please. I need you."

With a single, fluid motion, Fire Dancer lifted her in his arms and trudged through the snow toward the safety of the cabin.

Chapter Twenty-Seven

"I knew you would come for me," Mackenzie breathed. She threaded her fingers through Fire Dancer's cascade of inky black hair, and beckoned him with her eyes. She slid back on the narrow rope bed, aching to feel Fire Dancer's arms around her.

"I would follow you to the fiery pits of your hell," he answered as he climbed onto the bed.

They had locked themselves inside the cabin and added wood to the fireplace so that the room was warm, despite the drafts. In silence, they had shared a meal of dried venison, and berries and strong tea Mackenzie made with herbs Fire Dancer carried in his pack. Outside the chilling wind whistled around the eaves of the cabin, but inside Mackenzie felt safe and warm—safe because Fire Dancer was here with her.

"He did not hurt you?" Fire Dancer opened her arms and she crawled into them.

"No. He . . ." she sighed, understanding intuitively what he meant. There was so much to tell Fire Dancer, but she didn't want to talk right now. She wanted to feel the physical evidence of his love. "He wanted me to come to him of my own free will."

"When I came into the cabin, he—"

She caught his hand and kissed his palm, her green eyes luminous. "He'd lost patience because I had attempted to run away."

He held her hand in his and kissed the pad of each finger. "You fought him off."

"I cut him. I didn't mean to cut him there, but he wrestled my arm down. It was luck the blade hit flesh."

He kissed the pulse of her wrist. The inside of her elbow. "This man would not blame you if you had sunk the knife in his black heart."

She rose on her knee to face him. "Shhh." She pressed her finger to his lips. "Let's not talk about Okonsa right now. Let's not talk about any of this. I just want you to love me." She searched his black eyes for sympathy. "To make love to me."

Sitting sideways on the bed, he slipped his arms around her waist and pulled her onto his lap. He tugged at the ties of the bodice of her dress and the soft doeskin fell open to reveal her breasts that rose and fell as she took a ragged breath.

"Those nights and days alone as I walked through the snowy forest, I thought of nothing but these *opahla*." He nuzzled the valley between her tingling breasts. "This hair." He caught a handful of her bright red tresses and lifted it to his nose to inhale. "These lips." He brushed his mouth against hers in a gentle caress.

"I thought of nothing but these hands," she echoed as she laced her fingers through his. "These eyes." Her gaze met his. "This heart." She slid her hand into the folds of his hunting tunic and caressed his bare chest. "I knew Okonsa couldn't come between us because of the love that binds us."

Mackenzie rested her head on Fire Dancer's shoulders and sighed as he slipped his hand inside her dress and cupped one breast. She wondered if he would notice they were swollen because of her pregnancy. The tenderness had passed, as Laughing Woman had said it would, but her breasts were larger than they had been.

He seemed not to notice as he took her nipple between his teeth and gently tugged.

Mackenzie moaned and she looped her arms around his neck and arched her back. The first waves of excitement washed over her and she gave into them with every inch of her being.

"Mack-en-zie. Mack-en-zie," he breathed, his hot breath a caress on her cheek.

Their lips met and she opened her mouth to welcome his tongue, to taste him. She writhed in his arms, spirited by the caress of his bare hands on her bare flesh.

Fire Dancer tugged her dress over her head and let it fall to the floor. She laid back and allowed him to remove her knee-high moccasins one at a time, and then her leggings. Completely naked, she pushed back on the bed until she leaned against the wall. "Now yours," she whispered and pointed with a finger. "Take your clothes off for me."

Fire Dancer stepped back from the bed, his gaze locked with hers. His fingers found the ties at the neck of his tunic and unlaced it. She sighed with admiration as he slipped the quilled leather over his head. Fire Dancer's chest was broad and planed with taut muscles. A small scar ran beneath his left nipple.

"The rest," she encouraged. She moistened her dry lips with the tip of her tongue. Watching him like this made her skin tingle with anticipation.

He pulled off his moccasins.

Mackenzie's gaze shifted to the tight, leather fringed leggings that were all that separated her from his naked flesh.

His gaze did not stray from her face.

He unlaced the rawhide ties and slid the leather over his narrow hips, down his long, suntanned legs. He wore a loin cloth.

Mackenzie had not expected that.

The soft leather pouch between cupped his bulging rod.

"Let me," she whispered as his leggings fell to the floor.

He took a step forward and she slid to the edge of the bed. She reached behind him and stroked his bare, muscular buttocks.

He groaned with pleasure.

She ran her nails down the backs of his legs.

He groaned again.

With an experienced hand, she untied the leather loinskin and his burgeoning rod fell into her hands. She cupped the sacs in her palm with a gentle, experienced hand. His hands fell to her shoulders with another moan.

She stroked him, marveling at the softness of his flesh and the urgency of his need. Between her thighs she could feel a wetness . . . the same need.

Mackenzie stood up and pressed her hips to his. Because she was nearly his height, they fit together perfectly.

He slipped his hand around to the nape of her neck and pulled her to him in a hard, insistent kiss.

She parted her lips, and reveled in the feel and taste of his tongue thrusting into her mouth.

He pushed her gently onto the bed and she parted her thighs. He caressed the dampness with one hand, the other supporting him over her.

She closed her eyes and moaned. His hair fell over her face in an ebony curtain. "Love me," Mackenzie whispered.

He used his hand as guidance, and slipped into her. "Always."

She lifted her hips to meet his first thrust with a cry of relief.

He lowered over her, supporting himself with his elbows. "I will love you always and forever, *kitehi*. No matter what."

She raised her hips to meet another thrust. "No matter what," she panted.

Fire Dancer pressed hot, wet kisses to her breasts and she savored the feel of his mouth and the pleasure it produced. Her entire body pulsed as the tension mounted. She could feel herself drawing closer to climax. She could feel his body tensing over hers.

He called her name again and again. She stroked the muscles that corded his back and shoulders, his forearms, and chest. She was bathed in perspiration, lost in the ecstasy of each stroke.

His body was so hard and hers was soft. They melted in the heat of their passion and molded as one.

Again and again, he lifted her to a peak of pleasure, only to carry her down before she reached the summit. He teased and taunted her with each stroke of his manhood. He used it as a tool of delicious, torturous pleasure.

Unable to stand the glorious suffering no longer, she moved faster under him. He lost control and she gained it. She dug her blunt fingernails into the flesh of his buttocks, lifted her hips, and pulled him deeper into her.

"Mack-en-zie."

"*Kitehi,*" she breathed in his ear.

They came together in a surge of ultimate pleasure and flashes of light and darkness. He groaned and thrust one last time. Her muscles contracted. She cried out in pleasure and he moaned.

Fire Dancer sagged on top of her. She laughed, panting, and pushed on his shoulder. "Get off, you big oaf," she teased as he slid over against the wall.

She wondered impulsively if she should tell him about the baby right now. She decided not to. Another month hadn't passed. He had so much to worry about. And his cousin's body lay at the bottom of the ravine. Tonight wasn't the time. She would wait until they returned to the village. She'd keep her secret a little longer.

Mackenzie heard an eerie sound and she tensed.

It was a howl . . . echoed by a second.

Fire Dancer didn't say anything, but she knew he heard it too. He pulled the doeskin blanket over them both and tucked it under her chin.

"Wolves," Mackenzie whispered.

Another howl echoed off the mountain, splitting the night air with its haunting cry.

Then came yipping. Mackenzie was familiar enough with wolves to know what that meant. They'd found meat. They were zeroing in on their kill.

Another wolf howled and Mackenzie jumped in her skin. "Should we—"

Fire Dancer wrapped his warm arms around her. "There is nothing that can be done for him now," he whispered.

She snuggled closer to him. "Fire Dancer, Okonsa killed Tall Moccasin," she said softly.

She felt him tense. "He what?"

"He told me he killed Tall Moccasin and threw him down a ravine." She rolled over so that she could look into his eyes. "I don't know if it's true, but . . . but I think it is. The way he said it, he wasn't boasting. Just stating a fact. He said he would do the same thing to me, too."

Fire Dancer's gaze was hard and distant.

"I'm sorry," she whispered.

"Did he say why he would kill an innocent boy?"

"No."

Fire Dancer sighed. "This man guesses we may never know now." He slipped his arm around her waist and pulled her close to him. "Sleep, wife, and dream of happier times." His voice was sad . . . distant. But also hopeful.

"Gone," Mackenzie said staring over the edge of the ravine at the place where Okonsa's body had lay last night. There was nothing but a little blood mostly covered by new-fallen snow. "His body's gone."

Fire Dancer stared over the cliff. "A fitting burial for my cousin who I called brother, do you not think?" His tone was cruel and mocking. "In the belly of a wolf?"

Mackenzie rested her hand on her husband's arm. "You need to let go of your anger. He's gone. If you hold onto it, it will eat you up, and Okonsa will win after all."

Fire Dancer made a fist. "This man does not understand why Okonsa would do these horrible things."

"Maybe you didn't know as much about Okonsa as you thought you did," she said gently. "Sometimes the mind is unable to recover."

"He was a traitor, a thief, a liar!"

Mackenzie sighed. "*Ah*, but he said things to me that made me understand why he was the way he was."

Fire Dancer threw up his hand and walked away, back toward the cabin where they'd left their packs, ready to start for home. "This man does not want to hear it. There is no excuse."

She followed him, realizing it would be better to tell Fire Dancer about Okonsa's rape as a child in a few days when some of his bitter anger had passed. "Let's just go home," she called after him.

At the cabin, Fire Dancer lifted his heavy pack and placed the lighter one on Mackenzie's back. "Let us not speak of He-Who-Was-Eaten-By-Wolves again, shall we, wife?"

Mackenzie thought she could comply with her husband's wish, but she had one question. Somewhere in the back of her mind Okonsa's words still haunted her. Okonsa said Fire Dancer killed her father. She knew it wasn't true. She debated even asking Fire Dancer about the ridiculous accusation. It would make him angry that she would even think for a moment that he could have done such a horrible deed and then lied about it. Just the same, she felt like she had to ask, just to chase away the demons.

Fire Dancer set off through the snow, south toward home. Mackenzie fell in behind, walking in his steps. "Fire Dancer," she called softly.

He ducked under a snow-laden pine branch and lifted it for her. *"Ah´?"*

"Fire Dancer, Okonsa said something."

"We will not speak of him."

"I have to ask you. I don't know why he would say such a thing." The snow crunched beneath her feet. "But . . . he said." She exhaled and then just blurted it out. "Fire Dancer, Okonsa said you killed my father."

Fire Dancer halted on the path, but said nothing.

Mackenzie stopped directly behind him in confusion. Why had he stopped? Why hadn't he said anything? Why wasn't he denying the horrible accusation?

His back was still to her.

She touched the sleeve of his cloak. A lump rose in her throat. Suddenly she wished she hadn't asked. She should have just let it go. But he couldn't possibly have . . . "Fire Dancer?"

He turned to her slowly, as if he was an old man.

The breath caught in her throat at the look on his face. "No," she whispered.

"Mack-en-zie——"

"No," she said louder, her voice echoing off the snow-laden trees. "No."

"This man meant to tell you."

She took a step back shaking her head. It couldn't be true. It was a lie. She loved Fire Dancer. He loved her. He wouldn't have . . . he couldn't have!

"You meant to tell me?" she managed to croak.

"*Ah*. From the first day you woke only . . . only you were weak and then Snake Man ordered the wedding, and then—"

"You meant to tell me," she shrieked. Mackenzie's first impulse was to turn and run. Instead, she ripped the pack off her back and hurled it at him. "Bastard! Bastard!" she screamed. "You killed my father and you never told me!"

He put up his hands to deflect the pack.

"This was all a lie, then," she shouted, fighting the tears and feeling of betrayal. "You don't love me. You never loved me." Despite her efforts, the tears streamed down her face. She kicked snow at him. "You married me out of guilt, you bastard. Out of that Shawnee sense of honor."

"*Mahtah*. No. It is not true, and you know in your heart it is not," he defended. "That is why I did not tell you. Because I—I—"

"Don't say it! Don't say it!" She grabbed up her pack from the snow and pushed passed him. "Don't say another word. Take me back." She plowed through the heavy snow, her tears blurring her vision. "I'm going home. Home to the Chesapeake."

"Mack-en-zie, listen to this man. This makes no sense." Fire Dancer followed her to Josh's horse that was burdened with supplies. Robert Red Shirt's mount stood there too, laden with Mackenzie's paintings.

"Makes no sense?" she said softly. "No. What makes no sense is why I ever thought this could work between you and me." Mackenzie tied her bag to Josh's horse. She didn't cry because she had no tears left.

Fire Dancer had killed her father. He'd admitted it. Even

Josh admitted it, when she forced him to. She was almost as
angry with Josh as she was with Fire Dancer. He'd known and
he hadn't told her. He was going to take Mary and return to
the tavern on Chesapeake, without ever telling Mackenzie that
her husband had murdered her father.

Bastard.

The both of them. They had conspired together against her.
It was just like men.

Mackenzie yanked on the leather strap that tied her bag to
the horse. "Pardon." She slid between Fire Dancer and the
horse and walked to the other side to adjust the balance of the
pack.

The weather had broken and she, Josh, his new wife, Mary,
and Robert were all leaving this morning. The sky was clear
and it hadn't snowed in days. Robert Red Shirt was confident
they could made good time as they headed south and get out
of Penn's Colony to warmer climate before the next snowstorm
hit.

"Mack-en-zie." Fire Dancer followed her.

She didn't look at him. She hadn't been able to since he'd
told her the truth. At first, her heart had ached until she thought
it would physically break. She had loved her father dearly and
now he was gone, dead at the hands of the only other man she
had ever loved. Now she just felt numb. Numb and determined
to get the hell out of here.

Laughing Woman had tried to convince her that she was
being irrational, that self-defense wasn't the same as murder.
She even suggested that her pregnancy was clouding her logic,
controlling her emotions. When Laughing Woman suggested
they tell Fire Dancer about the baby, Mackenzie refused and
made her swear that she wouldn't tell.

One by one all of the Shawnee whom she had become so
close to had come to say good-bye and to ask her not to leave.
Each one declared Fire Dancer's undying love for her, until
finally she didn't want to see any of them. Even Mary, Mary
who had always wanted to live among the white men and would
now finally get her chance, tried to persuade Mackenzie that she
belonged with the Shawnee. Mackenzie would not be swayed.

"Mackenzie, this man does not understand your actions," Fire Dancer pleaded. "This man has said he is sorry. I explained that it was self-defense, just like you defended yourself. Joshua told you—"

"I don't want to talk about this. I don't want to talk to you at all. You killed my father."

He grabbed her by both arms and forced her to meet his gaze. *"Ahˋ*. This man killed your father in self-defense, but I still love you."

Tears sprang in her eyes. She wanted to tell him, *Well, I don't love you.* But she couldn't. Not even in the midst of her pain. Not even for revenge.

She jerked away from him.

Josh and Mary approached, their arms linked. They had been married yesterday by Snake Man and Red Fox. When they reached the Chesapeake, a traveling clergyman would marry them again, in a Christian ceremony.

The Shawnee ceremony had been so beautiful, that halfway through, Mackenzie had escaped. She couldn't bear to watch because it brought back memories of her own wedding such a short time ago.

"I'm ready," Mackenzie called to Joshua, trying to sound as cheerful as possible. "Let's go."

"Are you sure you want to do this?" Josh asked her quietly.

Fire Dancer stood off to the side and watched them make their final preparations to depart. Standing alone as he was, he seemed detached, not just from Mackenzie, but from the Shawnee . . . from the world.

"Ahˋ. I mean yes. I want to go home with you and Mary. I won't be a burden in the tavern. I swear I won't."

"That isn't what I meant, and you know it." His nut-brown gaze met hers. "It's your place. You have a right to be there. I just think you're making a mistake."

"Why does everyone think they know what's best for me?" she flared.

Josh sighed and dropped one arm over Mary's shoulder. "Have it your way."

Mackenzie turned her back on them as they walked to Fire Dancer, but she could hear what they were saying.

"This man wishes you would not go. There has been fighting very near to here. The French and British have taken the opportunity of good weather to kill each other."

Josh sighed and ran one hand through his thinning brown hair. "Mackenzie's set on going and I'm afraid if Robert and I don't take her, she's liable to set off on her own. You know how stubborn she can be."

Fire Dancer grunted. "Take care then . . . brother."

The men must have embraced.

Fire Dancer appeared at Mackenzie's side. "Stay until spring when the forest is safer. The French call us to fight beside them. I may have to, because we are already committed."

"I have to go now," she said flatly. Mackenzie could feel her heart breaking again, the wound opening anew.

"You have to go." For the first time since Mackenzie had learned the truth of her father's death, Fire Dancer spoke harshly to her. "You do what you must, and I will do what I must."

He strode away, and for an instant Mackenzie wanted to turn around and run after him. But she didn't. She couldn't.

Chapter Twenty-Eight

Fire Dancer sat on the edge of his sleeping platform and stared at his portrait, overwhelmed by suffocating sadness. *Mack-en-zie.* His wife, his heart was gone. Now he had nothing left of her but the picture. He wished desperately that she'd painted her own face despite the Shawnee taboo against it. Now he would have to rely on his memory and he feared his memory would fade over the years.

"This man said he was sorry," Fire Dancer said to her picture. He touched the streak of red ochre paint that was her hair. "If this man had been given choice, he would not have killed your father. This man had no choice."

She didn't answer.

Fire Dancer got up off the bed and kicked a wooden bucket out of his way. He hopped when he stubbed his toe. He hated being here inside his wigwam now . . . now that she was gone.

In the first hours after Mackenzie left yesterday morning, Fire Dancer had considered going after her. He had taken her captive once. He thought of doing it again. But after having her come to his arms willingly, he couldn't bring himself to force her into coming home. She no longer wanted him, no longer loved him. He had to accept fate as fate was.

"Fire Dancer?" Gentle Bear called in Shawnee. "Are you home, brother? I come with important news."

Fire Dancer wiped at the moisture that gathered in the corners of his eyes. He reached for his bow hanging from a rafter and dropped his leg through it. "Come in, friend. This man but tightens his bowstring."

Gentle Bear walked in and glanced at the bow, unconvinced. Fire Dancer set aside the bow. "What news do you bring?"

"A messenger comes from the French fort."

"Ah ?"

"The commander asks that we send men immediately."

Gentle Bear's tone tapped Fire Dancer's attention. "Men?"

"Our orders are to attack a fort tomorrow at dawn, along with others from the north."

Fire Dancer felt an eerie flash of premonition. Something told him he already knew where the Shawnee warriors were bound. "Which fort? There are many forts within a day's running distance."

"We attack Fort Bel-va-dere, friend."

Fire Dancer studied the toes of his quilled moccasins for a moment, then glanced up with resolve. "Let us go, then."

"You're willing to fight?" Gentle Bear took a step forward toward his friend. "Fire Dancer, Okonsa is dead. Many of his men were killed in that skirmish. If you approached council again, you could easily persuade them that we must break our ties with the French. We never agreed to fight their war for them."

Fire Dancer grabbed his quiver and began to count the number of arrows it held. "Council agreed we would ally with the French. If they fight." He lifted one shoulder to shrug the same way Mackenzie always had. "This man fights."

Gentle Bear gave a humorless laugh. "You sound as if you do not care if you live or die, Fire Dancer."

"I do not."

Mackenzie kept her head down so no one would see her tears. It was noon, the day after they'd left the Shawnee village.

The further Mackenzie got from the village, the less sure she was of her decision. Finally, after days, her numbness was wearing off.

Fire Dancer had murdered her father. Well, perhaps murder was too harsh a word. Killed him ... albeit in self-defense. She was angry with him not just for committing such a crime, but for not telling her.

She told herself she hated Fire Dancer. She had clung to that emotion for nearly a week. Now, suddenly, it was melting away like the icicles that dripped from the tree branches in the noonday sun. Beneath the anger, and the hurt, and the pain, she feared she still loved him. She hated herself for betraying her father's memory, but she couldn't help it. Her body, her mind, her heart ached for her husband.

"Someone approaches!" Robert Red Shirt startled Mackenzie from her thoughts. "Stand here."

Mackenzie drew her hunting knife from its sheath and halted beside Josh's horse. Mary peered over the bags packed on the mount, her eyes wide with apprehension. Josh, his musket in hand, turned his back on the women to protect the rear.

"Wait here for this man." Robert Red Shirt darted off the elk path they had been following south, into the thick of the forest.

Fear of the unknown made the hair prickle on the back of Mackenzie's neck. Her senses were alert and on edge, her muscles tense. She heard the chatter of a flying squirrel that had ventured from his tree hollow. She smelled the wet moss where the snow had melted in the sunshine, and the scent of a buck nearby. She could taste the cold mountain air on the tip of her tongue.

"Do you see anything?" Mackenzie whispered to Josh.

Mary slid her hand over the horse's neck to take Mackenzie's. "It could not be soldiers," she whispered. "We would have heard them many hours ago."

Mackenzie flashed a smile of reassurance. "You are right. The *manake,* they are so clumsy in the woods." It was not until she had completed her sentence that she realized she had said it in Shawnee and not English.

Mackenzie's cheeks grew warm with embarrassment. She had left the Shawnee life behind. She was one of the English-speaking *manake* once more and she had no right to speak of her own kind in such a derogatory way.

"It is all right," Robert called from the forest. A moment later he appeared with a trapper at his side, laden with muskrat furs. "This is Ebeneezer."

The older man with a grizzled gray beard nodded. "Ye scared me half to death. I thought you was Indians." He eyed Mary carefully. "Where ye headed?"

"South to the Chesapeake," Mackenzie said as she returned her knife to its sheath.

The old man's laugh sounded more like a cackle. He was missing his two upper, front teeth. "You best high tail it out of these parts. The French and the Indians is crawlin' all over the place. The mid-winter thaw musta brought 'em out. Word is, there's gonna be fightin'."

Mackenzie glanced at Josh. "How far is Belvadere from here?"

Josh walked to her side, his musket resting on his shoulder. "I was thinking the same thing. I don't want to get caught out here with you women in the middle of a battle. Robert?"

Robert Red Shirt chewed on a twig as he squinted and stared up at the sun. "Turn a little further east and we could reach the fort by dark if we hurry."

Josh looked to Mackenzie. "What do you think?"

"I say we turn southeast and get our tails moving." She grabbed up the reins of Josh's horse, weighed down with her paintings. Indian attack? The trapper's words didn't scare her as much as she knew they should have. She was just thankful to have something to think about other than Fire Dancer. "Let's go, Mary. We've still got a long day ahead."

Mackenzie's second arrival at Fort Belvadere was nothing like the first. Although less than six months had passed since she, her father, and Josh had made their journey from the Chesapeake, it seemed like six centuries. Mackenzie felt none of the eager anticipation of her first arrival. Today she felt numb—and sad.

The gates were thrown open when Josh announced his identity to the guard on duty. As the small party traipsed across the muddy compound, Harry appeared.

"Mackenzie?" he shouted from the walkway of the partially re-constructed main building. "Mackenzie Daniels." He ran through the snow and mud in his stocking feet, his arms outstretched.

Harry had lost weight since she last saw him and his military jacket hung loose and wrinkled on his frame. His red beard, left untrimmed, had grown as wild as a tangled vine.

Mackenzie laughed. "Harry. Have you lost what little sense you ever had?"

He grabbed her in his arms and lifted her off the ground in a suffocating bear hug. "I'll be damned. I'll be Goddamned straight to hell. You did it, boy. You brought her home."

Josh, embarrassed by the attention, dropped his arm casually over his new wife's shoulders. "Told you she was alive."

As Harry released her, Mackenzie glanced gratefully over her shoulder at Josh. She was so glad he hadn't spilled her entire story of the past months here in the middle of the compound with half the fort looking on from the palisade. She wanted to tell Harry what had happened, but privately, in her own words.

She gave Harry's beard a tug. "What ails you? Can you not find a razor between these walls?"

"You haven't changed a bit, Mackenzie. I swear by all that's holy, you're prettier than you were when you left. Come into my quarters and share a drink with me." He called over his shoulder. "Get your animals settled and you join us, too, Josh. You and your friend and Mary."

Josh tipped his hat and led the animals away.

Harry steered Mackenzie toward the log building. He shook his head and wiped at his eyes. "I just can't believe,"—his voice cracked—"it's you, sweetheart. Can't believe it."

"You really won't believe it when I tell you my tale," she

said with hint of irony in her tone. Truth was, she could hardly believe it.

"So tell me. I've got no place to be and a hind of venison roasting on the spit."

Mackenzie slipped her arm through his and gave him a pat on his shoulder. "Save any of that Madeira?"

He winked. "Just for you. Just in case."

Inside Harry's private quarters Mackenzie sat on a stool by the hearth to warm herself and dry her damp clothing. She shared a glass of the wine and related to Harry the entire story of what had happened to her since the night she disappeared over the fort wall in Fire Dancer's arms. She recounted the tale, fact for fact, without a single tear or even an inflection of emotion . . . until she confessed she was pregnant.

Then the tears flowed so that she couldn't stop them.

"Ah, sweetheart." Harry rose clumsily from his chair to offer her his handkerchief. "Don't cry, Mackenzie. I don't know what the hell to do with a woman who cries."

"I'm sorry," Mackenzie sniffed. "I . . . I haven't told anyone. Not even—" she hiccuped softly "—Mary and Josh. I . . . just . . . just couldn't."

Harry knelt in front of her as she dabbed at her eyes.

"I . . . I don't know what I'm going to do. Go . . . go home to the tavern, I guess. Run the business with Josh, I—" she paused for a hiccup "—guess."

Harry ran his hand through his hair, a look of helplessness on his face. "You . . . you could marry me. I'll have the child, half redskin or not. With my older brother being dead, I'll inherit all of my father's lands. Hell, with enough money, a man can legitimatize Satan himself."

She looked up from the balled handkerchief, the seriousness of his offer sinking in. "Marry . . . marry you?" she asked in disbelief. Then she laughed, though she didn't know why. It wasn't funny.

He clasped her hand. His was so much larger than Fire Dancer's. Fleshier.

"A man makes an honest marriage proposal on his knees and you laugh?"

She took Harry's hand and brought it to her cheek. His offer was an answer to her problem. And she loved Harry. But when she lifted her head and her gaze met his, she knew she couldn't accept his offer. It wouldn't be right. It wouldn't be fair to Harry. Because, though she loved him, she could never be in love with him. Not like she was in love with Fire Dancer . . . even now after all that had transpired.

"Thank you," she whispered with a sniff. "But I can't." She released his hand. "I can't, Harry. I got myself into this problem. I have to deal with it myself."

He rose from his knees and walked away to refill his glass. Mackenzie could tell by his silence that he was hurt . . . disappointed, and it surprised her. Had Harry had feelings for her all this years and she had not known it?

She rose. "Harry—"

He raised his hand, his back still to her. "It's all right, dear. I understand."

She sighed and gave him a pat as she walked past him. "Thank you. I'm going to turn in for the night. I'm exhausted."

"O'Donaho will find you a place to bunk down." Harry's voice sounded small. "Good night, sweetheart."

" 'Night." Mackenzie left Harry's quarters, her heart heavy.

The first musket shot cracked and Mackenzie bolted upright on the camp cot. *Redcoat manake,* was her first thought. *Come to attack the village.* Then she felt the coarse, moth-eaten wool of the army blanket flung over her and she realized she was no longer home, in the Shawnee village. She was at Fort Belvadere . . . and it was under attack.

Mackenzie leaped out of bed. It had been so cold in the small storage room that she'd slept with all her clothes on. Even her moccasins. She grabbed her knife sheath from the floor and strapped it around her waist on her way out the door.

Mackenzie spotted Harry pulling up his breeches as he raced down the hallway with Private O'Donaho attempting to catch up. "Get inside and bar the door," he ordered.

"Who's attacking? The French?" Mackenzie followed him.

Be damned if she was going to hide in a storage closet and wait to be burned out.

"I don't know," Harry hollered over his shoulder. He took the ladder up through the ceiling to the palisade, two rungs at a time. "Damn it. Didn't I tell you to find cover, Mackenzie?"

She scrambled up the ladder, her unbraided hair flying loose over her back. "I'm not one of your soldiers. You can't order me to do anything."

A musket ball ricocheted by and Mackenzie, Major Albertson, and Private O'Donaho all ducked at the same time. The lead ball hit the wall behind them, shattering wood and mud plaster.

Up on the palisade the air was already thick with blue musket smoke and stank of the black powder of the cannon on the walls.

"Archer! I want details!" Harry shouted, crawling along the wall toward one of his officers. "Who is it? Who's attacking us?"

A flaming arrow shot over the palisade and embedded in the wall behind them. The young private yanked it out and extinguished the fire with the sole of his boot.

"Indians, sir," said Lieutenant Archer. He had to be new. Mackenzie didn't recognize him.

Harry rolled his eyes. "Obviously, it's Indians. Are you addlepated, Archer? I can see that it's Indians. What Indians?"

Archer paled. "I don't know sir. Just Indians."

As Mackenzie sat on the log plank floor, a strange feeling came over her. Musket balls ricocheted all around her. The cannons boomed and flaming arrows soared through the air. Soldiers ran in every direction, carrying fresh ammunition and buckets of water to put out the fires.

"Fire Dancer," she whispered.

"What?" Harry had been talking to his officer, but stopped in mid-sentence. "What did you say?"

"It's Fire Dancer."

"He followed you here?"

She felt numb. "No. He thinks I'm headed for home, but

it's him, all right." She rested her hand on her belly that was now slightly rounded. "I feel him."

Harry looked at her strangely and then patted her hand. "Best you get inside then, eh?"

She pushed herself off the rough floor. "No."

Harry tried to grab her arm and pull her down but she swayed out of his reach. "Get the hell down, Mackenzie! You'll be killed."

She walked like a sleepwalker along the palisade wall. Like a sleep walker coming out of a deep sleep. Suddenly everything was clear to her.

Muskets cracked in the air and soldiers put out their arms to stop her, but she pushed them aside. Harry and the private followed, running as they crouched below the top of the jagged wall.

"Mackenzie!" Harry shouted. "Get down!"

Mackenzie stopped abruptly. She was above the front gates. "He's here," she whispered.

She carefully turned over an empty water bucket and stepped up on it so that she had a better view of the scene below. It was a beautiful morning, cold and crisp. The sun had just peeked over the forest horizon.

"Fire Dancer," she called.

Indians raced below. Some Shawnee, others from tribes further north that she didn't recognize by sight.

"Fire Dancer of the Thunder Sky," she repeated, her voice clear and strong.

The arrows ceased to fly.

The British soldiers inside the fort stopped firing to stare at Mackenzie with fascination.

"Fire Dancer."

The Indians below shouted to one another. They ceased firing their ancient fire locks and wheel locks.

"Mack-en-zie?"

He appeared below as if by magic. Dressed in a tunic and the leggings she had repaired recently, he carried a musket on each shoulder and two knives on his belt. He held a bow in his hand. His hair blew; long and free over his shoulders in the morning breeze.

"Why are you here?" He looked shocked. Afraid. Relieved. Suddenly, everyone was listening to her, redmen and white.

"Fate," she said simply.

Fire Dancer lowered his bow. "This man does not understand."

"Nor this woman. All I know is that fate caused our paths to cross once and now they cross again. It has to be for some purpose. You and I both know that nothing happens without purpose."

Gentle Bear stood near Fire Dancer and translated softly to the Indians around them.

"And what is the purpose now, Mack-en-zie."

His black-eyed gaze penetrated her heart . . . her soul. "The purpose is two-fold. We meet again so that this woman can tell you of her love."

There was a collective gasp from both sides of the wall.

"And to tell you that your men must lay down their arms and walk away from this place."

Another gasp. A few whispers.

"This battle is not yours, Fire Dancer, nor is it yours." She pointed to the redmen below who stared up at the white woman with obvious interest and confusion.

"If the French and the British are bound on fighting each other, then you must let them fight. To enter into the dispute will only mean lost lives for the Shawnee, the Lenape, the Huron, the Onieda and the Onadaga."

Fire Dancer handed his bow to Gentle Bear. "And tell me, wife, why do you say these words now? Now, after you have left my side, to join the white *manake* again?"

"Because someone must stop you and make you think, Prince of the Shawnee. Because someone must tell you that you have the courage to know when to fight and when to lay down your weapons. Because someone must build a path between the redmen and the white for the child I will bear you."

For a moment Fire Dancer could form no reply. He just stared at her with wonder in his eyes. Then he shifted his gaze from Mackenzie on the wall above him, to the men that stood at his side.

"Brothers," he said in English. There were whispers as men translated what he said into the various languages. "This man has long thought on this matter, and it is only now that I find the courage to speak up. To insist. The Shawnee of my village will not fight for the French against the British. We will not fight the French for the redcoats." He stood proudly, the breeze ruffling his blue-black hair. "This man will return to his village and try to make peace with his neighbors, both red and white."

Once again his black-eyed gaze was all for Mackenzie. "This man will take his wife home, if she will go." He lifted his hand.

Mackenzie turned away and scrambled down the ladder behind her. "What the hell are you doing?" Harry asked, following her.

She raced down the ladder and out into the compound. "Open the gates," she ordered. "Let me out."

"Mackenzie!"

None of the soldiers made a move to open the gate.

She spun around. "Tell them to let me out. My husband leads the Indians. They will not attack. I swear it."

Harry stared into her eyes for a long moment, then with a sigh, gave a flick of his wrist. "Open the gates. Let her out and close them."

As she heard the creak of the iron hinges, she caught a glimpse of Mary and Josh standing on the palisade. She smiled and waved.

They waved back.

Mackenzie lifted her chin and walked proudly through the gates. They closed behind her with a resounding finality. She knew she had stepped from one world to another, never to return again.

Fire Dancer appeared before her, and she ran toward him, her arms outstretched. "Fire Dancer," she whispered, almost too emotional to speak.

"Mack-en-zie."

He clasped her in his arms and lifted her off the ground in his embrace. "This man loves you."

"How much?" Mackenzie asked. The white clouds spun overhead in the blue sky as he twirled her.

"As much as this man loves the child his *kitehi* carries."

And then she laughed and their mouths met in a kiss of forgiveness . . . a kiss of promise for the future.

Epilogue

Winter 1801
Pennsylvania

"You exaggerate my heroics, *kitehi.*" Fire Dancer walked up behind Mackenzie's, dropped his arms over her shoulders and kissed the top of her head. "Do not listen to her, grand-daughter. She is old and—" he tapped his temple lightly "—was once injured in the head, you know."

Abby laughed and leaped off her stool. "Oh, Grandmama, that was the best story I ever heard." She hugged herself.

"What tales do you spin for our granddaughter, wife?" He came around the chair and clasped her hand.

"No tales, only truth." Mackenzie smiled saucily. After all these years—after the wrinkles and the childbirth, Fire Dancer's mere presence still excited her.

"Grandmama?" Abby approached them, a board in her hand. "Is this sketch of Okonsa?"

Linked arm and arm, Mackenzie and Fire Dancer stared at the portrait.

"*Ah`,*" Mackenzie said softly.

"I can't believe the wolves ate him," Abby breathed in awe.

Mackenzie's gaze met Fire Dancer's, hesitant. "Well, that was what we believed happened at the time."

Abby's black eyes widened. "He didn't die?"

Mackenzie smiled, memories tugging at her heart once more. She laced her fingers through Fire Dancer's. "You'll have to ask your mother about that, sweetheart."

Fire Dancer kissed Mackenzie full on the mouth.

Abby groaned and walked away. "Oh, yuck. Are you two going to start kissing again? My mama and dada are always kissing. Yuck." She wiped her mouth with the back of her hand as she left the room.

Mackenzie chuckled at her granddaughter and then turned to gaze into her husband's eyes. "You return early from hunting, husband."

He lifted one shoulder in a shrug. "This man missed the warmth of his lodge." He slapped her playfully on her bottom. "And the warmth of his woman."

Mackenzie laughed and whispered with a wink. "Then come to our bed and let me warm you."

Please turn the page for
an exciting sneak preview of
Colleen Faulkner's
newest historical romance
ANGEL IN MY ARMS
on sale in April 1998

Chapter One

Carrington, Colorado
June, 1867

Fox MacPhearson stepped off the train with a leather satchel in his hand and a strange sense of hope in his heart.

The Baldwin locomotive's whistle wailed, and the wheels screeched as it pulled through the station behind him. In a puff of smoke, the train was gone, and Fox was alone on the wooden platform.

So what now? Fox brushed his hand over his bare chin. He'd worn a beard and mustache for years, but on impulse had shaved it off the morning he'd left San Francisco. A cleansing ablution. As he washed the facial hair down the drain, he'd washed away his past. Here, in Carrington, he hoped he would find the start of a new life.

He removed his father's letter from inside his dusty wool tweed overcoat. Plum Street—that's where he was headed. That was where his new life would begin, number 22 Plum Street.

Fox deliberated on the platform and stared at the rickety depot steps that led to the street below. For some reason, he was hesitant to go. Not just because in going to his father's home he would have to deal with the emotional baggage of words left unsaid, but because . . . because . . . He sighed. Hell. He didn't know why he was standing here.

Fox took the warped steps two at a time. He reached the wooden sidewalk that kept pedestrians' shoes out of much of the mud of Carrington's rutted street and made a decisive right turn toward the false-fronted stores lining both sides of the road through town.

It was mid-afternoon, but there were few people on the street. Many of the store's window shades were drawn shut. The community did not appear to be the bustling gold mining town that, in his letters, his father had led Fox to believe it was.

A creaky sign, hanging by a nail from a corner post read: "Apple Street."

Fox nearly laughed aloud. After the bustling city of San Francisco, with its port of call, opera houses and art museums, Carrington was little more than a crossroads, a slum near the docks of the bay city. From the look of the loose shingles and broken windows, Carrington hadn't seen gold in years. Maybe that was why Fox had been forced to wait two days in Denver for a train passing through.

He passed a boarded-up store front. "Smythe's Emporium" the peeling painted sign stated over the door. He walked past several private homes. Tinny piano music filtered through the open door of "The Three Cabarros Saloon." He passed the saloon, though his heart pounded and his palms broke out in a sweat at the thought of a shot of rye whiskey. But he no longer drank. Drinking was one of the vices that had brought him to this pathetic one-horse town to begin with.

A half a block ahead, Fox spotted the first humans he'd seen in Carrington. So, it wasn't a ghost town, after all. There was a big woman dressed in waves of red crinolines. She had a rather prominent nose, but pretty blue eyes and a come-hither smile. Her rouged red lips and cheeks gave ample evidence of her profession. The woman standing beside her, laden with brown paper parcels, was barely more than a girl, with a fine mane of wheat-blonde hair. A whore, too, but a natural blonde whore. Fox had known enough bleached women in his life to recognize a natural one when he saw her.

The blonde was dressed in a shimmering sheath, not the billows of skirts and protruding bustle common to the day. The gown met tightly at her ankles so that she had to take tiny steps to walk. On anyone else the outfit would have been ridiculous, but on this woman, it was exquisite. Up until a few months ago, she would have been just the type he would have taken for a tumble in bed.

"Good afternoon, ladies." Fox swept off his bowler hat and gave a slight bow.

"Afternoon to you," the woman with the big nose responded warmly. "Just come to town on the four-thirty, I see." She offered a gloved hand. "Kate Mullen, but my friends call me Big Nose Kate."

He hooked his thumb in the direction of the train depot. "Guess the stop's not long. The conductor nearly pushed me out the door as the train passed through."

The young blonde woman laughed shyly. Her heavy rouged and the thick blue shadow on her eyelids detracted from her ingenuous beauty. "Have business in town, sir?" She shifted the weight of the bulky packages from one slender arm to the other. Her steady gaze made no excuses for her appearance nor for her vocation.

"Um. Yes." Fox hedged, hesitant to say why he was here, just yet. "I suppose I do. I'm looking for Plum Street."

Big Kate's blue eyes lit up as if she were privy to some secret. "Plum Street? Expected there, are you?" She studied him more carefully.

"Yes, as matter a fact, I am."

The wooden sidewalk creaked under her weight as Big Nose Kate took a step toward him. "We could show you, if you want. Not that this sniveling town is so big a fine, smart man like yourself couldn't find your way on your own."

For a moment Fox thought she would reach out to stroke his coat, or perhaps his cheek, but she didn't. For a whore, she had a touch of class. He replaced his black wool hat on his head. "Just point me in the right direction and I'll be on my way. I don't mean to trouble you."

"Wouldn't trouble us a bit if you stopped by Big Kate's Dance Hall tonight," the blonde said in a finely textured voice. "I'm Sally, Silky Sally." She managed once again to blush beneath her heavily rouged cheeks.

"I just might do that." He smiled and winked. He had no

intentions of frequenting a whorehouse. That fragment of his life was gone, washed down the drain with his beard. "Plum Street?" He lifted his brow.

Kate pointed a red lace-gloved finger. "You're headed in the right direction, handsome. Two blocks south. If Petey, the town drunk, is passed out on Plum and Peach, just step over him. He's harmless."

"Thank you. I'll do that." He tipped his hat and passed the two women on the plank sidewalk.

"Big Nose Kate's is on Peach Street," Kate called after him. "Can't miss it. It's one of the few places still open on that side of town."

Fox waved over his shoulder, but did not turn back. Two blocks down, he turned right onto Plum Street. The wooden sign at the corner had a plum painted beside its name, only the purple had faded to a pale blue. The street seemed to be mostly residential—white clapboard houses with varied roof lines, elaborate porticoes and gingerbread moldings. Each home was trimmed in a different confection color: bright pink, seafoam green and lavender. The houses appeared to have been no more than ten years old—built during the town's short gold boom, no doubt.

Plum Street was a pleasant, tree-lined street, out of place in a desolate, muddy town. He smiled to himself as he passed an empty porch swing shifting in the breeze. No wonder his father had liked it here.

At Peach and Plum, Fox did not encounter the town drunk. He read the numbers on the houses as he walked, amused that the townspeople would actually anticipate the need to give the houses numerical addresses, as if they had expected the town to grow to the size of Denver or Colorado Springs. But the practice served his need.

Number 22, Plum Street. He halted on the wooden sidewalk to study the white frame house, trimmed in sunshine yellow. It looked almost identical to the other houses, except that while some of the others appeared abandoned, this one was obviously occupied. While many of the others had been left to deteriorate, someone had obviously taken care of this house. The clapboard walls had been painted recently. The shutters hung straight. The glass on the windows was squeaky clean, unblemished by cracks or breaks. A stone walk had been laid and flowers planted on either side of the walk. It was like a house out of a child's fairy tale.

Fox halted on the stone walkway, feeling somehow undeserving. Would his father be disappointed that he intended to sell the home? Surely he hadn't expected Fox to live here in Carrington. Fox who had traveled the world, Fox who had once owned townhouses in San Francisco and New York City at the same time.

Fox chuckled. Maybe the joke was on him. Who in their right mind would buy this fairy tale house in the middle of a ghost town?

He walked up the painted white steps and across the porch. A swing drifted back and forth in the breeze at one end. To his left were a row of flower pots filled with dirt, zinnias or daisies yet to be planted in them. A trowel lay beside the pretty clay pots, as if recently abandoned.

His father's cryptic letter had said he would leave someone to watch after the house. Apparently, he'd had the good sense to hire a man as caretaker, or perhaps a spinster nurse had stayed on after his death to watch after the house and gain a roof over her head for a few months. Fox wouldn't evict whoever it was immediately. He would give him or her a few days to find lodging elsewhere.

Fox's first impulse was to walk right into the house. After all, it was his inheritance, one of the few things his father had ever given him. But he didn't want to startle the caretaker, or worse, be shot for an intruder. He rapped his knuckles firmly on the paneled oak door, his leather satchel still in his hand.

A dog barked wildly, and he heard the padding of the animal's four paws as it approached the door from the inside.

Fox heard footsteps behind the door—light footsteps; confident, yet feminine. It swung open and his gaze met with the clearest green eyes. *An angel.* A green-eyed angel with a halo of red-gold hair.

Fox had never experienced before such an immediate attraction to a woman. It wasn't his way. If he'd been asked only a moment before if he believed in love at first sight, he would have denied its existence with a cynical chuckle. Suddenly, he thought otherwise.

A large yellow mutt thrust its black nose through the open door and growled. Obviously a guard dog, it kept its hindend pressed into the young woman's billowing skirts.

For a moment Fox didn't know what to say. This had to be Celeste, the woman his father had mentioned in his final letter. *Celeste, the heavenly angel.*

A whore. The moment Celeste's gaze met Fox's, for surely this could be no one but Fox MacPhearson, she wished desperately that she was not a whore. She wished that she was once more the young socialite of Denver, her reputation unblemished. For the first time in her life, she desperately wished she could turn back the hands of time.

"Mr. MacPhearson?" she asked with a catch in her voice. Silver whined.

Celeste smiled at the stranger as she dropped her hand to her dog's smooth head to let him know the man was welcome. Silver had been John's dog, only now he was hers. "You are Mr. MacPhearson, aren't you?" she asked when he didn't respond immediately.

"Uh, yes. Yes, Fox Macphearson."

He seemed older than his thirty-some years, but not in a negative way. His handsome, angular face had the look of a man of experience. She was pleasantly surprised to see that he was clean-shaven, unlike most of the men that passed through Carrington. He didn't even have long side-whiskers, which were popular with city gentleman of the day. He had the same black Indian eyes as John, the same smile that could make a woman swoon, even a whore.

"Come in." She stepped back, self-consciously smoothing her cotton day gown. She'd been gardening and felt rumpled. She nearly stumbled over the dog as she stepped back into the foyer. "Silver, back, boy."

"How . . . how did you know it was me?" He followed her into the marble-floored foyer.

"Well, we don't get a lot of strangers here in Carrington, not since the gold petered out in the gulch," she answered, trying to get past her silly embarrassment. "And you look just like John, I mean your father, I mean Mr. MacPhearson." She stumbled over her words, not understanding her reaction. She had been expecting John's son for weeks. Why was she suddenly so clumsy?

He laughed, his smile radiating a warmth of sincerity. His voice was deeper than John's had been, rich, heady, like the oak of a good Chardonnay wine. "No, I don't suppose you do get a lot of visitors."

He removed his hat, and she hung it on the oak hook over the mirror in the foyer. Unlike his father's black hair, his was dark brown, and without a sliver of gray.

"I'm sorry, I . . . I didn't introduce myself," she stumbled, still feeling awkward. "I'm Celeste—"

"Celeste Kennedy. Yes, John told me in his letter."

She felt a strange sinking in her heart. She also noticed that he referred to his father by his first name. It sounded so impersonal and uncharacteristic of the man that stood before her. "He . . . he told you . . . about me?"

"Not exactly." Fox set down his leather bag and pushed back a thick lock of hair that fell boyishly over his forehead. "You know John, he could be vague when he wanted to be."

She smiled hesitantly, and met his gaze. *He doesn't know who I am . . . or at least what I am. John didn't tell him, the sly old bird . . .* And Fox hadn't guessed. Overwise it would have reflected in his dark eyes. It always did with men and women, though the look was different. With women, it was accusing, bitter and a little envious in some bizarre way. With men, it was lust, pure lust and lack of respect. The lack of respect had always bothered Celeste more than the lust.

"I'm sorry. How ungracious of me to keep you standing in the foyer. I was making myself a cup of tea." She motioned down the hallway, toward the kitchen. "Would you like one?"

"I would love a cup of tea." He removed his overcoat and hung it on the hook beside his hat before Celeste could take it for him.

She liked a man who could fend for himself. She walked to the kitchen, Silver leading the way. Never once in her life had she seen a man hang his own coat, not even John. "I . . . I was planting flowers. Summer's going to come early to Colorado this year."

"Is it? To San Francisco, too. That's where I came from."

"I know." She indicated a white kitchen table where he could sit and retrieved an extra teacup, saucer and white damask napkin.

Silver circled Fox, watching him with curiosity.

"Lay down, Silver."

The dog obediently slid to the floor and rested his muzzle between his front paws but kept his gaze fixed on the stranger.

Celeste turned her attention back to Fox. "John . . . your father talked about California often. He used to say he was headed back that way."

Fox chuckled, but his dark-eyed gaze reflected a shadow of pain.

"Always searching for that mother lode, wasn't he?"

She smiled at the memory of John. This was just small talk, something she'd gotten good at in the last few years. But Fox was easy to converse with. He made her comfortable. Maybe it was just because she liked the idea that he didn't know she was a whore. Of course, she would have to tell him the truth, but the fantasy was so pleasant that she let it go a little longer. It had been a long time since she'd felt this kind of freedom with a man—the freedom to just be herself and not have to worry about saying what he wanted her to say . . . or doing what he wanted her to do.

She watched Fox study the bright white and yellow kitchen. Sun poured in through the west window and cast golden light across his face.

"You've taken excellent care of the house," he said.

She lifted a kettle of hot water off the black, cast iron stove and crossed the kitchen to fill the flowered china tea pot. "It's a beautiful house. All the modern amenities. Gas lights and a flush—" She blushed as she replaced the lid on the tea pot and walked back to the stove. "John loved modern conveniences. He was always reading the newspapers to me, telling me what's been invented. He used to swear we'd be riding in horseless carriages in another ten years."

Fox chuckled with her and reached for the tea pot. Celeste reached out at the same instant. Their fingertips brushed. She lifted her gaze to meet his across the kitchen table, feeling a connection with him that went beyond John. A strange tingle arced between their fingertips.

Celeste pulled back in amazement. *Must have picked up static electricity on the hall carpet,* she thought. But she knew better. The moment he had touched her, her reaction had been emotional as well as physical. In her line of work, emotion was dangerous.

"I'm sorry," Fox apologized. "I thought I would serve you." He studied her warmly. He was such a true gentleman. "May I?"

Celeste couldn't take her eyes off Fox. This felt so strange. She had cared for John deeply, perhaps even loved him on some level. She had shared a bed with him many times, but she'd never felt this way about him, never felt this immediate attraction that she felt for his son. A little frightened by the thought, she glanced away. Celeste had worked hard to isolate herself from men, to protect herself, even from John. She'd never felt like she was in danger of cracking before . . . before now.

She watched as Fox poured the amber tea into her tea cup with the expertise of a parlor maid. "You do that well," she said as he poured himself a cup.

"Thank you." He smiled. "Thought I might find myself a job in a London tea house serving crumpets sometime."

He doesn't take himself too seriously, she thought. That was admirable in such a successful man.

She laughed at his silliness, and he laughed with her as he reached for the cream and sugar on the table. He had large, broad hands, clean, and steady. Celeste had always thought a man's hands told much about him. She could see that Fox had not worked manually for a living, as most men who passed through Carrington had. And judging from the newsprint stains on his fingers, he also read a great deal.

"Nice dog." Fox indicated the big yellow mutt with a nod of his chin.

Celeste glanced at Silver. "He likes everyone. John used to take him wherever he went. He used to say Silver had seen every saloon west of the Mississippi and east of the Nevadas."

"Silver?" Fox raised an eyebrow. "The dog is as yellow as a nugget of Colorado gold."

She chuckled. "Silver was John's—I'm surprised you didn't know about him. Surprised you never saw him. They'd been together for years. It seems John won him in a poker game. Originally, his name *was* Gold, but John said he wasn't a prime dog, not worthy of the name, so he called him Silver, after the lesser metal.''

John nodded. ''Sounds like something he would do.''

They both sipped their tea in a comfortable silence.

''Oh.'' Celeste glanced up at him. ''I'm sorry. I just don't know where my manners have gone today.'' She rose from her chair, feeling a little unsteady on her feet. It had never occurred her that she might be physically attracted to John's son. It had been a very long time since she'd been physically attracted to anyone. Whoring did that to a woman.

''Would you like a slice of cake? Mrs. Tuttle sent it over with her husband. He's the reverend here in town. Joash keeps an eye on me.''

Fox took a sip of his tea and pushed back in his chair, casually propping one ankle on the other knee. ''I'd love a piece of cake.''

''It's angel food.'' Celeste sliced off a piece and placed it on a china dish she drew from the cupboard overhead. ''Light as a cloud in the heavens, Joash says.'' She took a fork from a drawer and set it and the plate in front of Fox before retreating to her chair on the far side of the table. She felt safer there.

''You're not going to have any?''

She shook her head.

''What? Another woman who doesn't eat?'' He cut off a bite-size piece of white cake with his fork and brought it to his mouth.

Celeste watched him part his lips, mesmerized by their full sensuality. ''Uh . . . no.'' She laughed, the spell broken. It's not that I don't eat, only that I've had three pieces today already.''

He laughed with her again and their voices echoed off the punched-tin ceiling.

Fox took another bite of the cake and Celeste sipped her tea, and watched him over the rim of the tea cup, fascinated by how in some ways he was so like John yet in other ways so different. Many of his mannerisms were the same as his father's, like the way he slipped the fork out of his mouth, his lips pressed to the tines. But, while John had often been crude in his table manners, Fox was smooth and obviously comfortable with the silver plate and the fragile china. She had no doubt he had been served tea in London. While John had been a simple man, Fox was obviously a worldly one. He reminded her of the men she had known in Denver, men who had wooed her. That had been more than eight years ago. It felt like eight centuries.

Fox finished the cake and wiped his mouth with the linen napkin before taking a sip of his tea. "Well, Miss Kennedy, this had been very pleasant, but I suppose we should get on with business."

Celeste set down her tea cup with a slight clatter. "Business?"

He made a motion with his hand meaning to get on with it. "Of John."

That sinking feeling came back again. For a half an hour's time, she had been a woman sharing a cup of tea with a handsome man. In a moment, she would just be a whore again. "Your father, you mean," she said softly. "You haven't called him your father, only John." She didn't mean to criticize but, to Celeste, it seemed disrespectful.

For a split second, Fox looked uncomfortable. "Y . . . yes, my father. It's just that I never called him that. Only John. We both preferred it that way."

"Even when you were a little boy?" She was amazed by his confession. It seemed so unlike John. And there was the way Fox explained it. He said he had preferred it that way, but their was something in voice that expressed otherwise. "John never told me that."

Fox uncrossed his legs and pressed both hands to his thighs, leaning forward slightly. "Miss Kennedy, you seem to have known, or think you knew my father quite well." There was an edge to his voice, now. "Will you tell me exactly what your relationship was with him?"

ABOUT THE AUTHOR

Colleen Faulkner lives with her family in southern Delaware and is the daughter of a bestselling historical romance author. Colleen is the author of seventeen Zebra historical romances, including FIRE DANCER, TO LOVE A DARK STRANGER, DESTINED TO BE MINE, O'BRIAN'S BRIDE and CAPTIVE. Colleen's newest historical romance, ANGEL IN MY ARMS, will be published in April 1998. Colleen loves hearing from her readers and you may write to her c/o Zebra Books. Please include a self-addressed, stamped envelope if you wish a response.